In praise of RED JUMBO:

**Elegantly written; weaving together Magic Realism
and crazy hopefulness amidst very dark stuff.**

Red Jumbo hooked me from the elegantly California start.
There are tons of literary Easter eggs hidden in this book—I
can feel it. I'm thinking nothing is left undone here, it's a web
of interconnectedness; it's immediate, of the now, yet also
acknowledges the histories of things remembered, and I love
the guest appearances.

I sailed through this book! It has great flow, and I loved being
along on that very communal ride after all this time being in
pandemic mode. It's interesting how Coulson wove all the parts
together; there's claustrophobia and the weight of personal
pasts, and then it opens up into expanding spaces ... the open
road ... Kansas ... Aunt Arctica's endless mansion of
inclusion, *so* many symbols and sign posts, even death has no
hold on those who supposedly crossed over—even egregious
sins can maybe be forgiven.

The magical realism is fabulous! It's also crazy hopeful, amidst
some very dark stuff. Bravo!

— SARA GARDNER-GAIL, artist

RED JUMBO

Also by Chris Coulson

Nothing Normal in Cork
The Midwest Hotel
Go With the Floe
A Bottomless Cup of Midnight Oil

RED JUMBO

Chris Coulson

PINEHEAD PRESS

www.chriscoulson.net
cover, book design, and
oil pastel illustration by Chris Coulson
author photo by Susan Emshwiller

PINEHEAD PRESS
www.pineheadpress.com

For Rosie

and any other woman or man
who feels a little illegal
and a lot alive

And for Susan Jenny !

Soon we'll be away from here,
step on the gas and wipe that tear away.

"You Never Give Me Your Money"
— The Beatles

RED JUMBO

Coyote

Coyotes prowling in the cool blue evening under the Colorado Street Bridge grin and drool and drag a body into the bushes of the arroyo.

One of them chomps down slavering and excited into a hand but a CRACK! cracks in her mouth; this hand is not soft, luscious flesh, but wood or plastic, something hard. The other coyotes hear that CRACK!, look at the body, and their hungry grins droop into still drooling but now bored grins as they creep away off to something or someone to eat somewhere else.

One of the coyotes stays behind, keeps trying to eat, trying other parts of the body. He bites into the dress and drags the body halfway across the low-running creek, where it gets caught in the current and starts floating downstream. The dress rips off ragged in the coyote's mouth, so he gives up on the body and follows the pack into the woods. He walks a bit apart from the others with his treasure that may or may not be something to eat later, in private, or at least something to sleep with tonight.

Above, on the Colorado Street Bridge, leaning on a lamppost, watching coyote tails tail off into the trees, is Officer Serge Controllente of the Pasadena Police Department, smiling and laughing softly.

"Coyote," he whispers. "Yo soy un genio!"

His police car is behind him, lights flashing, engine purring, radio buzzing about some new crime in Pasadena he should go check out. He ignores that, gets his camera out of the trunk, and zooms in on the body (still floating downstream); zooms in on the head, the shoulders, then he zooms in on a dark blur of writing—**Macy's - Women's Evening Wear**—stenciled in black between the shoulder blades, before the body floats away forever around a turn of the water.

Officer Controllente looks for his phone, finds it in the car under some hamburger wrappers, and beeps in some numbers. Smiles and waits while it rings.

"Hi. Feeling photogenic? I have an idea. We'll need to do a grisly little photo shoot tonight, before we lose the light. You'll get a little wet, a little rumpled and twisted, a bit gnawed-on. You'll understand. Maybe you already do. OK? Good. I'll come pick you up, I'll be there in about 15 minutes."

Serge gets into the car, hits the siren and the gas, and the driver's side door slams shut with the sudden forward motion.

PART ONE *Out of the basement*

Moon

I came up out of the basement, walked out of the house, and looked at the moon. The dogs were with me. They were sick of that basement, too. I looked down at them. They looked up at me. Two hot-wired terriers; one steel-woolly gray, the other one white, wild, and fluffy.

"Look at the moon tonight," I said to them. They looked at the sky vaguely, wagged their tails specifically. "She's not supposed to be full until Saturday night. But even now she's got earrings on!"

I thought it was kind of a nice line, poetic. And I had just come up with it, out of the blue. The dogs waddled off into the dark and pissed on the night-blooming jasmine. I was kind of night-blooming myself at the moment.

An *almost* full moon night in California—and I was waxing in that direction, too.

I was sick to death of the internet, Facebook, TV, news; sick of trying to fill myself up with all that. It wasn't working, but I was plugged into the wall for it, my eyes whirling into the screen, staring empty, no food, lots of drinking.

I was plugged in, and I could barely walk. I *couldn't* talk.

I'd go for days and nights and weeks in that basement. Facebook. Porn. Angry, hopeless news. Liquor store. Facebook. Dogs sleeping all day. Me not sleeping at all. Sixty-one years old. Drinking anything, no stopping. No food. Liquor store. Avoiding mirrors and lamps and windows and neighbors.

That night, down in the basement, drunk and trying to write down (and maybe find out) what was going on, what I was going to do next—what I was *feeling*—I fell asleep at the screen, my finger fell asleep somewhere on the keyboard, and the screen traveled down maybe hundreds of empty pages before the computer made some sort of warning noise and woke me up. I sat up, saw the bottom edge of the moon dip an inch or two into my basement window, and I *stood up*.

The dogs saw something in the way I stood up, and wildly wagged their tails for the first time in decades, though Kansas was only five and Missouri was six. We all went upstairs, out of the basement, out of the house.

The moon was BIG, and white. The night sky was long, wide, starry, and deep; late-night BLUE.

We stood in that cool moonlight awhile that night, breathing in the fresh desert air, and while the dogs messed around in the bushes and rolled in the grass, I went inside, down to the basement, and unplugged the screen. The sound of the computer being unplugged was like a long, relieved, *exhale.*

The moon was way up over the hill passing behind palm trees and silky clouds and the sky was soft blue. *Kind of Blue* was playing inside my house and there was a cool sea breeze, though I was all the way over there, inland, up in the hills of Los Angeles, in a small town called Eagle Rock. That breeze was like lying down on cool sheets with no clothes on, with somebody else, with no clothes on. Blonde hair, or black hair, or brown hair, or red hair, or even no hair … and earrings, in the moonlight.

Well, I could go on and on. I was in the mood for love, and I was getting carried away.

Earrings, sheets, perfume, moonlight, the sea breeze. And nobody here but the dogs. With no women around, these kinds of images were bringing on a kind of tennis elbow lately (I didn't and don't play tennis, or golf. What for?). The dogs still needed their flea lotion rubbed on and I had an appointment in the morning. An interview. Maybe it would lead to a new job. Not bartending again, or writing obituaries for the newspaper, taking bodies to the morgue, doing telephone customer service in windowless rooms full of cubicles, working as a movie extra in Hollywood. No, something else, this time.

But on this night—finally up and out of the basement—the moon (with her earrings on) was getting to me. I rubbed the flea lotion on the dogs and the three of us went to bed.

Night blooming jasmine also Miles Davis blowing lavishly through the blue air, and I was thinking about women. Their eyes, thighs, and otherwise.

I was a night-blooming jazzman.

Hot

In the morning the phone rang and the dogs answered it. I was glad. I always wake up a little unsociable. Ask anybody. Well anyway, ask the dogs. *Anybody* wasn't there.

They attacked the phone leaping up on the table in the breakfast nook, knocking it on the floor, where it slid under the stove, saying, "Mr. Jumbo? Are you there, Mr. Jumbo?"

I could see and hear all this up on one elbow in bed, my tiny bedroom just off the tiny kitchen, in my 1925 bungalow. Such little rooms; they were all spinning and I didn't know why. I thought I had gone to bed early, and I had. But then I had gotten up again. What had I done, then? I didn't know. My brain wasn't even up on one elbow yet.

"Mr. Jumbo?" It was a woman's voice, kind of tinny and sharp-edged, I thought. But maybe that was because it was under the stove. The dogs were scratching for the phone, just beyond their paws. "I can *hear* you," she said.

I was up on both elbows now. One of the dogs, Kansas, the fluffy wild, white one, started whimpering. The wooly-gray one, Missouri, was panting very near the phone. Then they went for the water bowl, with the accompanying slurping sounds, tags clinking on the bowl.

"Oh my God. Mr. Jumbo. I hope I'm not *interrupting* anything. Ok ... well, you just call me when you're *up*. When you're *ready*. When you don't have *company*. I mean, oh never mind, you have my number. And please call, Mr. Jumbo. Private texting on Facebook makes me nervous and anyway, who advertises services on Facebook? I guess *you* do. Maybe I'm behind the times. I hope this isn't a mistake. I'll need to see your license upon arrival. Please call me. I notice you've not been on Facebook the last few days. Again, this is Mrs. Hamptons."

There I was, smiling so early in the morning. Something new. A new career. My first job in my new line of work. Detective. I'd never been one before, but I thought I'd give it a try. I didn't have a detective license. I did have a *card*.

So there was washing and shaving and dressing up and eating and then calling Mrs. Hamptons, a quick chat, she was talking fast, but I deciphered (or detected) something about her maid; she was missing or maybe something worse, maybe something *dark*, so *"I'm on the way!"* I said to Mrs. Hamptons, then I loaded Kansas and Missouri into the van. I was wearing a black pin-striped double-breasted with a white shirt and a red tie underneath. It was 100 degrees out there, but I was going to *South* Pasadena, and I was going, looking *good*.

As I drove along in my black suit, Kansas and Missouri with their faces in the air conditioner vents and their ears blown back, I hoped Mrs. Hamptons wasn't going to say that stupid thing *some people* always say: "Aren't you *hot* in that?" Who knows why *those people* have to watch the rest of us and how we're living, how we're doing things. The car in front of me stopped and I swerved hard and Kansas tumbled onto the floor. Missouri hopped down and gave her a lick so she wouldn't feel too embarrassed by the tumbling down. Such a compassionate dog.

I crossed the high, picturesque, Colorado Street bridge and looked at the mountains up near the sky, clouds gliding white and feathery across the tops. It would be cool and piney-smelling up there. But me and the dogs were going to South Pasadena—the mansion district.

The appointment was in Pasadena at a house on El Molino Avenue, close to the Lanyard Luxury Hotel. It was only the week before that I drove to that hotel for just one drink and it cost me $48. Or would have. I pushed it back at the bartender, my old friend, Justin Case. Justin wanted to make the drink *on the house,* but he'd just been hired at the hotel and didn't want to get in trouble. I tipped him heavily anyway, said goodbye, went back out to the van, woke up Kansas and Missouri in the backseat, paid $25 for the parking, and drove straight up North Lake Avenue all the way to the foothills of the San Gabriel Mountains, just a few feet under the stars.

Up there, I pulled three cold bottles of beer out of the Igloo in the back of the van, poured two new silver bowls (from Target; fancy and shiny, but cheap) full of cold mountain stream water (glimmering by) for the dogs, and we looked down on the hotel and all of Pasadena. The beer, the bowls, the water, and the view totaled around $17.

Something else happened that night.

As we looked down on the skyline of Pasadena at all the bars, cafes, restaurants, museums, and stores along Colorado Boulevard, my woozy eyes came down like fluttery pigeons to the roof of the famous Vroman's Bookstore. I already had the three bottles of beer inside me, but my mind was still spinning, and I knew that a good book would slow it down. Nothing political, nothing historical, something psychological, something comforting. Maybe one of the Winnie the Poohs.

We all got back in the van, wound down the mountain road to Colorado Boulevard, and I went inside Vroman's. Kansas and Missouri had fallen asleep, dizzied-out and dazed from all my curvy driving.

I walked to the *literary book* area, my favorite area, and saw a familiar head floating around above the shelves in the adjacent poetry section. Was it? I wondered; was it *her?* It *was*; what a thrill! Linda Lee Bukowski, at the *B* shelf, neatening up some of the books there. I didn't hesitate. Keeping one eye on her floating head I found her row easily and walked right up to her. I started off with how good she had been in the recent documentary about her long late husband, *Charles* Bukowski; she smiled big, blushed bigger, tried to steer the conversation back to him, but I was doing the driving!

"You were great in the film, you were funny and wise and warm," I said, and she was.

She went from smiling to sniffing.

"Do you smell … alcohol?" she asked.

Now I was blushing.

"Yeah, it's me, uh … I was just up in the mountains drinking beer with my dogs, I guess I shouldn't really …"

"No, no, I smell wine," said Linda Lee, then I did, too. Linda Lee was smiling affectionately, looking over my shoulder, and I felt something go by behind me. I turned and there was a rustling blur of papers or pages of *something* flashing by—I saw it was the racing form from Santa Anita—carried by a burly, battered but beautifully handsome man, who smiled affectionately back over my shoulder at Linda Lee, winked at me, and headed for the front door of Vroman's.

"Ah *Hank*," said Linda Lee.

I watched the man go out the door, watched the door slowly close.

"I miss your husband," I said, "but sometimes, like when I read those poems … I feel him close, you know what I mean?"

"Sure do," she said, gazing off toward the bookstore door.

I thanked Linda Lee Bukowski for talking with me, asked her to autograph one of his books, she hugged me, we both had tears in our eyes, I wasn't embarrassed about smelling of beer anymore, I said goodbye to her, headed out the door, set off the alarm, came back and paid for the book.

That had all happened a week ago. Now I was back in the neighborhood.

I drove down Orange Grove, cut across California Street, turned right down El Molino, and drove up to the gatehouse at the Hamptons address.

A man in a white coat and a gold name tag that said *Fyodor* stood there and didn't greet me. Maybe he was thinking. Pondering something else, or in the middle of an out-of-body experience. He seemed extremely wise, possibly playful, anywhere from fifteen to fifty-five years old. Probably closer to fifty-five. I didn't feel anything unkind coming from Fyodor; his eyes were soft blue (a little shy, maybe fearful) beneath yellow hair and eyebrows as bushy Vincent Van Gogh's haystacks.

He finally came over to the van, but kept his distance, because Kansas and Missouri were panting and slobbering in *his* direction. I zipped down the power window, thinking that might impress him some. It didn't seem to.

"Yes?" Fyodor smelled like the first floor at Bloomingdale's, the men's cologne department. Could a gatehouse guard afford the top colognes? Maybe he'd taken all those free samples stuck into magazines, and rubbed them all over himself this morning. How could I know? It was certainly something *I'd* done in the past. Wondering about this, I offered him my card and his eyes popped!

"Mr. *Jumbo?* Mr. *Red* Jumbo? Detective?"

I'd had the cards printed in a bold, black, distinguished font (even before I knew I had the job) so I'd appear to be a serious detective, but he'd read it out loud like it was the announcement of the circus coming to town. The dogs were trying very hard to get across my lap to Fyodor.

"That's what Mama called me. Mrs. Hamptons is expecting me."

Fyodor stared at me. He panned his zoom-lens eyes up and stared at my hair.

"Why?" he asked.

"Well, I am here to discuss that with *her*. It's all hush-hush, at this point. You understand."

"No. Not that. Why *Red?* You've brownish hair, you know."

I laughed. It was a humble sort of laugh.

"Well, you know, I mean … what can I say?" If I'd been standing outside the van, I'd have kicked one of the tires and said shucks. "Mama was … *grandiose.*"

Fyodor was looking and *looking* at me. Missouri went into the backseat to sleep while Kansas helped me stare back at Fyodor, who surprisingly stopped staring and started laughing. He wagged a finger at me, playfully scolding me.

"And Jumbo? Surely not your family name, no no, couldn't be, certainly, no. *Right?*" Then he stopped laughing and was staring again, swaying a little, like the tops of the palm trees (it was a windy California day) high above both sides of the long driveway up to the Hamptons mansion.

I was anxious to get up there.

But I took my time with this guy. Maybe I'd need him, later. Some kind of *Detective* need I didn't know about yet.

"Well yes, Fyodor. It is. My surname. I come from a long line of Jumbos. My father, Jasper "Jumping Jack" Jumbo, *his* father, Joe Jumbo, my great-great grandfather, Gerald Jenkins 'The Gypsy' Jumbo. It goes way back."

Fyodor held my card, backed into the gatehouse, and picked up the phone. "A *Mr. Red Jumbo* to see you, ma'am ... Yes ma'am, I will." He clicked down the phone and came out, still looking at my card.

"Hey, what about the alliteration?" he asked, turning the card over and looking at the back, nothing there. "What about that?"

"The *what?*"

"The alliteration? Your father was Jasper Jumbo, your grandfather was Joe Jumbo, your great-grandfather was Gerald Jenkins 'The Gypsy' Jumbo. And here you are, *Red* Jumbo. What about that?"

I smiled at him, lightly punched him on the arm. "Ah, you know how it goes. Win some, lose some."

Fyodor almost smiled, tried to lightly punch me back, but missed.

"She'll see you now, Red. Uh, Mr. Jumbo. *Sir*."

"Red. Jumbo's my *sur*name, but you needn't call me *sir*. See you on the way out, Fyodor."

The drive from the gatehouse to the mansion seemed as long as the drive from my house to the gatehouse. There were ducks and gazebos and statues and sprinklers along the way and Mexican gardeners who waved back. I drove slowly up to the front door and a woman walked out in a pink muumuu. She stopped and stood, feet spread wide, in black ballet slippers, a gold scarf around her neck, one end falling down to her knees, floating in the breeze.

The woman was maybe 60, tall and thin with long, skinny arms, hands on her hips, the hands twinkling gold, flashing silver, glowing white with (I'd bet on it, *real*) diamonds. Her long hair was red shading towards orange, blowing frizzy, a bit brittle, but still free in the wind. She stood there like she was in charge.

It was a great entrance, except I thought that it was *me* doing the entrancing. Or, entering. Not that I minded her standing there looking like she was in charge, I didn't mind her *being* in charge—I admired her confidence—I just didn't want to get knocked over by it, on my first day, a little unsure in my new career direction.

But it's ok, I thought—the morning is young.

I backed the van into some deep shade along the driveway, opened all the windows, spilled some kibbles and bits on the floor, and Kansas and Missouri got busy grazing. I stepped out into the driveway, said *Ok, here I go* out loud, and started walking towards her, slowly. *Two can play at this game*, I also said, taking my time and still far enough away so she couldn't see me talking to myself.

"Mr. Jumbo?" She was looking at me kind of funny, like something was wrong. Her eyes were small and green, a little filmy, like old green marbles.

"Yes, Mrs. Hamptons? Red Jumbo. How nice to meet you." I put my hand out to shake and bowed slightly, sort of *regally*, I was thinking. She was still looking at me funny.

"Aren't you *hot* in that?" she said.

Seaweed

We went inside the house, through the foyer—a lot of antique echo.

The living room was wide, long, and dark. The ceiling was so high I couldn't see where it stopped, only dusty gold chandeliers dangling down, humming, glowing dull. We sat in stiff chairs and stared at each other across a huge distance and nothing happened. I thought I heard footsteps in the far, dark end of the room, but it may have been the antique echo, creaking. I was looking around the room for something about the Hamptons feng shui to compliment, to break the ice, when Mrs. Hamptons got up from her chair and walked back to the front door again, gesturing for me to come, or maybe "*git,*" like a dog. Anyway, to follow her.

"We'll have iced tea on the front porch, Mr. Jumbo." So we sat down again, on the porch. Far in the distance, across the Hamptons grounds, I saw a pair of joggers on the street as we waited for the tea.

"I used to do that," I said.

Mrs. Hamptons frowned at me. "What?"

"Run."

Now the frown made a line between her brows like an irrigation ditch. "You? You don't look like the type to run."

"Well, I never did, *formally*. Just when the police were behind me." I thought that was pretty funny. She looked at me like I was a poor person's poodle—no grooming, no perfume.

"So what's going on here, how can I help you, Mrs. Hamptons?"

She shifted in her chair, indicating a change of subject.

"We could have the iced teas," she said. "Or would you like a *drink* instead?"

I could feel the jet engines rising, ready for take-off. Of course, the natural answer to that was yes. And had been for years. But maybe I should be a good guy, responsible, and refuse, insist on a gentle iced tea. Exactly. *Gentle iced tea,* I thought—a healthy, fresh, nice yellow slice of lemon floating there like a playful friend, ready to squirt …

"What are *you* having?" I asked.

She smiled. "Martini. Dirty," she said.

Now we were on the same wavelength. If Kansas and Missouri were watching from the van at this moment, I knew they'd sense that too, and wag their tails. But hang on, I thought. Take it easy. I was starting to forget why I was there. Someone missing. Someone dead? Someone Mrs. Hamptons knew, employed, and here she was in her pink muumuu offering dirty martinis.

"I'll have one too," I said.

"Then let's go back inside, shall we? We can talk properly inside, and besides, it's too hot out here."

So, back inside, and into our chairs again. I was getting out of breath from all this movement.

She smiled at me and shouted. "*Alberto!* Martinis, por favor!"

Alberto came in, looked right *at* me, he and I nodded, some kind of understanding there already, maybe remembering each other from past lives. I looked at him like: sorry, we're probably the same age, you and me, we could probably talk about our first and favorite Beatles records, but this is how the deck got shuffled this time, so I guess in *this* life, it's *your* turn to serve me with this woman thinking she can order anyone around, and …

"Señor Jumbo?"

I liked Alberto's face. His dark, sparkly eyes looked like he was *just about* to start laughing, at *something*, and his teeth were so white I smiled a little smaller. His hair was thick, brown and sort of *choppy,* like the ragged end of a handmade cigar, and his short, blunt mustache was the matching cigarillo on his lip. His fingernails were the color I recognized from the Lowe's paint department as *Dusty Rose.*

"*Tecate*, por favor," I said, changing my order to be in league with Alberto.

Mrs. Hamptons didn't like it. "Cheap *Mex*ican beer? That's what *they* drink, for heaven's sake! Oh, Alberto! I'm sorry. Did I just *say* that? Still, I'm certain there's not a drop in the house."

"I have Tecate in my room, in my refrigerator, OK, Señor Jumbo?"

I smiled and nodded yes at Alberto, he bowed his head slightly. I stood up, bowed my entire body right back, and we both laughed. Mrs. Hamptons made a rude sound with her lips, shifted sharply in her chair, crossing and recrossing her legs; it was a lot of body language—she was doing some kind of punctuation. Alberto started off to somewhere *behind the scenes*, so to speak, for my beer and her martini.

"I'll bet he does," she frowned after him. "*Have some* in his room. He hides, he slinks, he's sort of secretive."

I really wanted a stronger drink, like hers, but to hell with her. I didn't want to drink *with* her, with *her* drink.

10

"What was her name, Mrs. Hamptons?"

She looked at me, really lost. "WHO?" She blinked like the odd, *un*-wise owl.

"Your cleaning lady. Or, your domestic. Your *maid?*"

She stared and stared. Then she opened a drawer in a table next to her, pulled out papers, and went through them one by one. She dropped the papers in her lap, reached into the drawer again, and pulled out an old Rolodex.

"Jesus fucking *Christ*. You have to look it up?" I said it a bit too loud. I guess it was a stage whisper, but then I'd never been an actor. Wanted to be one, I even had a SAG card from a dog food commercial where I was instructed to go WOOF WOOF off camera to get a dog's attention. And right there and then, I got my card. It all happened after midnight, way after midnight, in Big Pine, California, and I heard all the people on walkie-talkies back and forth with each other: "Jumbo's said his line, notify SAG in the morning!" My acting life was about to open up and begin right there, that night, then it would be sushi with Tilda Swinton, shoemaking with Daniel Day-Lewis.

"Excuse me?" Mrs. Hamptons.

"What?"

"You said Jesus Christ. Or rather, Jesus *mm-mmm* Christ."

I was looking for Alberto and the Tecate to come, *stat*. But I went on and said the next line, clearly and politely. "Well, Mrs. Hamptons, with all due disrespect, I can't believe you can't remember the woman's name without checking your Rolodex. Also, I can't believe you still have a Rolodex."

"MISTER Jumbo, I *do* remember her name and … wait a minute … did you just say with all due DISrespect?"

Alberto came back, just in the nick of time. He lowered his tray with a frosty mug and the bottle of Tecate. "Your cerveza, pocho."

Mrs. Hamptons looked like she wanted to rake the backyard with her fingernails.

"*Pocho!* What is this? You know each other?"

I looked at Alberto and said cheers as I drank from his private stock.

"Alberto, what was her name?" I asked.

He straightened up and looked off in another direction like we all do when we don't want to start crying. "Rosalita."

Mrs. Hamptons dropped her papers and jumped in her chair like hot popcorn. "Rosalita, *yes,* that's it!"

Alberto walked over to her with her dirty drink. Then, he was gone, back behind the scenes of the house again.

Mrs. Hamptons took a *long* sip of her martini. She swallowed and came up for air. "They discovered her under the Colorado

Bridge," she said. "Actually, it was just one officer, Officer Serge-*somebody*—right, Alberto? Alberto? Oh, there he goes, *sneaking off* again. Anyway, I spoke with *Serge* when he called that night, he was out patrolling alone, found her body, her remains, her whatever, and called the house for the next of kin, Alberto, to come down and identify the body. Obviously, *I* wasn't going to go, wouldn't want to be involved with that. *God.* Who knows what she was doing down there under the bridge. The officer said that she was all muddy and messy, her hair all in her face. All twisted around, arms and legs. Serge said that she fell from the bridge. Or jumped. Or was pushed. Then he said that she may have been attacked by a coyote. Still, he said all of the evidence was inconclusive at that point. Seemed pretty conclusive to *me*. Foul play hasn't been ruled out. He has some crime scene pictures, he wants to bring them over at some point, but I don't need that."

I heard a door close, softly, somewhere in the house, somewhere behind the scenes.

"And *foul play* is the only reason you're here at all, Mr. Jumbo. But really, who would want to kill her? She was always so dramatic, she seemed so sort of SAD all the time. I *tried* to help her. I reminded her of how lucky she was, so *blessed,* to be in this wonderful country of ours. But she always had that long face. Suicide? Well, of course! That was *her*. But, um. There's another thing ..."

Mrs. Hamptons was drinking her martini quickly and getting pretty drunk, pretty fast. It wasn't her first drink of the day. I could tell by her eyes and slightly trembling hands. Her face looked like mine does when I step out of the shower and try to see my reflection in the fogged-up bathroom mirror. After I've been drinking all night.

"I had a feeling that there was some tension between her and my husband. I don't know what was happening, what she did. But it felt and *still* feels awkward around here, and I don't like it. I was binging on Netflix and Facebook the other night trying to escape, get away from the feeling in the house, the feeling inside me, and when I saw your post on Facebook, offering your services as a private investigator, it was perfect timing. Odd, but perfect. So I reached out. I wanna know what's going on."

"Mrs. Hamptons, is your husband around?"

"Who?"

Here we go again, I thought. "Your husband. You remember *his* name, don't you?"

"I beg your pardon, Mr. Jumbo?" she asked, slowly standing up, but wavering.

I couldn't resist. I had to say it. "Maybe you should check your files." Here I was, first day on the job, and probably a few seconds from being fired. I drank my beer. All of it. Why not get as loaded as Mrs. Hamptons? She was standing there, glaring down at me, but she seemed to have lost her train of thought, and she started swaying, like seaweed.

Alberto came back in with his tray. "Mrs. Hamptons, another?"

She was swaying and staring at something behind my back. Alberto looked there. I turned around and looked too, but there was nothing back there but a wall. A painting on the wall, a formal portrait of a woman, looked like Mrs. Hamptons, but older.

"Mama," whispered Mrs. Hamptons.

She fell back into her chair and held her empty glass up for Alberto. He took it and went off somewhere again. I heard ice cubes from the next room, Mrs. Hamptons fell asleep in her chair. Alberto came back in, saw her, sat down in the chair next to her, the tray with her drink on his lap. I nodded at the drink, he shrugged and took a sip.

"I *knew* it, Mother, I'm like you after all," said Mrs. Hamptons. "I love you. *But why did we both ...*"

She burped softly, fell back to sleep. There was a long silence. My Tecate was gone, Alberto started to get up but I waved him down.

"I'll get it," I said. I pointed at the door he'd come and gone through, he nodded yes, so I walked over and pushed it open into dim, blue light. The lights were off, but at one end of the long kitchen was a window, and beyond it, a swimming pool, which was shimmering blue onto the high ceiling, and reflecting on glass cabinets full of china and glasses. There were shiny stainless steel appliances lined up on the counters, everything clean, but it seemed to me they were no longer being used, just put away. I felt serene in all that subdued blue light; I wanted to stay in there, relax, maybe reconsider my new line of work, maybe *not* have another drink. My eyes were still adjusting to the low light, so to get a sense of where to walk—to get my bearings—I looked to the floor, beautiful black and white tiles arranged in patterns that reminded me of some of the paintings of Paul Klee, and my eyes followed one particularly playful pattern of tiles that led to the opposite wall. On that wall was a floor-to-ceiling liquor cabinet.

I made myself a strong drink. I only had a few days left of this drinking, I thought, I was about to finally quit, *I hoped*, so I made a strong one. A Long Island Tea; I poured everything I could reach into a glass, iced it up with the silver tongs from a silver ice bucket on the silver countertop, and walked back out to Alberto and Mrs. Hamptons. She was snoring like a vacuum cleaner. Alberto looked very down in the dumps, very sad. *Very.* Very *very.*

"Is this how it goes around here?"

Alberto nodded.

"Where is Mr. Hamptons, Alberto?"

He shrugged.

"You miss Rosalita, don't you?"

He nodded. It was a big, slow, *profound* nod.

"Was she your wife?"

He didn't nod or shrug or say anything, so I knew that she must be. Maybe.

Alberto took a sip of his drink, I sipped mine, and we looked down into our drinks. We continued looking into our glasses. Mrs. Hamptons stopped snoring. I froze in the heaviness of the silence, and what felt like Alberto's tremendous sadness that I was picking up, empathetically. A bartender in Pasadena had suggested to me one night that I was empathetic, and I thanked her for saying that, but I wasn't sure she was right. Maybe I was just getting drunk and mushy.

Something moved in the room. A tiny flicker of something in the stillness. I looked toward it and saw Alberto, looking at me.

It was only a second, or less, but I thought I saw the glimmer of a smile.

Maybe.

Bubble bath

We finished our drinks, had a few more and finished those, then Alberto and I carried Mrs. Hamptons to bed, shut the blinds and her bedroom door. That bedroom smelled like perfume and liquor and like nobody else was ever in there but her.

We came back into the living room, which was sliding into a dim golden, late afternoon light. Alberto asked if I wanted to watch a movie. I said sure, he went off somewhere for the movie, and I thought, *now what?* I should be asking questions about *the case,* but then he came back with *The Treasure of the Sierra Madre.* Alberto told me the final scene always cheered him up, no matter what going on in his life, no matter how hard it got.

"The gold blows away and those guys just laugh!" said Alberto.

"Alberto, I know that scene, I love it, it's inspirational, but can we do that later?" I needed to get out of the room, out of the house. It was all a lot for my first day.

"Yes, Señor Jumbo."

"Red. And we can talk about Rosalita some more, ok?"

"Si, Red."

I shook his hand, gave him my card, looked him in the eye, and said goodbye. He *looked* sad, but his eyes were clear, more or less dry (of tears), and he kept gazing off into space, *almost* smiling. He looked like he needed to see that movie, share it with someone, so I almost changed my mind about the screening, but kept moving out the door, down the front steps.

When I got to the van, where I'd parked in a deep, green-tinted pool of shade by a cluster of bamboo trees, Kansas and Missouri were passed out on the front seat, but one of them had thrown up on the driver's side. That's not a nice smell or sight in a car. Especially when it's where you're sitting. But I love those dogs. I swiped the mess out onto the Hampton's estate, for fertilizer.

There was a howling in the house.

It was Alberto. Alone in that house with nobody but his drunken, sleeping boss, he let loose a howling and some Spanish words I couldn't quite translate from the driveway. He was sobbing and moaning in there. I ran back to the house and saw him in a window, just off the porch. Alberto *jumped* a little, surprised, waved me off, smiling and shrugging—*I'm ok!*—so I smiled and shrugged too, turned around, got back in the van and drove away, across the grounds down toward Fyodor, waiting at the gate.

"Hi, Mr. Jumbo. How'd it go?" asked Fyodor.

"It's a bit sad back there at the moment. I'll come back later. Kind of an odd feeling in there."

"It's always a bit *sad* around here," he said. "And odd."

"Where's *Mr.* Hamptons?"

Fyodor looked up at the mansion."Somewhere, in there."

"No shit? I mean, he *is?*" I looked up at the mansion.

"Yes. Somewhere."

We looked at each other.

"See you later," I said.

"Take it easy, Red."

I stepped on the gas, the dogs barked goodbye.

I drove around the corner and up the Arroyo Parkway to the historical Trader Joe's (the first one) and bought the family-sized plastic jug of vodka (the last one, I hoped, that I'd ever buy), a bottle of bubble bath, and some "Charlie Bear" dog treats for Kansas and Missouri. I drove home, driving slowly, watching the signs and signals and mirrors, watching also for the police. The dogs were watching me. They knew I'd been drinking.

I got home, through the front door, locked it behind me, made a big vodka drink, and started to bubble the bathtub. I was going to get in the bubble bath and make notes about the day. I threw the dog treats on the kitchen floor and the dogs skittered after the feed like chickens.

Deep down in the bubbles, my drink on the porcelain sink with a clink, I wrote: *Rosalita, dead under the Colorado Bridge. Mrs. Hamptons, drunk. Alberto, crying. Mr. Hamptons, somewhere. Alberto and Rosalita???*

That was the extent of the notes. And that was my first day as detective.

I got out of the tub, dried off, went to bed and slept awhile, but at three in the morning I woke up, hearing Alberto's howling and crying again, in my dreams. So, I had a shot of vodka and some Valerian and floated back to sleep.

Kansas and Missouri slept through it all. Lucky dogs.

Forever

So, by sunup you might imagine how I felt. Not a hangover really, but my stomach felt like it was full of barbed wire. It was time to stop drinking but would sobriety interfere with my creative detecting process?

I don't care, I'll do it, I'll stop! It'll be a new day, a new life. I'll start right now. One day at a time, as they say. Enough of these mysterious stomach pains and waking up all night. This is it, I thought, and got out of bed. The phone rang. I said hello.

Really, really long pause on the other end.

"Buenos Dias!" I said next, trying to sound international.

"Is this ... Mr. Jumbo?" a male voice asked.

"Si, señor," I said. Another pause. I was international, but maybe in the wrong country.

"Mr. Jumbo, I am not a Mexican. I am an American. And my name is Hamptons."

Uh oh.

"You were at my house yesterday and upset my wife greatly."

I was looking in the mirror. I had no clothes on. I wondered what he was wearing. I wondered if he had a first name. I wondered if there was any vodka left. But no, *that* was over forever.

"I'd like to talk to you. How about a drink?"

"Sure, I'd love a drink, Mr. Hamptons." One forever at a time.

"Meet me at the Lanyard Luxury at noon."

Oh shit, not the $25 to park, $48 to drink place, again.

"I have a table there."

I bet he has a *floor* there.

"Have the captain guide you to the Red Saddle Room on the first floor. Listen, Mr. Jumbo, I'll buy you a drink, I suppose I owe you that for *trying* to be helpful, though you were most definitely *not*. And anyway, I want to meet a man who calls himself ... Red *Jumbo*."

Now, a *really* long pause. I'd heard him, but still, something in his voice—something a little angry, and a lot *in charge*—made me wonder what he wanted to talk about. He sounded like he wanted me off the case. Looking in the mirror, I wondered what to wear. Obviously, I wasn't going in the nude.

"See you at noon *sharp*, Mr. Jumbo," he said, and hung up.

If it was going to be *sharp*, I was definitely not going in the nude. I decided to wear the suit from the day before. And I'd quit drinking right after the meeting. But I knew I wouldn't quit this case. I felt that Mrs. Hamptons needed me, though she seemed at first leery, then weary of me. Maybe she was just weary in general. And I really wanted to stick around for Alberto. Besides, this was only *Day 2* as Detective Jumbo.

Vera Similitude

The phone rang again.

"*So* Red, listen: the corduroy soldiers from the civil war chased marshmallows around Times Square with shopping carts comedy people drama people Black people white people Chinese spider monkeys and then when I turn the tv set back to the right time zone I really want to fly Air France and have champagne for free but not anymore of course and not with a movie about where my mom went when she asked for more Vienna sausages especially after the toll booth opened on the Golden Gate Bridge for the last shift and really especially after her granddad molested mom on her birthday."

It was my friend Vera, from the Briar Patch Rehab Clinic. We'd checked in there on the same night many months before, and we became friends *that night,* right off that bat, because—the nurses said later, I don't remember—we were constantly laughing. We laughed at everything, probably to keep from being scared, or ashamed, and we laughed a lot as we *very* eagerly waited near the nurses' station— *very* friendly, they said, *very* talkative—for the next round of meds, asking also for pretzels, Beer Nuts, sometimes singing together.

We'd both relapsed since that night, Vera many times, including an ugly, damaging car crash, just her and a tree. I told her to call me, anytime.

And she does. *Anytime.*

"Good morning, Vera. How much longer are you in there? You must be almost ready to go home, eh? And isn't it a beautiful, cool, sunny day?" Well, that was probably one too many questions, I felt I'd overloaded her with information, and sure enough, a long silence followed.

Then ...

"When horns blow and Charlie Parker writes on cocktail napkins and Louis Armstrong does his laundry and passes out wooden clothesline pins to the Kremlin he has three hamburgers and four Budweisers before he says enough is enough and goes on a white egg diet for coloreds only and uses the whites only bathroom and hears his next door neighbor Memphis Minnie giving birth to Nora

Jones and the sun comes up with Don's rosy fingers and rings around her posy!"

"Wonderful, Vera, wonderful! You sound great, very *up and at 'em!*"

"Swing low sweet chariot and that's all I ever said before until *now.*"

I needed a favor from Vera. She had worked at the Lanyard Luxury Hotel for years, she'd been a cocktail waitress in the Red Saddle Room. I told her that I was a detective now, working on my first case, and I stopped there, just to let that information ooze into the spin-cycle of her brain. I heard her panting for a few minutes, and then, as her panting decreased to smooth and easy breathing, I continued.

"Vera, do you remember a man named Mr. Hamptons?"

The breathing suddenly stopped. *I've killed her,* I thought.

"You can run but I'll tan your hide and if you take the A-train and go back to the 5th-floor maternity unit where the nurse is wearing a Christmas tree dress and her eyes don't blink don't have eyelids and her eyeballs roll down the nape of your neck you'd better stay away from Mr. Hamptons."

Uh oh, *again.*

As I was about to hang up, Vera said, "Hey Bud, you any wiser? The cat's outta the bag and the cards are on the table now! So Bud! You any wiser?"

She had used that witticism on me again and again, and I laughed, again. She started laughing and her laughter was loud and out of control, atonal laughter, sounding like a recording of a sheep *baa-ing,* the record skipping. Laughter so loud that I heard the door in her room open and voices mixed with the laughter, probably nurses. One of them saying, "Now Ms. Similitude, *calmly* now, glad to see you so chipper, but simmer down a little, ok? ... a little *loud* this morning."

I held the phone closer and raised my voice.

"Nope, this Bud is *almost* wiser, but ... not quite there yet. Had some vodka with the dogs last night. Stopping sometime soon, and forever, too. Wish me luck, Vera."

"Blue cakes of soap bubbling along are the realistic navy looking for Morrison and now breakfast with styrofoam separate from the hash browns and no more yesterday papers. Ok, Bud? Good luck, Red. *Bye!*"

And that was that; she'd hung up.

I was standing there still naked and it was time to get dressed and on to the Lanyard Luxury, the Red Saddle Room, and the meeting with Mr. Hamptons. It was quiet in the kitchen, quiet in the house. I looked around for Kansas and Missouri. I saw them out the window playing in the front yard with an empty plastic vodka bottle. Kansas had the mouth of the bottle in his mouth and he was swinging it around like a carousel, Missouri barking at him. The neighbors were watching and laughing, then they saw me in the window, in the nude.

I waved, like Mister Rogers, then got dressed.

Well on the way

She's in bed, sitting on a smoothed-out red and blue patchwork quilt, circled by fun and familiar objects: her books (one of the books —Naked Lunch, by William S. Burroughs—in her hands tonight) and clothes and cell phone, a box of music and movies, and her schnauzer puppy, Felix, rolled up like a biscuit and sleeping at the end of the bed. She's been up all night laying out her new, temporary space, and now she's well on the way to cozy.

It's a small room, a bed in the corner of a detached garage built after the turn of one century but way before the turn of this last one, a room big enough for a Model-T Ford. That car's gone and the bed is piled high with big fuzzy red blankets and blue flannel sheets and puffy white pillows surrounded by candles lighting up—smoky reddish-brown—the wooden teepee of a ceiling, above.

She smiles, sparkly-smart eyes in the candlelight. Devilish and free.

"I've never felt this alive in my life," she whispers up into the ceiling, where it echoes in the beams; old wooden witnesses overhead, confirming her.

She blows out the candles and drops softly to sleep in the pillows, peacefully, for the first time in a long time. Good morning; good night.

Tick

Mr. Hamptons was late, so I sat at the bar. Justin Case looked up from a glass he was polishing, did *at least* a double-take, maybe triple, and walked over. Justin had kind of a crush on me, I think, off and on, and though I let him know he was barking up the wrong dead-end street and tree, he liked to flirt. Which, dead-end or no, was fun and felt good from him. And Justin—a former Danish casting director and distant cousin to Finnish filmmaker Aki Kaurismäki, *he says;* Justin Case, who'd moved to America and changed his name— has good taste.

"Hi, Justin."

"Hey there, Mr. Jumbo! What are you up to in those clothes? Very elegant for this time of day."

"Detective now. New career. As of about 48 hours ago. Meeting a client. Here. Never met. How do you like my detective patter?" I reached out, shook his hand, and he held it, slow to release me.

"Snappy. Staccato. *Vague.* Sexy. Who are you meeting?"

"Mr. Hamptons."

Justin's eyes slid sideways, he was watching something. Then *he* slid sideways. "There he is," said Justin, walking away. He was gone, the flirting was over. I turned around.

Mr. Hamptons was very tall, an older man (or anyway he seemed older than *me*, maybe late sixties), and *big*; a big silvery ex-football player, with that kind of ex-jock walk, hair combed back smooth and metallic like the hood of a long, gray limousine. He walked right to me, hand out, no smile yet, maybe there wouldn't be one; checking me out.

"Mr. Trumbo?"

I started to put my left hand out since my right smelled heavily of Justin's cologne, then switched back to the right, and we shook hands. I felt, and probably came off, very confused and awkward. Still, I knew my name.

"*Jum*bo. Red Jumbo."

He squinted at me. He wasn't wearing glasses, but he seemed to be; his large, square face seemed made of glass and metal, and his tiny, distant eyes were like two windows in the side of a jet plane, as seen from the concourse. He was cold; to throw in another simile, it was like standing near a refrigerator—the door open.

"What kind of a name is *that*?" he said.

"Colorful, eh?" I laughed.

He was tall, and the more he squinted at me, the farther away he seemed to get.

"Talking to you I feel like I'm standing in a ditch!" I said, still laughing, trying to break the ice (the door open, nothing melting). His remote, fuselage eyes were taxiing away from me, ready for take-off.

A long pause. I could smell Justin Case, and not from my hand. I knew he was somewhere nearby, but he was out of sight. Maybe hiding behind the bar.

"Mr. Jumbo, are you a drinking man?"

"Not yet," I said. Justin laughed, somewhere.

"What does that mean?" Mr. Hamptons was staring at me, and smelling his hand, as he led me to *his table*. "Drinking problem?"

"Me? Naw. Hey. Let's have one. Or two. What'll you have?"

When we sat down he was *still* taller than me. Justin appeared, red-faced and watery-eyed, really trying not to laugh. And failing.

"Drinks? Sir?" he giggled, but professionally, deferentially, to Mr. Hamptons.

Hamptons looked at me, still smelling his hand, looked at Justin and said, "Canadian Mist."

"Canadian Mist," repeated Justin, clicking his heels. "And for you, handsome?"

The table, this whole side of the Red Saddle Room, was smelling more and more like the Macy's cologne department up on Lake Street.

"TNT, Justin. And hold the first T."

"Yes sir, Mr. Jumbo. Is that the *Tanqueray* T, or the *tonic* T?"

"Yes, Mr. Case, the Tanqueray T. *Thanks.* Hey, that's another T!"

"Very good, gentlemen. Coming up!"

Hamptons watched Justin enthusiastically stride back to the bar, snapping his bar towel at a bar stool, whistling.

"That's so sad," he said.

"What's that?"

"The pain of that lifestyle."

"What, bartendering? Or is it bar *tending*. Anyway, I don't know about painful, I doubt it ..."

"You know what I mean, Mr. Jumbo. *Alternate* lifestyles. Very painful, I'd think. Through the ages, it's been tragic."

"Not anymore. Just ask Justin. Anyway, times change, thank God."

"Do you believe in God, Mr. Jumbo?"

"Sure, I'll bite. But what's that got to do with anything?"

The jet plane eyes turned slowly on the tarmac, the dark cockpit windows now taxiing right *at me.* "It's got everything to do with everything," said Mr. Hamptons.

"Well, what I believe in—my religion, I suppose you'd say—is very *loose and lively,* with loads of *leeway and love.* Fear and shame on the ground, behind you. I'd say the Ten Commandments are more like those orange construction cones in the road, like *Watch out over here! Slow down up ahead!* And I picture God as a playful and powerful young woman—imagine Greta Thunberg at the bow of a ship, with those fierce, beautiful eyes and the sea spray in her hair, sailing straight into any storm—*how dare you fuck with the earth!* Not that she's a god, she'd probably laugh that off. Or maybe a playful old man—Louis Armstrong blowing his horn right back at all the hate in front of him, wiping it off of him with his perfectly elegant snowy white square of cotton, and laughing, *you can't stop me!"*

Quiet, stillness; *not* serenity. Mr. Hamptons staring at me.

"Amen, huh, Mr. Hamptons?"

I looked over toward the bar. Justin hadn't brought bring the drinks yet; they were made, but he was watching, and apparently listening to me, from the bar with a couple of waitresses, tears in their eyes. Justin gave me a covert thumbs-up signal.

I tried to break more ice with Hamptons."I guess I got carried away. Anyway, as I said, times change."

"Some things never do, nor should they. You mentioned the Ten Commandments. Do you know the Bible, Mr. Jumbo?"

"Well, you know ... I, uh ..."

"Times may change but some truths hold eternal."

Mr. Hamptons leaned over and whispered, "I do feel sorry for your friend over there, I have nothing but pity for him, but what he does is wrong, by the Bible, and always has been. That is the sole source of his pain." This close he was even larger, also soapy-smelling, like a locker room. He leaned back, crossed one leg over the other, the body language of: *It is finished.*

"I don't care about the Bible," I said. "Or, to put it another way, I thought God, religion, by extension—*the Bible*—was all about Love. Or, to put it even *another* way—speaking of extension, and love—as my old girlfriend Fanny used to say, 'don't point that thing at me if you don't intend to use it!' "

Now the drinks came.

"An N-*T,* for Mr. Jumbo, and, for you, sir, a Canadian Mist. Will there be anything else, gents? No? Well, if *times change,* lemme know!"

Now that the mood was completely uncomfortable, I decided it was time to move on to the case.

"Now, Mr. Hamptons, about the case ..."

"The Pasadena Police Department is on this case. Have you even spoken with them? Not that I'm aware. I called and they've never heard of you. No, Mr. Jumbo, *you* are not necessary."

"My own mother used to say that to me, can you believe that?"

"What I mean is, your *services* are not necessary. I want you off this case."

"Off the *case?*" I asked, a little startled, a little too loud.

Justin Case walked over.

"Yes?"

"No, we were talking about *our* case, Justin," I said, literally patting him on the back. He smiled affectionately at me.

"Just remember that *I'm* your Case too, if you need me. If either of you need me that is, I'm right over there and ... well, anyway ... I'll get out of your hair." Justin started back to the bar, stopped, and looked at me. "You know, Red, I've always liked your eyes. They're *so* blue, so *clear*, with just a splash of green. As if Paul Newman had used a shot of Creme de Menthe as an eye wash. I don't know, maybe it's just the bartender in me, or that I'm cuckoo for Paul, like all of us. What am I saying? *Ha!*" He rejoined the now laughing *out loud* waitresses at the bar.

Hamptons looked a little lost. "What did he just say?"

"His name is Justin Case, Mr. Hamptons," I said. "He's my pal."

Hamptons drank his whiskey drink, one gulp. "*Those people* have no boundaries," he burped.

"Yeah, I know, goddamn bartenders—always in your hair ..."

"No, I meant—*listen, Jumbo*: you're off this case! You've already upset my wife, who called you and trusted you, for whatever misguided reason. And I was having a nice day until I got here, so that's it. I am simply trying to make everything alright again. Everyone seems to be crying at my house. Rosalita didn't deserve any of ... whatever happened. I had no idea. Of *course* I felt for her. But you're off the case. I will pay for your—*tonic water*—but this is the end. Right here. Mr. Jumbo, I just can't understand you. I don't know what makes you tick!"

"Tick?"

"Tick."

"Maybe I *did* order a TNT, because you and I are starting to sound like a bomb about to go off! Get it, Mr. Hamptons?"

"Yes, Mr. *Red Jumbo*, I get it. What a name. And Justin Case. What is it with the names around here, anyway?"

"By the way, Vera Similitude sends her love."

"Who?" Hamptons was so upset his shirttail had gotten pulled out of his pants and his tie was askew. "I'm outta here!" he said, pounding the table, knocking it over, the drinks splashing me. I was laughing, but I thought I saw tears in his eyes, looking around wildly for a way out of the bar.

Justin rushed over. "Help you *neaten up*, sir?" Justin went for the shirt tail but Hamptons was already lunging across the room toward the door (or the end zone; once a football player, always a football player, he had that about him), a couple of chairs falling as he rushed out of the Red Saddle Room.

"Well, there goes your detective career."

"No, Justin, this is just the beginning. I'm just warming up with the Hamptons. And I want to find out about … *Rosalita.*"

I said that last line to myself, under my breath. This guy Mr. Hamptons wasn't going to scare me that easily. What he didn't know is that my mother really had said that to me when I was a kid. That I was not necessary. But the good thing about something like that is that later, if you can get away from it, clear out, clear your head, and keep going, nobody can *get you* anymore.

"And so now, Justin: how about another TNT?"

"TNT?"

"Yes."

"Or just the second T?"

"Yes. Just that."

"Good, Red."

"Thanks, Case."

"Great patter, Jumbo."

"Shucks."

Justin walked over to the bar; new clean glass, fresh ice, and some bubbly, fizzy tonic. He placed the drink in the center of a small round silver tray, came back, uprighted my table, pulled the bottom of his vest straight, straightened his tie, looked at me and gave me the thumbs up again. The waitresses did the same—*three* thumbs up!

It was great to have friends. And the case was just beginning. I wouldn't quit on Rosalita. Because somebody *got her.*

Sunday

I drove home, thinking and thinking. Thinking too much. I missed my dogs. When I pulled up to the house, I looked for their heads in the window, looking for me. But no, nothing, *nobody*.

I'd left the TV on for them with the sound off, a Duke Ellington CD on repeat, playing over it, so when I walked into the house they were riveted to the screen, watching Pee Wee Herman's Playhouse as the Ellington Orchestra played "Lady of the Lavender Mist."

I got out of the suit, into my blue jeans, and onto the couch. Mr. Hamptons was no fun. He was grouchy, rich, homophobic, and seemed to be loaded with that *old-time religion.* Mr. Hamptons also seemed loaded with anger.

All this told me that it was time for a day off. Time to turn my brain off. If I could.

What happened to Rosalita? I imagined her falling from the Colorado Street Bridge. Did she jump? Or did someone take her there, push her off? It made me sad, a little mad.

Kansas and Missouri jumped on my chest, and I was back to my day off.

I made a big cup of coffee with heavy cream, changed the music to the Oscar Peterson and Count Basie collaborations, and lay down on the couch with a big, fat 564-page hardback book, Kansas and Missouri dropping into their positions: Kansas on my leg, Missouri swaddled in my suit on the floor. Mrs. Hamptons was right, it *was* too hot.

All three of us took a deep breath—*This is it, this is the life!* we said.

I opened the autobiography of Keith Richards to page three, and thanked God—*Greta* in my case—that I'd only had tonic at the Red Saddle Room. I read the first paragraph of Keith's book, then stopped and looked at the dogs; little furry ribcages breathing slow and easy.

It was a cool, beautiful, early Fall day. October, my favorite—the real beginning of the year for me, no matter what's supposedly dying outside. Cold nights, pumpkin spice all over the place. I looked out the living room window through the bare branches of the young trees out in my tiny front yard, to the BLUE sky. It looked *soft* blue, like soft blue cotton, like my new Levis. I was in that kind of a mood, the expansive mood when my new blue jeans begin to look like big, blue, open sky—or, the other way around. Either way, Kansas had his head on my thigh. Or my *sky*.

I listened to the music, "S & J Blues," put the book down, closed my eyes, and breathed like the dogs. (I thought about the basement under me for a few seconds, so many of my addictions down there, so I stopped thinking about it, and kept it *under me*.)

"This is great—*right now*!" I said out loud, to the house, to the dogs. "A beautiful day, music like this (I'd had a dream the night before with Fiona Apple talking to Count Basie in a cafe—about his music, him asking her what she thought of it, her telling him his music had "the sound of *inclusive mutiny*," both of them laughing— and I was their waiter!), hundreds of pages of good ribald literature, and you dogs. This is it, right here, the great, slow, *Sunday afternoon ease*. Maybe not quite *all* of it, maybe something's still missing, some*body*, a woman, maybe someday I'll meet her, but this is good. And you guys know how to stop everything and do *this,* don't you?"

One of them, Missouri maybe, exhaled yes, in his sleep.

It was Thursday, but *we* didn't care.

Power and Light

In Kansas City—standing behind the bar, his bar; standing in the golden sundown bars of light coming into the Union Station windows from the west, the west he stares at like it's a magical direction—Roscoe smooths out a clean sheet of white paper on the backbar, just before happy hour starts, and thinks: I need to send this poem to my friend Rosie. She'll get it. If anybody will get this, Rosie will. I'll send it right into that light, into the west. I'll use the post office, of course, but with my heart I'll send it right into that light.

My heart and a stamp.

Kansas City CockaDoodle Do

Blue-Black man in crisp white shirt
(that shirt GLOWS his whole bedroom!)
in the morning sun in Kansas City
with his new (old) chest of drawers
... he takes a moment.

He found the chest on the street,
dragged it down to home
planed the top, polished it
cleaned out the top drawers,
has his keys and his glasses
and his watch
the one he thought he lost
up in those drawers
he made new knobs
screwed them on the drawers
he knows where everything is now,
he's going to work.

He spreads his fingers
on top of the furniture
the clouds are gone
out of his nails and nothing's

shaking. He fingers
the pomade jar, gets it just right,
then

He folds the old paperwork
and the crumbling orange wristband
and those shoe laces and that belt
into the second drawer down,
he'll keep it there.

Buttons his cuffs
pulls them straight
adjusts his watch, dial up,
polished crystal
over old gold granddad numbers
and now, to him, this morning

The sun is *so yellow*
The sky is *so blue*
and the fall leaves
Redder than ever! Blowing Around!
And the dog next door
who's barking at him
even his teeth are *so white!*

On the way to work
first day
at the Union Station Bar
the man is right on time.

And taking it.

*Roscoe smooths the page with his long cigar fingers, ruby red
cuff links flashing in the setting sun like shiny gold and red cigar
bands (this could be Roscoe's next poem, maybe it already is!), then
he folds his poetry into tonight's menu and shelves it in the backbar
whiskey bottles. He turns around, prepping the bar for happy hour.*

*Roscoe had a little birthday party with the waiters, cooks, and
busboys after closing a few nights ago; he'd turned sixty, an age he'd
been dreading since he turned fifty, but it seems alright tonight, sixty.
He'd been thinking of writing about that in his next poem, bringing
in some lines about him being a "setting sun," but he knows better
than that now, because he feels better than that, now.*

Roscoe looks through the north windows into downtown K.C., sees the top of the Power and Light Building warming up, beginning to light up for the night.

"Power and Light, man. Power and Light," he whispers.

And this is the first line of his next poem.

Fire

I woke up early Friday morning, refreshed and ready to detect something.

I stretched, yawned, and the phone rang; Mrs. Hamptons wanted me to return to her mansion. I got this message via answering machine, via Fyodor, who told me she wanted to have a "sit-down" with me. I heard this as I was *lying down*, in bed.

So, I got myself dressed, a bit less formal this time; my new blue jeans and a green corduroy coat (brown leather elbow patches) over a black T-shirt, and an Irish cap, black and white herringbone. I thought I looked snappy, sort of *French detective*. I fed the dogs, who'd been patiently watching my fashion routine.

We all walked out to the van and took a look at it. A good ride, creamy white, new tires all around, all the hubcaps missing, a Beatles bumper sticker on the back bumper. Kansas and Missouri studied the van too, then Kansas walked up and pissed on the rear, left tire.

"I hope there aren't gonna be any car chases on this caper," I said to Missouri, below and by my side. He looked handsome this morning. He was wearing his new leash and collar ensemble—blue leash and red collar—so he looked like one of the Budweiser Clydesdales. Of course, the reminder of a Budweiser Clydesdale played flashback hell with my new, brief life of sobriety, so I looked at Kansas instead, with his dull brown collar, and got in the van.

E, read the gas gauge as I started up the engine. I headed to Fire's Gas Station.

When I got there, Fire was writing in a black leather notebook on top of one of the pumps, nobody around, no customers, very quiet. He was so into the writing he didn't hear the van drive in, didn't hear me get out, didn't hear Kansas and Missouri barking. He didn't even know I was there until I walked up and touched his writing arm.

This startled him wildly, and his writing hand made a mark on the page that wasn't a word, or even a letter, but a violent black, downward slashing line; it could have been the graphic art from a front page story of the *Wall Street Journal,* with words like PANIC! STOCKS CRASH! BLACK TUESDAY! surrounding it.

But it was only Friday, so Fire relaxed and smiled when he saw me.

"Fill 'er up, Mr. Hosé!" I said, and patted his shoulder, the non-writing one. He folded up the notebook and started filling the van's tank.

Fire's Gas Station was the last full-service gas station in Pasadena. Fire even wore a bright white canvas jumpsuit as he served, with *Fire* stitched in red thread on his chest. He said this made some of the customers a little jumpy as he pumped their gas, but we thought it was funny; of course, it *had* been my idea. The jumpsuit, the name in red thread, also the name.

Fire Hosé is pronounced Fire *José* because his real name is José, José Orinar. Just after I'd met him in a Pasadena pub (Lucky Baldwins; both of us singing, loudly, both of us getting thrown out) and after a long period of what Fire said had been "the high fun," he began limping badly and found out (from a shocked orthopedic surgeon, who asked him, "What have you been *doing?*") that he needed a double hip replacement. I drove him to the hospital, waited in the waiting room, and hung out with him all the days after surgery while he slowly healed.

One night, when I had come by to check on him, he was on so much morphine that he was having some *high fun* again. He was on his feet and we were walking up and down the halls (I was trying to keep up) when he noticed a fire cabinet in the hospital hallway that said: FIRE HOSE. He thought it was the funniest thing he'd ever seen, and he kept repeating it: *Fire José! Fire José! Fire José*! and laughing, dancing up and down the halls. I suggested it as a pen name.

José Orinar is a poet, and he'd always wanted a flashy poetic pen name, instead of what he called "my pedestrian peso-a-dozen name."

"Fire Hosé!" he screamed that night. "Who needs Juan Ramón Jiménez when you can get the even wilder, lyrical work of *Fire Hosé?* Hosé practically *pisses* poetry! Highly flammable!"

When he checked out of the hospital, the staff even paged his exit over the intercom, using his new name.

But back to the case.

Back to the gas station.

I pointed at his notebook on top of the pumping gas pump.

"I really like the way you write, Fire. You working on your autobiography today or is that more poetry?"

"Poetry, Red. I'm proud of it. I think I've found my niche and I intend to scratch it."

Silence settled over us. Fire pumped gas into the van and looked off toward the snow-topped mountains. I did too, following his gaze to a line of tiny pines up there, bending sideways in high wind, blowing snow. Kansas and Missouri growled. A breeze came by. Out of the corner of my eye, I secretly looked at Fire who kept on looking at the mountains, philosophically; I could see he was about to say something.

"That was pretty good, wasn't it?" he said.

"Well, yes, I was just about to say that. And I think you should, too. *Scratch it*, I mean."

Out of the corner of my other eye, I saw that Kansas and Missouri were looking up at the mountains, too.

"I will. I'm going to write my life and some poetry and stand here and pump gas and I don't care what *anybody* says a poet is supposed to be doing for a living!"

The van's tank filled with gas and the pump clicked off; Fire pulled the nozzle out and slung it back into the pump holster like a Mexican movie cowboy.

"Ok?" he said. He was looking me in the eye.

"*Ok*! I'm *with* ya, Fire! Keep pumping!"

The silence came back on a new breeze, Fire and I looked up at the mountains again, but this time Kansas and Missouri started barking. They didn't want to go through all *that* again. I handed Fire my Visa card, he beeped it on the pump, handed it back, and I slid into the van, behind the wheel.

"All I know is that you're Fire Hosé, *poet and petrol man*, and that I'm Red Jumbo, *detective*. And I'm ready for action."

"You're a detective now? When did that happen? Do you have a case, a client?"

"The Hamptons. I'm on the way to their little 25-room shack over by the Huntington Library now. Someone killed their maid, Rosalita. Or, it was suicide. Or, *something.*"

Fire leaned in the van window. Kansas licked him. "Be careful, Red. I know that guy, Mr. Hamptons. He gasses up here all the time, then goes next door for pie and burger."

"Dangerous?"

"No. I don't *think* so. But condescending."

"That *is* dangerous."

"Careful, Red. Really condescending. Or at least he is with me."

"Don't worry about me, Fire. I was born for this case. And anyway, how much longer were we going to wait to be who we *are?*"

Fire pulled out of the van window, stood up, and shook my hand. After all the *high fun* of his life, he'd never smiled so brightly.

"Go Jumbo, go! I know you'll solve something!"

"Keep pumpin', Fire. *This is it! This is us!* From now on."

In the rear-view mirror I saw his silver pen move and twinkle in the sunshine over the gas pump as I drove toward the Hamptons.

Drool

Fyodor looked worried as he came out of the Hamptons gatehouse. His eyes met mine when I drove up, but they didn't look like they wanted to pop out of their sockets and shake hands with me. I turned off the ignition.

"What's the matter, Fyodor?"

"I don't believe in 'tough love,' Red. Or in 'reality checks' or in anybody telling me anything 'for my own good,' as they say. I don't want any of that."

"Well, I wouldn't either. What brought all this on?"

"My wife, Ruby, her *brother*—he told me last night that I was too smart for this job, that I was wasting my potential, that I was taking the easy way out, and that his sister was probably going to get bored with me sooner or later. He kind of cornered me last night with all this shi, uh—*stuff*—then he hugged me, first time for that, and gave me this book."

Fyodor handed me the book. On the cover was a giant pastel rainbow, trying to be psychedelic, the arches covered in words, making the title:

"Going for the BOLD in Your Life; How to Grab the Brass Ring and Ride it to Personal GOLD!"

"Wow, Fyodor. Long title," I said. "And," I looked at the back page, "677 pages? Who has time to go for the bold when you're stuck in a book this long? And look at the footnotes!"

"And then, after he hugged me, he said that he was just saying all this for my own good, that it was a bit of tough love: a reality check, he said."

"So he really got all those cliches into one sentence? That *is* a lot of shit to be cornered by."

"Yeah, Red. A mouthful, huh?"

"I'll say. I guess he really read this book. Well look, Fyodor, do you like this job?"

"Yeah, it's ok. It *is* easy, though."

Kansas and Missouri were sniffing at the cover of the book, licking and nuzzling the spine.

"What's wrong with easy?"

Fyodor snapped brightly alert. Kansas and Missouri, together, each with a corner of the book in their mouths, carried it to the back seat.

"Gee, Red. I've never heard anybody say that before. Not my parents, none of my school teachers. Certainly nobody in a church."

"Those people are sometimes just in the way. Take it from a friend, hell—take it from yourself. Easy is good, Fyodor, it eases the way—*being easy*—and it may be a way of … *blooming*. I'd say you're doing just fine. But *you* know that, you knew it all along."

Fyodor looked out over the grounds, toward the Hamptons mansion; butterflies and birds and chipmunks and slow-moving skunks on the long green lawn; past the grounds up to those mountains again, miles to the north, clouds and fog moving over the top of them like a Japanese ink wash painting.

All beautiful; Fyodor began to smile.

I heard a noise and checked the rearview mirror; I saw the dogs' heads jerking up and down in the mirror in the back of the van, making kibbles and bits out of the tough love book.

"But what about you, Red? Is your job easy?"

"So far," I said. "Of course, who knows what's next with the Hamptons. She's expecting me, right?"

"Yes she is, Red. Actually, they both are, and they're mad, too. They're mad at *you*."

I looked up the driveway and saw something flashing in one of the large lower windows—Mrs. Hamptons jewels, maybe. Waiting for me. *Let them wait*, said some new voice, inside.

"Hey, Fyodor, how *about* your wife? Ruby, you said? Everything ok there?"

"Ruby, yes. We're so much in love, Red. She works here too. She's the landscaper and gardener, supposedly *in charge* of the groundskeeping staff, though I doubt the staff can tell, and she couldn't care less. She's only ever used her authority once, but upwards, in the direction of the Hamptons, getting raises for the staff a week after she got her job, along with new work boots and straw hats. And the parties!—we have backyard parties nearly every weekend with the groundskeepers, which are so fun and *musical* that they've formed a mariachi band! The leader of the band, Peter Márquez, has a beautifully rich, deep voice, a vibrato that rattles drinking glasses, and he dances with his guitar like a matador. He's trying to get them recorded out in the valley somewhere. It's a strong and talented band, for a bunch of gardeners!"

"Well, why *not* gardeners, you know? Do they have a name, this band?"

"Sure do, Red. They're called, *Pete Mas*. As in—Peter Marquez *and* his wonderful band, right? "

"*Pete Mas*. I like the sound of that. So, you and Ruby have a really good life together."

"We do. We live a few stations down the Gold Line, so when we get off work, we get on the train, go home and watch movies all night. Well, most of the night, until we start making movies of our own—if you catch my drift."

Fyodor smiled, I smiled, then we spent a few minutes trying to out-wink each other about *that drift*.

I looked at the freeway in the distance, below the mountains, and saw the long, slow line of cars in late morning rush hour, creeping along.

"If you want a reality check from me, I'd say *your* reality looks awfully good, Fyodor. Very full of love and friends. And music. Nice and, *easy?*"

"Yeah, Red. Most people I talk to, it's always about how *hard* it all is. Being happy, I mean. Or being whatever you want to be."

"Most people. My grandfather—"Jumping Jack" Jumbo—had a thought about *most people*. A little nasty, coming from him; I never knew a more cheerful, kind, or encouraging man. Colorful too, he got crazier and crazier, which in our family meant more and more *optimistic*, the older he got. He loved turning ninety! I loved all that about him, but I guess he felt that most people didn't understand him, and maybe they'd been a little nasty to *him*. Still, he never went bitter. Though he did say that one thing about *most people*."

I started up the van.

"What did he say, Red?"

"The majority drools."

I put the van in gear and started up the drive toward the waiting, *mad-at-me* Hamptons; Kansas and Missouri in the back, chewing, hacking, and coughing on wet pulpy bits of tough love and reality.

Enflowerment

I drove up the hill, into the circle drive, gently coasted to a stop in the deep, cool bamboo shade, poured a bottle of water into a bowl for the dogs, left them with some biscuits (as a complement to the appetizer of the self-help book), and walked up to the front door. Mrs. Hamptons opened it before I could knock, and she was all smiles. She seemed energetic, cheerful, not angry at all—even happy to see me again.

"Mr. Jumbo! So good to see you again. Golly, you look ... different, today. A tad *European?* I was thinking, before you arrived, that though we have some talking to do, concerning the *case,* I was wondering—would you like to see my electric dresses? It may have some bearing on the case. Or ... *not.* Come in, *come in,*" she pleaded, pulling me in the door and bursting into wild laughter, *loud* laughter, seemingly out of proportion to anything going on in the foyer, or anything going on anywhere. I tried to laugh along with her, just to be pleasing, but then she stopped, and we stood in strange and sudden silence. I thought I detected the scent of Tanqueray, but it may have been the scent of various other botanicals casually splaying out of all the hand-thrown pottery in the foyer.

There was a knock on the front door. Mrs. Hamptons swung it open to Fyodor standing there, also all smiles, and very out of breath.

"Fyodor? What are *you* doing here?" she asked, in what sounded like a state of shock, or emergency, her smile had disappeared, and she was looking at Fyodor with such contempt that I stepped between them.

"Electric dresses? Yes, where *are* they? I'd love to see them. Well, WE would, wouldn't we Fyodor? Yes, please, show us ..." I said, enthusiastically smiling, trying to distract her from Fyodor. Too late for that, though, he was already in the house (and for some reason, softly humming "Don't Cry for Me Argentina" behind me), a clear violation of *something.* Sensing that I'd set off some sparks in Fyodor, I kept talking.

"Are they upstairs, in your walk-in closet?" I asked. "Let's walk up, and walk *in*, Ms. Hamptons."

"Why *Ms*. Hamptons?" she asked. "You know how married I am to *Mister* Hamptons. How *happily* married." She nodded to the far corner of the room.

Mr. Hamptons was at a massive, wooden, gold-trimmed desk. He looked up from behind a computer, looked across the room with those tiny, expressionless, fuselage window eyeballs.

"Oh well, I was just being *modern*, calling you Ms., Mrs. Hamptons. It was by way of being respectful. Plus, I'm always tuned in to the feminist wavelength, thanks to my Great-Grandmother, Jezebel Jumbo, who walked with Elizabeth Cady Stanton. Anyway, what's the idea of an electric dress?"

"The electric dresses are part of an overall theme," said Mrs. Hamptons, staring at Fyodor. Mr. Hamptons was also staring at Fyodor from across the room. "People thought I was joking, or out of my mind, but after the men put in the electric fence around the house and grounds, I asked one of them—in coordination with my husband's personal tailor, up on *Green* Street, of course—if they could wire my wardrobe as well. It has to do with the ongoing and insidious illegal alien problem. They are *everywhere*, now."

"So you want them off your grounds and off your body?"

I heard this sentence but I hadn't said it. I *wanted* to say something like this, but hadn't dared. I looked around the room, up to the chandelier, along the baseboards, and the hand-thrown vases, trying to see where it had come from. Everyone was looking around to see who'd said it. Everyone but Fyodor.

He'd said it!

I had skydived once, a long time ago, under much pressure from a church group I had been part of temporarily, involuntarily; skydiving was going to open up my spirituality, they said. I was scared out of my wits to do the skydiving, but I had met the skydiving church group at the church for "jump day," driven out to the airport with them, and I'd gotten on the plane.

The way I felt in the door of the little plane, just before I jumped out, was how I felt now, after Fyodor said what he said. But now, I was ready to jump with him.

"Yes, *Miss* Hamptons, is that it?" I said, jumping. "You trying to solve the immigration problem *electrically?*"

I leaned to get closer to Fyodor and loudly whispered: "Of course, I don't see it as a *problem*, you know. More just the natural course of things. People, like animals, just roaming where they please. Where they desire. Cleaner water over the next hill, more arable soil over the rise, friends and family, cooler shade across the mountains. *Natural*, you know, Fyodor? The way it *should* be."

I leaned back, straightened my posture, and smiled at Mrs. Hamptons.

Mr. Hamptons small eyes flickered like tiny blue pilot lights on a cold stove. But I only sensed that peripherally; my attention was to Ms. Miss *Mrs.* Hamptons.

The silence in the room was like a giant pane of glass, scotch-taped to a ceiling, going to break any second.

"FYODOR! WHAT are you doing in here!?!" screamed Mrs. Hamptons.

"What do you think happened to Rosalita, Mrs. Hamptons?" I asked.

I was starting to feel like a detective, if only for this one job. Or this afternoon. Or however long it lasted. But I liked this feeling, this clarity. I loved being sober now, off the alcohol. I felt so good I wanted to celebrate with a drink or two. Now *that's* ironic, I thought, standing there. *Meanwhile ...*

I looked between Mr. and Mrs. Hamptons, him sitting at his desk, her standing in the middle of the foyer, eyes glazed over. Fyodor asked me, in a whisper, *"Now what?"*

"Um," said Mrs. Hamptons, finally. It was a start.

She went on: "Tempers seem to be flaring, let's be civil and talk like *people* do." She was on the move, towards a group of chairs by a big, floor-to-ceiling bay window full of the Hamptons grounds, mountains in the distance, and my van (my sleeping dogs' legs up in the air and relaxed) in the middle distance.

"Follow me, won't you," she lured, and slurred, "to the *conversation area*?"

I whispered to Fyodor, "Let's give it a try, ok?" He was with me; we walked over and sat down. The "conversation area" was two or three feet lower than the rest of the room and sort of *elegantly* darker, with groups of wingback chairs facing each other.

After we sat down, settled quietly for a moment, Fyodor started jiggling a foot, then he sat up, was about to speak, so I asked Mrs. Hamptons, "What's *your* feeling on what happened to Rosalita?"

"She jumped off the Colorado Street Bridge, Mr. Jumbo," she said, looking at Fyodor like he was about to ignite and set fire to the room. "We've been here before. You know all this. Did you talk to the police? I realize there is scant suspicion of murder, she was very, very VERY depressed, as you can imagine, with her life, her *heritage*, however, I wonder about foul play. A must say, I miss her to this very day."

I watched my watch; my goal was thirty seconds on the sweep secondhand before I'd respond. A technique to keep control of the interview. At fifteen seconds I cracked.

"What do you think, Fyodor? How did Rosalita seem to you?"

Fyodor was surprised by being addressed by me but straightened up in his chair and cleared his throat. He seemed to like being in the catbird seat, at last.

"She always seemed as happy as a clam to me."

"And clams *are* happy, eh, Fyodor?"

"They *are*, Red."

"And she was too, yeah? Rosalita?"

"Happy? Oh yes, Red. Very."

Maybe Mrs. Hamptons felt left out; she interrupted us.

"Please! Fyodor, what are you *doing* here? Who's watching the gate?"

He looked at me.

"Don't look at *me*," I said.

"Mrs. Hamptons, I wanted to talk to you about something," said Fyodor, looking less in the catbird in the seat and more like the mouse under it. "But I don't know if this is the right time, with Red —with Mr. Jumbo—at work here."

Fyodor and Mrs. Hamptons looked at me.

"No please, go on, you two, I'm the investigating detective here, but I can fade to the background for the moment, no problem."

Thinking of background, I wondered what Mr. Hamptons was up to, in the dark corner across the room. The pilot lights in Mr. Hamptons eyes flickered like someone had walked past the stove, but he said nothing. I settled back in my chair and yawned a little, signaling to everyone: *fading to the background now.*

"Well, Fyodor?" Mrs. Hamptons asked. This was probably new territory for Fyodor, a unique social situation for him, but he jumped in.

"I'd like to work *less hard* here at the house, Mrs. Hamptons."

This surprised Mrs. Hamptons. Me too, and I liked it. Mrs. Hamptons leaned forward. "You *what?*"

"Yes, I ... I'd like to concentrate a bit less on work. I mean, get the work done, of *course*, to be sure, but I'd like to focus not so much on work as on ... blooming ... exploring my options, like the *enflowerment* of my soul, you know? Is that a word, Mr. Jumbo?"

This was getting better and better. I didn't want to say anything or rain on Fyodor's parade, so I nodded at him as if to say: *Yes, go on!*

He saw the nod, and did.

"So listen, Mrs. Hamptons," he said, commandingly.

She put a hand in the air: then, one finger. Fyodor and I knew a point was about to be made.

"Fyodor! You've always possessed such a, such a magnificent ... *work ethic*," she said, turning and sneering at me. "What's become of that?"

"Oh, c'mon, Mrs. Hamptons. Aren't we past that? What a boring thing to discuss. Or even think about."

This was a jolt for Mrs. Hamptons, I think. She *looked* jolted. I was having fun watching these two. Meanwhile, Fyodor was now focused on the wall on the other side of the room, a painting there. It was a beautiful work, alright. I recognized it. It looked like an original. The Hamptons certainly had the money for it, if maybe not the taste. Fyodor, noticing me noticing it, leaned a little closer to me.

"Red. That painting there. Isn't that a Utrillo?"

"De Kooning, Fyodor."

"Oh yes, Red. You're right, of course." He sighed. "All those motels, as a kid ... my mom and dad and brothers and sisters, we traveled so much, crammed into motel rooms, one Holiday Inn after another, splashing in the pool, *Magic Fingers* ... everything starts to look the same after awhile ..."

Mrs. Hamptons looked wired enough to get electrocuted in one of her electric dresses, if she had one on. And Mr. Hamptons was slowly rising from his desk. His pilot light eyes were still flickering blue and his stove looked lit. Normally, I would've been frightened by his body language, but I was having so much fun with my imagination, with the pilot light image in my mind, that I was actually quite relaxed.

But here he came, stepping down into the conversation area. We all stood up—maneuvered around the chairs, changing places and making room for him, a very large man—then began to sit, in slow motion. Mr. Hamptons was the last to sit; he waited for us, then sat. He was in charge, but his pants were unzipped, which marred his presence a bit. We were seated in a kind of circle like we were about to play cards. His presence dealt us a great silence from the deck, and we all sat there, looking at our hands.

Now I *was* nervous, too nervous to look at the secondhand of my watch to watch how long this silence was lasting, or going to last. The woman in the De Kooning painting looked like she was about to scream.

"Why are you here, Mr. Jumbo? I distinctly remember telling you you were not necessary." Mr. Hamptons looked at me like I was going to give him the wrong answer no matter what I said and he was ready to attack.

Fyodor was laughing. "A *Red Jumbo* is always necessary!" he said.

This was the place in the card game where someone is shuffling the cards, but they fumble the deck and spray the cards all over the room. Mrs. Hamptons looked jolted again. She *had* to be wearing one of those electrified dresses.

"Oh baby."

We all heard it; nobody moved. I thought I heard deep breathing, wondered if anyone else heard it. Yes (I was thinking), that is *definitely* breathing, and a kind of *gasping* breath at that, but when I looked around at the others, everyone seemed to be holding theirs.

"Oh ... *baby*." Me and Fyodor were looking under our chairs.

"Oh baby baby baby *baby* ... I want, I NEED your GREAT! BIG! COCK!" Me and Fyodor were searching the room for clues. This wasn't coming from *Mrs.* Hamptons, but *Mr.* Hamptons was on his feet, the pilot lights in his eyes blown out, and he was on the run. Towards his desk.

"I need you to *fill* me, baby, fill me with your sweet cream of meat!"

Mr. Hamptons was a large man, but he slid into his desk like he was stealing third base.

The computer was turned away from the room, but as he sat down to it, Mr. Hamptons face, aside from being highly startled, was bright red and purple and kind of *swirling*, from the glare of whatever was on the screen. With a click of his mouse, those colors left his face and he looked over at us. There was still a breathing sound, a kind of slurping noise, but with another click, that too was gone.

Mr. Hamptons looked pale. The red and purple swirling had now transferred over to Mrs. Hamptons face. Mr. Hamptons put his hands on top of his head in what *looked* like disgust.

"Where do these things come from? The internet is ... so vile, and so *invasive.* And a man like me*,* receiving *this* trash! I'm going to get off the internet for good! I'm sick of it, just *sick* of it!"

Mr. Hamptons had kind of rumpled himself running to his computer so quickly, his jacket pulled slightly off one shoulder, and as he stood up, his pants fell down. (I *thought* his pants were unzipped, so this didn't surprise *me.*)

There was an awkwardness in the air now which really slowed down time and killed the conversation. Mr. Hamptons *did* rejoin us in the conversation area, but it seemed to take the rest of the afternoon for him to zip up and walk over.

Fyodor and I watched as he sat down and looked at his wife, who was smiling, but it was a sad smile, her eyes glazed again. She was looking out the window.

This reminded me of something, and I too looked out the window. There, about fifty yards away, in the bamboo shade, were Kansas and Missouri, awake and looking back at us from the van. They have very acute hearing and must have heard all the running, heavy breathing, and slurping.

I waved and smiled at them. They smiled back, no waving, looked peaceful. I knew their water bowls were full, the van parked in a calm, cave-cool shade.

I looked over at Mr. Hamptons.

"Where were we?" he said, breaking the long awkwardness.

I looked at Fyodor, sitting next to me, whose eyes were very big —very *engaged* in the situation.

"I think we were about to discuss whether or not I'm on this case," I said.

De Kooning

Another awkward silence oozed into the room but I was getting used to awkwardness, becoming daringly *at home* with it, even looking for it. I didn't know what I was going to say next and that was *fun.*

But then the phone rang and broke the silence. Mr. Hamptons looked relieved; he was very daringly *not* at home with awkwardness. Too bad for him; I was ready to swim in it. I was on the way to a new way of life.

Mrs. Hamptons, shifting into business-like gravitas, reached for the phone on the table in the gravitational center of the conversation area.

"Yes?" she said.

Yes? for the rich. *Hello* for the poor. *Don't answer it!* for the very poor.

"200 cases of Budweiser to Cedar City, Utah ... 150 cases of Vive Clicquot to Truckee, California ... the old hotel there ... yes, *that* one ... next, the wine cooler shipment to Eureka, Arkansas, and then order 77 cases of Boulevard Beer, by rail of course, in Kansas City. Thank you. Oh? He what? *Again?* Ok, terminate him. No, today. Alright. Goodbye."

Mrs. Hamptons hung up, made some notes in a Moleskine on the arm of her chair, and looked up at us.

"Had to let someone go, eh?" I asked.

She gave me a *none of your business* dirty look, but answered. "Yes, Mr. Jumbo. One of my shipping clerks has been sampling the wares, so to speak."

"Ah, that's tough. Couldn't give him a second chance, I guess?"

Now she just gave me a dirty look, *mean.* Mr. Hamptons, out of the spotlight for a moment, chuckled softly, but kept quiet.

"No, Mr. Jumbo. I don't believe in that. Though Enrique was one of our oldest employees, he was with us from the start in the shipping department. Worked his way up from our backyard. He was once our gardener. Even then, though, I thought he was *tippling through the tulips*, as it were."

Mrs. Hamptons looked over at her husband to see if he'd heard her pun. He had, and his smile was *big*, a painted-on circus clown smile; at the moment, literally caught with his pants down, he was eager to laugh at anything she said.

I went on, in defense of Enrique. "Hard, though, firing someone, I guess, never had to do it myself. But it's also hard, when you've got that drinking need. I mean, it's *fun*, drinking. It can really broaden your outlook, for a while anyway, or until it flattens you out completely. But if life is a black and white summer re-run, a little drink or two can make it a wide-screen technicolor extravaganza. But then I suppose it gets to where you have an extravaganza *every day*. Day and night. And then, when your dad dies, you need it, or if it's Easter, you need it, or if a bird flies over without the rest of the flock you feel sad for that lone bird and you need it. Well, Mrs. Hamptons, *Mr.* Hamptons (I didn't want him to feel left out), I know you have a business to run. But it's just *too bad* for Enrique."

I'd gotten a little worked up. I hoped I hadn't exposed myself with my speech about drinking.

"You seem to know something about this 'drinking need' yourself, Mr. Jumbo," said Mrs. Hamptons, who was studying me from head to toe.

A bank of clouds had rolled over Pasadena (and the Hamptons estate) (and the cool bamboo shade of dogs, probably cooling it even more) during this conversation, the room had gotten dark, but now the sun came out and lit up the great white wall—De Kooning and all —behind Mr. and Mrs. Hamptons. It was a dramatic moment; I wondered if it was symbolic. With all the abstract expression going on in the conversation area, mine included, I decided *yes,* it was symbolic, but of what?

"Shall we call it by its name," said Mr. Hamptons. *"Alcoholism."*

They were both studying me, but only my head at this point, not the toes. I could even feel Fyodor's peripheral survey of me. I made a mental note to write down "peripheral survey" later that night, for future detective conversations.

I became casual in my body language before responding to Mr. Hamptons.

"Oh, you know, I googled it. Alcoholism, I mean. Handy knowledge, in my job."

The doorbell rang.

I had a feeling the conversation area was about to expand.

Fyodor went to answer the door while I simultaneously excused myself to the nearest bathroom, first asking the Hamptons where it was. From the bathroom, just around the corner from the foyer, I could hear the visitor at the front door announce himself.

"Officer Serge Controllente, Pasadena Police Department, to see the Hamptons."

Marble and cottage cheese

As I peed, I heard some superficial small talk in the foyer, then Mrs. Hamptons brought Officer Controllente into the house, and as they passed near my bathroom door, she asked him a question.

"Care for a drink?"

"Yes," I said to myself, in the bathroom. Where'd that come from? *Who said that? Shhh!*

"Why yes, Mrs. Hamptons," said Officer Controllente, "why not? Maybe a glass of wine? A nice Bordeaux, maybe? Why not let my hair down a bit? I'm done for today, after I'm done here, with my update about Rosalita."

The conversation seemed very relaxed, considering it was with a policeman, and about someone who'd either killed herself or was murdered. I wanted to get out there, so I zipped up and checked myself in the mirror. I looked good, but funny how I'd said yes to a drink from the bathroom.

Careful, I said, to the mirror.

I rejoined the conversation area, nodded at Officer Controllente, and we all sat down. Officer Controllente sat on our side of the room —between me and Fyodor. He was a smiling, handsome guy, friendly eyes the color of Tootsie Rolls, with thick, shiny black hair, combed straight back, reflecting the wall sconces and chandelier that Mrs. Hamptons had just switched on (getting dark in the room again). There was a flash of silver in his sideburns and deep widow's peak which gave him a lot of *dash*. Fit and energetic, he looked to be anywhere from forty-five to fifty, and he wore his police uniform loosely, a little disheveled, his badge slightly askew, and he smelled of what I recognized as my favorite men's cologne: Gio, by Armani. I wasn't certain of that, also it seemed unusual for a cop to wear cologne, on duty. I wondered if it was unusual for me to notice cologne as keenly and as often as I do, but I knew it had to do with my life in the Midwest, where sensual extravagance of any kind is unusual, especially with men. So I'd come to appreciate and applaud it with men.

"Uh, officer, is that Gio, by Armani?

"Acqua di Gio, yes. You know it?"

"Yes, I do. I'd have some on now, but I ran out of it."

"Macy's over on Lake Street, *on sale* right now."

"Hey, thanks. I'll head up there later."

The Hamptons were glaring at us, but saying nothing. I figured we were waiting for Serge's glass of wine to arrive. There were a few moments to think. What I was thinking—what I was wondering—was why was I always noticing colognes and perfumes? I'd be the first to say that no one *has* to wear cologne or perfume—I liked it, enjoyed the sensual, romantic playfulness of it—but it's not a *should* for anyone, men or women. I decided to accept it, and perk up my nose even more.

"By the way, who are you?" asked Officer Controllente.

"Officer Serge Controllente, of the Pasadena Police Department, meet Red Jumbo, private detective," announced Mrs. Hamptons, in her *foyer voice*. "We thought maybe you two might compare notes on the case?"

The sun gave up under the clouds again, the room darkened, and the painting on the far wall raged up red and yellow under a white pin light. Officer Controllente gave it a curious, curatorial look. "Nice," he said. "Kinkade?"

"De Kooning," I said, just conversational. Casual. No need for snobbery with the police department.

"Oh? Thomas De Kooning? I think I just saw one of these at the Glendale Galleria."

"No, not him. This is his brother, *Willem* De Kooning."

Officer Controllente crossed his legs, to get a better view of the art, I thought.

"Oh yes. Of course, now I see."

I was right about the legs.

The glass of wine arrived by Alberto, who nodded at me, glanced at Fyodor, and *really* glanced at Officer Controllente; they seemed very friendly, very familiar. Probably not, though. Just a couple of friendly guys. Then, Alberto was gone. Officer Controllente took a slow easy sip of the wine, and stared into the painting. He sighed.

"Good?" I asked, nodding at his glass.

"Oh yes, Mr. Jumbo. I always like red more than white. Less sweet."

"Red."

"Yes, that's right," said the officer.

"No, I mean, call me Red."

"Oh yes, of course. I was still thinking of the wine. Call me Serge."

We shook hands. We were becoming friends already.

"Yes, Red, this is a very good wine. Very floral and frisky. Of course, I'm no expert. But I *am* in a good mood! Aren't you having any?"

"No, thanks. Too late in the day for me."

Serge uncrossed his legs and sat up, suddenly frisky, like his wine.

"Mrs. Hamptons, *Mr.* Hamptons ... *you guys* (looking at me and Fyodor), this case—what I wanted to talk about this afternoon—I *have* gotten somewhere with it."

"Thank God!" cried out Mrs. Hamptons, picking up her Moleskine and pen again, ready to take notes.

"Good work, Officer, we knew we could count on *you,*" said Mr. Hamptons, aiming his emphasis on the word *you* at *me,* but meaning *Serge.*

"What's going on here, Officer Controllente?" I asked, feeling, I'll admit, suddenly competitive with my new friend Serge. "With the case, I mean."

He took another *slow motion* sip of the wine and set the glass on the coffee table in the center of the conversation area, with a distinct clink.

"Coyote," he said in a very low voice.

"Coyote?" I asked.

"Coyote," Serge reaffirmed with a nod.

"*Coyote?*" asked Fyodor.

"Coyote," Officer Controllente repeated, keeping the motor running. "Coyote, *dead* now."

"Explain," Mr. Hamptons instructed.

"Do," said Mrs. Hamptons, the conversation getting increasingly haiku-like.

"As you know, the body was under the Colorado Street Bridge—she fell or jumped—we may never know—she may have survived the fall but I doubt it. As she lay there, she was partially eaten by a coyote. Hopefully, she died before the coyote came."

Mrs. Hamptons put her pen down. "Oh dear."

"If you would like to see her, or the photographs, for that matter, though it's not really procedure, that can be arranged. Only Alberto needs to view and identify the body—*Rosalita*—him being her next of kin. But you may, Mrs. Hamptons. *Mr.* Hamptons, if you need a moment with her, for closure. I don't recommend it, however. The coyote really bit into her, ate her."

"No, no, no need of that," said Mrs. Hamptons, quickly. "I thought she had committed suicide. She *was* very sort of mopey though, you know. I always told her to count her blessings. I thought we had very much *involved* her around here, wouldn't you say so, Fyodor?"

Fyodor glared at her, didn't answer.

"I will pass on viewing her body. Of *course,* she was illegal," said Mr. Hamptons, laughing and standing up. "Most of these people are *born* illegal."

I felt my arms go hard.

"What does that mean, Mr. Hamptons?" I asked.

He couldn't stop laughing; he ignored me and walked over to Serge. "So officer, the case is closed?"

"Yes, Mr. Hamptons."

"Good. We can all move on now. I'm tired of all the long faces around here," he said to Mrs. Hamptons. "Let the dead bury the dead, as they said in that movie—what *was* it, Precious, the title?"

Precious? I didn't want to look at these people anymore so I stared into the flaring red and yellow swashes in the De Kooning painting. I loved the painting but I wanted to rip it up.

Mr. Hamptons was standing and looking at me but I couldn't look back. "Anything *you* have to offer, Mr. Jumbo? Any sophisticated politically correct National Public Radio liberal-type tolerance philosophy you'd care to enlighten us with?"

I thought, ok—*fuck it.*

"Sure, Mr. Hamptons. I do. Are you ready? You may want to take notes."

Mrs. Hamptons lifted her pen. "Oh *do tell*, Mr. Jumbo," she said.

I reached for Serge's wine glass, still a sip on the bottom, but stopped.

"Fuck you. Both of you."

"WHAT?" screamed the Mrs.

"Um, I don't think I quite heard that, Mr. Jumbo," said the Mr., walking slowly closer.

"Let's get out of here, Red," said Serge, squeezing my arm and standing up. Fyodor was standing up too. So was I, but I wasn't done yet.

"I said fuck you, you rich, marble-twatted bitch, and as for *you,* you entitled, bloated, bigoted lump of caucasian cottage cheese: Fuck *YOU!"*

I made another grab for the wine glass as Serge pulled me toward the door and Fyodor pushed me from behind.

"We'll be leaving now, Mrs. Hamptons, Mr. Hamptons. Call me if you have any questions or concerns," said Serge, in his Officer Controllente voice. "And—sorry for your loss."

"Loss my ass!" Mr. Hamptons yelled. We didn't lose a goddamn thing. And get *him* out of here! Jumbo—*you're fired!"*

"You're an ugly man, Mr. Jumbo," said Mrs. Hamptons, "I thought so from the beginning, ugly in every conceivable way. And your name is stupid, too. Go somewhere and get drunk, stay drunk. Stay by yourself, away from *good* people. You are fired!"

I was being pulled and pushed out of the house by Fyodor and Serge; I was very carried away, in general.

Mr. and Mrs. Hamptons were windmilling their arms around, very red in the face, trying to get at me. Mr. Hamptons fell across the coffee table, Mrs. Hamptons flopped over him, their arms and legs waving all around for some traction to get up and come after me. It was a wild sight; I was feeling angry, confused, and what Mrs. Hamptons said hurt my feelings, but it was funny seeing them entwined and writhing on the floor.

"LOOK at them!" I laughed, pointing at them from inside the tangle of Serge and Fyodor. "They're doing *Caligula!"*

I was crazed, laughing, and then we were out of the house, us three; Fyodor and Serge holding onto me, walking me to the van.

Then, for the first time in a long time—I started crying.

Serge patted me on the back and kept me moving, away from the house. I couldn't see where I was going through my tears.

Fyodor had tears in his eyes too, seeing me crying. "Are you alright, Red? You sure got mad in there, in a flash. It happened so fast. I'm used to the Hamptons, I guess, and used to being in that position. You know, *servile,* and insulted."

"I know, sorry. I'm ok. I think maybe it's a PTSD thing."

"I didn't know you too were in the police department."

"That's LAPD, Fyodor," said Serge.

"Oh, you said *PTSD,* ha! Of course, my mistake! There's so much going on, I misheard you—*hell*, I probably have PTSD too!"

"Who doesn't?" said Serge, "Oh and I *did* like the Caligula reference, Red."

"Did you ever see that movie?" I asked him, sniffling and wiping my eyes.

"Yes, in a hotel ... on my honeymoon, I think. And by the way, I do know the *slight* difference between Willem De Kooning and Thomas Kinkade. I was just playing with the Hamptons. Who probably think the closest someone like me comes to *Art* is through a can of spray paint. Can you drive, Fyodor? I guess maybe *you're* through here, too? Job-wise? Can you drive Red and follow me? We'll go get coffee at the *Crème de la Honky.* I need to talk to you guys." He gave me a squeeze on the shoulder. "Ok, Red?"

"Sure, ok. Thanks, Serge. I could use a coffee. And I don't want to go home, after all that. I could use some company, too. That stuff in there—those motherfuckers, fucking ugly goddamn shit, they don't care, this fuckin' shit just keeps going on, generation after generation—but yeah ... ok, let's go," I said.

"Come on, man. You don't know what's going on yet, Red. You either, Fyodor. Let's get out of here."

I got in the van, passenger side, and Kansas and Missouri jumped in my lap, happy to lick the tears. Then they saw Fyodor's wet face and started in on him as he followed Serge in his police car.

As we caravanned past the front door, Mrs. Hamptons ran out.

"Fyodor, where are *you* going? There's no one at the gate! Come back here!"

"*No!*" he yelled back, and paused—then, "Hey! Mrs. Hamptons —" Fyodor turned to me for a second, braking the van softly. "What did you call her? Oh yes. Marble-twatted bitch? I like it, Red—it's good, I'm pissed off, and I *don't* like her, but it seems too harsh, and insulting in the usual sexist way. Marble-twatted bitch. I want to insult her, but in an equal, *gender-free* way. Ruby and I were talking about that in bed after watching some stupid movie from the seventies. I'm trying to change all that stuff in me, you know?"

I did know, and I knew he was right.

"Me too, Fyodor. I'm changing even as you speak. Anyway, you worked for her, and a lot longer than *I* did, so you say what you need to, in your own way." Fyodor let off the brake and turned back to Mrs. Hamptons. "I don't like you, you ... *jerk!*"

He drove away from the estate and through the grounds, for the last time.

"I can't believe I just said that to her," said Fyodor.

"You were great. How did it feel?"

Serge was stopped up ahead where the Hamptons driveway met the road, waiting for an opening in traffic on South Oak Knoll Avenue. Fyodor half-saluted the gatehouse as we passed it, and flicked on the right turn signal.

"It felt new, I guess. For me, anyway. I wonder what's going to happen now, Red?"

"We'll find out," I said. "More *new*, I think."

Power and Light, Part Two

In her garage room, cozy in a worn, flannel robe—she's worked her way through a stack of Merchant-Ivory movies, starting with "Room with a View," finishing with "Remains of the Day," which reminds her of the old days working for the Hamptons.

Sort of.

"I was almost Anthony Hopkins there for a minute!" she says aloud to herself, laughing, relieved to be free; now identifying with the spirit of the Emma Thompson character.

In this spirit, she dials her cell phone. Two rings, then,

"Good evening, Union Station Bar, this is Trixie, how may I help you?"

Wow, TRIXIE! You don't hear that name much anymore, she thinks. Certainly not in Merchant Ivory films.

"Hello?"

"Oh yes, I'm sorry, is Roscoe there?"

"One moment please." The line clicks and there's music, Duke Ellington's "East St. Louis Toodle-Oo."

Then, a low, oak barrel voice,

"This is Roscoe."

"Roscoe. Hi."

"Hey baby! Well, damn, what's going on? I mean ... are you still with those people, or ... where are you? You still in California? To put it another way—is this it? Are you ready? You made your move?"

"I'm out, Roscoe. I quit."

"But I thought you couldn't. Or they'd turn you in."

"I'm dead, Roscoe. Rosalita's dead."

54

Mist

Fyodor drove us to the Crème de la Honky coffee bar and parked by Officer Controllente's police car. Officer Contr—or Serge—as I was calling him now, was already inside, probably getting a table and ordering us coffee. I looked at Fyodor. "I think we're about to find out about something."

"Yeah, Red. I think so, too."

"I wonder what? Serge said we didn't know what was going on."

"I usually operate in that mist, Red. Not knowing what's going on, I mean."

"And now we're both out of jobs. That must be the world's record for the shortest first detective case, and I didn't even solve it. I didn't even really work at it very much. And I feel bad about Rosalita."

"I really liked her. I missed her before she was dead—I didn't get to see her all that much around the Hamptons place, me stuck at that gate—but now I *really* miss her, Red."

"I miss her and I never even met her," I said. "I guess I *just missed* meeting her."

"Which maybe is another kind of *mist*, you know? Emotionally."

"And that feels sad, Fyodor." Well, fuck it, I give up, I thought. Because now I wondered if talking to Serge was even worth it. He'd found out about the coyote, cracked the case, Rosalita was dead, I was fired, it was over. I'll go in, tell Serge I was taking Fyodor home, that I had something else to do, see you later, Officer Serge, thanks, nice to meet you, etc. There was nothing I'd find out today, or maybe ever, that would change this feeling, an old feeling.

The *fuck it, I give up* feeling—that I used to get lying in bed, as young as twelve or thirteen, probably younger, in the Cloverleaf Gardens Apartments off the highway cloverleaf behind the Holiday Inn in Kansas, listening to my mother's TV set laugh track through the wall all afternoon and into the night, day after day after day and more days way past high school—*that* feeling.

I didn't want to give in to it, all dull and hopeless. But I didn't *really* give in to it back then.

Anyway, that's what the Shawnee Mission Kansas Police Department said after taking me to jail *again*, for trespassing past the barbed wire and the angry-foaming guard dog into the Shawnee Mission Salvage Yard, to beat up junk cars.

"The kid's got spirit, I'll give him that," I overheard one policeman say to the other in the station, after locking me up for the night. "Kinda weird, though, pounding away on cars in a salvage yard past midnight. But at least he's not pounding on other kids. Or his girlfriend."

Those cops, drinking coffee and talking about *me* like that. It gave me some hope. (And hope for a girlfriend.)

But the hell with it, I thought, back in the parking lot of a California coffee bar, not in Kansas anymore. I was a detective, now I'm not. I still have Kansas and Missouri (snoring again, in the back of the van). Still, I didn't want to go home yet.

"I guess we should go in," said Fyodor. He didn't sound very lively about it.

The sound of a BIG engine hovered, above and behind us. It woke up the dogs. It reminded me of something, this sound. I'd been out to LAX the week before, stuck in traffic on the Imperial Highway, close to the main runway. It was that sound; I wondered if a UPS cargo jet was about to make a coffee delivery.

Of course, that wasn't it.

It wasn't *that* big, or high.

But a very big and polished black truck rolled up next to and high above us, turned, backed up and pulled forward, backed up again and parked parallel to the front door of the coffee bar, taking up several parking spaces, the two left wheels up on the sidewalk.

On the back bumper, I saw the sticker: FREEDOM ISN'T FREE!

That's what *he* thinks, I thought.

The truck shook. Nothing to see behind the black-tinted windows, and then all the doors opened, and out came four men in matching sleeveless T-shirts, seemingly matching arm muscles, expressionless except for the matching scowling, behind four pairs of black sunglasses. That made for eight mysterious eyes, more mystery than even Fyodor and I could come up with, put together.

The men stopped near the van and stared at us in their dark glasses, then walked into the Crème de la Honky, moving in the usual middle linebacker-abominable snowman swagger. None of this was very scary, it looked to me like a scene from *West Side Story*, I was waiting for them to start singing. I looked at Fyodor, to see how he was doing.

"Ready?" he asked.

"Ready!" I said. And we were. We were ready for anything. And I had a feeling that's what we were about to get.

Power and Light, Part Three

There's a click, then Duke Ellington again. This time, "Things Ain't What They Used to Be." Another click. The sound of dishes, glasses, silverware banging around, voices, laughter and splashing water, then Roscoe's low, sneaky laugh.

"Sorry to put you on hold. Had to boogie back to the dish room for privacy so we can talk about the plan. Ah man, the fun begins!"

"I'm dead. And Roscoe, I've never felt more ALIVE!"

"Mmm-MMM! Dead! Right on. Still illegal, too, I take it?"

"Oh yeah!"

"Rosie, Rosie, Rosie. Remember baby, Power and Light, always! Now—here's what we're gonna do ..."

Whirlpool

The anything, ready or not, came gradually.

We sat with our cups of coffee and let calm settle on us; it had been a wild hour just gone by.

Serge was quiet, smiling, slowly savoring his latte, looking like he was thinking about something. Like maybe it was someone's birthday and he had a surprise cake coming. The four guys in sunglasses were sitting at the next table looking at us, looking at *me*. They'd finished off their drinks and paid, and now they were just lingering. I put my shades on and gave them a *smile*. A sort of *un*contagious smile. I saw that Serge was watching this.

"That smile has some history, doesn't it, Red?"

"Sure does, Serge," I said.

One of the sunglass guys turned in his chair, creaking it under his big linebacker body, and swung his legs out toward me. "I bet it ain't *American* history," he said.

"Well, no. It's more personal history really," I explained. "It has to do with something between me and my mother."

"Huh. Yeah. Well, I bet your *mother* was an American, at least."

I hadn't looked at Fyodor in the last few minutes since we'd come inside, so I did now, for variety. He didn't seem to want to get involved, so he asked me to pass the cream. I passed it to him. "Here you go, Fyodor."

The other three guys turned toward us in their chairs. "What was that name you just used?" one of the other men asked; this one had a tattoo of the Declaration of Independence coming up out of his T-shirt, spreading across his neck.

I couldn't believe it. "Wow, is that what I think it is, there on your neck?" I said, in a friendly way, and really astonished.

The guy looked like a fullback, about to go offside. "Yeah! It's a very important American document. Ever heard of it, sir? How about you—*Fyodor?*"

"Well, *sure* I have," I said. "I mean, I know the Decoration of Independence when I see it, but what I'm wondering is—is it *all* there? I mean all the fine print and all the signatures? That big old

John Hancock must be all across your belly, or—somewhere down around there." I pointed lower.

Four big men; their table was still, but getting restless.

"That must've really hurt, that tattoo."

Four big men; their table and chairs were beginning to creak. Serge pulled his badge out of his jacket and set it down quietly by his coffee cup.

Everyone quietly noticed it.

The tattooed man sat back in his chair, took a deep breath, and exhaled, slowly. "Freedom isn't free," he said. He was big but he was pouting.

"Got that right," said one of the others.

"Aw c'mon, fellas. Of *course* it is," I said. "Should everything lead to conflict? Must everything be gained through violence? Must everything be *gained?* Even now you guys look like you're ready for conflict, with *us*. Why? I bet you were taught that by someone, somewhere. Dad, grandad, coach? And man, those lessons, gone unquestioned, really stand the testosterone of time. *Get it?* Here, I'll even pass you the cream—*free!*—from the sacred cow of brotherly love and compassion. Fyodor? Please pass the cream."

There was a moment, nothing happened, and then they got up and left the Crème de la Honky. All was quiet until they got in the van, there was the loud rumbling of the engine, and they were gone, leaving a lingering cloud of blue smoke.

"Fun to be undercover sometimes. Please pass the cream, Fyodor," said Serge, and he put the badge back in his pocket.

Fyodor passed the cream.

"You know, I feel kind of bad about that, those guys," I said. "Seems like lately, I'm either crying or confrontational. Up and down, I'm too volatile. And now the first case of my new job is over and I didn't do very much. I could use some good news. How about you, Fyodor?"

"Yeah, me too. I'm probably fired, which will probably get Ruby fired too, and poor Rosalita … " said Fyodor, at length, after a long pause. Then, he said, "I don't—oh, *hell*—I don't understand *anything* anymore. This isn't much of a good day. I'm like you, Red. I'm either mad at myself or everybody else, or scared, or both. I worked for those Hamptons way too long, hated it, and didn't quit. But I think I just did, so now what? I guess I could use some good news, too."

I patted Fyodor on the shoulder and we looked over at Serge. He was gazing at a travel poster on the wall behind him; gazing and simultaneously stirring a whirlpool in his latte, not spilling a drop. Fyodor and I made eye contact—mutually amazed by this smooth and steady stirring without looking—then we looked up at the poster.

It was a sunset picture of the cliffs and surf off the west coast of Ireland somewhere. Written in the early evening sky over the cliffs in the poster was the line:

Dingle is Waiting for You
O Come, Come and *Dream!*

Serge turned around, blew on his cup, and took a sip. He reached for a beat-up paperback on the next table, *Nothing Normal in Cork*, and flipped through the pages with a smile.

"I should do that, go there. I really oughta do that, someday," he said.

Fyodor and I smiled and shrugged at Serge like yes, he should, *we* should, we probably *won't*. Serge swallowed, smiled, and said, "She's alive, you know."

Then he said it again.

"Rosalita's alive. And *very* well."

Illegal

"She's alive?"

I couldn't believe it. I was confused. I wondered if I was back on the case again now, or if there was a case, or *what?*

Serge smiled at me. "Yes, Red. She is. And not far from here. At my place. Would you like to meet her? She would like to meet you. And I'm sure she'd like to see Fyodor again."

"She knows about me?" I asked.

"Yes, she does. She left a message on my phone as I was driving over here, checking in, to see how things are proceeding, so I called her back—I described the scene at the Hamptons a little while ago. She likes how you stood up to them, told them off. She especially liked your line about the *marble-twatted* ... well, you know ... that thing you said. She's glad to know that you are so much on her side."

"Her what? I mean, yes, I am. I mean, I thought she was dead, so yeah, I guess I was, or am, on her side, but—*wait a minute* ... "

"Let me call her back and set up a meeting. You guys got anything going on this afternoon?"

I started to look at my watch, but what for? Fyodor and I looked at each other and couldn't think of a thing we might have going on.

"Sure, today's good for me," I said.

"My dance card's clear," said Fyodor.

"Ok," said Serge, and dialed his phone.

"I'll be right back," said Fyodor, on his way to the men's room. He was smiling, he had tears in his eyes.

I was confused and looked it I guess because Serge reached over and squeezed my arm.

"You'll understand all this very soon, don't worry." He was waiting, listening to Rosalita's phone ringing. "You're already a hero, Red."

That felt good to hear. But how? I wondered why he said it. I wondered if it was true. I always wanted to be a hero, do something heroic. It wasn't something anyone had ever looked at me and expected. I couldn't remember, when I was young, anyone really *looking* at me. So, when I was young, I started disappearing, and alcohol helped, kept me company. But after what Serge had said, I started trying to feel proud of what I had done, but I wasn't sure what it was, didn't even know where to start to figure that out.

I said: "Well, Serge, I don't know what to say," and that was true. But my confidence was building, in spite of my confusion. And it *did* feel good, telling off the Hamptons. Also afterwards, when I started to cry. I felt a little *cleaned out* from the crying. That had surprised me, it came out of the blue, but it also came out of many years of being *me*.

Serge was smiling at me, then he put a hand up and held the phone closer to his ear. "Rosalita? Yes ... *yes!* ... yes, that's how I feel, too ... great ... and Kansas City? Good, good ... and *now* we have Detective Jumbo with us! ... yes, he's here with me now, we're at the Crème de la Honky, also Fyodor ... yeah, he's fine, and he's so happy to know you're ok, *alive*, as is Red, though they're both a little confused, needless to say ... haha ... oh, and you should've seen the Hamptons! ... I've never seen Mrs. Hamptons that color before! ... haha ... yeah, she was even redder than Red, here! So I was thinking we should meet, like this *afternoon*, and all get on the same page, what do you think? And probably it's best to get away from this side of town for a public meeting since you're considered dead over here ... yes, let's celebrate! ... yeah, just a few more steps, some details to hammer out and it's all over ... what? Wow. What a nice surprise. Ok. I didn't know *that* part of the plan, which seems to be ever-evolving! ... under his name ... ok, got it. What's his name again?"

Serge looked around on the table, picked up an elegantly embossed paper napkin (*Crème de la Honky*), and started writing. "Roscoe ... G.T. ... Towne. Got it, Rosalita."

Fyodor came back from the men's room and sat down, his eyes red and moist.

"Serge is talking to Rosalita?" he asked.

"Yes. Are you alright?"

"Oh yeah. I'm glad she's alive. I don't know what's going on, but I'm glad she's ok. I barely knew her, but she was—*is*—really cool. I like her. Kind and witty. A very nice face. She used to bring me coffee, out to the guardhouse. Can you tell what's happening?"

"Rosalita sounded good, so relieved, and anxious to see you two guys," said Serge, taking out a credit card and waving it cheerfully to the waitress. He noticed Fyodor's eyes. "Fyodor? *Hey*, amigo ..."

"Oh no, I'm alright, I'm just so glad she's alright, I'm glad she's away from them, the Hamptons, especially *him*. He *was* flirtatious with Rosalita, which made her nervous, and I think he wanted something, or he did something ... to her. I don't know. He's creepy. But what about her citizenship status, and all that? She's still illegal, isn't she, Officer?"

Serge put on his sunglasses, leaned across the table to Fyodor, got very close to his face, and lowered his voice.

"First off, Fyodor—the name is Serge. Ok?"

"Ok."

"Second off, as an officer of the law, me and Detective Jumbo over here, well, we don't care about *citizenship status*."

I had no idea what was happening, but I was liking it.

"Do we, Detective Jumbo?"

"No, Officer, we don't." I was staring up at Ireland on the wall, in a kind of happy trance.

"Thanks, Detective," said Serge. "Protect and serve, Fyodor." Serge put his hand out for Fyodor to shake, then held Fyodor's and smiled. "And sometimes—to be completely human—get a little *illegal*."

I blinked back from Ireland.

"Let's go. We're heading out to see Rosalita now. We're spending the night in a hotel," said Serge.

Fyodor shook his head. "I can't afford that. Especially now that I'm unemployed. And my wife, Ruby, she won't know where I am."

Serge folded the napkin he'd written on and handed it to Fyodor. "It's all paid for, by this man, Rosalita's Kansas City friend. And Ruby is invited." Serge stood up. "We've got to cross Hollywood, got some driving to do. And some talking. I'll call from my car, Red, turn on your speaker. I have a little story to tell you guys, about coyotes and a mannequin from Macy's."

Pretty in Pink

We followed Serge's police car along Sunset Boulevard and turned right, right behind him.

Serge pulled over to the side of the road, zipped down his window, and waved us ahead. "You guys go first, Jumbo, I'll follow. Don't want to make them nervous with my patrol car." I nodded and drove ahead through misty-cool sea air under blowing, bending palm trees …

… into *Pink*.

The entrance to the Beverly Hills Hotel, the Polo Lounge, the footpaths, even the men running towards us in polo shirts; everything pink. I had a flash of something, a feeling I couldn't place. A flashback—*have I been here before?*

Fyodor turned to me and scrunched up his face. "The Beverly Hills Hotel? God, I hate this part of town. I always feel like *staff* over here and it gives me the blues. You may not know that feeling, Red, because you look a little more white. White doesn't get that kind of blue, Red."

Kansas and Missouri in the rear-view mirror, peeking over the seats, giving me a *look*—the dog version of *what-the-fuck-are-we-doing-here?* A good question. The overkill of pink had a sort of blunt but dazzling effect on my senses, maybe the dogs felt it, too. Fyodor, in the passenger seat, seemed absolutely dazed by it.

I rolled down the driver's window and there again—all this *pink* smiling at me!

"Good Evening, sir! Welcome to the Beverly Hills Hotel! How may I be of service?"

Pink; polyester perfect white teeth polite very personable and … *pink!*

"Checking in!" I said enthusiastically, contagiously.

"Yes, sir!" he said, asking if I needed valet service and, because of the pressure—there was someone behind him, another behind him, another guy behind that guy, all assisting each other in serving me—I knew that I had to say yes. One of those guys *behind* passed a small computer to the head man in pink.

"Just to expedite things, sir, may I have your name?"

"Red Jumbo." He tapped rapidly on the small keyboard, all the keys—*in pink.*

"Jumbo, Jumbo, Jumbo ... hmmm ... "

Fyodor nudged me.

"Oh yes, *sorry.* I'm Red Jumbo, but it'll be in another name."

"Of course, sir. And *that* name, if I might?"

Fyodor dug into his pants pocket and handed me the folded napkin. I unfolded it to the name *Roscoe G.T. Towne* and passed it to the valet.

"Towne, Towne, Towne ... *Towne,* aha, *yes!* Roscoe G.T. Towne! Very fine, sir, *excellent.* I have it. Reservations for—let's see ... ah! *You* sir—*Red Jumbo*—as you said, then ... Fyodor—that's *you,* sir?"

"Yes, I am Fyodor."

"Good, then we have the names Ruby *T.*— just a last initial, Rosalita and Alberto, and Officer Serge Controllente?"

"All coming, on the way or ... *here,* " I said, pointing back at the police car rolling up behind us.

"There's Officer Controllente. We call him Serge. He just came from work, as you can see. After we check in, we're headed to the Polo Lounge for drinks!"

Meanwhile, the dogs—oblivious to all of this, except possibly the last part, about *drinks*—began loudly lapping up the bowl of Evian water I'd bought for them in a liquor store on the Sunset Strip. The pink valet team heard this lapping, saw Kansas and Missouri in the back of the van, and went into a huddle.

"Uh oh," said Fyodor.

"I know. Now what?" I wondered.

"Do they take dogs?"

"So far."

"But why shouldn't they?"

"I don't know, but don't you get the feeling they *wouldn't*, in a place like this?"

"Come to think of it, yes. I do."

"I never imagined I'd be staying at this hotel. And all paid for by this mystery man Roscoe."

"*That* was a surprise. Kind of fun, though, eh, Red? What a day. *Who knows* what's next?"

"Uh-oh, here they come."

The huddle broken, the pink man *in charge* came running back to us, the other three guys running behind him, then splitting off in different directions, in a hurry.

"The hotel allows one pet per guest, gentlemen." The valet nodded at Kansas and Missouri, then looked over at Fyodor. "I take it one of these sweeties is yours?"

Fyodor smiled proudly, nodded yes dishonestly. The lapping continued behind us.

"Oh, that's awesome sir, wonderful! Also, are your little friends trained? Another policy of the Beverly Hills Hotel."

"Oh naturally, absolutely," I said, getting into the enthusiastic rhythm and deciding to go all the way with it. "Mine is awesomely trained. Yours is too, right, Fyodor?"

"Oh yes! He's *so* trained!"

"That's fine, sir, and one last bit of business and then we'll get you taken care of ... are your dogs under 40 pounds?"

"Yes!" I said and waited, enthusiastic, but there was a brief pause, and I had a feeling there was still trouble coming, something ... *disqualifying*.

"Well then! I can tell from here that they are quite *chien petite,* if I may be so bold! *Very* fine sir, excellent, so happy to be of service! I'll be glad to assist in getting you each checked in, and our *Canine Concierge* is awaiting your arrival inside, you can't miss her, she'll be wearing a sort of *coral* pink blouse. I can take care of your vehicle, and, *Mr. Jumbo?*"

"Yes," I checked his flashing golden name tag, "... *Mr. London?*"

"Have a great stay!"

Rolling easily with all of this now, I had been accepted into the Beverly Hills Hotel; feeling right in tune, spontaneous like jazz, and a little behind the beat.

I nodded at Mr. London and said, "I will. I'm *in the pink,* now!"

Confident as all get-out.

Bloody Club

After saying goodbye to Kansas and Missouri, having gotten them safely to their complementary seemingly mandatory shampoo and clip in the Pink Polo Pet Palace, I was off to the Polo Lounge.

I was in a good mood, even excited, and surprisingly a guest of the Beverly Hills Hotel. Walking briskly, *brightly* down the hall toward the bar, only a minute or two from the Pink Polo Pet Palace, but already I missed Kansas and Missouri, worried about how they felt being in this hotel, a place very unlike our house in Eagle Rock.

Then I walked into the lobby and had a flashback. Or it was deja vu? One or the other, and it hit me like a ton of (pink) bricks. I saw the potted plants and stopped, dropped away into the past. Some blurry evening when I was dragging potted plants around the lobby, through the hotel? *Did I?* The potted plants said yes. I walked on to the bar.

I thought *one last drink* (or many) would break the flashback, brisk and brighten me back up again. But also I knew many drinks (because it wouldn't really be *a* drink) would only flatten my emotions and make me pee. I stepped up to the bar. Flashbacks again.

The bartender was coming, wiping her hands on a towel and smiling at me. I had my eyes on a Tanqueray bottle.

"What will you have, sir?" she asked.

"A Bloody Club, please!" I said, a little too loud, a lot too cheerful, fighting flashbacks.

"What is a *Bloody Club?*"

I stared at the red seal on the Tanqueray bottle, it looked like a dab of dried blood.

"Blood orange juice and a splash of club soda."

I was coming back from somewhere. Somewhere gin was being served forever.

"Well, *wow*—ok! A Bloody Club. I kinda thought you were going to say something about juniper berries, but *no no*, my mistake. Bloody Club—I can do that, so ... Hey. Wait a minute. You, are *you* ... ?"

"No, people *say* I look like him, but no ..."

"I remember you. Yeah! You're the guy that did the potted plants that night, aren't you? Like, dang, ten years ago? Hey Sonia—it's *The Potted Plant Man!*"

Sonia came over and they both stared ... and remembered ... and smiled. I smiled and remembered too. Me, back then, wildly drunk, laughing, singing, too loud, knocking drinks over, throwing my credit card at the bartender and staggering out to the lobby, and something about potted plants. I thought there was something familiar about the Polo Lounge. Sonia handed me the Bloody Club.

"Cheers!" I saluted.

The women looked at me, then laughed and laughed. Looked at me again. And laughed some more.

"Oh *ho ho ho,* that's not what you were cheering with *that* night!" said Sonia. "When you came in you looked like trouble, but you were friendly, kind of cute—we liked you—but then you were drinking anything and everything and really *mixing* things. You passed out on the floor once, and everyone just stepped over you. I think they thought it was a movie, that you were acting. I remember them looking around for cameras, a film crew! And you had a friend, I remember he was from out of town, and he was *trying* to talk to you ... but ..." Sonia shrugged at me, started laughing again.

"I can't believe it's *him* again, Sonia," said the bartender, looking me over, up and down.

"... and then he left, your friend, he looked upset, and then *you* got upset, paid your tab, I think you tipped us about forty percent, so yes—*we liked you!*—but our manager went after you because you'd left your Visa card on the bar, and she found you out in the lobby attacking the potted plants and dragging them by their leaves around and around the foyer, around and around, a potted plant in each hand, out in the parking lot, into the restaurant, and down the hall! With the staff in hot pursuit, but not quite catching you! They said you were singing "Jingle Bells" ... and it was summertime! Fourth of July weekend. We thought it was pretty funny! Kinda worried about you, though, getting home that night. But, hey—*welcome back!*"

"Thanks, Sonia. Good to be back, and I won't go anywhere near the potted plants tonight, I promise."

"What's your name? I'm Sonia, as you know, this is Annette ... and *you are?*"

"Red Jumbo."

"You're kidding."

"No, it's my name. I come from a long line of Jumbos."

"You *do?*" asked Annette, swizzling my drink with a tiny polo mallet swizzle stick. "That's a family? That's a *bloodline?*"

"Yes, it's true. My great-aunt was an actress, Genevieve Juniper Jumbo—she had a stage name but it escapes me now—she was on contract at Warner Brothers, and I think she came in here *a lot*."

"Hey listen, can you say it again, your name? Do you mind? Wait, I want to get ready ... ok, you ready, too, Sonia? Ok, go ahead: *Say it.*"

"Red Jumbo."

A felt a tap on my shoulder and turned around. A beautifully brown woman was looking at me with what I saw as a *dare* of a smile. She wore a Pacific-blue dress and a silver jeweled barrette flashed in her long shiny black hair. Her eyes were also brown—I was thinking her eyes were like freshly-made latte when you look down into the cup and see the cream swirling around a highlight and splash of rich, deep, *brown* coffee, steaming warmly, fluidly. Laugh lines twinkling back from her eyes, she looked maybe sixty years old. She stood there with sixty years of confidence.

I inhaled softly, smiled subtly. I *thought*.

"It's Coco Mademoiselle, by Chanel. My favorite perfume. You are Red Jumbo?" she asked.

I turned to Sonia and Annette; they nodded that I was. I turned back and nodded the same to this woman. She smiled white all the way across, flashing earring to flashing earring. There was something familiar about her.

"I thought so. Good to meet you. I'm Rosalita."

More Bloody Club

And behind Rosalita stood Alberto!

He was wearing a two-tone suit, red pants and gold jacket, and *shiny*; I could see the threads shining red and gold, like finely woven steel fibers. His hair was slicked back shiny and black in gleaming brilliantine!

"*Tres Flores*, Señor Red!" said Alberto, noticing me admiring his hairdo. He looked great, they looked great together, Alberto and Rosalita; I shook hands with Alberto and though I had never kissed a woman's hand before (that I could remember), this seemed like the right time.

I was very glad to meet her, I was very glad she was *alive*.

Behind *them*, in a far corner of the Polo Lounge, looking this way, Fyodor and Serge stood at a table with a large bottle of champagne and glasses lined up on a bright white tablecloth. Together—a perfectly choreographed chorus of two, I was impressed —Fyodor and Serge swept two glasses high, almost into a chandelier overhead, and toasted.

"To *ROSALITA!*" sang Serge, actually singing each of the four syllables, a trill on the last one, looking as if he'd already toasted everyone else in the room, including two tables of white-haired women in red and white polka dot bandannas (a *Rosie the Riveter Remembrance Convention,* I saw the sign out in the lobby, flanked by potted plants); also including Annette and Sonia, who were, of course, *still laughing*, behind the bar. Fyodor took a long sip and waved us over to the table.

On the way over, I threw a soft playful punch at Alberto's shoulder.

"You *knew*?" I asked him, "all along?"

"Oh yes. I am *in on it*. I was always in on it! Did you like the way I cried the other day? Do you think I am a good actor? Even Mrs. Hamptons was almost feeling emotions for me! *Almost*. Maybe. Maybe not! I don't care anymore!"

I stopped and looked around at everyone. Everyone seemed *in on it* but me. Then I saw Fyodor, getting bubbly with champagne, pouring himself another glass.

"Were *you* in on all this?" I asked him.

"No."

I looked around at everyone again. "Why'd you leave Fyodor out of the plan?" I asked.

"It's alright, Red," he said. "I understand. I can get a little emotional, a little upset. You saw me today at the Crème de la Honky."

Serge laughed. "I talked to Ruby and she told me *not* to tell Fyodor about the plan, not yet, not until we were all together, that he might have gotten so worried about Rosalita not getting away with it, that he might have blown the whole thing somehow." Serge laughed again, and smiled affectionately at Fyodor.

Fyodor gave Serge a look, a shrug, then turned to Rosalita, "I'm just so glad you didn't really die, Rosalita."

"Call me Rosie, buddy," she said. "We're all together now, yes?"

I saw that Alberto had tears in his eyes, and he wasn't acting.

"Well," I said, "I'm getting the impression that *getting away* is the point. So, Alberto, is this a day off from the Hamptons?"

"Yes, I just came from there," said Alberto. "I snuck away from the Hamptons—after you guys left, they had their eyes on me—then drove over to Serge's house, picked up Rosie, and we got a taxi to here. Today is a day off, and tomorrow, and the next day ... and ... so yes, this was my *last* day."

"Do they know that?"

"They *will,* Red. When they notice me not around tonight. When they go to our empty room, where Rosie and I used to live, and find my note. I wrote in the note: *Dear Hamptons, I cannot face this house with Rosalita's memory everywhere, I must go away and mourn her. I know you understand. Goodbye.* I almost wrote, *thanks for everything,* but no. I wouldn't. I wrote the note, closed the door to our room, and tip-toed down the creaky back stairs, out to our car."

I pictured the Hamptons estate: the front door, the foyer, the kitchen, the *conversation area*, and the De Kooning painting, looking down on Mr. and Mrs. Hamptons, sitting there. Wondering what just happened.

"Who's there now, Alberto?"

"Fantasmas," he said.

"Not mine," said Rosalita.

"I'm glad of that," I said. "We all are."

I pulled a chair out for her, one for Alberto, and we all sat down. Serge poured champagne, skipped my glass, Rosalita waved him off, I turned and Sonia was right there, holding a tray with a pitcher of margaritas, waiting for me. "Your *usual,* Mr. Jumbo? A Bloody Club?"

72

Fyodor, Officer Serge Controllente, Alberto and Rosalita—my new friends—heard this and looked up.

Rosalita, going with the flow and sailing free in her Pacific-blue dress, asked, "A bloody *what?* I'll have one, too."

The candle man and the plan

Sonia stepped away, whistling the song I realized she'd been whistling off and on since I'd walked into the Polo Lounge, a rather ambitious song to *whistle,* "Nights in White Satin" by the Moody Blues.

Or, as I'd first heard it, always thought it was called, "*Knights* in White Satin."

"You thought *what?!*" Sonia shrieked, coming back to the table. I must have been thinking out loud.

"Every time I hear that song," I explained, "I see these *knights* ... like, *Arthurian* knights, hanging around ... in *white satin!*"

Sonia, laughing at me again, or *still,* dropped her tray and the pitcher of margaritas, which bounced, landed, and exploded sideways in the direction of a table of Rosie the Riveters. The margarita liquid and ice fell short of the table, but the spray excited the women in bandannas, who also exploded with a delighted *"Wheeeeeee!"*

"Well, that's what *I* always thought," I continued, "I mean, I could tell it was this great, heavy love song, I could hear the romantic longing in it, and ... listen, I remember kissing a girl—the head pom pom girl in high school—we were in the back seat of my Chevrolet, kissing, and that song came on and I couldn't stop laughing! Ruined the whole night."

"What did *she* do? The pom pom girl?" asked Annette.

"Well, it ruined the romantic mood, obviously. She got out of the car and went inside her house, turned on a light in there and didn't come back out, so there I was, alone in the back seat of my first car, but still laughing."

Sonia was also still laughing, down on the floor, mopping up margaritas and ice.

Fyodor was having fun—"This is great! I didn't know I was going to wind up *here* when I woke up this morning. I *appreciate* it!" —and pouring more champagne.

Alberto looked very *on top of the world* in his red and gold shiny suit, sliding his free hand back along his pomade, looking around wide-eyed at the Polo Lounge.

"All paid for, all taken care of—for each of you," said Rosalita.

"We have a *Roscoe* to thank for this?" asked Fyodor.

"Yes," said Rosalita. She reached over, took Alberto's hand, and kissed it. "Roscoe G.T. Towne, of Kansas City. Poet and bartender at the Union Station Bar, in that order, as he says. He's another conspirator in *the plan*. A plan which is a little loose, I'll admit, but with a focus on getting out of LA as soon as possible."

"Roscoe G.T. Towne?" I asked.

"Yeah. Great name, huh? He's a great man, a generous man, kind of a Santa Claus type—kinda dresses like that too, except with a bit more bling."

"What's the *G.T.* stands for?" asked Serge.

"Roscoe loves his mother and father. They love him back, always have. When he was born—like, one hour later—after all that beautiful broth of birth and blood had been wiped away, and Roscoe rolled his little brown eyes up at his mother and father and *smiled*, his father said that all he was missing was a top hat and cane and a little baby-size red and gold ring. And that he was ready for the world; that he was *going to town!*"

This table felt great. Was this really happening? All this fun and friendliness?

"And so the name," she concluded, "Roscoe G.T.—*Going To—* Towne!"

A man, standing very still—a very tall *thin* man all in white with a black bow tie and tiny black mustache; he looked like a dinner candle that had been blown out and left to stand in honor of something or someone—this man stared at me from a corner of the Polo Lounge.

He came to the table.

The talk at the table stopped like it too had been blown out, and the man bent down, close to my ear.

"Kansas and Missouri are finished, sir," he whispered. "No rush whatsoever, whenever you're ready. They are happy and sleeping."

And then he was walking straight down the hallway out of the lounge, the candle getting shorter and shorter as he walked, until he became a tiny children's birthday cake candle.

We all watched him leave, then Rosalita looked at me. "What was *that*, some sort of secret, your-ears-only, detective message?" she asked.

"No, that was about my dogs. But my ears would love to hear about *the plan*."

"Good. Because I'd like to talk to you and Fyodor. Hey Fyodor, where's Ruby?"

"She's on the way. By the way, Rosalita — "

"I'm glad. I like Ruby. So, about *the plan* ... oh ... yes, Fyodor?"

"— I like what you just said."

"What did I just say?"

"When you spoke of *the beautiful broth of birth and blood.*"

"Yeah, Rosalita. I liked that too," said Alberto.

"Me too," I said. It *was* a striking image.

"Oh thanks, you guys," she said. "Anyway, the plan. Me and Alberto, Ruby, Serge, and Roscoe already know most of it, some more than others, so again, *Fyodor*—please don't feel excluded. I've played a lot of my plan close to the vest, but now the vest is off. And there have been some changes, we're still improvising—you, Red, are the newest piece of improvisation, you too, Fyodor, and I want to talk to you both about it. But Red, I have a question."

"Fire Jose, I mean, *away!*"

There was a brief pause at table, they all looked at each other, Rosalita looked at me.

"Friend of mine, doesn't matter. Please, Rosalita, go on."

"Would you drive us to Kansas City? Alberto and me? I'm illegal here in California, I'm illegal everywhere, Kansas City, too, but it's dangerous here, with the Hamptons and ... the angry climate lately. With Roscoe, in Kansas City, we'll be safe. Maybe even happy."

I didn't see this coming. I didn't know why she was asking *me* to drive, but I liked it; I was back on the case again. Or back on *something ...*

"This Roscoe, he has some ideas, Rosalita?" I asked.

"Oh yes, he has some ideas alright," she said. Serge and Alberto chuckled low and conspiratorial. Fyodor looked at me and shrugged. I shrugged back; we were still out of the loop, but I had a feeling the loop was about to lasso us.

"Roscoe, he has ideas, but to get to those ideas and our plan, I need to get to Kansas City, and that's where I need you, Red. Or rather, *want* you."

"I'm not saying no, Rosalita, not at all, but why me?"

She looked right *at* me, no blinking, then she smiled slowly. "Because I like you, Red. *I always have*, I mean, ever since Serge told me about how you told off the Hamptons today, which I've never seen anyone do, and then he said you began to cry, well, I like that. You have fierceness, but *feelings* too, no?"

I couldn't say no. To any of this.

"Roscoe will pay expenses. For you, Red, and you too, Fyodor. You and Ruby. And, everybody. I like our little group. I trust all of you. Serge tells me he can take vacation time at the police department, so ... but Red, do you think we can all fit into your van?"

I laughed, wondered that myself, and looked across the table at Fyodor. "What do you think, Fyodor? Want to go? Can Ruby come with us?"

"*Oh yeah,* Red. I mean, she may already be fired, because of me. Anyway, adventure is Ruby's middle name. But Rosalita, what *is* the plan?"

Rosalita, looking very relaxed, laughed at the question. "The plan isn't very complicated really. It's mostly a matter of ignoring everything they—whoever *they* are—say we should be doing, and start living *our* lives. The way we want to. Not much to it. But of course, who does that?"

Now I *knew* I was in on it.

"In other words, Fyodor, what I am going to do is run—make my big entrance, *into my own life!*—and laugh. Laugh off anyone trying to stop me. Laugh at life, laugh in joy. Wake up laughing! There wasn't much laughter at the Hamptons, was there?"

"Yes. I mean no," said Fyodor, "but I mean, you're illegal, and ... isn't there something you, that is, *we,* can do, so that this won't be like ..."

"*Crime?*" asked Rosalita.

"Yeah, *that.*"

I took a long swig of Bloody Club and watched the human chess pieces at the table glance at each other; Rosalita, Alberto, and Serge. Probably Fyodor, too. I guess they'd been at this chess game off and on for years, their friends and family too, and I suppose they knew it was a game never-ending, with them always the pawns, never the kings or queens, never winning, someone else setting the rules, making them play.

"I'm in, everybody, truly," said Fyodor, "I'm with you, but I heard on NPR that they're really cracking down on immigrants, the border patrols, ICE agents, all over the world, it's so scary now, and ..."

"I don't listen to NPR anymore, the other acronyms, or anything else much," said Rosalita. "There is a life outside of all that, and I want to go *there.*"

There was a big glassy crash at a table on the other side of the Polo Lounge and we all looked. A woman—it seemed to me that she had six or seven purses and enough jewelry flashing to land a flight out at LAX—this woman must have knocked over her cocktail and it had crashed and tinkled, all around on and under her table. She was flashing and dripping.

The tall, thin candle man was back from somewhere and on the way to help.

Without even looking at him, the woman pointed at the floor and said: "Yes, just, get—*that.*"

Then she answered one of her six or seven cell phones. I *think* I saw that many, one for each purse, I guess. And day of the week.

The candle man very quietly swept the glass, and then himself, away.

"You see, Fyodor," said Rosalita, staring at the spot on the floor where the candle man had knelt and cleaned up, "life is too short, or maybe it's just *too good*, to wait for progress to get progressive."

Existentialism

Later, 1 a.m., up in my room, Kansas and Missouri asleep on the bed, all eight of their newly perfumed legs in the air, me by the window watching the tail lights on Sunset Boulevard go back and forth like fireflies.

I was pondering and brooding and romanticizing, which I *am* good at. I was pondering what going back to Kansas City was going to feel like after twenty-five years away. I'd run from there one morning with a movie production company I'd hired onto (set painter and movie extra, playing a vaguely criminal hobo); the movie was called *Kansas City* (accurately enough), the film company was returning to Hollywood, they needed a driver for one of the production trucks (it was a *non-union* show), so—in an overnight decision at the wrap party, with less than five hundred dollars, the Bible Belt cutting off my air, the relatives all dead—I ran away with the circus.

The brooding, alone in a hotel room, was about alcohol. A drink. But though I was shaky, wanting anything, gin, wine, a beer—I stopped. That felt powerful, like if I can *stop* this, maybe I can *go do* anything. And this evening I had not been alone, not back in my dark, concrete basement in Eagle Rock, hiding. There could be other people around, now.

Also, alone in a hotel room, I was romanticizing, about perfumed legs up in the air, and not from the Pink Polo Pet Palace. I thought about Sonia and Annette in the bar. I *liked* those women, but I remembered (I checked) seeing their wedding rings. I wanted to fall in love with someone. *Tonight!* (I romanticized), there must be *someone* in the hotel.

The phone changed the subject and rang.

"Hello," I said, in the dark.

"Red?" Rosalita.

"Yes, hi, *good morning.* Everything alright, Rosalita?"

"Oh sure, I just can't sleep. I conked out for an hour or two, but I had a dream so *real* I woke up real *hungry.* I think I'll have to check out the room service menu. And I'm a little nervous but excited about everything, so I was thinking of you and wanted to thank you for being a part of, everything, all of this."

"Of course. This will be quite an adventure, and I need one!"

"I know we haven't gone over all the details, like why I was dead and now I'm alive, what happened at the Hamptons ... or why I had a dream tonight of the sauce at Bryant's Barbeque, hahaha ..."

"Bryant's Barbeque!?" I said, *really* in the dark. But salivating.

"Oh ... yeah, well, we'll get into *that* later ... I haven't actually been to Bryant's Barbeque, but Roscoe talks about it so much I can almost eat it, *in my mind*. But we haven't talked a lot about what's next ... everything Alberto and I own was in a little pile of boxes in the garage at Serge's house in Hollywood—which, as you may know, was my temporary hideout after I left the Hamptons—and I've had those boxes shipped to Kansas City, where Roscoe is waiting for us. With *his* plan. So, Red ... how soon can you be ready to go?"

"I only need to go pack some bags for me and the dogs, lock up the house, turn on the porch light; I can be ready pretty quick. When do you want to go?"

"In the morning. Roscoe only paid for these rooms for tonight. Or is that too soon?"

This *was* happening fast! Was I ready?

"I'm ready, Rosalita. Tomorrow we'll swing by my house, get some things, and go! Get some sleep, partner. *In crime!*"

"Good night, partner! Good night, *Red*."

I hung up and the phone rang again; I smiled and picked it up.

"Bryant's Barbeque, may I take your order?"

"Red, are we really doing this?" asked Fyodor.

"Yes, we are! You want to, right?"

"I do. So does Ruby, my wife. And she's with me in the room now, just got here, a little tipsy. She had a friend drive her over, and I think they had some fun down in the Polo Lounge."

"Great, buddy, I think we may need a gang on this job. And it might be a romantic adventure for you two."

"I can't wait for you to meet her. She was an exotic dancer, once. She still goes by her *stage name*—Ruby Taillights. With two l's."

"That's a *marvelous* name, Fyodor! It's refreshingly grandiose! And I'm glad she's coming with us."

"She's very cool, Red. I love her. I may even change my last name. Fyodor Taillights? But now I feel badly for you."

"Why?"

"Well, it'll be romantic for us—me and Ruby, and Rosalita and Alberto—but what about you?"

"Ah, thanks Fyodor, but don't worry about me! Maybe I'll meet someone in Nevada or Utah or Colorado or Kansas, somewhere along the road. I used to know a college math teacher in Glenwood

Springs. What a woman. She taught me about infinity one night, but I'll tell you about *that*, later. Goodnight friend, get some sleep. Say hi to Ruby. I'll meet her in the morning."

Fyodor said goodnight. I heard the cars swish by outside on Sunset. The phone rang again.

"Jumbo, here."

"So you say," said *someone. Some man.*

"This *is* Jumbo."

"Maybe you are and maybe you aren't."

I turned on a light. Somehow I thought maybe the voice was in the room, not on the phone. The bulb flickered the room *lit*; there was no one in the room.

"This is *Red* Jumbo. I guess maybe you're making a sexy phone call to somebody, big boy, but I need some sleep, so goodnight."

"This is Hamptons, big boy. And I know what's going on."

This was a surprise. But I played it cool and *getting sleepy.* "So you say," I yawned.

"Oh, I do."

"Maybe you do and maybe you don't."

I wondered if he noticed a pattern in our conversation, but in any case, I was bluffing, calling his bluff, and I was ready to play this bluff right off the edge of the cliff.

"You were seen at the Beverly Hills Hotel today, Jumbo."

"I was?"

"You was. Were."

"By who?"

"Whom, you mean?"

"I mean who. Yes."

"What?"

"Stick to the point, Hamptons!" Now I had him, and I was gaining ground. "*Who* saw me? And why are you calling so late, I need sleep, it's been a long day, and you loomed large in it!"

I threw all this at him to throw him off, and sure enough, a long silence followed. I could almost hear Hamptons catch up to the end of my last sentence. Then he started yelling.

"I don't know what you're up to, *or maybe I do*, or why you're over on that side of town, in the Beverly Hills Hotel. You certainly can't afford it, we didn't even pay you. And hear this, sir: *We never will!* The case is closed!*"

Another surprise. And relief. He knew where I was but didn't seem to know what was going on.

"I don't like you, Jumbo. I don't believe you. I didn't like your looks from the beginning, when we met at the Lanyard Luxury Hotel. You are smarmy, obsequious ..."

"Gee, you really *don't* like me, do you?"

"*And* I don't trust you. You are obnoxious, a *liberal*, a loose cannon, and I think you might be dangerous."

"Dangerous? You just called me a liberal, and yet you think I'm dangerous! Fuck, I mean *gee*, I don't even have a gun!"

"Mr. Jumbo, I have a man at the hotel tonight, and he will be watching you in the morning if and when you leave. He was watching when you checked in with my *ex*-employee, Fyodor. You will be followed. You have *been* followed since just after I met you at the Lanyard Luxury. That is how much I don't like you. My man spotted you yesterday at the Crème de la Honky with Fyodor and Officer Controllente. And this man watching you is a *real* detective. Also a gentleman, his conversation devoid of your ghetto language. The f-word, for example. He is a member of Mensa. Furthermore, he has never heard of you, he doesn't even think you *are* a detective."

"Well, I *am* new," I said.

"I don't know what you are, Jumbo."

"It's a big question, alright."

"Come morning, my man will be watching you, he'll be covering your exit from the Beverly Hills Hotel."

"I think he'll be covering my exist*entialism*, Hamptons, since no one knows what I am."

Hamptons hung up, I hung up, and turned off the light. I took a deep breath and tried to ease up, relax my brain, which was running fast. I was relieved that Hamptons' man hadn't seen Rosie, that she was alive. Hamptons would've told me that. Wouldn't he? *Shhh*, I said to my brain.

I sat down by the window and watched the fireflies go by. Whatever was going on, I was going to stay on top of it. I knew I could, now.

Polo Lounge Trojan Horse

I went back to the phone to call Fyodor. Kansas and Missouri were on the bed, spooning. Probably in deep REM sleep.

"Red?" said Fyodor, on the first ring.

"Still up, eh?"

"Yeah, can't sleep, this is all too exciting. Ruby and I are in bed watching *Doctor Zhivago*."

"Oh yeah? The remake?"

"Is there one?"

"Probably. Anyway, I need to tell you something. Hamptons just called. He knows I'm here."

"Just you?"

"No, you too, and Serge. We were seen at the Crème de la Honky, then we were seen checking into the hotel. Hamptons has a man on the job, on *me*. This man is somewhere in the hotel, and will be watching tomorrow when we leave. Who knows, maybe he's on my floor, next to my room right now."

Long, long pause. The sound of a balalaika in the phone.

"Fyodor? … You there? … Hey, don't worry, it'll be ok."

"Oh, sorry—I lost my train of thought; I'm crazy about Julie Christie! She's so sexy when she gets into her fur there in Russia in the winter, my *God!* Of course, she *is* British, and *British women*, you know …"

"Fyodor—"

"No, I heard you Red. So, what do we do?"

"We have to sneak out of here in the morning, somehow we— you and Ruby and Serge and I—have to get Rosalita and Alberto outta here, and not through the front door."

"Shall we try it now, *under cover of darkness?*"

"No, I think we wait until it's busy, right in the middle of the day, when there's more foot traffic around the entrance, the lobby, and somehow slip right out of here."

"Maybe disguises, Red."

"Maybe. I don't even know where this man is, or where he'll be. Hamptons just said he'd be watching. He can*not* see us, and *really* not Rosalita. Which makes me wonder if he saw the rest of us in the Polo Lounge …"

"We need a Trojan Horse solution, Red."

"Right, right ... interesting thought … let's see …"

"How well do you know those women at the bar? They sure liked you!"

"I wish they were here right now," I said.

"They're there right now? Oh good, ask them if —"

"*Of course* they're not here right now!"

"Easy Red, *easy*. Gee, someone needs some sleep!"

"Hell *yes*, I need some sleep! It's been a long day! I'm finally in the Beverly Hills Hotel—I know *you* don't like this side of town, but I've always dreamed of staying here. I had no idea when I woke up this morning that I'd be here tonight, or did I say that already? Or did you? Anyway, all I've got are these dogs in bed with me. And I haven't even *gone* to bed yet. And you're over there with your wife, Ruby Taillights, not to mention Julie Christie."

"You know, Red, I bet she stayed here, with Warren Beatty, back in *those* days."

He was right, I *was* tired. I switched on the bedside lamp and saw a small Miro painting above the bed. Childlike, sophisticated, playful; red and blue with black lines, a small white crescent moon dangling amid the abstract composition—I liked the painting. I thought maybe if this *detective thing* goes south, I could go home and be a painter. Stay home, don't leave the house, and paint. I was *so* tired.

I felt like that moon in the Miro painting; a lonely moon, dangling amid abstractions.

Hey! *Write that down,* I thought. And I did; I got the Beverly Hills Hotel stationery out of the bedside table drawer and wrote it down! So I wasn't that tired, after all, if I could still come up with a poetic line. I was beginning to feel a change again ... just by writing that down ... *something* ...

"Red. Hello?"

"Oh, hi Fyodor, what were you saying? And I'm sorry I snapped at you."

"Maybe you could talk to those women tomorrow, what are their names?"

"Sonia and Annette."

"Ask Sonia and Annette if they could steal us some staff uniforms. We can all dress up as staff, food service or the housekeeping department, whatever, maybe Rosalita and Alberto still have their clothes from the Hamptons job ... come to think of it, *I do!* I wore it over here yesterday! My official Hamptons Gatehouse Suit and Tie, so to speak, which certainly spells STAFF as far as I'm concerned, Ruby can dress as a hotel gardener, and then Serge can go out the door as a cop, in *his* uniform ... so really it's down to just you! Maybe Annette and Sonia can dress you up as a bartender, and then we can all sneak out through the service entrance. There's got to be a back door, side door—*employees entrance,* right? Would they do that for you, you think? For us?

I liked it. Painting could wait.

Hippie Trojan Horse

When I woke up way past sunrise, after a night of vivid (rough) childhood dreams, it was like I'd been asleep for months, and I didn't remember where I was; I felt like I was already over *east,* in Kansas City. But there were those palm trees out the hotel window, moving like elegant, sensual, very flirtatious hula girls, and the sea air was blowing through the room ... the sweet, melon-eating breath of those hula girls.

Not Kansas City.

And how about that? I'd heard the expression "all roads lead to Rome," but Kansas City? And here I was, about to drive these people there.

I smiled and stretched in bed, sucking in the tropical hula girl breath, feeling completely refreshed; feeling, like last night, a change coming on, something *new,* anticipating something, like the first cool night in October (which it was), something big and cheerfully *out of control!* I thought about what Fyodor had suggested last night about uniforms and subterfuge and disguises and escaping out of the hotel.

Time to go! I thought, flying out of the sheets like a parachutist in reverse.

I pulled on the Levis, stuck my head out the hotel window as a form of washing my face and combing my hair, and snatched up the jingling car keys—*on the move!*

But before I got to the door, I heard what sounded like a lot of people in the hallway, moving my way. Now I was the parachutist again, but dangling in tree limbs, waiting. Who or what was this gang of people? The hotel staff? Hamptons henchmen or henchwomen? The gang stopped, there was a pause, then knocking; I dangled in the breeze and waited.

"Red? It's me, Fyodor!"

I opened the door and there he was, with Rosalita and Alberto, Serge, and a hallway of smiling, multi-colored hippies! What a relief! I always like seeing hippies, does my heart and soul good, especially *this* morning, in the Beverly Hills Hotel. And they were carrying signs, like

CLOSE IMMIGRATION DETENTION CENTERS!
(Now, goddammit!)

"What do you think, Red?" asked Fyodor. "This is our Plan B, what you might call our *Hippie Trojan Horse*. They'll walk us right on out of here, out of our rooms, down the hall, down the elevators, through the lobby to the van ... and then we'll drive the hell on out of here."

Kansas and Missouri had slipped past me and were out in the hall, licking the legs of a hippie woman—or, as her T-shirt said, HIPPIE CHICK—and the entire gang was smiling at me, waiting for me to say yes.

I smiled yes, I *said* yes, then I said, "One second, please," called the front desk and asked to have *Mr. London* bring the van around to the front door. The hippies swung around in the other direction and started running, towards the elevators, Kansas and Missouri charging and jingling ahead. As we arrived at the elevator doors, two elevators arrived and *dinged* simultaneously, and when the doors slid open, a woman was inside one of them, leaning languorously against the back wall, with red and yellow-streaked hair, wearing green Cat Eye sunglasses, red *Hello Kitty* high-top sneakers, a blue leather mini-skirt and a black T-shirt with **BLACK LIVES MATTER** blazing across the front in red.

"Hi, handsome," the woman said to Fyodor. "I got *both* elevators up."

"Red Jumbo, meet my wife, Ruby Taillights."

In one elevator, dinging out the floors going down—Fyodor, Ruby, Kansas, Missouri, and I hid inside one circle of hippies, the circle in the other elevator enclosing Serge, Alberto, and Rosalita—I discretely whispered a question to Fyodor (the whispering unnecessary because Ruby and the hippies were singing "Uncle John's Band" in full voice), *"Where'd these hippies come from? And do we still refer to them as hippies? I only use that word as the highest possible compliment."*

Fyodor, suddenly playing it cool, eyes straight ahead, possibly showing off for Ruby, who he was clearly in love with, whispered back. "Ruby and I were down in Venice, having a *Leaving LA-Road Trip-Celebration-Eye-Opener*, waiting for you to wake up ... by the way, how did you sleep?"

"*Great*. I haven't slept like that for weeks. Months. Years, maybe."

"Good, good. I'm glad. You look better, somehow. *Clear*, in your eyes. So anyway, while you slept in, Ruby and I orchestrated the hippies. I mean, there we were on the beach, in a surfer bar called

The Inn of the Wave Riders and the Crest Fallen ... yeah, that's what *I* thought, try to get all that on a cocktail napkin, you'd love the place, Red ... where was I? Oh yeah, so here come these hippies into the bar ... and yes, I think we *do* call them hippies, there will always be hippies, thank goodness ... anyway, there we were and here they came with their signs, and I thought: bingo! *Our way out of the hotel!* I bought them a round, asked them if they wanted to move the demonstration to the Beverly Hills Hotel. An LAX Super Shuttle driver was in the bar too—off duty, I guess—he was watching and listening to us, he's Guatemalan, his mother knew a woman whose house had been invaded in the middle of the night by ICE, was horrified by what she'd seen, and so he drove us back to the hotel for free!"

The elevator dinged LOBBY.

"And so here we *are*," said Fyodor.

The doors opened and Kansas and Missouri got out first, the hippies following them, bringing us along. We met, then blended with the circle coming out of the other elevator; I saw Rosalita—very bright-eyed and laughing, *enjoying* this—and as one big, loud, colorful, musical, mismatched yet unified and anarchic gang (six of us concealed, plus dogs), we moved toward the front desk, toward the front door.

Looking across the lobby, out the hotel entrance, beyond the red carpet, through our multi-colored human camouflage of hippies, I could see my white van in a far corner of the parking lot, a smiling pink and khaki valet starting the engine. The other cars in the lot looked empty, I didn't see the *other detective*, but I knew he could be anywhere.

I looked at Fyodor.

"And so here we *go*," said I.

Porte Cochère

I did a quick count of the hippies in the lobby. I counted twenty, but with the scintillating colors, vibrating energy—not to mention all the smiling and laughing, playfulness, hugging and kissing and singing—it seemed like one hundred and twenty! The women and men behind the front desk were smiling at us in their playful (but professional) pink hotel uniforms, but they were also looking very serious, hands near phones.

The hippies, enclosing all of us in one big circle, moved us toward the front door. The dogs were calm, looking up at us, wagging and wondering, but slowly strolling with us, one paw at a time, toward the door. I noticed Rosalita talking very seriously to a hippie; I couldn't hear what was being said until the hippie said, *"oh yeah, we can sing that!"* and Rosalita and the hippies broke out in smiles. Rosalita broke out; the hippies never *stopped* smiling.

Then—the circle through the front door and outside, beneath the gold-trimmed porte cochère—the hippies broke out in song: "The Girl from Ipanema." Beginning softly, singing louder and more festive as my van flew towards us, the entire circle *dancing*, Samba style; even the dogs were running in circles. The van slowed and gently eased inside the circle. At the wheel was Mr. London himself. He was waving at me, looking a bit overwhelmed by the singing hippies, but waving at them, too. Mr. London jumped out of the van, flashed peace signs all around, and as I approached with a tip, he said, *"Groovy,* Mr. Jumbo! Simply groovy!"

There was an idling police car, its headlights looking right at us. The two officers inside waved. Serge waved back, said they were friends of his from the Pasadena Police Department, that they were there to shuttle his car back to Pasadena, that they knew he was on "vacation*"* and that they "owed him one."

A couple of security men near the front desk ran outside, red-faced and yelling into their cell phones, aggressively waving at the hippies to MOVE! Serge, still in uniform, walked calmly over to calm *them,* got into an argument, fingers pointing back and forth between the three men, all very funny with the hippies still singing, *"... tall and tan and young and handsome ..."*

I felt *someone* watching. There was a black SUV up the hill, at the top edge of the parking lot.

I overtipped Mr. London and gave him the peace sign. Serge stepped neatly out of the argument with the security guards (who were now arguing with each other), came back to the van, made eye contact with me, then with Fyodor, the three of us going back and forth with eye signals, then they nodded at me and got in up front, Serge behind the wheel, Fyodor in the shotgun seat.

With the group of hippies surrounding the van, Rosie and Ruby and Alberto stayed hidden and slipped into the far back, lying flat with Kansas and Missouri. Years ago I had removed the last row of seating in the back, so with everyone trying to find some way to fit in this small space, the van was rocking back and forth like a rowboat, rolling them tumbling around on top of each other.

I had my eye on the black SUV, parked quietly, windows blacked out. Then I made eye contact with Serge to start driving, and as the van eased away from the hippies, out from under the porte cochère, very carefully threading between a black Bentley and a black Range Rover, a black limousine, and a pink golf cart, I started walking slowly in the direction of the SUV. I heard its motor start, and I stopped, making sure whoever was inside the SUV saw me, then I flashed the peace sign, smiled, and turned around.

The hippies were floating behind the van like rose petals after a wedding, waving goodbye as it rolled around the side of the hotel, then they turned in a big bouquet, and smiled up the drive at me.

"Meet me under the porte cochère," I yelled, smiling and gesturing toward the front door of the Beverly Hills Hotel with a casual toss of the head.

We casually gathered there, casual, but maybe alarming the incoming hotel guests, who were staring. I looked around in the crowd for Mr. London, and when I saw he was standing right behind me, I told him that we were about to leave, it was almost over.

"Alright, Mr. Jumbo. *Please*." He flashed me one final peace sign, then trotted to a Mercedes that had just arrived. The black SUV was idling, waiting.

"What now, Red?" asked one of the hippies.

"Now that Rosie and the van are safely gone, I gotta get out of here, too. Can you all *sing* me out of here?"

"Oh yes we can! We have a guitar or two, you want one?"

"No no, just back me up." The lights on the SUV switched on.

"What shall we sing?" someone asked. " How about 'We Shall Overcome,' or maybe 'Hallelujah.' "

"I was thinking about the George Michael song. 'I Want Your Sex.' Know it?"

"Oh yeah, sure! Of course, we don't have an organ, which looms large in that song, but we have a lot of percussion instruments, to get that primal rhythm, so yeah. *Let's do it!*"

The drumming started, bongos and cowbells, someone had a snare, I got out front and started singing, I knew all the lyrics, surprising the hippies (and me!) who all kicked in lasciviously, full sexy voices, completely game, uninhibited; the hotel guests, the pink valets, and the security men froze and stared at us; and I led the hippies away from the porte cochère, away from the hotel, down the side road the van had taken, the hippies fanning out and spreading like rose petals across the lawn around the hotel, and I *disappeared.*

Mr. Hamptons told me he'd had me followed since our meeting at the Lanyard. If I was being followed, let *me* be followed. And now I was gone.

I was running, cutting this way and that across the hotel grounds, under the palm trees, through the bougainvillea, listening and looking behind me for the black SUV, up ahead of me for my van.

A rooster crowed. Text message alert! I pulled out my phone, kept running, read the text: Van, *ahead!*

Looking back, I saw that the black SUV had stopped, driver's side door open, and now a man in black was running straight towards me. I shot ahead, flew over a hedge, landed in a rolling somersault, ran to the road where the van was just slowing, dove into the back and we tore outta there just as the man in black somersaulted *into* the hedge, flailing his arms around, angry, growling like Tom Waits, trying to claw his way out of the greenery.

Rolling and tumbling in with the rest of the gang, I yelled. "I'll pick up the extra seats when we swing by my house. Sorry, but I wasn't *ready* for this!"

Serge stopped after a couple of twists and turns. We all got out, laughing and stretching. I got back in the driver's seat. The road was open in front of me. Rosalita looked at me in the rear-view mirror; we held each other's eyes until we cracked up laughing.

"Go ahead," she whispered. Then she yelled, "*Floor* it!"

I did!

I *floored* the van on a narrow one-lane road, the palm tree hula girls bending and blowing in a wind picking up tropical steam, *swung right* and sped up the hill, *up* the whiplash of Benedict Canyon Drive to the longer whiplash of Mulholland Drive, top of the Hollywood Hills, *but ...*

... hold on, I thought.

I want to pull over and feel the moment. Something BIG is about to happen.

Yes, I will, I thought. *I'll pull over.*

Don't rush this moment, it won't happen twice. Or will it? Something even better, moment-wise, later?

But stop, now.

I pulled over to the side of Mulholland at the top of the hill; Hollywood sparkling in the sun below, the horizon line whispering, calling, saying *something* to us, in the east.

We sat there, nobody talking, the eastern horizon in the distance —waiting, luring, rising—and I thought: *Where am I going? Who am I? Not in any big, Dalai Llama on the Mountaintop way, though there was some of that, but more in a sort of—now what?—way.*

I looked over at Serge beside me. I looked in the rearview mirror. Everyone's eyes were on the next few dozen yards of Mulholland Road winding out ahead; eyes philosophical, serious, and introspective.

Or, maybe they were waiting for me to drive.

Rosalita was looking at me, not blinking. Then, she winked.

There was a coyote in front of the van, about ten yards ahead. He winked and smiled at us, and shot off towards the Marlon Brando-Jack Nicholson compound.

I took my foot off the brake ...

Beverly Hills Hotel to the Hotel Colorado

... the road inhaled us, east; we curved along, Hollywood on the right, the San Fernando Valley on the left, past the Hollywood Bowl, Serge says he can see Van Morrison down there in his black hat checking out the mike stand for a show that night, up the Cahuenga Pass (Fyodor, suddenly excited, says, "Wow, Van the Man! Hey, that gives me an idea ...") and down the neck of Barham Boulevard ("... if Hamptons has some detective watching us, maybe we need a *code-name* for this van ..."), past Warner Brothers, right on Forest Lawn Drive past the cemetery, all of us waving at Bogart, him blowing smoke rings out of his grave back at us ("... so, let's call *this* van— *Morrison!*"), merging onto the Ventura Freeway to my house up in Eagle Rock, me in the house, around and around, checking doors, windows, grabbing dog toys, the "Goodbye Yellow Brick Road" CD, my top hat (found on the floor in the concert hall of the Los Angeles Philharmonic one Christmas Eve) and teddy bear (from a London toy store when I was a baby over there), some of my favorite blue jeans, wide-wale corduroy pants, and flashiest clothes, the back row of van seats for *Morrison*, everyone installing them as I flick on the porch light, go out the front door, lock it, check it, should I leave the porch light on?—yes—who knows how long this will take, then up past the Rose Bowl to the 210 freeway, off at the Lake Street exit, up the hill to Altadena to Serges's sister's house, a small, rose-covered bungalow, Serge and Rosalita hop out and up to the front door, a woman comes out with a little creamy puppy (looked like a little biscuit, *breathing*, I thought) in her arms, ears up and happy seeing Rosalita, passes the puppy to her, "Thanks, sis—*later!*" says Serge, hugging her, then back down Lake, back on the 210 east ("I didn't want to take Felix to the Beverly Hills Hotel ..." Rosalita tells us, cuddling her pup, "...too *intimidating,* he's never been out of Pasadena!") and goodbye downtown Los Angeles, getting smaller; rolling out into the flats east and past a gas station, a California Pizza Kitchen, a Home Depot, a Verizon store, east, then UP the 15, climbing, pines and hawks and sun-hot desert, toward Las Vegas, the sky a lot bluer up there, rolling, rolling along, Rosalita in her shades now, smiling a playful *come and get me!* smile, through the candy neon of Vegas, all those lights on in the late afternoon, jets soaring very close above the van ... St. George, Cedar City, Holiday Inn Express, Starbucks, another Verizon store, *gas up*, pee break, corn nuts and ice tea and ice at the station at the BIG RIGHT TURN EAST on 70; long slabs of brown Stonehenge all around up there, hot out there, Indians out there, Mexicans out there, all the color of the brown Utah Stonehenge, selling handmade jewelry and handmade carne asada and carnitas tacos wrapped up hot and tasty in shiny silver foil (says their homemade sign in Sharpie) at the rest stop, we buy a bit of it all; driving on through this massive dry ocean bed, rolling, rolling east, evening sliding blue and gold and glowing pink in the long sky; we cross the Colorado line into light lacy snow spinning across the highway, *gas up* again, about 100 miles to Glenwood Springs, which we make in a couple of hours—most of us asleep, including almost, *me*— just after midnight, large snowflakes falling wet and heavy on the windshield, snowdrifts piling up, us pulling up, under the *next* port cochère, to the front door of the Hotel Colorado.

Heavy shots

A beautiful, high blue sky day at the Rose Bowl Flea Market, Saturday afternoon, early spring, wild, fresh wind blowing high and low, over and through all the shoppers, blowing a few hats off. The first time they've breathed deeply all winter, and they are invigorated by it, bright-eyed, twinkly, and friendly.

One woman especially so, in a big red cowboy hat she just bought at the market, walking briskly, almost up on the toes of her shoes, she's flashing colorfully through the crowd. She sees her friend Agata from the Unitarian church, waves, and walks over to Agata's booth full of paintings.

The women say hi, hug, laugh, hug again, look at the paintings together, the woman in the red hat buys one, and says goodbye to Agata, see you later, maybe breakfast next week? Then she turns from the booth and sees a friendly-looking stranger smiling at her. She smiles back, walks on along through the flea market, sees another friend, says hi, moves on, looks back and sees the friendly-looking man behind her in the crowd, still smiling at her.

The wind sweeps down hard, she holds onto her hat and starts out in the direction of her car, leaving the flow of the crowd, less and less people around. She looks back, the man is gone.

It's a long way across the parking lot. She sees her car in shade under pine trees at the edge of the lot and begins to walk faster; her cowboy hat blows off and she's chasing it, laughing, running, catches up to it, sweeps it up onto her head at a cocky angle; threading through parked cars, she gets to the back of her Toyota hatchback, unlocks it, lifts the hatchback, places the painting on a blanket, folds the ends around it, unfolds another blanket and spreads it over the painting, feels a hand on her back SHOVE her, and she falls forward onto Agata's painting, ripping it, cracking the frame beneath the blankets.

She hurts, turns around and the friendly-looking man is there, close and on her, his hands on his belt buckle, his zipper, then he reaches in and takes off her new cowboy hat, puts it on his head, shoves her deeper into the car, grips her arms, flips her around on her back and climbs in, on top of her.

"Hello sugar," he says, a big, heavy man, sweaty, smells bad, the woman is thrashing her legs and arms, but he's on her, smothering her, opening her shirt, his pants down, clawing at her, claws her pants and panties down, scratches her legs with his sharp nails, opens her bra, pulls it off and tosses it into the front seat, roughly pulls her shoes and socks off ("gonna suck these little toes, I LOVE me some gurrrl feet ..."), tries to push inside her, bends against her, only slightly erect, pushes again, less erect, begins pumping his crotch hard against her, the hat falls off, he keeps pumping against her, keys and loose change spill out of his pants down around his ankles, he stops and fumbles out of the car.

"You yummy," he says, gets back in the car, straddles her, and starts slowly tugging on his penis, drooling and licking his lips, making slurping, sucking sounds, drools on his hand and pumps himself faster ("I want to milk you, want you to milk me"), twists her nipples once each, hard, she flinches and cries out, her hips recoiling down into Agata's painting, the man still mostly flaccid but keeps tugging on himself, rubbing himself on her, trying to get inside her but he's bending soft and small, jerks harder on himself, grabs her hand and sucks her fingers, clamps her hand around his penis, left hand hard on her chest, holding her down, masturbates hard with his right, comes in spurts and globs and keeps coming, all over the woman; her bare feet, thighs, crotch, belly, breasts, still coming in heavy shots all over her face.

He leans down close, misses but kisses near her mouth.

"I so love you, Mamacita," he says, pulling his clothes on, sloppy, zipping up and smiling, just a friendly guy again.

"Fuck you," she says, crying, raging, pounding the windows and the roof with her hands and feet, wedged in the back of her car on top of Agata's shredded now broken painting.

"Hopefully, you will. Maybe I'll see you here again sometime, hmmm?" He turns and walks casually back toward the flea market, shirttail hanging below his creased, smelly suit coat.

Pulling her pants up, putting her shoes back on, looking around for her cell phone, the woman sees a silver business card case in the twisted blankets. It has an ornate H engraved on it.

Inside the case, the top card says:

The Hamptons Group
Distributors, Liquor/ Entertainment
C. J. Hamptons, CEO

She closes it, drops it in the blankets, dials 91— on her cell, stops, looks at the Rose Bowl across the vast parking lot ... many people, far away, having fun.

It's still a beautiful high blue sky day, but for Rosalita, the sky gets colder, comes down lower.

PART TWO *Over the Rockies*

Open the door

I feathered the gas pedal, feathered us away from the hotel, and rolled to a snow-crunchy stop in a far corner of the parking lot, under some low, snow-laden pine branches. It was quiet in the van. I looked over my shoulder at the rest of the gang.

"I'm going in, or my name's not *Red Jumbo!*" I said. "Stay here, everyone."

They seemed fine with that idea, wiping peepholes clear in the steamed-up windows to watch me, go in.

I got out of the van. *Cold.* Snow up my ankles. Snow less festive than an hour ago, but while festive is my middle name, this snow was allowing me to be … *furtive*. Shrouding the van, and me, outside the hotel.

I crunched along in the dark, walking across the parking lot toward the yellow glow from the porte cochère of the Hotel Colorado. I heard crunching behind me and turned around.

It was Rosalita, heading my way.

Take the money, fucking run

A small lime-green lamp was switched on low, glowing lime behind the front desk, but no one was around. There was faint piano music on in the lobby, something classical, playful. Maybe Mozart.

Rosie looked around. "Where is everybody?" she whispered. "We *do* have reservations. You hear something?"

I thought I heard something too, something creaking. We waited, but nothing else happened, no one arrived at the desk. Just Mozart, tinkling in the dim lobby.

"We may not need reservations. It's pretty empty, this hotel, I think," I whispered back. "*Quiet.* Why are we whispering?"

There was a bell on the front desk. I was thinking about ringing it. We waited, listening for more creaking.

There was a little hour sign on the front desk. *Back in Half an Hour.* Rosie texted Alberto telling them to go get coffee or *drinks,* we'd wait here. The van drove off and Rosie sat down on a couch in the lobby.

"Rosie, can I ask you something?"

She nodded.

I sat beside her. "Why, do you think, the Hamptons hired you, when they seem to hate immigrants?"

"I don't know. I *was* polite, so to speak, cheerful, a good housekeeper. So there was that. But I suspect they could feel the rebel in me, and they—she mostly—tried to drive it out of me. Maybe Mr. Hamptons thinks that I ... no, never mind, I don't know."

"There are always people around who want to drive it out of you. Crush your confidence, your spirit. They haven't got the spirit, so they can't stand it in someone else. But you know that. Was it also because you're Mexican?"

"Well yes, Red, there's that. And I'm an *illegal,* as Mrs. Hamptons calls it. As he calls it. As many call it. She really hates *that.* Says we're all coming up to steal jobs from white people."

"She said all that to you?"

"I overheard her giving a speech to Mr. Hamptons one night, and she was screaming! She was drunk, and it was ugly, though he didn't say much. Those two are politically wired into California Republican power, and way against *any* immigration, *any* citizenship policy…"

"But what *about* that, how is it that you were in their employ?"

Rosalita gave me a look.

"Ok, yes, sorry Rosalita—that *was* a stuffy phrase—*in their employ.* I think spending last night in the Beverly Hill Hotel is getting inside my soul. I was just wondering why they hired you if they're so against immigration, and especially *illegal* immigration. *And,* on a side note, how is it immigration anyway, going from Mexico to Mexico, or … as some call it now … *California?*" It felt good saying all this, I was on a roll, even if I was whispering.

"You're funny, pocho."

"What *is* that word, Rosie? Alberto used it with me in Pasadena."

"Buddy."

"I am that, Rosie."

"I know you are … *pocho.*"

Silence in the hotel, high up in the Colorado mountains, past midnight, then a little wind on the windows. I didn't know what to say next to Rosalita, so I waited for her to say something.

"He fucked me," she said. "No, he *raped* me. It was almost ten years ago. I don't want to talk much about it. Ok?"

"Yes. Of course, Rosalita."

She was staring at the front desk, she looked at me, she looked behind us, out the windows. Back at me. Still very quiet all around.

"I was at the Rose Bowl Flea Market, and it happened fast. He was gross, a slob, and he's a stupid man—he accidentally left his business cards in my car."

"He did?"

"Yeah. A month or so later, I called him. I reminded him of who I was. It scared him, I had to wait while he ran out of the house, away from Mrs. Hamptons, I guess. He was all out of breath. Asking what I wanted. How did I get his number. I didn't say anything. I was about to hang up, maybe call him a motherfucker or something and hang up, but I couldn't speak. Froze up in anger. I didn't want to cry. Then he offered me a job. I didn't see *that* coming. He offered me a job as what he called a domestic. I said *how much?* There was a moment of silence, he said: $1,000 a month. I said $5,000. He said yes. And he offered me my own living quarters in a private wing off the side of the house. The use of one of his cars anytime, because I told him my Toyota hatchback was dying. Which it was. Not to mention, depressing to even sit in. I said *yes.*"

"How could you stand to be anywhere near him?"

"I was broke. *"

"Good reason."

"No money left. No job. Lost my apartment. I had been working at a Unitarian church doing gardening, I was *good*, too, they loved me. My friend from church, Agata, she knew my situation, got me a job there—they were paying me under the table—and I had a key to the church, so I slept in a little window seat up on the top floor down a side hall where no one ever went, had a beautiful, sparkly view of Pasadena at night! But then someone *else* found out, the church board or somebody high up in the church, I think it was the choir director, that I was an "undocumented worker." So, they had to, quote, *let me go*. Though I *was* allowed to stay in my Chalice Circle group. I started working for him the next week, and that was ... about ten years ago."

"Wow. $5,000? That's a lot. Was he really that worried you'd turn him in?"

"Yeah, I think so. I'd gotten to know a lot of people in the church; he didn't know about Serge yet, but I let it drop to both the Hamptons that I had a policeman friend there, and I hung out in Old Town Pasadena a lot, so I think he was worried about his *standing in the community*. Which was pretty funny, actually, because most of the time he had a problem with his standing, and his standing *up,* in his own house. They're a real boozy pair. And after nine years of working with them, I was too. I needed to shut out that pain. He came to me and said Mrs. Hamptons wanted to fire me. He told me he'd pay for me to go to rehab. I took that offer."

"So, you worked for them until you couldn't stand it anymore, and decided to get 'dead.'And Mrs. Hamptons never knew what happened? What about Alberto? He must know."

"*Alberto.* A very bright spot in all of this. I met him at the Hamptons. He was already there, working for them. We fell in love very quickly. I liked his eyes. They're like puppies. Not puppies' eyes, his eyes are like actual puppies, if that makes any sense. And yes, he knows. When I told him, he wanted to kill Mr. Hamptons. I told him I'd rather visit him in our bed than in jail. He cried off and on for days. Not so the Hamptons could see him. Still does, he gets triggered almost as easily as I do."

Speaking of Alberto, I wondered if he and the others were coming back soon. I looked out the window, heavy snow coming down, no sign of the van. I wondered if *they* knew she'd been raped.

"And Ruby, of course," said Rosalita, "we got close very soon, working at the Hamptons. I told her it was alright to tell Fyodor, who never mentioned it to me, but he was always warm and kind when I saw him around the property. Very sensitive man. And as I said, I met Serge at the UU church. I liked him, trusted him from the start. I told him all about it. He was so sweet, really tender with me as I told him, and he just listened, but I could tell he was angry about it, too. He asked a lot of real police questions and finally, sadly, determined that with no rape kit done, no physical evidence, and the passing of time, the word of an undocumented Latina was not going to mean shit against the word of a white pillar of society. I would probably be deported if I tried to get justice. Serge was mad when the UU church let me go from my job and stayed in touch with me, after. We'd have coffee sometimes. He and Alberto are buddies now. But no, Mrs. Hamptons never did know. She was drunk most of the time. Then, Mr. Hamptons started to get like that, too. Drinking, I mean. Losing his *standing*. And the old Hamptons business and family money kept rolling in, some of it now to me. I put it away, invested it through the advice of a friend of Serge's at his bank, and every time we passed a Bank of America ATM on this trip, in all the big and little towns, I imagined each of them lighting up and saying, *Hi Rosie! Everything's gonna be alright!* Which was a phrase I picked up from Roscoe."

"Rosalita, on that day at the Rose Bowl, did you call the police? Was anyone around?"

"I sat there in my car awhile, staring at the stadium, watching the crowds walk around, way off in the distance, not even crying yet, then I called 911. The cops came, I showed them the silver case and his business cards, and they intimated that a man 'of his standing' wouldn't do such a thing and I must have found, or stolen, the silver case. When they asked, I lied and said my green card was at home, they laughed and suggested I go back where I came from and find it. They wrote some stuff down, told me to comb my hair, straighten and button up my shirt—to the highest button! As if that bit of neck had been the thing to provoke this!— and left. I drove home, and *then* I cried. And cried. I cried hard. And couldn't sleep. Nothing ever happened, the cops never even called back."

"Fuckers," I said.

"Yeah. And telling me to comb my hair. Fuckers. Can I tell you something?"

"Of course, anything." I leaned forward in my chair, elbows on my knees, to listen to Rosalita, but I heard creaking again, somewhere around the corner from the front desk, down a dark hall.

"When I called him, I didn't even imagine Mr. Hamptons would offer a job, but when he did, I said yes. You may wonder about that, think it's weird, or maybe you think I was wrong to do that. Or weak."

"I don't think any of those things."

"Let me try to get the rest of this out, Red. I need to say this. Because I've accused myself of all those things. Many long nights, wide awake in bed. And long afternoons, serving him, serving *them*. Feeling subservient. But then I thought—if I'm not going to tell his wife that he raped me, if I can't get the fucker arrested, if screaming at him, or trying to beat the shit out of him wouldn't do anything but get me deported, and if I can't do anything about immigration laws and the racist thugs that enforce them, or about cops that tell a woman to comb her hair and button the higher buttons on her shirt after she's been raped—if I can't do any of that, I can damn sure take his money, make a plan. And fucking *run!*"

"Right on, Rosie."

"I said all of this to Serge, too, at the time."

"What did he say?"

"He said, *Right on, Rosie.*"

Creak. We both heard it, and footsteps, like a drum beat kicking off the rhythm of a bright, uptempo jazz song coming down the hall towards us, followed by the long, very formal, and pointed clearing of a throat, and a man walked into the low limelight of the front desk, in wingtip shoes, no socks, a black and red check robe, and hair slicked back, parted in the middle.

He peered at us like maybe he wanted to scold us, checked his watch, and said, "You wouldn't be the *Red Jumbo* party by any chance?"

"Me and Roscoe put it in your name, hope you don't mind," whispered Rosalita, then, whispering at an end, "HELLO! Yes, Deckle, it's us, sorry we're late."

The man was standing sideways to us, one foot forward pointing at us like a scolding finger, one eye squinted, looking ready to ask us *where have you been at this hour?* then everything changed and he spun on his shiny heels and started walking, smiling wide and gleaming, a very grandiose presence, I thought—*like the Golden Gate Bridge at night!* The lobby was large, it was a *long* walk over, we watched him as he headed to us, heels clicking closer and echoing in the dark.

"Isn't his face, his smile, like a photograph of the Golden Gate Bridge at night? Can you see it, Rosie? Like the spanning cables are the upturned parts of his mouth, all the car headlights his teeth ..."

Rosie looked at the concierge—he was about halfway across the lobby, then she looked at me.

"No, Red, I don't see that at all."

I was confident about this image, and ready to argue for it, but then the concierge was right in front of us. His cologne arrived a second later; his name tag, of the *Hotel Colorado*, said: Mr. Edge.

"Hi and welcome, folks! How may I help you? My name is Deckle and *WELCOME* to the Hotel Colorado!"

His cologne continued to arrive, and Deckle's eyes and smile got very large, this close to us: the bridge all *lit up.*

"Ah yes, and how could I forget the *Jumbo* reservation, placed just last evening, by a Mr. Roscoe G.T. Towne, of Kansas City, I think? *Oui?*"

"Oui!" I responded, with a burst of energy, Deckle's enthusiasm and French very contagious. "Reservations for we. I mean, *us* ... I am Jumbo, and this, as I think you may know, is Rosalita."

The front door stormed open, perfect timing, and in came the snow and the rest of us. It couldn't have been rehearsed better.

"And *that* is Alberto, Serge, Fyodor, and his wife, Ruby Taillights. What do you think, Mr. Edge—*rooms ready?*"

"Call me *Deckle*, please! And yes, Mr. Jumbo, ready, of course. Mints on all your pillows! We'll have you upstairs, *bedded down,* and luxuriating in mere moments!"

He said all this musically, with many high and low notes, ending with gleaming eyes and *that smile,* which he seemed to be beaming straight at me.

"Forgive me, ha ha," laughed Deckle, breaking out of his beaming, "it's just that *voice* of yours. Such *resonance*, quite rare. It's as if a grizzly bear got inside one of Bach's grand organs, if you will."

"Yeah, Red ... the Golden Gate ... I can see it now," said Rosalita.

Deckle suddenly clapped his hands in a festive *Christmas morning!* sort of way.

"Well!" he said. "Follow me, and we'll see about those rooms, shall we?"

And he pulled us along, in the grand elegance of his heavily cologned jet stream, up to the front desk.

Couch surfing

Outside, a car was crunching through the snow, up to the Hotel Colorado. We all stood still, didn't turn around. Then we slowly turned around.

Coasting to a stop in front of the building was a shiny black Jaguar XJ with California plates and a bumper sticker for the Los Angeles Philharmonic, with, in bright red letters:

DUDAMEL DOES IT WITH A BATON!

We all stared at it. I whispered sideways, to Rosie, "Is that their car? You don't think it's them, do you?"

Rosie nodded yes, whispering to me, "If they think I'm alive, if they found out somehow, maybe from their *other* detective guy, they may be after me. They treated me badly while I was alive. And now that I'm dead—or they think I am, or maybe now they know that I'm *not*—they don't seem to want to stop. It looks like they want me, dead or alive."

The Hamptons were staring at my van, Kansas and Missouri barking wildly at them through the window; then they were coming in from the parking lot; then they were under the porte cochère; then they were at the front door. Staggering a little.

I made a dive for one of the lobby couches, got behind it, Rosalita got behind me, the rest of our little band behind her.

"Mr. Jumbo?" asked Deckle, so softly his voice was like smoke after someone has blown out a match.

I popped my head up for a second, checking the front door ... the Hamptons were almost in the lobby ... flashed a quick, sneaky smile at Deckle, "*Shhhhh* ... don't tell that couple, the Hamptons, we're here, Mr. Edge ... it's a *surprise*. They haven't seen their kids in a while, this is our anniversary present to them! *Shhhhh* ..." then I popped back down again; Rosalita, Alberto, Serge, Fyodor, and Ruby —all my *Hamptons siblings*—staring at me.

Deckle seemed game. I peeked back and saw him flashing the thumbs-up, with *both* thumbs. He grabbed the edge of the front desk and propelled himself around it, toward the front door.

"Gotcha, Mr. Jumbo! *Will do!*" he whispered quickly as he passed by the couch, just as quickly changing faces, into his louder, concierge voice, "Ah, welcome to the Hotel Colorado! I am Deckle Edge, your host this evening! And you are?"

We all laid low, on all fours, behind the couch.

There were mumbling, shuffling, stamping-off-the-snow sounds from the front door, echoing across the lobby, Rosalita looked worried, right behind my hidden-behind-the-couch ass, *then* ...

"My name is Hamptons, and I know that van in the parking lot," said Mr. Hamptons. "And those goddamn dogs. He is here. Red Jumbo is here."

"R e d ... JUM*bo*?" Deckle sang my name, in three different notes. "Gee, what a name!"

"Is he in this hotel, Dreidel? *Tell us!*" yelled Mrs. Hamptons, obnoxiously.

"It's Dreckle, my dear," stated Mr. Hamptons, authoritatively.

"Deckle, actually," clarified Mr. Edge, politely.

I was on edge.

"Yes or no? Is Jumbo here ... *Deckle?*" Mrs. Hamptons said the name as if she was holding it as far away from her body as possible —with her voice.

"I couldn't say," said Deckle.

"You couldn't say? Well, you'd better say! I can see your name tag from here, and I'll report you! By the way, why *can't* you say, Deckle?"

I wanted very much to peek over the couch again, but Rosalita had me pinned down, sitting on my legs. Serge, Alberto, Fyodor, and Ruby were behind her, all of us looking terrified.

"It's the uh, *element of surprise*, Mrs. Hamptons," said Deckle.

It was like listening to a radio drama. I was imagining those three faces countering back and forth out there in the lobby.

"Element of WHAT?" squawked Mrs. Hamptons, like a tuba.

"Surprise, Mrs. Hamptons. You'll thank me in the end!"

"*I'll* thank you in the end!"

Something in her voice, and the sound of shoes moving fast on the lobby floor, and I *had* to take another peek over the couch. So I did, slowly rising, Rosalita coming up with me, and we caught a snapshot of Mrs. Hamptons, one leg drawn back like a field goal kicker for the Denver Broncos, in mid-kick, aiming for Deckle's butt —

"Mrs. Hamptons! I'm on *your* side!" yelled Deckle, dodging her kick. Mrs. Hamptons yelled something back, then both of them ran toward the elevators!

Rosalita yanked me back down behind the couch, a finger to her lips. *He's turning this way!* she mouthed, just a wisp above a whisper.

It was quiet in the lobby. Mountain winds blowing outside the hotel, creaking the old building. Running footsteps, Deckle and Mrs. Hamptons probably, far away down a wing of the hotel, or upstairs, somewhere.

But closer, footsteps coming across the lobby. Towards us. One step, another.

Slowly, step by step creaking closer, someone coming, stepping on a board, so close—*that same board sagging under me.*

Rosalita's eyes filling with tears; scared or angry or both. It made *me* angry, seeing her eyes, but I kept still, quiet.

"Perfume." Mr. Hamptons voice, whispering. "It's *hers.* Could she be—alive?"

Rosalita's eyes *so* scared. Her hands were trembling.

"Red Jumbo is here, somewhere ... upstairs," Hamptons said. "Is *she?*" Then there was a long silence—no creaking, no moving, no breathing, nothing but the wind outside—finally, Mr. Hamptons footsteps walking away from us, DING—the elevator arriving for him ... and he's gone.

After a minute, we all stood up, slowly. Just us, in the lobby.

"Let's get out of here," I said, looking at Rosalita's eyes.

"Yeah. But not too far," she said. "I don't know what they're doing, but I want to keep an eye on these, on *this* ..."

"Fucker?"

"Yes. Fucker. *Those* fuckers. And I've hidden behind my last couch. Ok, Red?"

"Ok, Rosie."

We all walked out from behind the couch, softly, trying not to *creak* the floor, tip-toeing towards the front door in a unit, like a balletic dance company. It was snowing again, big flakes floating against the windows and around the streetlights. We heard the sound of footsteps returning; hurried ones.

"Like you said, Red—let's get out of here," said Ruby, opening the door.

"I want to drive," said Rosalita. I handed her the keys.

We walked as fast as we could toward the van through fresh snow, getting deeper; we all got in, Rosie got the motor running, our three little dogs in the van windows, bright-eyed and barking, wrapped up in blankets on our laps. I turned the heat to *high.*

"Floor it!" I said.

She did, we spun in place for a few seconds, the tires found traction, and we fished-tailed away from there.

110

Rume Service

Next morning was beautiful. Tranquil. Frosty white and sunny blue sky.

I woke up in a little Estonian motel, with Estonian music (I guessed) floating down the hall, the high, strong, soaring voice of a woman, no idea what she was singing, but feeling higher and stronger myself because of her (even soaring, for so early in the morning), along with the friendly brown smell of coffee and the gregarious golden smell of fresh-baked bread. Which all made me immediately happy! My life before this morning hadn't been much like this; days and nights and then more months of days and nights like that, all the same, emotionally snow-blind, cold and alone down in my basement. I hadn't often *broken bread* with many others, or hardly *any* others, but I knew that there were *many* others in the motel this morning!

I leaned up in bed, only my eyes and nose peeking out into the cold but cozy room, deeply breathing in these swirls of smells, my eyes blinking, focusing, following the swirls of white sheets and blankets covering me, out through the frosted window at the foot of my bed, into the swirls of snow going up the side of Glenwood Springs into the mountains.

A knock at the door, *"Housekeeping!"* and a woman's head popped in. *"Terre hommikust!"* It sounded like good morning, *looked* like good morning on her face, which was friendly, really awake and very *alive*, with shining dark eyes, shiny red lips, and teeth white as the snow outside.

"Good morning! Who is singing?" I asked, from my fuzzy warm snowdrift of a bed.

"Oh! Liisi Koikson! She's singing 'Varjud.' You like it? It is not *Guns and Roses*, ha ha ha!"

"Oh yes. It's mysterious, and romantic, full of longing, the sound of yearning through the long winter, so to speak. And yes, she has a nice voice. Of course, I have no idea what she's saying. Sorry, but I don't know Estonian. Like most Americans, I only drive in first gear."

"Ha ha, oh my goodness, funny, and ... *Wow!* You know Estonia, I think! We *are* like that, longing through the long winters and long days, but you talk more than many Estonian men—they are very *stoic*, very *stern!*" She said these last couple of words trying to toughen her face up, frown and *harden* it up, which only made both of us laugh."

"Well, yes, I do go on and on sometimes. You know: blah, blah, blah, but I *do* like this music! Also this motel. I just came across the country from California, from Los Angeles, from the Beverly Hills Hotel!"

"Oh, fancy-*pantsy.* Or is it fancy-schmancy? I don't know, ha ha ha," she said, coming into my room now, fresh towels over her shoulder, over her T-shirt, over the big red lips of the Rolling Stones logo, coming in with her.

"Fancy, yes, but cold. A little snobby. Ickkk!" I made a face too, on that last word, and we both laughed again. It was nice to be laughing again instead of running and driving and diving behind couches. "Like down the street, at the Hotel Colorado."

"You were there?"

"For a few minutes, last night, in the lobby. Then we came here, my friends and I. *Better here.*"

"Better here," she whispered and winked. And laughed. "You stay with us tonight, too?"

"Maybe, I don't know the plan."

"I hope yes stay," she said, saluting me and smiling. "Your nose, too, sir. Very strong nose, a handsome feature. Don't take it wrong, but your nose would be good snowplow for our Colorado mountain roads, they get so snowy! MISTER Jumbo. Wow wow wow; some name!" she said, shaking her saluting hand like it was *red hot.*

Then she was gone, down the hall, whistling, in Estonian.

Kansas and Missouri were snoring somewhere in the bed, so I slid back down in the sheets, just my eyes peeping out of my linen snowdrift, unzipped my brain, relaxed and opened it up, thinking back over the days.

It had been another refreshing night of deep sleep, like the night before at the Beverly Hills Hotel, except there I'd felt like a stuffed Elizabethan miniature *man* figurine in a dried-out diorama. Or my peasant version of that. It was nice to see my old Polo Lounge friends, Annette and Sonia. But I had new friends, and I was out of Los Angeles and going ... who knows where?

I'd wanted a change that night—when I staggered drunk out of my house in Eagle Rock, looked up at the moon, sick of TV, and internet, Facebook, my cell phone—and I was getting it.

Another knock, *"Breakfast,* Red?*"* This time, Rosalita, calling through the closed door.

"Yes, Rosie, I'll be right down, but give me a few minutes, I'm ruminating. And *good morning!*"

"Ruminating, eh? Don't break anything. Maybe you should call Rume Service. Ok, see you downstairs. Let's talk about what's next, and about those two down the street at the Hotel Colorado. And good morning to *you!*" She stepped away and I heard her footsteps moving down the hall.

She was right about that: *don't break anything.* I decided then and there that *too much* ruminating was over. It was one thing to luxuriate in the luxuriously crisp, clean, snow-white sheets, but I have a way of getting lost in thought, lost in space, and if I stayed in bed any longer, I'd be checking the thread count; counting the threads, one at a time. Ruminating had brought little illuminating, I'd found out the hard way, the long way around, in my own life.

So, I was decided. And I felt a sudden squirt of energy, maybe from that newly glowing part of my brain, and before I knew what I was doing, in what you might call full voice—*full verve!*—I yelled,

"Yeah, Rosie! Let's *do* talk about what's next."

Her footsteps, fading away down the hall, stopped. I heard them do a leather twist and pivot.

"Oooh, Red—I like the tone of your voice!"

Even the dogs stopped snoring, now they were running around under the white sheets like Halloween ghosts, trying to get out of bed. Rosalita was walking back down the hall to my door and she stopped just outside it again.

"There were a couple of times back in California when you sounded a little like a piccolo, no offense, Red. But now you sound like a tenor sax! Nothing like a good night's sleep, out of town, eh?"

"That, and the influence of *sparkly women*, first thing in the morning!"

"Hey Red, are you *decent?* Are Kansas and Missouri up yet? Are *they* decent? Let's get outside. Because speaking of *sparkly*, it's looking sparkly out there! Let's get out and walk the dogs, they've been cooped up and transported cross country, probably they have *van lag*. I'll go get Felix and Alberto. Let's have a break, let's have some fun, it's a beautiful morning!"

"You think we should show ourselves outside, with the Hamptons in town, maybe watching?"

"Sax, Red, *sax.*"

"Oh yeah. I was going piccolo again, wasn't I?"

"I know you're sax at heart! And I'm tired of acting scared, even if I am, a little."

"See you outside, Rosie."

"Si, Señor Jumbo. I'll go wake up Serge and the *Taillights Two*, and get coffee!"

"Bye for now, Rosie. See you in a few minutes."

Then there was the leather twist and pivot of Rosalita's footsteps down the hall to the landing again, and someone coming *up* the stairs.

"Terre hommikust!" said the other sparkly woman so far this morning.

The best sandwich in the world

Roscoe unbuttons his vest as he approaches the tin-silver order window at Bryant's Barbeque in Kansas City.

While he waits for the cook to come, he studies that window; a soft, silvery sheen of silver, brushed by lots and lots of ribs over lots of years. He's going to write a poem about that order window. The cook's face comes into it.

Roscoe leans down into the window, undoes another button on his vest, and orders "Beef and fries," pouring the words to the cook slow and sumptuous, like pouring BBQ sauce, he thinks, like pouring poetry, too. A cell phone rings in his vest.

"Hello?"

"Mr. Towne? This is Deckle Edge again at the Hotel Colorado. How are you this morning, sir?"

"Hungry, Mr. Edge! I'm about to have breakfast! So now, did the gang arrive all safe and sound?"

"Yes, Mr. Towne, they were here last night, but they left. We were talking in the lobby, their—I guess, parents—came, who Mr. Jumbo said they wanted to surprise, they even hid behind a couch!—then, they were gone. I looked all over the hotel last night, but I can't find them."

"I'll have an ice tea please."

"Um ... excuse me, Mr. Towne?"

"Oh, sorry Deckle—hey, call me Roscoe—I'm ordering breakfast here, but go on. You say they're gone? And their ... parents ... are there?"

"Oh. I see. Sorry to interrupt. I can call back ..."

"... side of fries, man, yeah, perfect!—no no, Deckle, go on ... "

"Well, yes, Roscoe, they're gone, Red Jumbo and all the gang. Mr. Hamptons—I guess he's their father?—asked me this morning if I'd seen them last night, he thought they'd be here, in the Hotel Colorado. Asked me if I'd seen them, I said I hadn't. I hope I did the right thing. I didn't know about the element of surprise component. But anyway, Mr. and Mrs. Hamptons are looking for them. Oh, and I'm afraid Mrs. Hamptons is a little put out with me. Shall I cancel your reservations for the Red Jumbo party?"

"Yes, please do. I'll call Rosalita. Did you meet her last night? I'll call Red, too. I'll find out where they are and tell them that their —parents—are looking for them. Hang on a second, Mr. Edge," says Roscoe.

Roscoe slides his tray from the order window down to the cashier's window, pays her, and carries his food to a long red Formica table by the front window, under a big blown-up photo of Count Basie in Bryant's, tickling the ivories.

Roscoe sits down at the table with a deeply satisfied sigh and sees his own ivories smiling, reflected in the glass of the Basie portrait. Then he remembers he's still got Mr. Edge on the phone.

"Oh sorry Deckle, to keep you waiting. You say Mrs. Hamptons is put out with you? Between you and me, she's a bit of a snob, a bit of a narcissist."

"Oh dear! An arsonist! Well, she is a rather animated woman, she kicked me in the butt and chased me all over the hotel last night, but still, wow!"

"No no, I said she's a narcissist."

"Oh. Oh, ha ha. Well, Roscoe, that's a horse of a different color, ha ha. Ok, then, I'll get on the computer and cancel the reservation. It's been nice talking to you. Have a nice breakfast."

"Well, thanks again, Deckle. May I call you Deckle?"

"Oh, of course, Mr. Towne. Bye now. Give a call if you hear anything."

"Goodbye, Mr. Edge. I certainly will. But let's keep it between us, don't want to spoil whatever Red and Rosalita and the rest of the gang have planned. Have fun in Colorado. What a beautiful state! I gotta get back out there!"

"Yes, come on out! And call ahead when you do. If you just call when you hit the Rockies, I'll fix you up with a room here by the time you come down the other side! Goodbye, Mr. Towne."

Roscoe ends the call, pulls up Rosalita's number but stops, smiles, breathes deeply, sets the phone back down on the red Formica, on a corner of the table away from the plate piled high with beef and fries—out of the juicy line of fire—lifts his sandwich, takes a small bite, and chews and chews and chews ... nice and slow.

He's going to eat this—slowly.

He remembers the old days, running in here, impatient in line, eating fast, hitting the bathroom, back to the table, eating fast, drinking a pitcher of beer, bathroom again, then the parking lot, driving too fast, swerving home in his car, the bathroom, bloated and peeing and then, asleep. After all the years of eating too fast, drinking too fast, choking on it ...

He's trained himself, and is enjoying everything.

Like now.

Here he is, in one of his favorite (what he calls) Eating Establishments in Kansas City, but it feels like it's the first time he's been here. And maybe it is, at this slower speed. It's different, this morning. Small bites of the sandwich, tasting the beef and the fat and the sauce, the crisp brown flavor of the potato skins on the thick fries, one fry at a time.

He's holding the best sandwich in the world. His table is at the front window of Bryant's, looking out onto Brooklyn Avenue. There's a puffy white cumulus cloud like a pillow bouncing around silently over the Kansas City skyline, and a little kid with her black and white kitten chasing a red leaf skidding on the sidewalk. Roscoe has been hard on himself; lived hard, worked hard, worried hard, hardly slept for years, and finally even meditated hard to get to a day that's this easy. Now, it is. He feels a little like that cloud bouncing, or that leaf blowing down the street. It's easy, now.

A police car pulls up and parks in front of Bryant's. The policemen sit ... and sit. They get out, slowly, hitch their belts, touch their guns, almost in unison, come inside, and get in line.

Small bites, Roscoe says to himself, watching them. Easy.

Parade on 6th Street

That morning in Glenwood Springs got even better!

It *was* sparkly outside when we all got out there on 6th street with our cups of coffee; Rosalita in a University of Colorado ski cap, Alberto in a black cowboy hat, Serge in blue-mirrored aviator shades (I'd slept late, *they'd* gone shopping), Fyodor with a black wool scarf wound around his neck and mouth—*Doctor Zhivago* style—and Ruby Taillights, in her *Hello Kitty* sneakers, with Kansas, Missouri, and Felix out in front—in University of Colorado dog sweaters—all of us making tracks in the fresh snow.

We looked like a parade, beautiful all around us, and above, the cold wind blowing powdery blasts of snow off the tops of the mountains, the ski lift zipping cars up and down; I got an idea and called the small parade to a halt.

"Hang on a sec, I need a hat too. I mean, a *hat*. You'll see," I said, and turned back to the motel.

"Hey Red," yelled Ruby, in the clear Colorado air, "we need pictures of this—for Facebook!"

"Naw. I don't think so, Ruby. *We* know how good this is, you know?"

Ruby put her chin in her hand in mid-air, *thinking wise*, paused, cocked her head sideways and smiled.

"Red, you're right!" she said. I gave her one of my thumbs *up*, she gave me her two-fingered peace sign and walked over to Fyodor. "He *is* right, isn't he? I like your friend. He's unusual. He's fun."

"I told you," said Fyodor. "He *is* unusual. And kind of brave."

"I sense a sprinkling of the iconoclastic," Ruby whispered.

The air was so clear at that altitude that I could hear this exchange even way down the street, so I bent down to *untie* then tie my shoes in case they were going to give me some more compliments, but that was all of it, so I tied my shoes, went down to the motel, upstairs to my room, got my top hat from the philharmonic, and walked back up the street. I brought the teddy bear from London, too.

The parade continued up 6th street, with me in my top hat, the teddy bear riding Rosalita's dog Felix, who seemed proud to carry him, taking ever higher steps with his front paws. The wind came down out of the mountains down the street fast fresh and *cold!* in our faces.

We leaned laughing into it, Rosie's phone jingled and she pulled it out.

"Hello? *Roscoe?*" she said, laughing, trying to stay on her feet. "Yes, it's *cold!* We're all out walking across town ... yes, we were there last night, the beautiful Hotel Colorado, but then the Hamptons showed up, right behind us, in the lobby, and ... how did you know we hid behind the couch?"

We were puffing up 6th street when I saw a black SUV driving and stopping, driving and pulling over, pulling over and parking, a few blocks behind us. But the driver unfolded a map and spread it on the dash, so maybe she or he was lost. Funny thing though, I thought: a *paper* map.

"Oh, Deckle told you. Right. What a guy, eh? Yeah, he played right along with us, right up until the moment he literally got his ass kicked by Mrs. Hamptons! He told you about that, too? Ha ha! Excuse me? Well, Red says the Hamptons had someone watching him at the Beverly Hills Hotel, but Red shook that someone off our tail—some man in black, in a matching black SUV—but not before he tipped off the Hamptons, and it looks like they followed us to Colorado. Or they followed *Red*, I'm not sure they know that I'm alive, or who *else* is in the van."

I was watching the SUV. The driver folded the map and flung it into the backseat, then made a quick turn off 6th street. Serge was watching too, we both shrugged.

Rosie's phone made a ping sound and she looked at it, "... so, I'm looking at this picture of stacks of pork and beef, and towers of Wonder Bread! ... Bryant's Barbeque? Mmmm-mmm ... *Hello? ...Roscoe?*"

Black and white

Roscoe watches the two policemen go back outside, get in their car with bags of barbecue, put drinks on the dash, and settle in for lunch.

Like Roscoe, they eat slowly, faces turned toward Roscoe, sitting in the window. Both of them behind sunglasses, Roscoe can't be sure where they're looking, but he can't eat anymore.

He's scared. He's on the phone with Rosalita but he's frozen; sure they're watching him. He knows two reasons why. One reason is a million dollars. The other reason is racism.

The black sunglasses hide the eyes of these cops, but not their white skin.

Alcoholics, notorious

Serge looked at me, I looked at him, and we both looked up the street to where Fyodor and Ruby and Alberto were making snowballs and playing with the dogs. My teddy bear had slipped off the dog, Ruby was brushing snow off the bear and remounting him on Felix, who immediately dived over a small snow drift, leaping and springing through the snow and the high mountain air; teddy bear's first rodeo, and hanging on!

Serge smiled, watching that. But he looked worried. Rosalita was still on the phone, waiting, not saying much. "No, Roscoe. You can't do that. Roscoe?" She put down the phone. "Roscoe hung up. He's worried about some cops he thinks are watching him."

"Roscoe's not into anything, right?" asked Serge.

"*Into* anything? As in, *illegal?*" said Rosie. "Aside from—being Black. Which is always a little illegal around *some* people."

"Yeah. That's what I thought. Sorry for the question. Funny, I was a cop again there for a second. Not that cops are *all*, you know ... oh the hell with it. You know the rest of that sentence. You know *me*. We're not *all* racist pricks."

We stood there looking up at the mountains.

"God damn it," said Serge.

The dogs came trotting down the hill and dropped close to me, dropping their heads on their paws in the snow. Fyodor, Ruby, and Alberto followed, slowly strolling down.

"Roscoe said he wants to order a beer. They have Budweiser on tap at Bryant's—*his beer*—and he says he wants one. I told him he can't do that."

"Why not?" I asked. Seemed perfectly reasonable, even to me, an alcoholic.

Rosie shook her head at me. *"Red, Red, Red,"* she said. There was something familiar about the way she was wagging her finger at me. "You don't remember me, do you? Or Roscoe, for that matter. I recognized *you* the second we met at the Polo Lounge. I couldn't believe it was *you* that was showing up as the investigating detective. When Serge told me about a *Red Jumbo* at the Hamptons, I thought *no,* not the Red Jumbo I know from rehab. But I knew there couldn't be two! I didn't know you were a detective, Red!"

The sun was starting to come up. The one in my mind, not the one already up and shining on the Rocky Mountains.

"I didn't either," I said. "You and Roscoe were ..."

"Roscoe and I were in rehab, too. I remember the week you were admitted to Briar Patch. But those first two weeks you were on the floor, heavily medicated, falling out of your chair at the meetings, so I don't expect you to remember a lot. I think I left Briar about the time you were coming out of the fog. But do you remember me? A little?"

My mind was clearing, getting light; the snow on the Rocky Mountains was brilliantly bright!

"I do, Rosie. There were so many others, and all those doctors and counselors. I didn't know who was who at first. I remember Vera."

"We *all* remember Vera!" Rosie laughed, and we gave each other a hug. "Anyway, I'm worried about Roscoe. He sounds vulnerable right now, I hope he's ok ... he sounded scared ..."

Serge took off his blue-mirrored sunglasses. His eyes were red, looked mad. *"God damn it,"* he whispered.

We didn't know what to do next, this side of the Rocky Mountains, and the entire state of Kansas, from Roscoe and the police car.

Rosie's phone rang.

"Yes, Roscoe. I'm here. Oh ... they did? They're *gone?*"

Serge and I didn't know what else to do but shake hands, so we did that.

"So Roscoe, they just drove away?"

"No beer, tell him," I said.

"Red says no beer. Hahaha, yeah, well, he *sort of* remembers us. Yeah ... good, I'll text you the name of our new motel here, a lot cheaper than the Hotel Colorado or the Beverly Hills Hotel, and *thanks again,* from all of us! ... Oh yes, and thank *you,* Charlie Parker! But why don't you get on out of there now. Ok, Roscoe? Ok. Bye for now. Bye. You, too."

It was getting colder with weather coming over the top of the hill, sudden cloud banks sliding across the mile-high (at least) blue sky, and coming out of that blue—breezes of snowflakes flying down 6th street. Speaking of something from out of the *blue,* I wondered what Rosie meant, that *thank you,* to Charlie Parker.

"I have an indelicate question," asked Ruby, and her eyebrows jumped over her sunglasses.

"Yes?" I said.

"Is anyone around here *not* an alcoholic?"

Rosie and I started laughing; Serge, then Fyodor, finally Alberto —one at a time, slowly—raised their hands. The dogs kept their paws down, stayed low to the ground.

"Let's get back to the motel, coffee—or whatever—on me," I said. The dogs, seemingly understanding bits of this sentence, took off first, losing the tumbling teddy bear, which Alberto picked up and piggybacked down the street. I heard tires crunching snow somewhere, and looked behind us. Serge looked too, sliding his blue shades on. It was that SUV again, a *black* SUV, still stopping and starting, black gloves messing with the map on the dash.

"Why is it always a black SUV?" wondered Serge. "You know, like in the movies."

The crunching was fading, and when we casually, both of us whistling (*just out for a walk, just taking the air, just looking around*), turned to look, the SUV was gone.

"Well, anyway, they're probably not cops. Like you, Officer Serge."

"Or detectives, like you, Detective Jumbo."

Sinu Hääl

We got into the motel cafe just in time; the breezes of snowflakes coming over the mountains and down the street had turned into a windy wall of snow!

The woman who'd brought me towels that morning greeted us inside, seated us at a table, and when she saw me, she stopped short and said, "Wait! Music! *Estonian,* since you like it!" and then she was gone, into the kitchen. Music came on through the little speakers above and all around us. A woman's voice. Singing something Estonian. Everybody looked at me.

"Don't look at me," I said.

The woman returned, beaming, dancing a little with the music. "This is called 'Sinu Hääl' which, in English, says, 'Your Voice.' Oh, and I am Klarika! Would you like something to drink?" (*Good morning again,* she whispered to me, on the side.)

"We all want coffee, yes?" I asked the gang. "On me."

"Americano," said Rosalita. "Hi Klarika, I'm Rosalita. You can call me Rosie. Can we have our dogs inside here?"

"Hi, Rosie! Oh yes, of course, we don't mind that at all where I'm from. Would they like some coffee, too? Haha, I'm only kidding. Where are they?"

"Down here under the table, keeping our feet warm."

"You like this song, Rosie? I like it so much. It is a woman talking to someone, someone who is not there, someone very far away I think, even in another time zone. She is not talking on the phone or on Zoom, she may be writing a letter. She's making small talk, but it's sweet, talking about the weather where she is, the rain and the apples getting ripe, trying to tell this person how she feels about him or her, how much she cares about them, how the person's voice makes her happy, asking if the person hears her … but I don't know if she will ever see the person again. Oh dear … this song. So sweet, so sad. It touches my heart. I am so glad my love is just up the street here in Colorado! What would your dogs like to drink? Vodka? Hahaha, I am *funny* this morning!"

"You are!" laughed Rosalita. "Just milk all around, ok?"

"Yes! Oh, and ..." Klarika looking around the table, her eyes finding me, "... *Red Jumbo*, yes?"

"Yes, that's me!"

"A man Roscoe called to put your rooms on his credit card, I just spoke with him, and we did it all on the phone, for last night and tonight, too? Ok? Maybe more nights?"

"*Maybe*, Klarika."

Klarika went around introducing herself to everyone, asking Ruby where she got her *Hello Kitty* shoes. She straightened up, hands on her hips, twisting with the Estonian music, and smiled at us.

"Well, I go get coffee, and *vodka* for dogs!" said Klarika.

It was cheerful and warm within the white walls and yellow lights, as snow filled the window panes.

Off with the ski cap

I looked outside and noticed that my van, Morrison, was beginning to disappear in the snow. The headlights looked like eyes, shivering *"Help me, I'm cold!"* The grill was chattering *Brrr.*

"Morrison is cold," I said.

We all watched the blizzard cover the parking lot and the van and the surrounding, steeply drifting hotel grounds.

Alberto, who hadn't been talking very much since we got to Colorado, asked, "Say, Red—why do you call your van Morrison? Oh. Never mind. Now I remember."

So Alberto, a man of few words (but lively eyes!), was able to ask and answer his own question in one sentence.

"Rosalita, *Rosie* ... how is Roscoe paying for all this?" asked Fyodor. "It's generous of him."

Rosalita pulled off her University of Colorado ski cap and shook down her long black hair.

"I think I'd better tell you more about Roscoe. And about something he found. Underneath Union Station, in Kansas City."

Charlie Parker's Cocktail Napkin

There was a moment of silence, we heard snow slide off the roof of the cafe, then Rosalita broke into what I'd call the *smile of a lifetime,* though I'd only known her a few days.

"I'm going to my room to get something," she said, standing up.

She *spun* into a pirouette, once around, walked right out of the cafe, on her way, but then she was right back, or her face was, smiling in the door, "I'll be right back!" and then there she went, gone again. Very energetic!

But what was that big smile about?

The Estonian song faded out, there was a gap in the cafe music loop, or someone turned it off, so there was another moment of silence. And it was ... *quiet* ... in the cafe, just one other customer at a table by the window, all bundled up, with a cup of coffee. We sat waiting for Rosalita to come back, and there was music again: "Close to You," by the Carpenters. We looked at each other like: well, ok, *yes*—we *were* getting close to each other on this adventure from California, Fyodor and Ruby were already *very* close, as was Alberto to Rosalita—so the look was yes, we *do* feel close.

Karen Carpenter was wrapping up the song when Rosalita came back to the cafe with a piece of paper.

"Roscoe found something one night underneath Union Station in Kansas City. He drank in the Union Station Bar all the time, now he works there as a bartender. Anyway, he found this thing down deep in the dark of the sub-basement. An old cocktail napkin, wadded up in the dust and decay, something written on it, in ink, and not faded away. Roscoe made photocopies of this napkin he found under the Union Station. He did that the day he found it. He was very careful with what he'd found, being gentle with it, and hiding it. He was very alert to do this, considering the condition he was in back then, which was—drunk, most of the time. Later, after I got to know him, this was when we were in rehab together, he gave me a copy. I'll pass it around. Charlie Parker wrote this. *Red?"*

She handed me the paper, I lay it down smooth on the dry (I checked, and wiped) wooden cafe tabletop. Black and white, crisp and clean, Rosalita had taken good care of her copy. Charlie Parker's handwriting. In strong black ink:

I passed the napkin to Fyodor.

"Roscoe says the story is that Charlie Parker left Kansas City for New York one night by freight train, from the yards in downtown Kansas City, and that *maybe* Parker wrote this that night, and threw it down in the basement of the train station, wandering around down there feeling *bad*—scared, sad, drunk, high. That night he left his mother, and his wife and son, Rebecca and Leon, in that house in Kansas City. That Olive address. Yes, this story has a *maybe* in it, but Roscoe took the napkin home, and he took very good care of it. He talked to some people at the Kansas City Jazz Museum, some local musicians, and then, through them, to some other, *out-of-town* musicians, who had some New York connections to jazz organizations, museums—which led to auction house connections. Some people from Sotheby's flew to Kansas City to see the napkin, which Roscoe had hidden because he doesn't trust banks, and within a few more months—Roscoe flying back and forth, Kansas City to Manhattan and back, visiting Birdland, staying in the Crown Center Hotel, some big, free dinners, and attending an auction—he got a check from Sotheby's for one million dollars."

The cafe was silent as a snow drift, and surrounded by many.

"My God, *one million dollars!*" I said, stroking Kansas and Missouri under the table. "I love Bird, and I like his cocktail napkin poetry too, his sort of, *declaration of independence.* May I have a copy of this, too? I relate to it, in these last few days. Escaping. Leaving everything. Don't you? But wow. *One million* dollars!"

"One million dollars, Red. People in Kansas City know about the napkin going to auction, that Roscoe got pretty much *all* of it, less some fees here and there, agents, and the Sotheby's people. Kansas City is very judgmental, and Roscoe feels increasingly resented around there. Especially at the jazz museum, which wanted the napkin, and from the local jazz organizations or societies, or whatever they're called. The jazz musicians in KC don't seem to mind, though. Apparently, Parker begged his second wife not to let anyone bury him in Kansas City. So, *there*, I would say. *That's* what Bird felt about Kansas City."

"You say Roscoe's feeling resented around there?" asked Serge.

"Yes. He still loves KC, but he says it's getting kind of cold for him. Socially. He says as soon as he started going to New York and the newspapers there, and later in KC, picked up the napkin story, with his name mentioned, he was getting weird, bad feelings from old, *quote*, friends."

"Oh yeah?" Serge was really zeroing in now. I watched him, thought I'd better pay attention to his technique, in case I actually became a detective somewhere along the line.

"Yeah. And they started calling him *New York Roscoe.* Asking him when he was leaving, isn't Kansas City good enough for you anymore? All that sort of thing."

Serge looked out the window at the snow. "Yeah, that's the kind of thing you get sometimes in those smaller cities. But Rosie, he's feeling threatened? Maybe that's why those cops outside the barbecue place unnerved him. I don't know, but that's a lot of money, all of a sudden."

"I also think he's lonely. And he told me that he used to have such fun there, a lot of friends all over town. I think that's all died down."

"Rich, but lonely," I said.

Rosalita nodded, looking a little worried for her friend. The napkin came around the table back to her. "Yeah, and that's how he can afford to generously fund this trip. I think he needs a cause."

"And, like Bird, some *friends*," said Ruby, from her end of the table, typing something into her pink *Hello Kitty* smartphone. What she was typing in was "Parker's Mood," which was interesting to hear (it felt lonely but *warm*, the melancholy blues) in a snowbound cafe in the middle of Colorado. We sat and listened; then Ruby turned down the volume.

"I know about those small towns. They can get even smaller when *you* start getting bigger. And I don't mean your money, getting bigger. I mean your, well—*soul*, getting bigger. Your bigger outlook on life. Your, what I like to call, *trickster largesse!*"

Ruby had a point. Serge, too. The whole world could be a small town like that, sometimes.

Klarika came back with the tray of steamy hot white coffee cups, and a smaller tray with three bowls of cream for our dogs. We sipped, the dogs lapped, Charlie Parker's "Mood" played again. "Is *good!*" Klarika nodded toward the phone. She walked over to the customer by the window, a man sitting alone, his back turned to us. He was in a huge parka with the hood *up*. I could just barely hear Klarika bend in close to him and ask if he wanted more coffee.

He didn't say anything for a few seconds, didn't move. Didn't look at her. Then, still not turning to look at her, said, "I've been waiting. This is cold. So, yes. I think I'd like some more coffee."

She flinched a little, but then Klarika straightened up, laughed, rolled her eyes, gestured at slapping her forehead, said "*oof,* sorry!" and walked toward the kitchen.

As she walked, the man turned, and watched her.

He was watching her walk, watching her legs, watching her hips, he was fixed on her body. He had to turn his head a little to follow her across the cafe. It was Mr. Hamptons. I looked down our table and saw that Rosalita had seen him, too. Klarika went into the kitchen.

There were some noises in the kitchen, something dropped and broke, Klarika said something very angry, very *Estonian* probably, I couldn't make it out, and Mr. Hamptons turned his face back to the window.

It got quiet again in the cafe, quiet in the kitchen. Then something else fell and crashed on the floor in the kitchen, and Mr. Hamptons sighed, loudly. He stood up suddenly, pulled on his coat, and, keeping his face forward and away from our table, walked into the kitchen.

The first voice in there was, maybe, the cook, "Can we help you, sir?"

"I'm leaving, I haven't got time for this," said Mr. Hamptons, from in there.

"Oh no, sir, I have your coffee ready, *here*," that was Klarika.

"I'm leaving," Hamptons.

"Sir, not that way! The exit is through the front door, please." The cook.

Then, more crashing and stomping from Hamptons, a slammed door, and quiet in the kitchen.

Quiet in the cafe. *All* of us knew—Mr. Hamptons had been there.

"He must have seen us," said Alberto. "Do you think he heard us?"

"Oh yes, my Querido" said Rosalita. "He hears. He sniffs around. He has *antennae*, feelers—like a roach."

Dead was ok

Mrs. Hamptons opens the blinds in her hotel bathroom just enough to do her makeup. She doesn't want the harsh light from outside, or the reality of the mirror on her face anymore. She's afraid to see herself that brightly, that directly, these days.

Maybe from now on. And yet ...

A very small part of her—gradually getting larger—knows that the mirror isn't reality any more than the light is harsh, it's something else making the walls close in, and as she starts with the eyeliner, the something else walks into their suite.

"Rosalita is alive," says Mr. Hamptons. "I just saw her."

"Didn't you believe our new, most recent detective? He told you he saw her in the Polo Lounge."

"I know. But it feels funny seeing her alive, since all this started."

"Funny? How do you mean? Do you care?"

Mr. Hamptons gets a beer out of a bag on the bed, pops it open and drinks. "No. I don't care anything about her. Dead was ok with me."

"Who else was there?"

"Red Jumbo, Officer Controllente of the Pasadena Police Department, and all OUR workers. All of them, our guy was right. He said they were all together in the Polo Lounge, drinking, but I didn't know they were all coming on this trip. And I overheard Rosalita talking about her friend in Kansas City, Roscoe somebody, who got one million dollars from Sotheby's for some napkin."

"A what? A napkin?"

"Some famous dead Kansas City musician wrote his family a letter on it or something."

"A million dollars?" she asks, in the mirror.

"And guess what. This man doesn't like banks. He's got the money stashed somewhere. I googled this guy and his napkin—his name is Roscoe G.T. Towne—but didn't learn anything much. We'll find out when we get to Kansas City. Come on, let's get going."

Mrs. Hamptons finishes with her eyes and moves on to her lips.

"So ... she's alive, Rosalita," she says, holding the lipstick. "And her suicide was a lie. And to think I hired this quote, unquote detective, Red Jumbo, to solve her big, tragic death. Why the fake death?"

Mr. Hamptons shows up in the bathroom door with his can of beer and his shirt off. His stomach hangs out of his unzipped pants, dimpled and pale, like cottage cheese.

"She could have just quit. I was about to fire her, anyway. She seemed to be making you nervous." Mrs. Hamptons finishes her makeup, smacks her lips, and takes a last look at herself. "Or maybe you liked her."

Mr. Hamptons looks at her in the mirror for a few seconds, then snorts and walks out the door.

"I don't know why you bother," he says.

Call from the Coast

We sat there in silence, no music in the cafe, none of us talking, then Klarika walked out covered in flour and anger, her hair a little bit wet.

"What a *jerk!*" she said. "What a mess he made back there!"

"Yeah, he's a jerk," said Rosalita and Alberto and Serge and Fyodor and Ruby and me, all in our own ways, sort of mumbling over each other.

"And he didn't even pay the check," Klarika went on, holding it away from her breakfast-splattered white blouse. I stood up with my hand out.

"I'll get it, Klarika. Are *you* alright? It got noisy out there in the kitchen."

"He was trying to push past us to the back door, trying to get out, he knocked some plates and food off the counters, threw food at us, found the exit and ran out. Odd man."

"Very," I said, handing her my Visa card.

"You know him?"

"Yes, a little. Rosalita over there, she knows him more. She used to work for him. He's been *odd* before, right Rosie?"

"That's right, Red. I *used* to. But I left. We can do that, can't we, Klarika? You're from Estonia, right?"

"Yes," said Klarika, smiling past me towards Rosalita like an old comrade at arms. "It is getting better, there is still what some call the 'Iron Ceiling' ... not glass, maybe it was just me that said that, but I think there were others ... so I left, for *Colorado!*"

"Good for you, Klarika!" Rosalita toasted, holding up her coffee cup.

"When is your birthday, Rosalita?"

"November 11. I am fifty-seven."

"Oooh, *Scorpio!* Oo la la!" said Klarika, fanning herself with a napkin. "I didn't say you had to tell me your age, though who cares? Are we ashamed? I say no way! Also, I can see it in your eyes, somehow, that you are Scorpio."

"How so?" asked Rosie. Klarika looked around the table and focused on a bottle of steak sauce.

"Ha ha, you are like that, I see—Heinz 57! 57 varieties, no? Ha ha ha! Passionate! Adventurous! Brave! That is only *three!* Ha ha ha! Such a lucky coincidence, or a *sign*, this bottle being here just now!"

"Why, thank you, Klarika," said Rosie. "Am I blushing?"

"Oh no. Not so that you can see. So … this man, this odd man, that you worked for. He is a peeg?"

"Yes, Klarika, very much a peeg. Wouldn't you say, Red?"

"Definitely a pig. I mean, peeg," I said. "Though I do like pigs, you'll notice I didn't order bacon for breakfast."

"Are you a vegetarian, Mr. Jumbo?" asked Klarika.

"I seem to be moving in that direction, more for the sake of the animals than *my* health. I hate to think of them confined and lonely, then slaughtered. And please, call me Red."

Now Klarika gazed at me, somewhat in the way she gazed at Rosalita. "This says much about your character."

"Oh, he's up to his ass in character," said Fyodor, laughing. I liked the friendly, casual way he said it; it seemed like years, not just days, since we'd met at the gatehouse of the Hampton's estate. We were old friends already. Klarika was still gazing at me.

"Also, I like your voice, *Red.* I feel better from hearing it. Makes me feel safe, and soft. But please! Don't take this as *flirt!* I am SO *taken,* ha ha ha!" she said, pointing out the window, and with her eyes, up the street; a tall house at the top, windows lit up, smoke pouring out of the chimney. We looked up there, then back at her. "Your voice eases me down like when I in the old days would lay on my Grandfather's chest at night and hear his *beeg* low voice through his rough, fuzzy shirt. You remind me of Grandfather, though maybe you are not really *that* old. No, you remind me of his chest. No! *Voice,* oh! You understand, yes?"

I did understand, so, feeling highly, even intimately complimented, and a bit self-conscious, I said, "Oh, I *do*, Klarika," my voice jumping a few octaves. *"Thank you."*

More snow slid off the roof.

"Klarika," Fyodor continued, taking a sip of latte, "this *peeg* we're talking about, was he already in here, early this morning, before we came in?"

"Yes, he was. And when he saw you all coming to the door, he changed tables to face the wall. He made a call on his cell phone. Whispering. Odd man. He *did* order bacon, a *lot!* So, he was hiding from you?"

"Yes, he was," I said, looking out the frosty cafe window, into the falling snowflakes, wondering what he was up to, wondering what was going on. Wondering where my van was in the snow.

"I was watching him sometimes, after you came in. When I poured his coffee or brought him his food, I saw he had the newspaper there, but I saw he wasn't *reading* it. I thought he was trying to listen."

Rosalita stood up and walked over to the window, rubbing a clear circle in the frosty glass. "Hamptons heard about Roscoe. About the cocktail napkin. And about the money."

Klarika poured me a fresh cup of coffee, and I walked it over to Rosalita and looked through the clear circle with her. Out the window, I saw the tip of my van's antenna sticking up alone, above the snow.

"I was surprised they showed up here yesterday. I was surprised that they were *that* pissed off at you leaving, that they would chase us here to —get you back, or have you deported, or—something. It spooked me. And when I saw how you reacted to hearing his voice, when we were hiding behind the couch, it gave me a chill. Also broke my heart. But I don't think you need to worry about him overhearing about Roscoe's money. They're already loaded, right? What do they care?"

Rosalita looked at me. "They care, Red. And I *am* worried. They are loaded, yes. Very rich. They have a liquor distribution company. She has some old family money. But they're greedy. So I am worried, Red."

I felt someone behind me. I was right. Alberto was right behind me. Also, Fyodor, and Ruby, Serge on the way. And Klarika, with the coffee pot.

I heard a rooster crowing, unusual in all this snow. Seemingly a small rooster, seemingly a *vibrating* one, probably trembling from the cold, but the crowing was coming from our breakfast table, coming from my cell phone.

I walked over to the phone as everyone stood by the window, waited, and sipped their coffees. On the screen of my phone was a number beginning with *626*.

"Pasadena," I said to everyone at the window.

Vera Similitude, a Space Odyssey

I sat down and listened to the message. I had a bite of my hash browns on the plate. I started laughing. My new friends at the window stopped sipping coffee. Klarika set down her coffee pot on the table where Hamptons had been.

"*That* was Vera."

Rosie sat down on the other side of the table from me. She put a fork into some of my hash browns, too. "Is she still in rehab?"

"She probably always will be. Or out, then back in again."

"I loved her. Really rich parents, but I don't think they ever came to visit her much. Just paid for her to be there. Automatic deposit. They sort of automatic-deposited *her*."

"I love her, too. She has a brother, but I never saw him. I offered myself as a brother, and she said ok. 'Brother and *friend?*' she asked, and of course, I said yes."

"Roscoe liked her, too. The three of us hung out; smoked, lined up for meds, couldn't sleep, went to all the meetings and classes and breakfasts together."

Rosie looked at my phone.

"What did she say, Red?" she asked.

I put the phone in the center of the table, in the dishes and cups, in the center of our circle, and looked around at everyone.

"Ready?" I asked. They were, and I turned up the speaker.

"*Hello, Red!* Top of the morning from the bottom of California! There's something right off the top of my head I need to get to the bottom of, Red, so here goes: California, Nevada, Utah, Colorado, the Tuileries, next, somewhere close to Paris but Van Gogh actually did not die the way they all say, no suicide and I'm glad ... he only sold one painting but he painted what he wanted which is the way a hero paints. Um, where was I? Oh yes—Paris. D'Orsay. Art and jazz and maybe only Paris treated Charlie Parker like a hero, he too painted what he wanted only what he wanted good red jazz music out of his saxophone, no matter how crazy they thought he was, throwing cymbals at him then symbols at him ... deconstructing him and with drugs, but he painted anyway. Then, *Bird's words*. Roscoe found his poem in the bottom of the Kansas City train station. He took it upstairs, out of Union Station, took it home, took good care of it, Bird's words. He sold it to the right people to take good care of it, made one million dollars, *one million dollars*, Red!"

There was a quiet second or two, snow slid off the roof again.

"Vera has a mind like a lint brush," I said. "It roams, moves like mercury, it shoots around like a comet, and it *hurts* a lot, too, I'd imagine. But it's very full, her mind, and amazingly sharp. It's also amazingly warm. There are whole worlds inside her. I don't think I've ever met anyone as kind, and—*immediately loving*—as she is. There's no wall; when I met her in rehab, she came right up to me ... no hovering, but no holding back. Was she like that for you, Rosie?"

"Yeah. Exactly. Then she starts talking, and you have to *strap in!* When she starts talking, it's like being in that scene towards the end of *2001.* I used to talk to her, late at night, about ... Mr. Hamptons. She was a good listener."

Rosalita sat up *quick!* pounded the table with her fist (catapulting her fork toward Klarika, who caught it on the fly), and smiled at all of us.

"One night, after one of those talks, I woke up, wide awake, starlight in my rehab bungalow windows, feeling *very* valuable, no, not good enough—very *alive!* Free. And I knew I had to leave the Hamptons. I didn't want them to turn me and Alberto into the Pasadena Police Department, or the INS, or the Border Patrol, or all of the above. I had to get away."

Klarika got up from the table, hugged Rosie (handed back her fork), went into the kitchen, and brought out more bowls of milk for Kansas, Missouri, and Felix.

"Maybe it's time to go to Kansas City," I said. "Time to get back on the highway. Time to cross Kansas."

"Maybe we should cross it at night," said Serge.

"Yes, I agree," I said. "I'd rather look at stars and moons than at flat and wheat and the Holiday Inn Express. And bible billboards."

The rooster crowed again, this time in my pocket.

I looked at my phone. "It's Vera again," I said. "Another message. Ready?"

I put the phone on the table again, the speaker turned up. Everyone leaned in.

"Red I think I said something about the Tuileries which brought in the *Telluride* Film Festival and the Mount Wilson Observatory *Telescope*, you know how we could see that up on the mountain at night above Briar Patch here in Pasadena, and then the Penn and *Teller* magic but no one has ever taken me to Las Vegas or any of those viola concertos of *Telemann's* or the William *Tell* Overture and

I think Mr. Hamptons made some overtures to Rosalita so he can go to hell and I do care about you and Rosie and I want you to TELL me how you are, if you're ok, that you're still clean and sober and that you and Rosie and Roscoe don't get hurt, please tell me how you are, and that you're all ok, *ok?* And also. Also ... I want to say ... I don't think any of us should be afraid of Mr. Hamptons."

There was a pause, she hadn't hung up, we could hear her breathing, rattling something, maybe some object on a tabletop where she was, then —

"I don't want you to be afraid of Mr. Hamptons either, Red. I want to say: fuck him. I *will* say it. Fuck him. I love you Red, give my love to Rosie and Roscoe and your friends and if you still have your dogs—*bye for now!"*

There wasn't anything much to say after that.

"Let's go to Kansas City," I said.

Her mouth in his brain

Down out of the Rocky Mountains, across eastern Colorado, Highway 70 looks like a straight line to Kansas City. Mrs. Hamptons is bored, and hungry. Mr. Hamptons is bored numb, and staring.

"I'm hungry. There won't be anything but trash out here, but I want to eat," says Mrs. Hamptons. "Pull over anywhere."

"I'll pull over anywhere," he says, staring.

"Pull over in Hays. That Applebee's over there," Mrs. Hamptons taps her lipstick case on the window.

"Do you want to stay here? Maybe a Best Western?"

"No! Drive all night, straight through, we'll take turns," she says. "I can't be out here."

"Ok, ok," he says.

Mrs. Hamptons taps with the lipstick, Mr. Hamptons turns on the radio; Miley Cyrus is singing. He knows her voice, he remembers the way she looks from TV—he remembers her mouth—and turns it up.

"Turn that off," says Mrs. Hamptons.

He turns it off and exits into Hays, Kansas; signaling, curving, and turning finally into the Applebee's lot. He parks by a red BMW, new, all the stickers still on the windows. The back door opens and a young Black girl, maybe nine or ten, jumps out excitedly. "Come on, Dad, let's eat!" she yells. "I'm HUNGRY!"

"I bet she is," says Mr. Hamptons. "Not as if she hasn't been fed, though, the chubby little brat. Kinda cute, though. They do have cute children, I'll say that. And I see they have a new car, too."

Still thinking about Miley Cyrus, Mr. Hamptons stares at the girl.

The girl, showing Dad and the rest of whoever's in her car how hungry she is, licks her lips. Mr. Hamptons watches. Then she runs inside the restaurant as her family gets out of the car and follows her in, laughing.

The Hamptons walk in behind them.

"I'll meet you at the table, I have to go to the bathroom," says Mr. Hamptons, by the hostess desk. He walks across the dining room toward a side hall of bathrooms, passing the booth where the girl and her family sit with menus. The girl bounces on the booth,

smiling, bright-eyed, and happy. Mr. Hamptons nods at her family, sees her mouth, and walks down the hall to the men's room.

He gets into a stall, tries to hear the Miley Cyrus song in his head, can't, tries humming it, remembers a bit of it, sees the girl bouncing on the booth, sees her mouth, her tongue licking and the pretty pretty white teeth biting, her lips sucking, licking, he gets his pants open, his cock is already hard, he pulls it out, rubs it against his thigh, rubs it, rolls it, rolls it harder on his leg, her mouth in his brain, the teeth biting down white on the end of his cock, humming the Miley Cyrus music, seeing Miley's lips, the girl bouncing, her lips, he wants to see his own face with hers, mashed together kissing, so he stands on the toilet to see over the stall to the mirror, sees his own face as he jerks off hard, his face red really getting purple as he jerks, standing on the toilet, someone's coming into the bathroom, he drops back down to the toilet bowl, hunches down, making himself smaller, quieter in the stall, still jerking, his pants down around his ankles, sees how purple his ankles are becoming, got to cut down on the cocktails, he thinks.

Mr. Hamptons comes hard, but very quietly, in the stall.

He cleans himself off and walks out to his table as properly as possible, not looking at the girl's table. He sits down with Mrs. Hamptons and reads the menu, which is large and overwhelming him, so when the waiter comes he orders a hamburger.

"I'll drive next," says Mrs. Hamptons.

"Good. I'm tired."

Snowflakes, like angels

We all agreed to maybe take a nap (no maybe about it for me, I was sleeping deeply, for a change, this high in the Rockies), pack, walk the dogs, check out of the motel, and meet later, back at our same breakfast table for dinner. The cafe was closed but unlocked, nobody was there yet, so I sat in the dark and rested my brain.

It was beginning to get dark outside, but I detected something moving out there. Still being *sort* of a detective, maybe on the last dregs of that, but still, trusting my instincts, I slyly focused on the *something moving*.

It was Klarika, perfectly framed in the window, walking towards the cafe. She was walking arm in arm with a tall, red-headed woman in a white fur coat. The woman looked like a red-headed snow leopard; she walked slowly, like a cat. The sun was just dropping behind the mountains, the light coming down the valley across the snow blueish-white, and in this light, Klarika and the woman turned and kissed each other. They stopped for a breath, Klarika holding the woman's head in her hands, and then they *really* kissed each other. They hugged, and the woman walked up the street to the tall house at the top. Klarika saw me watching from the window and waved. Then she bent down, made a snowball, threw it, and it hit me right in my window pane.

She came inside, out of breath, smelling like snow.

"Did you see us?" she asked.

"Yes, and she's beautiful!" I said.

"AND she's my wife!"

"AND ... *congratulations!*"

Klarika switched on the cafe lights and sat down with me. The blueish-white outside turned blueish-black, and we saw ourselves in the window reflection, laughing in the yellow cafe light.

"Would that I could go with you all to Kansas City, if I wasn't married and so much in love! And the cafe, of course. I must work!"

"Well, Klarika, we are friends, we'll stay in touch. Are you on Facebook?"

"No, I quit that."

"I did, too," I said. "One night, just a little while ago—I took my dogs, walked out of the house, and that was it for Facebook. The *end*. The moon was full that night, and I needed a change. It's a long story."

"But I give you my phone number, ok?"

"Of course, and I'll pass it around to the others. Maybe if we come back through here after Kansas City, we'll stop and see you again."

"And you meet my wife, Katrine, and our daughter, too!"

"Klarika and Katrine! It's fun just saying your names together! Maybe you could set your names to music. What's your daughter's name?"

"We have a favorite actress, she's Danish, her name is Sidse Babett Knudsen. So our daughter's name is Sidse Babett."

"What a family!" I said, and took out paper and pen. "Here's my cell phone number ... *and* the number to my house in California, if and *whenever* I get back there! But I think I will get back there—through here—so I'll call you, my friend."

"Yes, and you can stay with us," said Klarika. She smiled at me and put out her hand. "Is it a deal?"

"It's a deal!" I said.

Then Rosalita walked into the cafe, talking on her phone. "Yes, Roscoe, the Hamptons may be on the way already, or they're still around here somewhere, but now *we're* leaving, we're gonna drive through the night. The consensus here is that Kansas looks better in the dark. Yeah, I don't know what *Dorothy* was thinking, if I was her I would have said, *There's no place like Oz!* So anyway, again, the Hamptons don't know where you live, so don't worry about *that*. Ok ... Bye, Roscoe."

Alberto came into the cafe, then Serge, then Fyodor and Ruby. Kansas, Missouri, and Felix trotted in, off leash and relaxed, and flopped down under the table. Everyone sat down, Rosalita hugged Alberto, they all looked at me.

"Kansas City here we come, let's celebrate!" I said. "Fyodor, *you* look thirsty ..."

"Thanks, Red. I was maybe going to have a glass of wine, but since you put it *that* way ... Klarika, can you make me a *Moscow Mule*, please?"

"Why, of course, Fyodor. I am Estonian!"

"How *are* you, Red? You've done all the driving so far, since Beverly Hills."

"I'm alright, Fyodor. We'll take turns driving later, but I'll be your driver for the evening. So *everybody*, drink up!"

"Anyone else?" asked Klarika.

"I'll take a *Vodka Volcano* with cucumbers," said Ruby.

"I'd like a *Kiwi Pineapple Fusion Tequila Intrusion*," explained Serge.

"Tecate for me," Alberto ordered. We all gave him a look.

"Oh, wait ..." he said, noticing the look.

Our *look* was encouraging a mutinous sort of—*Let your hair down, Alberto,* we're in the middle of Colorado, buried in snow, out on the road for Rosalita, ready to strike a blow!—feeling. (Anyway, that's what *I* was encouraging.)

"Ok," said Alberto, "for me—a *Green Grinning Ghost's Skull of Gin!*"

Klarika seemed to know all the drinks, even that last one. She looked at me and Rosie.

"Coffee for me, please," I said, making steering wheel motions with my hands.

"I'd like some kind of sleepy tea," said Rosie, putting her hands together at the side of her head, tilting it, and closing her eyes. "Ok?"

"Yes. I bring you a pot of lemon chamomile tea," said Klarika, "I'll be right back. Oh, *look!*"

Klarika pointed out the window to the parking lot. Snow was falling lightly, like a Hallmark Card Christmas commercial, except it was real Colorado snow, and Morrison the Van looked like a big snowball. But something else was happening out there ...snow was being flung sideways ... then I saw the red-headed snow leopard again.

"It's Katrine! My wife. She's cleaning your windows! Oh, and there's our daughter, Sidse!" Around the side of the van rolled what I thought was a smaller snowball (with legs), and up climbed Klarika's tiny daughter in parka and hood, climbing up on the back bumper reaching a little snow scraper across the back window.

"What a sweet family you have," said Rosalita.

"I'm so lucky. Oops, I make drinks!" Klarika ran off to the bar.

"So are they!" Rosie called after her. "Lucky!"

"So are we," I said."

We watched Katrine and Sidse—tall and tiny—completely clear the windows, then begin building a snowman, except this one looked like a snow*woman.* Sidse was working, at ground level, on the feet of the snowwoman, while Katrine sculpted snow into a wild, flowing head of hair, like her own. Finishing that, she began work on an arm, a long arm of snow getting longer, a sleeve, a hand, then a finger, *pointing.* Katrine sculpted, poured some bottled water on it, making it frosty solid, shaped some more—sleeve, hand, fingers—and the one finger pointing.

Klarika came back with a tray of coffee, tea, and the drinks. *Rubbing their hands and wild-eyed*: that would describe Alberto, Serge, Ruby and Fyodor, as the drinks arrived.

Klarika served us, folded the tray under her arm, then walked over to the window to watch her wife and daughter; proud of them, in love with them. I made eye contact with Rosalita, we smiled, then grabbed our cups of coffee and tea, and went over to the window, too.

"What is it?" asked Klarika. "What is this smile?"

"We're enjoying the sculptresses out there, your wife and daughter," I said. "I can't believe she's making that arm so long, that it's not falling off. She knows what she's doing. She's good."

"She is very good, she just *jumps in*, you know? She'll try anything. She doesn't care about doing something wrong, she cares about *not* doing something."

"I wish you three could come with us," I said. I watched little Sidse outside, sculpting kneecaps on the snowwoman. Rosalita was watching Katrine put the final touches on the pointing finger.

"Klarika, what do you think she's pointing at?" she asked.

"I-70. *East.* Denver, through Kansas, to Kansas City. But maybe it will start to snow harder tonight. Don't you want to wait until morning?"

Rosalita and I looked at each other, then out the window.

"You know that man that was in here today?" asked Rosie. "So rude, so violent?"

"The peeg?" Klarika asked, shaking her fist. "Yes. He's hard to forget. I *want* to forget him, Rosie."

Rosie looked out the window.

"He's out there somewhere," she said. "We think he might try to steal from a friend. Maybe hurt someone. We have to stop him."

"Go stop him," said Klarika.

I buttoned my coat; there was raucous laughter at our table, the glasses were already empty, Klarika was going to the bar for another round; I *unbuttoned* my coat.

The cafe door blew open *cold,* jingling bells, and Sidse came running inside, Katrine behind her a few steps, stomping her boots and shaking the snow from her long red hair.

"So nice to meet you, Katrine," I said, standing up to greet them. "I'm Red, and this is Rosie. "And nice to meet *you,* Sidse! You made her feet so *good*, that snowwoman, and also her knees!"

"... *thank you* ..." said Sidse, in a shy, small breath, smiling with all her little white snowgirl teeth showing, red-faced from the cold outside, even redder now with blushing.

"Nice to meet *you,* Red. Your vehicle is ready!" said Katrine, with a strong, warm handshake. "Yes, you *do* have good eyes. They are blue as sky on top of the Rocky Mountains. And a nose that can plow through the snow."

"I like his eyes because I feel that they *see* me," said Klarika. "Oh Red! Tell Sidse your *full* name."

Our drunk and raucous table now went silent, and Rosalita went into a coughing (or laughing) fit. Sidse looked up at me.

"Red Jumbo," I told her, with a little salute.

Sidse got excited. "Mommy, like the elephant!"

"No, my darling," said Katrine, "that's *Dumbo*. This man is Red *Jumbo*."

"Yes, Sidse, that's me."

Sidse suddenly spread her feet (in her little slippery snow boots) as far apart as she could, put her hands on her hips, and *really looked* at me. She seemed to be taking a stand.

"Well, *I* like your name. It's silly, it makes me happy, and silly and happy is my philosophy of life!"

This was completely moving and delightful, and I must have turned as red as Sidse, because she looked up, took one of my fingers in her hand, and shook it. "It's ok, Mr. Jumbo. I blush, too. All the time."

Another round of drinks, a lot of latte for me, and the rest of Rosie's pot of sleepy tea later, I drove the van down 6th Street, turned right at the Village Inn, coasted down the hill, under the highway bridge, and turned left up the entrance ramp. We were on the 70 again. Night, and black, the highway all white ahead of us, snowflakes flying right at us at 65 miles per hour, but landing softly, on the windshield.

"Snowflakes, *like angels,*" said Rosalita, before she fell asleep.

Through the Rockies, and Kansas, by night

Then, they were all asleep.

A few miles up the highway, and after three (or *four?)* of Klarika's "generous" drinks, everyone was knocked out.

"Maybe it's the altitude," said Ruby, on *her* way out.

They were all so peaceful back there. I could see them in the rear-view mirror, the dogs splayed out on various laps, feet in the air (the dogs), as I carefully steered, carving through the snowy Rockies.

Rosalita was *way* out, deeply asleep, but singing something, in a dream maybe. It sounded like "Silent Night," but I love Christmas songs—*all year*—so I could've been imagining it. And it was hard to tell with the windshield wipers flapping their wings.

I drove, awake and alone, in what also felt like a dream, though it *was* happening; large, lacy snowflakes flying softly (angels!) in the headlights, onto the windshield; the white highway ahead, two tracks through the snow; me and the other cars and trucks driving very slowly up and down, curving through the mountains, and I was thrilled but it was *scary* driving through that blizzard with these giants moving around up there in the high and slippery, mountains like big, black shoulders rolling and shouldering around both sides then behind the van, so I was alert to keep us from sliding off into the dark and the deep *down below*; and I saw tiny lights up there—red, white, sometimes golden lights—*houses!*—in those shoulders; someone living there, in those houses, amazing to imagine that, living somewhere up there, so high and far away; whooshing through the Eisenhower Tunnel; later, not sure how much later in this dream time, driving into a rest stop at the top of the mountains, Denver all lit up below, letting the dogs out to pee in the pines and snow and gravel (*still* nobody waking up in the van, even the dogs looking back at the van as they peed, like they were thinking: *they are all so peaceful*); driving down into Denver like driving down into a giant Christmas tree in a white toy van ornament, rolling down one of the long branches of lights and pine needles and frosted colors, and then

A cell phone rang.

It rang to my right, down on on the floor, lit up. It was Rosie's phone, probably slid out of her hand when she fell asleep, and she was still *way* out, she wasn't waking up, not even moving, so I kept one hand on the wheel to keep Morrison in the tracks, not skid off the road, while my other hand found the phone, just as it stopped ringing.

The screen lit ROSCOE in the dark. I slid the phone next to mine in the cup holder. There was a little shifting and shuffling behind me, I could see Fyodor's mouth wide open and asleep in the backseat, then all was quiet again.

Down the mountain, down from the snow, down into Denver, the lights looked less magical than they had from the mountaintop; they looked more like the day *after* Christmas than Christmas Eve. I drove the van out of the city, toward the Kansas line, away from the lights.

Billboards came shining up out of the dark. Advertising the Denver Broncos, Holiday Inn Express, McDonald's, all thinning out as we got closer to Kansas. Then, almost at the state line, this billboard:

GOD and GUNS.
OUR DIVINE RIGHT!

"Well, you got one, you got the other," said Fyodor.

"Or, you have one, you don't need the other," said Ruby, yawning.

The van was waking up, dogs ears were flapping. Rosalita moved, took a deep breath, stretched, and asked, "Where are we?" Alberto and Serge were talking low and sleepy in Spanish. I detected a sneaky smell of alcohol in the van.

I heard Ruby say, "Oh! Why *yes*, don't mind if I do."

"What?" asked Fyodor. "Is the bar open?"

Everyone laughed, the smell got stronger.

"We are almost out of Colorado, about to cross the state line," I announced.

Ruby, in a voice loud enough and out of the blue enough and *out of the last who knows how many hours of silence* enough to nearly send the van off the highway, sang — "*OOOOO—KLAHOMA, where the wind comes sweepin' down the plain!*"

"Uh, wrong state, Ruby," I said.

"And the wavin' wheat—can sure smell sweet—when the wind comes right behind the rain! OOOOO—KLAHOMA ..."

Now they were all singing, except for Rosalita and me. But we were smiling.

We rolled along in the dark. Neon was coming up out of Kansas ahead; I turned around and interrupted the singing.

"Hungry? Breakfast?"

"IHOP!" yelled Alberto.

"Denny's!" yelled Fyodor and Serge together, louder.

"I see an IHOP at this exit," I said, signaling a turn onto the exit ramp. "Rosie, where's the parking lot? Do I cut through the motel and the gas station?"

"Yes, Red. It's next to the Starbucks. Turn ... hang on, almost ... *here!*"

"What time is it, anybody?" asked Ruby.

Rosie pulled back her sleeve and a small aquamarine dial popped on, then off. "One-thirty," she said.

"I *love* it! Breakfast in the middle of the night, just like college days!" yelled Ruby, tipsy to her toes and cracking me up, sounding like she was crawling around and climbing into the rear of the van to maybe exit through the tailgate. I heard my tire iron clang against something, Felix barked, I turned to look, and the van bumped suddenly to a stop against the IHOP dumpster.

"Oops," I said, "misjudged the distance."

"Wow," said Alberto, "*someone* needs a rest, maybe!"

"Well, it's a *longgg* way over the Rocky Mountains," Ruby was singing, "Red must feel like Lewis *and* Clark, ha ha ha ... *yahoo!* Pancakes for everybody!"

"You all ready? Let's go in and get a table," I said.

"OH WHAT A BEAUTIFUL MORNIN' ... *OH! what a beautiful day* ..." Ruby sang, getting out of the back of the van.

"Still the wrong state, Ruby," said Fyodor.

"I got a beautiful feelin' ... everything's goin' my way!" Ruby continued, hopping out into the parking lot with a Radio City Rockettes *kick!*

"Everything *is* going your way, Ruby. And I love you," said Fyodor.

"All of us do, honey," said Rosalita. We all started for the front door of the International House of Pancakes, and when we got inside there was a potted plant in the lobby.

Ruby saw it and smiled at me. "Red? Polo Lounge?"

"Polo lounge?" asked Rosalita.

"Yeah," said Ruby. "Red knows. I heard a rumor about Red at the Beverly Hills Hotel the other night. Something about potted plants."

"HELLO! And welcome to the International House of Pancakes!" The hostess had arrived, wildly friendly for the middle of the night, and seated us at a long table by the window, all facing the same direction, watching taillights go east and west in Kansas.

"Look, Ruby!" whispered Fyodor. "Taillights!"

Opening our menus, looking over the top of the menus, we noticed ourselves in the reflection of the IHOP dining room window.

"Hey man, we look like the Last Supper," said Alberto.

"But we need six more disciples, don't we?" agreed Serge, putting an arm around Alberto.

After two mountainous hamburgers for Alberto and Serge, stacks of pancakes for Ruby and Fyodor (Ruby infusing her bottomless cup of coffee with what seemed like a bottomless *flask* from under the table), Cobb and Caesar salads for Rosie and me, down the highway, sometime many billboards on the other side of midnight, I found some Bossa Nova music in the night air, from a college radio station in Lawrence, Kansas.

There was a long sigh from the back of the van. I thought the air was going out of one of the tires.

"Ahhh Red, that's *nice*," moaned Ruby.

"Yes. Yes. *Yesss,"* exhaled Serge, in ecstasy. "What *is* that song? I *know* it."

"Something about a quiet night and a quiet star," said Alberto.

"*Corcovado*," I said.

"Yes, that's it," said Serge. "*Corcovado*. Such an evocative song, I feel like I'm in one of those sexy spy movies from the sixties, you know?"

"Yeah, me too," said Alberto. "Like one of those scenes between the investigating and the traveling, the car chases and the arresting, and in the middle of it all, the spy has met a woman, at last! Or a man. In a hotel or somewhere. Walking on a beach. Like *that*."

"*Yesss*, Alberto," said Serge. "This is kind of like that. This music doesn't go with Kansas."

"What does?" asked Alberto. "Go with Kansas?"

"Kansans," I said. "Straight roads. Church music. Flat tires, old faded church bulletins, or something. Jello Mold. Potato Salad picnics in the heat."

Fyodor was snoring.

"Listen to that guy," yawned Ruby. "The way he snores. It's like, *zipper snoring*. You know? A sudden intake of air rattling in the back of his throat, sounds like a winter parka being zipped up frantically. Wow. I love that man. Alright, good night, I'm going to sleep now, *carry on*."

That was it, everyone rolled back into themselves, into sleep. I turned the music down a little, but up enough to Bossa Nova them in their dreams.

And I drove straight ahead, toward Kansas City.

Electric razor

Across Kansas, the sun comes up, beautiful across the land, dewy and fresh in the Flint Hills, but in Lawrence—it's scummy ashtray brown through the tan polyester curtains of their motel room.

On opposite sides of the queen bed, Mrs. Hamptons grunts and rolls farther to her side, as Mr. Hamptons, on his side, crawls out of the covers and stands, swaying. He sways to the TV set, turns on the cheerful, brightly lit Today Show; Mrs. Hamptons grunts louder, he turns it off.

Now it's dark again, but he sees a tiny point of light—the peephole in the motel room door—he goes to it, opens the door, and walks outside in his pajamas. He doesn't care that he's in public in his pajamas, it reminds him of strolling the grounds of his mansion back in Pasadena, waving to Alberto working in the gardens, calling out Buenos Dias! *to the lawn crew mowing the lawn, inspecting the perimeter fence, carrying a walking stick like the main man—Lord somebody—that he likes in Downton Abbey, but just now his pajama pant cuff has dipped and dragged through a puddle in the crummy motel parking lot, and he's not in Pasadena anymore.*

Dazed in his pajamas, trying to focus, he hears music, and voices. He looks toward the sound, up a hill, sees a car parked up there, two men playing the radio and dancing in their seats, bouncing the car. The men laugh, sing, bounce the car; Mr. Hamptons grunts, like his wife, and walks back into the motel room.

It's noisy in the room, the Today Show is back on again, loud and stunningly cheerful, Mrs. Hamptons is getting dressed.

"Where were you?" she asks.

"Walking, looking at Kansas."

"See anything interesting? Ha ha."

"A couple of fags on a hill, in a car—dancing, or something."

"Yeah. Or something."

"Shall we get breakfast, or do you want to push on?" he asks.

"Let's eat here, I've seen the highway restaurants of Kansas. Let's find something in town. On Massachusetts Street. I googled it last night. Massachusetts Street is the cultural center of Lawrence."

"Maybe of Kansas."

"Which would explain those fags you saw on the hill. They are just so DRAWN to the arts. They have taken over."

"Yeah. And the Jews, of course. It's always been that way. I guess the thing to be would be a gay Jew! That's so funny, ha ha."

"It is," says Mrs. Hamptons, not laughing. "How far are we from Kansas City?"

"Less than an hour. We're almost there."

"I'm glad. Let's not drive back. I can't take it anymore."

"We won't. We'll fly home, have someone return the car."

"Good. Let's eat. You ready?"

The Hamptons leave the Today Show blaring, lock the room, and get in the car. Mrs. Hamptons drives toward Massachusetts Street; Mr. Hamptons looks behind him, back up the hill at the car, still bouncing.

They find Massachusetts Street, pass the Eldridge Hotel, pull over, and park. The car is silent, they are silent, scanning the street for somewhere to eat.

MMMMMMMMMMMMMMMMMMMMMMMMMMMMMM

"What was that? Is it the car?" asks Mr. Hamptons.

"The car is off. So, no," says Mrs. Hamptons.

"I don't wanna get stranded in Kansas. Sounds like an electric razor."

They look around, they listen, but all is silent again. Mr. Hamptons stomach rumbles.

"So, that was you, before?"

"No, but I am hungry."

"When I was googling, I read about a restaurant here called Blanche & Mabel's Ambrosia Cafe. See, right over there. Across from the hotel."

"Let's go," says Mr. Hamptons.

After over-easy eggs and bacon and toast and V8 juice and coffee, they linger. The college students in the cafe talk about politics, music, personal psychology, and literature. Mr. Hamptons sneers. "What do they know?"

"Nothing." agrees Mrs. Hamptons, with her sneer.

MMMMMMMMMMMMMMMMMMMMMMMMMMMMMM

The students continue talking and laughing, young and exhilarated by what they're saying. The Hamptons look around, old and in a panic by the electric razor sound. They look at the students, the waitresses, the busboys; none of them seem to have heard that sound. The Hamptons look at each other, and deny it all.

"So. In your research the last night, does anything happen in Lawrence? Did anything ever? Has anyone of importance been here?"

"Paul McCartney," says Mrs. Hamptons, still sneering at students.

"Who?"

"Paul McCartney. Remember the Beatles?"

"Oh. Ok. Well, that's something, I suppose. I liked them until they got weird and anti-American and drug-riddled. None of their songs made sense after 'I Wanna Hold Your Hand' and 'Raindrops Keep Falling on My Head' ... that early period."

"Paul stayed at the Eldridge, across the street."

"Maybe we should stay at the Eldridge, too. I'd like to stay one more night here in Lawrence. Maybe we can check out this Massachusetts Street area, if it's such a cultural center. Anyway, I'm worn out from all this driving. I need a good ten or twelve hours of sleep tonight, maybe fifteen, but I can't take another night at that crummy motel. I don't feel comfortable with those guys on the hill, in the car. I think it's a gay motel. But why?"

"Why?" asks Mrs. Hamptons.

"Why was Paul McCartney here?"

"A tour. Playing Kansas City. Then a lecture at Kansas University."

"Anyone else?"

"Who? What?"

"Anyone else famous been here besides a Beatle?"

"There was some crazy homosexual writer, maybe he's dead now, but he moved here in his sunset years." Mrs. Hamptons appears to be thinking hard. "What was his name?"

"An old Beatle and, who? A crazy homosexual writer? Alright, I've changed my mind. Let's get out of here right now. What do I care about Lawrence? But oh my, I'm so tired," yawns Mr. Hamptons.

"William S. Burroughs. He moved here in his sunset years."

"Oh. Yeah. I remember him. A food writer, I think. He wrote some kind of a book about having lunch. He was in the Beat Generation. Has his sun set, or is he still around here?"

MMMMMMMMMMMMMMMMMMMMMMMMMMMMMMM!

Again, no one appears to hear the sound but the Hamptons.

"Shall we go check out of the motel?" asks Mrs. Hamptons.

"Shall we have drinks first? How about a Bloody Mary before we leave? That girl over there has one, and it looks good."

Mrs. Hamptons looks where he's looking, the nearest table of laughing students, and sees a young woman—chewing on a celery stalk—who greets the Hamptons with a V of her fingers, the peace sign.

Mr. Hamptons makes a V back to her. "Yes, let's have drinks," he says.

Later, after drinks, checking out of the motel and into the Eldridge, then returning to the cafe to drink for the rest of the afternoon, now Mrs. Hamptons snores in bed, while Mr. Hamptons sits by their hotel room's window and watches Massachusetts Street.

Wide awake, he contemplates the in-room TV porno, but he stays by the window, staring down, jealous of the sidewalks full of laughter and talking on both sides of the street. The sun is getting low in the west, but he can see the horizon line to the east.

It is flat. Just, flat.

A bunch of students comes down the street, laughing, cheerful, and he sees the young woman again, the peace sign girl. They go into the cafe and sit by the window, Mr. Hamptons can see her sitting there. She looks out the window, around the street and up, and she sees him. She squints a little, puts on glasses, and again flashes a V at him. Also, a very wide and warm smile.

Drinks come, food comes, they talk and laugh and talk. She talks, looks out the window, but not up at him anymore.

Time passes slowly, Mr. Hamptons thinks about pornography again, but he doesn't want to have to explain it later to Mrs. Hamptons, when she sees the bill. He stays at the window, pouring a small glass of white wine. Mrs. Hamptons coughs, breaks up her snoring, makes a smacking sound with her mouth and moans a little. She says, "Mama ... mama, I love you mama, am I your little girl?" Moaning, snoring again.

Mr. Hamptons looks down and sees the students rising from the table, passing the check around, exchanging cash. They come out to the sidewalk and begin to go in different directions, hugging and waving. The peace sign girl is still there, talking to a friend; Mr. Hamptons puts on his coat and tiptoes out of the hotel room.

He's down the elevator, through the lobby, and crossing the street before he knows it, before he's ready to talk to her, only a few feet from her and her friend when he begins to stagger, stumble, as he tries to slow himself down so he won't run into them.

"Hi!" he says. "I saw you, before. Earlier, I mean. In here. In the cafe."

"Well, hi," says the girl, smiling, but surprised. "Yes, I remember. And, up there, too!" she says, laughing and pointing at his hotel room window.

"Yes, up there, too. True. Well, I was just going inside for a drink. My name is, um ... Red. Red Burroughs."

"I'm Helen, and this is my best best friend Teri."

"Hi, Helen. Teri."

"Did you say Burroughs?" asks Teri.

"I did," says Hamptons, smiling and swaying on the sidewalk.

"Well, wow, I'm doing my thesis on William S. Burroughs, any relation?" asks Teri, teasing.

"Nephew."

Helen and Teri seem to believe it, not believe it, then believe it again.

"I don't believe it, c'mon, Red!" says Helen, laughing.

"It's true. And I've come to see him in his sunset years."

Helen and Teri look at each other, at Mr. Hamptons, and begin talking simultaneously.

"You may be too late!" says Teri.

"That sun done gone down!" laughs Helen. "Wait, but—I'm sorry—didn't you know he died?"

"Oh, of course!" says Mr. Hamptons. "Would you two care to join me for a drink?"

Teri is edging away, almost gone, toward home, but Helen's intrigued. "Well, sure. Ok." Teri edges a tiny bit back.

They go to the cafe door. Mr. Hamptons holds it open for Helen and Teri, looking up at his hotel room window as they enter. Nothing there but a very still curtain.

"What's that like? Being his nephew, I mean," asks Teri, nudging Helen, as a waitress brings drinks to the table.

"Oh yeah, what was that like?" Helen kicks in. "I love his voice."

Teri nods. "Me too. Since I started working on my thesis, I've YouTubed him a lot. That face, and that voice! He sounds like an electric razor. An electric razor reading poetry! Buzzz, brrr! MMMMMMMRRRRRRR, oh, I can't do it. What a character!"

Mr. Hamptons mumbles to himself, "Electric razor? I've been hearing that all morning."

"Cheers! Here's to William S. Burroughs," says Teri.

Mr. Hamptons raises his gin and tonic. "Here's to Uncle William! Well, Bill, since I'm family."

"Here's to Burroughs and Kerouac and Ginsberg and Ferlinghetti," says Teri, raising her cup of coffee.

"And to the City Lights Bookstore!" adds Helen, adding her wine glass to the toast. "And Joan Baez!"

"And Paul McCartney!" says Mr. Hamptons.

There's a pause, they hold their glasses, frozen in the toast.

Teri clinks her coffee cup to the glasses. "Well, sure," she says.

"Can't forget Paul!" says Helen.

"Wait a minute. What did you just say?" asks Mr. Hamptons.

"Can't forget Paul!" repeats Helen. "And here's to Ringo and Yoko!"

"No, you—Mary. What did you say?"

"Teri."

"Teri. About how he sounds like an electric razor."

"Well, it's just my simile. I've worked it into my thesis."

Mr. Hamptons takes a long drink of gin, rattles the ice cubes around in the glass. "Yeah, that. I've heard that razor sound. Today. Here, in Lawrence. I don't know, maybe not ... waiter!*"*

The sun is going down.

Helen and Teri have stopped talking, they're watching Mr. Hamptons. The novelty of him has worn off for them, disappeared entirely.

"I'm not a homosexual like my uncle by the way," says Mr. Hamptons, getting drunker and drunker. "Though he is an interesting man. Was, I mean. Good writer, too. We all liked him in the family. Proud of him. You know something? We'd have family get-togethers, and he'd invite that fag, I mean that gay *friend of his, just kidding, what was his name? Allen Greensberg, and it was weird, but we were proud of William. You know? I'm gonna go see him tonight."*

"Your name is Red, *you say?" asks Teri. "Red Burroughs?"*

"Yes. My name is Red. Red Burroughs. 'Cuz I love a vagina, juicy and red," he says. "And Burroughs because of my relationship to the writer, and because I like to ... burrow in." Mr. Hamptons stares at Teri. Under the table, he rubs his foot up Helen's leg.

Helen and Teri get up, get gone.

Mr. Hamptons tries to focus and follow them with his eyes.

He looks around on the table, which is moving, dipping left and right, finishes his drink, picks up a napkin, which is floating, he thinks it's the check, there's a hand on his shoulder.

"Time to go," says the waitress.

"Go where?" he says, handing her the napkin. "Here, put it on my tab ..."

"You already did that. Come on, let's go."

"Time to go?"

"Time's up."

"Ok. I guess this is Kansas. No sense of humor in Kansas, no sense of adventure, no live and let live, is that what it's like around here?"

"Yes. Whatever that means. And it's time to go."

"It IS time to go! And I'm going over to my brother's-nephew-uncle's house, William F. Burroughs. HE knows me! I am RED Burroughs, his UNhomosexual nephew brother, and even though he's

a fag, and doesn't give a shit about vaginas, I do, and we are family no matter what! But who the hell knows why he came to Kansas!"

Mr. Hamptons is on the street. In his eyes, the street moves in staggered shifts, side to side, like film caught in a projector. Across the street, he sees the front door to the Eldridge Hotel and tries to get there.

MMMMMMMMMMMMMMMMMMMMMMMMMMMMMM!

Mr. Hamptons stops suddenly in the middle of staggering toward the hotel, one leg swoops out in front of the other, and he goes into an unplanned and drunken pirouette.

"That sound," he says, scrunching up his face, thinking hard.

"Hey, mister."

Mr. Hamptons hears a low voice down at the end of Massachusetts Street. He looks down there and sees a thin man in a black suit and hat. The man stands still under a streetlight just warming up and glowing. "MMMMMMMMMMMMMMMMMM," says the man as he raises a long, silver-barreled handgun level and fires.

Mr. Hamptons, still scrunching his face and pirouetting on one leg, blinks, and a bullet zings somewhere behind him, down toward the north end of Massachusetts Street. He looks that way, and back south, toward the man. Everything is sliding and twitching in his eyes; he focuses on the man.

"You better stop fucking around with people, Mister," says the man. "With women, especially. I've about had it with you, goddammit."

Mr. Hamptons squints and sways, his head periscopes out ahead of his body, towards the voice, towards the man, and he says, "Who are you?"

"The name's Burroughs. William S. And this gun ain't empty yet."

"Those girls said you were dead."

"Could be, mister, could be. But I want you out of town. And I want you and your wife to stop fucking with people, people just trying to live and let live, as you said in the cafe. And I still say this gun ain't empty yet."

"What do you know about my life? What are you, the all-seeing eye or something?" Mr. Hamptons is talking to the man, but making drunken eye contact with the headlights of a Toyota pick-up truck, fifty yards out from him. The truck isn't talking. A window slides open in the hotel above.

"What's going on?" asks Mrs. Hamptons, sleepy but angry, rumpled from bed.

"I'm the all-seeing eye, alright. And I have another one at the end of this Smith & Wesson," says the man, with a lingering MMMMMMMMMMM vibrating down the street.

"Well, look ..." says Mr. Hamptons, as an intro, then loses the thread.

"What are you doing?" Mrs. Hamptons, a bit more awake now.

"... what if I don't care what *you say, you faggot? Even if you* are *William N. Burroughs, what about that?"*

"Welllllll ..." says the thin man at the end of the street, again raising his gun and aiming straight down the street at Mr. Hamptons, "what I say about that *is* this.*"*

And he fires the gun.

The flash lights up his end of the street and everyone dives behind parked cars. A kid on a bike goes into a metallic slide on the sidewalk and into some bushes.

"Oh shit!" yells a UPS man on the street, diving back into his van in a flash of brown.

Mr. Hamptons sees the gun smoke, hears the blast, waits, wonders, and feels a cool singe in his crotch. He looks down and sees a hole in his pants just to the left of his zipper. Blood comes to the fabric near the hole.

"You'll find, on closer inspection, that I've left you your pecker, sir, though I imagine it's about as twitchy and jittery as tinsel on a Christmas tree right now. And the next time you think to rape someone ... well, you just might wanna go find the bullet that came so close to your genitalia, down on Massachusetts Street there, behind you. Maybe you want to go find it, for a keepsake, possibly. A reminder."

Mr. Hamptons checks the blood by the hole, it's minimal, not spreading, he feels a cool burning on his inner thigh. He looks up at the hotel room window, no one is there.

"I'd advise you to get out of town. Before sunup, Mister. Like those Warner Brothers cowboys say."

The thin man in the suit and hat slides the gun inside his jacket and turns, moving like the old man that he is, bent and stiff, like an apple tree in wintertime, and walks south, out of the streetlight, towards home.

Faintly, Mr. Hamptons hears the MMMMMMMMMM.

He turns and staggers down the street and looks for the bullet— doesn't find it, in the dark—goes back to the hotel, into the lobby men's room, and checks on his wound. The bleeding has stopped, and there's a red slash across the inside of his thigh, scabbing over already. He zips up and takes the elevator up to his hotel room.

Mrs. Hamptons is packing, not talking, so he begins to pack. She goes to the car without him, he checks out, the desk clerk doesn't refund the night, Mr. Hamptons doesn't care or argue, he leaves the lobby, finds the car, and drives north, up Massachusetts Street.

Ten minutes later, on Highway 70, she asks, "Are you badly wounded?"

"It's just on the surface," he says.

"Lucky."

"Yes, I'm lucky. Just a little blood, and probably a scar."

"It's ok, I'll never see it. Neither will your college girls. Are you still drunk, too?"

"Yeah, a bit. But I'm alright to drive. Though I need to pee."

"Pull over and pee, then. You're lucky you can."

"Yes, lucky again. You want to take a little nap before we get to Kansas City? It's about forty miles to the Crown Center Hotel. Be there within the hour. You're not getting much sleep tonight."

"Me? No. I'm awake."

"Ok," says Mr. Hamptons. He looks in the rearview mirror and watches the low line of Lawrence lights crawl backwards into Kansas, into the dark.

Lawrence, by sunrise

I certainly didn't think I'd get lost.

Who can say why? Maybe I got lost because I was doing all the driving; the others were either asleep or drunk or singing. As long as they could sense *eastward motion* coming from me, they were at ease, but I'd been awake since Glenwood Springs, and somewhere out there that night in western Kansas I lost track of time. And direction.

I got *very* lost.

Who can say how? One major highway, straight across Kansas, and somehow I got off that highway, *way off,* onto a two-lane road, onto a dirt road, then right up to someone's house; right up to a giant American flag, stretching from driveway to second floor rain gutter, then greeted by the end of a shotgun. And a monotone: *good morning.*

Of course, I *do* know why and how I got lost, but I didn't want to tell the others. They'd slept through all of it.

One of my favorite movies from childhood (along with *Oliver!*, *Fantasia, The Great Escape,* even *The Sound of Music* once in a while), was *In Cold Blood.* That movie was screening black and white in my brain as I drove along in the dark, and I thought we might be near the town where the multiple murder of that book happened; western Kansas, south of the interstate a few miles, a small town called Holcomb. Since I'd read the book, I also thought I knew where the exit was; I checked to see if everyone was asleep, they were, so I turned off the highway. I thought it would only take a few minutes.

I drove south, it was dark, and flat, and wildly windy; no towns, no signs, nothing. I was feeling creepy, in the black blank screen of the windshield I saw the night-driving movie scenes of the murderers, and the gas gauge was dipping close to empty. I looked left, which was east, nothing, no lights. I looked right, west, nothing. Ahead, something square and low to the ground lit up. I slowed down, it was a homemade sign—GAS—painted in black on a sheet of wood, with an arrow pointing left. Didn't say where or how far, only an arrow, *left.*

I turned left, swung the headlights onto a wind-dusty dirt road that went straight off into the dark. I drove onto it with a bounce and scatter of gravel.

It was dark everywhere except for the few feet of dirt road in the headlights. The gas needle bounced with the bounce of the van on the rough road, but mostly hovered low. Objects lit up ahead on the right side of the road; when I got there it was a swing set, swinging in the wind, an air conditioner in the dirt, and a cardboard, life-size, standup John Wayne. After that, another homemade sign said GAS 200 YARDS.

After *that*, I saw something else ahead in the dark, looked like shiny metal, then it looked like glass, then I saw my headlights in the windows of an old, two-story house, getting bigger. There was a gas pump in front of it, with one last sign leaning on it that said GAS.

I drove right to the pump and the barrel of a shotgun came down from the porch of the house. Something behind it said good morning.

"Good morning," I said, yawning, trying to look friendly, everyone still asleep in the van. "Need gas, sorry it's so late."

"It *is* late, or early. Need gas, do you?" A short, round woman in a Kansas City Chiefs hoodie (over a long pink robe) and glasses came down the porch steps in fuzzy pink slippers. "Late," she said again, but lowered the gun. "Lost?"

"Yeah," I said, chuckling like a lost driver would, "on the way to Kansas City, but ..." I started to tell her I wanted to see where *In Cold Blood* happened, but she still had the gun, so I went in another direction, "... we needed gas, so I got off the highway."

"Do *what?*"

"Yeah, gas," I laughed, "all out. Think of that, in this day and age!" I didn't know what that was supposed to mean, but it sounded folksy and humble.

"You could've got it closer to the highway. You *are* lost, hon. But go on, get your gas. We have a twenty-dollar minimum."

She leaned her gun on the pump and stuck out her hand. I gave her my credit card, she pulled a device out of her robe and scanned it. I started pumping gas.

"Go back that way, turn right on 83, and get back on route 70 east," the woman said. "You got some driving to do. We ain't a *mo*tel, too."

She picked up the shotgun and *flap-flapped* her slippers back up the porch steps again, but before she went inside, she stopped, kissed her hand, and touched the corner of the massive American flag draping the front of the house. She dropped her head—then, that was over—so she went inside, the screen door slammed, the front door shut, and I heard the lock *click*.

I screwed the gas cap back on and drove away. I took her directions seriously because I was beginning to hallucinate; driving in a straight line in darkness, not even any stars above, just blank and black and flat. It got a little friendlier out there when I remembered to turn the headlights back on.

It seemed to take the rest of the night to get back to Highway 70 (I kept turning right too early), and lights, and other cars. I didn't know what time it was, or even what day it was, but after a few more hours of driving it was becoming morning—a pink line on the horizon to the east—and there was a sign: *Welcome to Lawrence, Kansas.*

Everyone was waking up, dogs too. They'd been *out* since just after the IHOP, sleeping like babies, even when the shotgun was on me.

"Did you get lost, Red?" Rosalita asked. She'd slept through it, but somehow she sensed it.

Rosalita was laughing, though she could see that I was angry. Who wouldn't be? Not really *that* angry, just cranky. I was a *little* angry. And tired. And hungry. But not lonely. So I wasn't in that condition I'd heard about in rehab, that warning acronym called HALT: Hungry, angry, lonely, tired.

"I'm just *Hat*, Rosie," I said to her, knowing she'd understand. (But again, I wasn't really *that* angry.)

"He wants his hat?" asked Fyodor.

"You had one on in Glenwood Springs, the *top* hat, walking up 6th Street, but I haven't seen it since," said Ruby. "Oh *here* it is," she said, rummaging around in the back in the morning sunlight. The tire iron clanged again.

"I need to sleep," I said, looking around for motels.

"There's one," said Rosalita, pointing at a sign: *The Jayhawk's Nest.*

"What a corny motel name," said Ruby. "Jayhawk? What *is* a Jayhawk? It must be endangered. This motel sure looks to be. I wonder if this road trip is."

"I'm pulling in," I said, pulling in. I started laughing, at nothing specifically.

"What's so funny?" asked Alberto. *"I think he's punchy,"* he said, as an aside to someone in the back.

"I like him, but I hope he knows what he's doing," Ruby asided back.

"Nothing, I guess," I said. "Nothing I can *point* at. And yet, everything seems funny. Also fuzzy, kind of pink, in the early morning light. But I'm not angry or anything. Sleepy, yes. I think I'd better crash."

"Yeah, I think you'd better," said Serge. =

We checked in at the motel office; I was cordial to the old guy at the front desk but yawning throughout the process—*Welcome to Lawrence, where are you all from? California huh? Hmmm. Well, have a good stay, lots to do here!*—then I waved as Fyodor got back in the van and drove the others off somewhere, to breakfast. I walked down the line of motel room doors to door 7. I got inside to the fresh, *new sheets-smell* of the room, the *cool blue-gray silence*, and shut the door.

I walked over to the bed and *Timmmberrred* into it, bouncing two or three times before leveling out; *this* bed had some action and spring! I lay still and breathed in the silence, ready for sleep. A long, deep sleep.

The last time I'd been asleep I was up in the Rockies. I was body-tired but my brain was whirring. Whirling. I looked up, and upside down, at the painting on the wall behind the bed. Utrillo. How did I know about art? How did I know about being a detective? And, why did I choose *that?* I didn't feel too good around police anyway, so why go into this line of work? Though, of course, I did like Serge. Serge Controllente. Officer Serge Controllente. Was that *his* real name?

(I was getting sleepy, but kept grilling myself, to get more so.)

I knew I wasn't really doing detective work anymore, *per se.* I was helping Rosalita get out of Pasadena, away from the Hamptons, to reunite her and Alberto with her rehab friend Roscoe, to some sort of safe haven they'd dreamed up, some kind of start toward a new life. *Different* life. Her life. This was all friendship now, not a job, with Serge, Fyodor and Ruby, and me—all along for the ride. I was getting the picture of the cruelty and secrets of the Hamptons, feeling the ugliness of it (I was getting sleepy alright, running all this information by myself, summing it up; what was this self-grilling thing I was doing, a relaxation technique, a *plot synopsis?*). It was amazing to me that we'd all take off cramped together in a van to help her, and her husband, start a new life, away from abuse ... and fear, and what Hamptons did ... it was amazing and there was something ... something so ... *poignant* about it. All of this out of simple kindness, compassion, humanity ... never been part of something like ... this ... so moving to me, but so *tired* ... and it renewed my faith in, um, ... a little bit hungry now but so tired looking up at the sparkles in the cottage cheese motel ceiling, renewed my faith in—

HALLELUJAH!

"FUCK! *What?*" I screamed sitting up wide awake in some room. That was *me* wide-eyed in a mirror at the end of a bed. I knew it was me that had screamed fuck but where was I? I'd heard classical music. Just a few seconds, and it sounded like a room full of people singing. Then it stopped. The next time it happened, a few seconds later, those same people were singing HALLELUJAH. They'd sing four or five hallelujahs and stop. I saw a cell phone blinking on the bed. It lit up and went HALLELUJAH again so I grabbed it and pushed the first key that looked green.

"Rosie?" a low, male, melodious voice.

"WHAT! *WHO?*"

"That *you*, Rosalita? What's wrong?"

"This is Red Jumbo!" I blurted. I *yelled*, is more like it. There was a long pause, then some chuckling, like a VW Beetle starting up. *Where* was I? In a motel in Kansas probably. (I'd read *that* detail on the back of the motel room door.) That chuckling kept going, then the voice said, "Red JUM-BO. I remember you!"

"Roscoe?" I had a sense, recognized something.

"That's me, Red! Good to speak to you, can't wait to see you again!" The chuckling. Slow and sly and warm. "I always did like that name of yours. By the way, do you know *my* full name? And, on a side note, why do you have Rosie's phone?"

"You mean Roscoe G.T. *Going to* Towne? I sure do," I said, also chuckling. "And no, I don't know why I have her phone …"

"Well, I have a question for her. Tell her to give me a buzz when you see her, alright? No rush. And hey, Red—how about these Hamptons? What are they like?"

"Fuckers. Both of them."

"So I gather. What kind of car do they drive? How will I know them if they come around? Rosalita seems worried they might."

"They know about your money, they know where you work, but I don't think they know where you live."

"They know how *much* money and where it came from, right?"

"Yes. Oh, and their car—a Jaguar, of course."

"Of course."

"You've seen one around there, Roscoe?"

"Maybe. Could they be here already? I saw a black car, maybe a Jaguar, definitely a luxury vehicle."

"They *might* already be there, I don't know. Try not to worry about it. *We* don't even know where you live yet. Anyway, we're in Lawrence—I got a little lost along the way—and I was just trying to get some sleep, but we're on the way."

"Good to know, Red. But get some sleep. I think I woke you up. Nice talking to you, again."

"Again?"

"You don't remember much about Briar Patch, do you?"

"Sorry Roscoe, you were there, too? Rosie said something about that yesterday, but …"

"Oh yes. You were in pretty bad shape when you first came in. About gone. And then you were medicated, of course, and in *that* fog for a few weeks, so I'm not surprised you don't remember us."

"That was quite a place. Quite a time, wasn't it?"

"Yes, it was."

"I'm looking forward to meeting you, Roscoe—*again!* I'll have Rosie call you, but, *question?*"

"Shoot, Red Jumbo."

"Can we go to Bryant's Barbeque? I haven't been there in years."

"You bet your *sauce* we can! You know the place?"

"Oh yeah. I grew up in KC, over on the Kansas side. As soon as I got my driver's license I crossed the state line. For the food, the music, and Harold Pener Men's Wear. Never went back—across the state line, I mean. In my heart and soul, anyway."

I heard the VW Beetle chuckling again.

"Mr. Jumbo, I think you and I are gonna get along just fine. Oh, wait a minute. There's a car. Hang on. There's a car out there, going around the block ... third time this morning ... oh never mind, I know that guy. I think. Later, Red. I'm gonna watch this car. Bye."

He hung up. It had been fun, I was glad to talk to Roscoe, but now I was gone, done, *tired.* I fell back into the sheets, dropped Rosie's phone onto its own pillow. I wondered why I had her phone. My brain was working again, but the sleepy tide was against it, and I was drifting. I'd find out ... later ... when they got back ... from break ... fast ... and ...

HALLELUJAH! ... HALLELUJAH! ... HALLELUJAH!

I sat up, and there I was in the motel mirror again.

"Hello?" I said.

"Red? It's Rosie. Why do *you* have my phone?"

"I was wondering about that, too. Also why you have Handel as your ringtone."

"Why, Red, can't you handle it? But don't worry, I have *your* phone."

"A little mix-up in the cup holder."

"*Sleep*, Red."

"Bye, Rosie."

It was soothing, lying there ... hearing the long trucks in the distance ... getting nearer ... louder, longer, passing, vibrating the motel a little, silence ... then ... another one ...far off ... getting nearer, louder ... then that one passing, vibrating the room, that one receding in the distance ... all quiet.

In the dark, I pulled up the western-style bedspread (covered with mountains and pine trees, stars and moons, deer and antelope at play), closed my eyes, and smiled. Sleep was coming at last, the first since that morning in Colorado, waking up to the sound of Klarika's bright humming and singing. So nice, so peaceful, so sleepy.

I was imagining myself in bed, somewhere else—in a log cabin in pine trees at the top of snowy mountains, windows all fogged over with warm yellow light inside, a radio playing, a little curlicue of white smoke floating up out of a red chimney drifting away into the blue sky turning flaring red toward the endless western sunset and beyond, into stars and moons—I could see all that like it was sewn into the bedspread, an inch away from my face. Which it was.

But my cabin was far away in the mountains, and I was dreaming of one of those for me, one for Rosalita and Alberto, one for Serge, one for Fyodor and Ruby ... all the cabins in a circle ... *far away* ...

AND HE SHALL REIGN FOREVER AND EH-EH-*VER*!

I didn't even move this time. I was more *still life* than the Utrillo on the wall.

"Hello?"

"Hey Red." Roscoe again. "Did I wake you again?"

"Uh, no, I was just sort of daydreaming about 18-wheelers and an Estonian woman, singing. What's up?"

"What's the name of that hotel or *motel* you're in, there in Lawrence? I didn't get a call back from Rosie, since you have her phone, but why not ask you? I called her last night to remind her to let me know where you're staying next so I can pay for it. She probably thinks she's gonna get away with paying for it. But in the holy name of Charlie Parker, I say—no way. It's gonna be *my* 'Salt Peanuts' on the line, not hers!"

I told Roscoe the name of the motel and we hung up. I tucked Rosie's phone into the other bed so I could get some sleep, and got back under the covers of my bed.

There was a knock on the door.

I staggered through the dark and opened the door to Rosalita. Kansas and Missouri ran between my legs with a strip of bacon in each mouth and jumped into the other bed.

"Phone?" Rosalita asked.

Back through the dark to the *other* bed, I petted the dogs, pulled her phone out from under the covers, and returned it to Rosie. She returned mine.

"That's cute, Red, you actually tucked it in. Here's some toast," she said, handing me a bag from Blanche & Mabel's Ambrosia Cafe. "*Sleep*, Red," Rosie kissed me on the cheek.

Back through the dark to *my* bed, like I was swimming to it, then I went deep underwater.

Ambrosia

Later, much later, during dinner at Blanche & Mabel's Ambrosia Cafe (blue linoleum floor, red Formica tables, long log walls with chinks full of tchotchkes, banjo music on a jukebox), someone across the dining room was looking at me.

I felt it before I saw it. Before I saw *her*. She was trying to catch my eye, get my attention; she got it and smiled, then started writing on a napkin. Maybe for *me*, I thought. She was reading *Last Chance Texaco* by Rickie Lee Jones, but had a fork in the book, marking her place, as she wrote her note. She finished, put the cap on her pen, looked up, straight at me, and *winked*.

I took note of her note and winked back.

She was *sexy*. Honey on ice cream sexy, hair and skin like that.

Then, she held up the note. It was a big, black

!

"Umm, *Red?*" said Rosalita, looking up from *her* book, *Naked Lunch*.

"Someone likes you, I think," said Ruby.

Alberto began softly singing "Bésame Mucho."

"That woman is very attractive, interesting look in her eyes, I like the shoes, the way she crosses her ankles like that," said Serge.

"Boy, you must be a *good* cop," said Ruby.

"I like how she carries herself, even while she's sitting down," Serge added, or concluded, I didn't know if he was finished. I was distracted.

"I feel good about this one, Red," said Fyodor, giving me a very warm look.

"*This* one? How do *you* know?" laughed Ruby, with a playful punch on Fyodor's arm.

"Hey, Red's my friend! I've known him longer than anyone here, we go *way back*, all the way to the gatehouse at the Hamptons mansion, so if I'm acting a little protective, then you can kiss my Jayhawk. What *is* a Jayhawk? Anybody seen one in Lawrence yet?"

The woman was waving her note.

"Anyway, I like her, Red," Fyodor continued. "She looks, I don't know ... *European.*"

"And friendly," said Alberto.

Someone's cell phone vibrated.

"Ah, it's Roscoe, excuse me!" said Rosie, and ran outside to Massachusetts Street. She ran back in, wrapped up some sushi in a couple of napkins, "For the dogs!" she said, and was on the run again, out the cafe door, still on the phone.

Everyone went back to eating dinner, a long platter of that sushi —shrimp, avocado, yellow tail, scallops and masago, eel sauce and seaweed with a lot of tempura, *the Flint Hills Roll*—and I waved back at the woman across the room. Now it was clear; she was waving at me, I was waving back, we were communicating. She was all those things my friends were saying. She was *very* interesting, she looked around my age, and I liked *that* because if we were already on this strong a wavelength, just looking at each other, I was getting excited about what would happen when we started talking! And while I hadn't necessarily focused on ankles in a woman before, not right away anyway, it was true what Serge said about hers—— crossed in some way confident, at rest. I could make out a tattoo around one ankle, a red ring of roses with green leaves and stems slipping into her shoe, another stem winding up around her leg and underneath her faded blue jeans. She wore a white blouse, unbuttoned a few buttons, loose around the neck; her neck and skin free, open to the air. All following on the general honey and ice cream theme and

I wanted to go over and *lick* her!

I had the feeling something very fun was about to start. So, naturally, I couldn't finish my *Flint Hills Roll.*

I looked over at Ruby, she too was trying to get my attention.

"*Go,*" she coaxed.

And I did! I got up and over to the woman's table faster than I thought I would, and so, there I was. Whatever I thought I'd think of to say along the way hadn't come to me, so now I'd have to be *in the moment* charming.

"You're like honey on ice cream, if you don't mind me saying so."

After I said it, she looked me over, and said, "Uh huh ... uh huh ... well, *I like it.* But first, here's what I saw, when I saw *you:* Blue eyes, blue jeans, overall pretty cool guy. But also—if I may, I don't mean to be presumptuous, and don't take it the wrong way, please, because I love your smile and what I'm picking up on as very happy energy, though all of us are *complicated,* sentient beings ... um, where was I? Oh yes—*also,* I see someone maybe a little *blue,* too. What's your name?"

"Red."

"Of course it is!" she said, crumpling up her note and doing a perfect hook shot to a bus tub in the waiter station behind her. "Don't need that, anymore. Have a seat. You caught my eye, just now. I hope you aren't with one of those women over there," she said, shrugging innocently, looking over at my table of pals. "If so, please forgive me."

Rosie had returned, she and Ruby gave me the power fist gesture, pumped it in the air, then they nodded what looked like encouragement to this new woman.

This was moving fast, getting fun.

"What's your name?" I asked.

"Jenny Sue. What's your *last* name?"

"Jumbo."

"Red Jumbo. Yeah, I can see that on a marquee."

"What's yours? We'll take care of all these details up front."

"Yes, let's do. My last name is Skiptewmaylewe."

"Jenny Sue Skiptewmaylewe. *Musical*. What country are you from?"

"Long Island."

"Is that a real name?"

"I bet you're not used to *asking* that question."

I laughed out loud. "True."

"Is yours? Your name?"

"Yes, but I like *your* name. It's provocative."

"Why would that be the case? *Provocative*."

"Jenny Sue Skiptewmaylewe. It provokes singing and dancing. By the way, do people go—*my darling*—after you introduce yourself?"

The charm was turning *itself* on now, and I was getting relaxed. Relaxed wasn't all I was feeling; my body had a life of its own.

"That depends."

"On?"

"Whatever's going on, Mr. Jumbo."

We stopped and looked each other in the eyes. Our hands—well, mine—wanted very much to *travel*, to move, and touch her.

"We're moving fast," she said.

"I'd say we're about neck and neck."

"Your friends, are they, I mean—what are you all up to? They look nice."

"Those are my friends from Los Angeles. We came together in my van, we're on the way to Kansas City."

"I came here from Long Island, and I live here, but the dream is to someday get to Los Angeles. Funny, huh?"

Jenny was staring at me and my heartbeat was speeding up. I wondered if she could tell. Her chin was resting on one hand, one sexy *Thinker*, elbow on the table. I was thinking too, as she slid on her elbow closer to me. I did that too and slid right into her cloud bank of perfume, which slid us into Paris, in *my* imagination.

"That *is* funny," I said.

"I have a nice little house."

"Is your house close?"

"It is."

She was curling a couple of her fingers around a couple of mine. I curled right back, we rubbed fingers, slid our palms together. Her skin was soft, moist—not honey or ice cream—but the morning dew skin of fruit in a garden, if we were out there in that garden in the morning, naked. But what the fuck was happening to my mind? Fruit? Naked, in a garden? I knew that guys, especially guy writers, were always doing this, turning women into food or fruit, then making them *naked*, to be poetical and romantic.

But this woman, these images—she was filling my head! I was wildly overwhelmed by her.

Our eyes were looking deeply into each other, moving closer, not blinking; if this was a kind of trance, it was a very sexy one. I was getting warm and trembly all over, I didn't ever want to let go of her fingers. She was filling my pants, too.

"I have a Volkswagen, *closer*," she said.

"Even *closer?*"

"Yeah. Kentucky Street."

"This *is* moving fast, isn't it, Jenny?"

"Faster than a victorian novel, Red."

"Pages and petticoats flyin'."

"Come on, I'll show ya my Bug. Let's go for a walk." We came out of the trance enough to stand up from the table. "Would that be alright with your friends? Just a little walk, and then we could come back here. I'd like to meet them." She laid some cash on her table and nodded *thank you* to the waiter.

Lightly brushing hands, holding fingers, and each other's eyes, she walked me toward the back door of the cafe. But before we got there, I looked over at my table of friends. They were looking discreetly in all directions but mine, and smiling *to beat the band!*

"Hang on a sec," I said to Jenny.

"Sure, see you in the alley. Oh. That sounds so raunchy," she said.

"My middle name."

"Red Raunchy Jumbo. Yes, I can see that."

"Just kidding. See you in a minute, Jenny."

170

I was walking toward my friends but they shooed me away, toward the back door. But as I reversed in that direction, Rosalita waved *c'mere* at me.

I walked over, she whispered, *"Roscoe just booked our rooms for another night. He says you sounded so tired this morning."*

"We're only going for a walk," I whispered back.

"Roscoe says you need rest *tonight, so try to sleep, tee hee. See you later!"*

I smiled angelically at Rosie and made for the back door, but along the way, I swung by the bus tub. The tub Jenny tossed her exclamation point note into. I saw it near a plate and puddle of pancake syrup and butter, and pulled it out.

I already knew I'd want to keep *this* note.

Lawrence, by sunset

The sun was still in the sky and shining but the moon was up, chasing it down, and we were in a hurry, too.

Holding hands now, not just fingers, we fast-walked down the red brick alley, stopped by a dumpster, and kissed. A sort of *test* kiss, just to see how good it was going to feel. I tasted her, breathed her in; we kissed lightly, touching lips, rubbing lips; wet, lingering, and exploring. Our first kisses. We touched noses. She gave my ear a tiny tug with her teeth, her hands soft and warm on my back; it felt good, it was *going* to feel good.

We backed off out of each other's arms, our backs to opposite walls of the alley, and smiled at each other.

"Jenny Sue?"

"Yes, Red?"

"You're looking rather incredulous."

"Can't believe this is happening. How good I feel," she said.

"You're also looking rather *incredible!*"

"Flattery will get you everywhere, Mr. Jumbo."

"Will it get me to Kentucky Street?"

"Yes. Maybe even farther. *Further?* What's right? But say—Mr. Jumbo—do you think you can get there? Can you *walk?* I mean, you're blushing, so that explains your *first* name, but ..."

"Take me to Kentucky, Miss? *Ms.?* What's right?—*Ms.* Skiptewmaylewe. My darling."

We pushed off the red brick walls with our butts, met in the middle of the alley, hooked little fingers together and walked, a little bit slower, out of the alley. We went *on* looking at each other, smiling, excited, moving a little bit *faster!*

Savoring; smelling it, touching it, our other three also incredulous senses wide awake and surrounding us, waving at us, trying to get our attention, too.

We walked west through downtown Lawrence, out of breath—or *Breathless*—like the movie, except not in Paris. I saw the sign for Kentucky Street, looked around for a Volkswagen, saw the front bumper and headlights just as she pulled me towards it; it was parked in an alley, and as we turned into the alley, the setting sun—level on the edge of the Kansas horizon—*blasted* us, shining straight through both the rear window and the windshield.

I looked over at her squinting at me, smiling, and I was either really caught up in the moment and seeing things, or the sun really *was* shining stars and comets off her teeth!

Probably it was a bit of both.

"What the fuck is going on here?! This is ridiculous! I LIKE you —like, *already!*" she said, laughing, pulling me hard toward the VW. We got to the car and she tried to unlock it with her house key. She found the *car* key, unlocked the door, saw what was happening around my zipper, and said, "Oh my god, am I in trouble now!"

"I think we're both in trouble now!" I said, standing so close to this *new person* ... her hair, hands, her fingers working the car key, her hips, savoring her voice, then, finding mine again ... "after what? About an hour? I don't know how I could like you even more, but I have a feeling I will!" We tumbled toward the backseat, pushing the seats forward, Jenny throwing *Amazon* boxes and a heavy, gigantic, Frida Kahlo coffee table book into the front seats, which dropped the front end of the VW low (we would soon shift the weight to the back end, however, and *in rhythm!*). I was trying to get situated for what we were about to do, however we were going to do it, in her tiny car; I turned around and, her face close, Jenny said, "here I come," and her lips were on my mouth, kissing, licking, tasting.

I joined in.

We were twirling tongues, staring at each other at close range, "such green eyes," I said, "such *blue* eyes," she said, kissing and feeling around on each other; I don't know what she was feeling— she seemed to be liking it—*I* certainly was, feeling this new woman, her soft, strong, curvy, squirming, warm body, under cotton and denim. I was looking for zippers and buttons.

We squirmed back to face to face again, smiled big, kissed hard. She pulled back for a second.

"You like my lipstick?"

"I do, I *do*."

She touched my lips, and licked them. "It looks good on you, too," she said.

The sun was down, Lawrence was getting dark.

Her shoes had come off, I kissed her toes, and somehow, while I was doing that, she'd gotten my pants off. Getting even, I pulled down the cuffs of her creamy blue jeans, which took her panties with them, and her panties took some of *her* with them—a couple of sticky strands of her—which snapped delicately, like a beautiful bubble. I breathed deep, inhaling her. She was busy with something too, elsewhere in the Bug.

"Such a *nice* penis," she said. "Such a nice shape, and ... *temperature* ... and aroma. Rather like a small baguette, you know? And how nice to have it unwrapped, *out of the bag*. I would be proud to walk around Paris with this under my arm!"

I was enjoying this, of course, also trying to get closer to her, but I was wedged into the floor of the VW, a little stuck, and I got a cramp in my back.

"You won't mind, then, since you've brought up food, what I was just thinking, *hoping* you'd want to do."

"Oh, I definitely don't mind," she said, tracing her fingers on my baguette, kissing the end of it.

"I mentioned honey, back in the cafe," I said, my cramp melting away. "Well ... watching your wet panties pull away from your wet hair, and your pretty wet lips ... was like watching the lid come off the honey jar ... long, sticky, sweet, syrupy strands ..."

"Yes, honey, it seems you have an apt—MMM! ... *mmm* ... a *very* apt visual metaphor for my ... *pussy*."

I had dislodged myself enough from the floorboards to *touch* her metaphor.

"... *mmm*MMM, Red ... how *nice*."

There was a siren far off in the distance, getting louder, coming closer, red and blue flashes all around us. Whatever few people were walking along this side street (I don't know if there *were* any people there, I wasn't looking) would be distracted by *that*, not watching *us* —so during all that noise and flash, we wriggled and kissed and slid around until she was on me and I was *in* her.

It was dark (the flashes had passed) but I kept my shirt on, she pulled my jacket around her shoulders. And she moved on me, her breasts floating in and out of the jacket, her thighs muscling and stretching, grinding me.

"Hey you," I whispered up to her, where she was grinning at the roof of the Volkswagen. She looked down and her hair covered her eyes, but I could see the grin.

"Yeah *you?*"

"You feel good."

"Oh, so do you. Nice to feel *all* of you, Red."

I moved up as far as I could, she came down as far as she could —all of her did, so *that* felt good—we met and kissed, a sweet kiss, her hands holding my head in her hands. She sat up again, high on her spreading knees—and *that* felt good, too.

Jenny went on slowly grinding me, but there seemed to be something she wanted to say. She flipped her hair back from her face and squinted at me.

"It feels so good with you. I mean, *already*. I mean—it's so fulfilling. But then again, it's also so *fill-fulling!* If you get me!" She

174

gave me a little warm squeeze and plunge, to drive home the point. "Get me?"

"Got you," I said.

"Maybe you do."

"Maybe you do, too."

We stopped talking, closed our eyes, and moved with each other; moved faster, hotter, wetter, all the chills and juices and shivers and squirts and tingles sliding and flashing through both of our bodies in and out faster and all of that in the both of us, then in the one of us, breathing hard, dripping, and bright-eyed smiling.

The Volkswagen stopped moving.

After some delicious, semi-naked rapturous moments of silence (I doubt the Kansas church across Kentucky Street would approve of this variation on the word rapture; too bad for them)—after I'd kissed her from head to toe, down both arms and all her fingers, and she looked like she'd gone to heaven, I know *I* felt that way—Jenny moved.

She stayed semi-naked, barefoot, some of her wild, electrified hair sticking to the ceiling, climbed over and through the seats to the front, and started the Volkswagen. It sounded like a sewing machine. She shifted into first and the Bug jumped into the street.

"I'm taking *you* home with me!" she said.

Wedged into her backseat like carry-on luggage, I was in no position to object. Not that I was looking to object. "Please do," I said.

She was shifting gears so fast down Kentucky Street that my hair was on the ceiling, too. Not that I minded; I was laughing and holding on tight!

"We'll be there in a jiffy, I live a few blocks south ... around the corner from the house where Williams S. Burroughs lived. You know his work?"

"Oh yeah. I love all his books, love *Naked Lunch*. I like the last one, written here in Lawrence. His journals from his last days alive."

"I loved my naked *dinner* this evening," said Jenny Sue, throwing her gear shift like dice.

"Did you just say *jiffy*?"

"I did."

"My grandma used to say that all the time. Wow. I just thought of something."

"What?"

"She kinda *looked* like William S. Burroughs, grandma, if she was a man, and if she was a Beat Poet. She had those glasses, and that voice. *And,* she said jiffy."

"I have those countryisms, though I'm from Long Island. I like 'em."

"I miss grandma when I think about her. Anyway, that book of Burroughs' final journals was moving. I *think* they were final. He's dead, isn't he?"

Jenny Sue ran a red light and kept shifting. "Oh yes. Awhile ago. Though a man got shot on Massachusetts Street the other night, was it *last night?* And people who were there swore they saw Burroughs with his pistol. And that he did the shooting."

"How can that be? That can't be. Who'd he shoot?"

"Some older gross guy, who was evidently drunk and getting sexual, in an icky way, with some students, some young women, in —well, where we met!—Blanche and Mabel's!"

"Well, good. I'm glad, then. Though I hate guns, and I'm generally a Buddhist. That's the first time I've told anyone that, Jenny. The first time I've said it out loud, even to myself. Well, anyway, is he dead?"

"Mr. Burroughs, yes. The gross guy, no." She turned at a corner down a new street and we nearly flipped over. "Bullet grazed the guy —*in the crotch,* they say! Here we are," she zipped the Bug up a short driveway to a garage door, turned off the headlights, and looked at me in the rear-view mirror. "You're *generally* a Buddhist?"

"Yeah. And what I call a *Neo-Buddhist.* Which means, I suppose, that sometimes I want to kill somebody."

"Would you?"

"No, I'm a softie. I get mad sometimes, you know. But I literally can't kill flies. But getting back to that other thing ... it must've been a man that *looked* like William S. Burroughs. Or a fan, a Burroughs imitator, you know—like *Elvis.*"

"Beats *me.* No pun intended. *"*

She turned off the sewing machine Volkswagen and we sat in silence, in the dark, thinking. There was the sound of a train in the flat distance.

"Maybe it *was* him," I said.

"Could be. Sometimes they come back, you know? Maybe he *had* to, just to shoot this creepy lech from out of town."

"Maybe. Anyway, I love those Beat books."

"Me too. Let's go in, Red. I'll make a fire in the fireplace, and we can find out how much else we have in common."

"I think there will be a lot," I said.

"Me, too."

Jenny's place—the first floor of the house, a long, wide room with a kitchen area in the corner—was warm, dark wood with dusty rose wallpaper, slightly sagging scarred wooden floors with red and green carpets pieced together and overlapping each other, a pink Formica table, a small wooden table, three fluffy couches, wood-beamed ceilings, a big fluffy bed by a BIG brick fireplace, framed expressionist paintings all over the place (we started talking about expressionism between kisses: "You have good taste!" "You taste good too, Red!") and over her bed, a lobby poster from the film *The Great Escape.*

"Well, *that's* a surprise," I said.

"What'd you expect? *Steel Magnolias? The Tree of Wooden Clogs? 101 Dalmatians?"*

"No, no, and no offense. You *yourself* are a surprise. And I love that movie."

"What do you love about it, Red? The camaraderie? The *esprit de corps?"*

"I hated my parents."

"Oh. Yeah, so did I."

"I was always trying to tunnel out of my childhood."

"Yep. And I always felt the big guard tower spotlight on me, from my father. Maybe I'll go into that later."

I was moved by what I thought she was probably saying. It seemed like every woman I'd ever known had been sexually abused at some point by a man: teacher, boss, father, or the *local* Holy Father. Also, I was moved—well, excited—that she'd said that word: LATER!

"Care for a drink? Beer? Wine? A can of pink grapefruit *Perrier?"*

"The can, please. My favorite!"

"It is?"

"Sure, *now*. I drank enough of that other sort of French drink, maybe a couple of arrondissements worth, over the years. Now, I choose Perrier—the *Bubbles of Vergèze!* Sometimes I'll have something called a Bloody Club, but tonight, please, bring on the Bubbles!"

"I drank up a couple of arrondissements myself. Have a seat by the fireplace, Red. I'll be right back with drinks and kindling."

On the way to the big fireplace, I walked by her big bed. There was a tranquil green bedspread, partly pulled down; I leaned down and smelled her pillows. I inhaled deeply, stood up, and started over to the fireplace again, but stopped again, at her chest of drawers. Jenny was in the kitchen, but I very quietly pulled out the second drawer down—it was partly open too, like her bedspread, I could see it was her lingerie drawer—and I leaned down again, into her perfume.

I felt a lick on my neck.

"Do I smell good?" Jenny was back.

"You caught me!"

"Yeah, you sneak! But it's ok, you can sniff my drawers."

Jenny was carrying a silver tray with my can of the Bubbles of Vergèze, a glass of red wine, a box of wood matches, a couple of sticks of kindling under her arm, and she was wearing a red velvet robe, a matching one over her shoulder, which she was somehow shrugging at me to take. Amazing, under the circumstances, with all that she was carrying. She was beautifully and dexterously laden. And *limber*.

I took the robe.

"That's for you. I bought these as a set, in a hotel in Belgium, in case something like this happened."

There was a price tag on the robe: forty-eight euros.

"Yeah. New. Never worn. Please," she said, and set down the tray. She pulled off the tag, and some of my clothes, I pulled on the robe. "I think it might be yours. I'll make the fire now. Then, we'll talk. I wanna know you even more. A *lot* more."

She built the fire, struck it alive with a wood match, glowing up high, hot, and yellow on the bricks. We sat down on the red rug in front of the red fire, our red robes reflecting the fire; there was lots of red flying around the room. Not me, though. I was still and peaceful. We began to talk.

About the unpredictable eccentricity of Tilda Swinton and, for Jenny, the delicious luxury of baloney sandwiches on Wonder Bread. Somehow it started there. We both loved that cleverly wild actor and I loved that Jenny loved that sort of sandwich. "I'm used to the granola girls," I said. Then ... we talked ... about corduroy, silky pajamas or none, silky skin, Elton John's clothes, the wise and playful voice and imagination of the wild Australian trickster—Sia, Barbara Stanwyck's chutzpah, the acting of Bette Davis and her eyes, the same with Emma Stone and hers, Kipper Snacks, Helena Bonham Carter, Mozart, Public Enemy, the Beatles, the Bangles, Mavis Staples, the Psychedelic Furs, Eric Satie, Ricky Lee Jones, the Clash, Siouxsie and the Banshees, Barbra Streisand singing in that tug boat, Bob Dylan blowing *against* the prevailing wind, the Stones, Blossom Dearie, Sinead O'Connor, R.E.M., Billie Eilish, Neil Young astride the Crazy Horse, Annie Lennox, Raul Malo and the Mavericks, Marc Chagall, Muddy Waters, Wynton Marsalis, Cat Power, Branford Marsalis, Pema Chödrön, David Hockney, Chrissie Hynde, Miro, Patti Smith, Van Gogh, Van Morrison (I told her about Morrison, the *van;* she asked if *my* van was grouchy), and music like the *Goldberg Variations,* anything sung by Bettye LaVette, *songs like Honky-Tonk Women, and Why don't we do it in the road?*; then we went into pine trees, candles, night lights, full moons, lunar eclipses, pancakes, Dutch Babies; we talked of taking all-night flights to

Europe waking up not knowing what time zone you're in, being in a country not knowing the language—not rudely, but adventurously *out of control!*; baby buds in spring, baby birds in their nests, wild blizzards at Christmas, the color green, the color blue, the playground crayon flamboyant color RED, the desert, the Sierras, pine log cabins and their *smell,* inside; the worldly, wild, sexy jazzy voice of Melody Gardot, the irreverently wild, warm, freeing humor of the Dalai Lama (we noticed that the word *wild* was coming up a lot), I brought up my *wild* bardic hero, Kate Bush, and Jenny said *Mr. Springsteen* with a pause of admiration; then we went into Charlie Parker jazz, Billie Holiday blues, Louis Armstrong *liveliness,* the mysterious Celtic soothing comfort of (I almost didn't tell her, thought I'd be embarrassed) Enya's music (but I did, and I wasn't); dogs, goats, polar bears, zaru soba, sushi, baloney and Wonder Bread (she said it again, to impress me, now that she knew that I already *was*), fried catfish, coq au vin; writers like Patti Smith, Ken Kesey, Jane Austen, Charles Bukowski (Jenny brought him up, when I told her I'd just seen him a Pasadena book store, she said, "But he's dead, isn't he?"—"Yes, *I know!"* I said) Tom Robbins, Erica Jong, William S. Burroughs ("He too is dead," I said, "but didn't some people just see *him,* in downtown Lawrence?"—"Yeah, I know ... spooky!" said Jenny), Margaret Atwood, and Ursula Le Quin; the movie directors Aki Kaurismäki, Mira Nair, Sally Wainwright, Spike Lee, Kaouther Ben Hania, Deniz Gamze Ergüven, Robert Rodriguez, Jane Campion, Pedro Almodóvar, Susanne Bier, cinema-crazy Quentin Tarantino, Paul Thomas Anderson, Jasmila Zbanic, Ava DuVernay, and Robert Altman; the film *A Room with a View,* also *Run, Lola, Run,* and *Pee Wee's Playhouse* plus all of Pee Wee's films; seaweed salad, pumpkin pie, ramen noodles, whipped cream, fresh bread, garlic, gardening (she had plants all around, flowers and trees filling her little backyard); our shared left-wing or liberal or socialist politics but not staying with *that* for very long; airports in the middle of the night, sleeping on trains, floors of old hardware stores, the ceiling at Grand Central Station, fireplaces in bedrooms, and then, one more thing we both liked, though surely we hadn't hit on everything, *another* thing we liked—was slow kissing, for hours, falling asleep together ... which ... then ... we *did.*

Sunup

There was morning sunlight on a fireplace. I didn't know where I was yet, but then I saw Jenny; we were all arms and legs and hair and sheets, wrapped up tight.

Light was flashing in the bed, I reached down into the covers and answered my phone.

"Hello?"

"RED. *You dog.*"

"Fyodor?"

"Buenos dias, *Señor Rojo!*"

"Rosie?"

"Hi, Red. Yes, it's Rosalita. We have you on speaker."

"You do? Well, I've got *you* on speaker, too."

Jenny smiled big in bed. *"Rosalita.* Makes me think of that song by Mr. Springsteen. Although this voice, *this* Rosalita doesn't sound like she needs any saving!"

"Hey, buddy!" Serge shouted, echoing into Jenny's house. "Where are you, anyway?"

"Yeah man, where *are* you?" Alberto asked, Rosie laughing in the background.

Jenny was *stretching* ... waking up. Bed-mussed hair in the warm sun, toes wiggling out of the sheets. *Whew.*

"Top of the morning, loverboy!" the phone said.

Jenny smiled. "Who is *that?*"

"Her name is Ruby Taillights."

"Hmm, wow. Ok, I like it," said Jenny.

"So, where are you, Red?" asked Rosie.

Jenny came up out of our tangle of arms and legs, kissed me, and leaned down to the phone.

"Hi, Ruby Taillights! Rosalita! Hello Fyodor, I'm Jenny. My address is 7 Kentucky Street. Just a few blocks north of your motel. Red told me you're over at the *Nest*. It's nice to meet you. Come on over!"

"Nice to meet *you*, Jenny," said Rosie. "Can we? I mean we have to check out, and all that ... and we don't want to interrupt you and Red, if you're just ... how should I say this ... *waking up*. Oh, and we have your Rickie Lee Jones book. You left it at the cafe, maybe you were distracted at the time."

"Maybe I was. I think I was seeing *Red,* as it were. But yeah—come on. I mean, take your time, but come on, when you're ready, Rosie. I mean, Rosalita."

"Call me Rosie. And you're Jenny?"

"Yup. Jenny Sue Skiptewmaylewe!"

A moment of silence on the speakerphone.

Then, Fyodor: "Did you hear *that?* "

Followed by Ruby: "I sure *did!*"

"You like that name?" asked Jenny. "You don't think it's too much, do you?"

"I like it, *a lot!*" said Ruby.

"So why don't you come over so I can meet you all face to face. And have you eaten? Or had coffee?"

"Well, no," said Rosie. "We were gonna go over to that Blanche & Mabel place again."

"Come here, instead. I'll get some coffee going in a minute, after I get unwrapped from our handsome mutual friend here, and I'll make pancakes. I even have fresh strawberries and cantaloupes! From the Farmer's Market, just yesterday."

"Sounds good. So, the address is ... *seven* ... Kentucky Street?"

"Yeah. There were three other numbers but they fell off sometime last winter. I don't care, the mailwoman knows where I am, and I don't need anyone else to! Oh, and Rosie—speaking of Blanche and Mabel's—I noticed yesterday that you were reading *Naked Lunch.* Did you know that Burroughs used to live in town, here in Lawrence? *And,* I was telling Red last night that some people saw him down on Massachusetts Street a couple of nights ago."

There was a pause. "Oh yeah?" said Rosie, curiously.

"Yeah. But I don't know how. I mean, the man is dead."

"Ah, but Jenny, you know—being dead doesn't stop *some* people!"

"That's true, Rosie. See you in a few minutes."

"See you soon, Jenny Sue!"

"Skiptewmaylewe!" added and encouraged Fyodor, who *really* liked this name.

"See you *all* soon," said Jenny, ending the call.

"You'll like them. You'll like my friends."

"I know I will. I already do. And I like you."

She kissed me again, stood up out of bed, and went to make coffee. Jenny Sue Skiptewmaylewe, naked in the sunrise! I got up, naked too, and went out there in her kitchen to help make pancakes.

Good morning!

Good Morning!

We were in a flurry in the kitchen, me and Jenny. Bacon sizzling, pancakes stacking up fluffy and brown, syrup bubbling on the stove, and a heavy, delicious cloud of coffee in the air. There were dabs of butter, flecks of flour on our skin, then I heard distant singing and barking dogs.

The dogs were barking their usual barking, but the singing, the song (full-voiced) was *Oklahoma!*

Jenny pulled on her robe. "What's that, a musical troupe?"

I pulled on my robe. (I had an erection, of course!) "Maybe, but I think it's my friends. Who knows why *that* song, but they've been singing it since we crossed the Colorado state line."

"Ah, so it's your friends, then. What are you all up to, anyway?" She handed me a University of Kansas apron.

"It's a long story, as the saying goes," I said, tying on the apron. "If it was a novel, it'd be over 181 pages by now, but can I tell you later? I want you to meet my friends."

She came closer and adjusted the apron so the bird, the Jayhawk, was in front, concealing the erection. I was *feathered in*. Still, all this activity only solidified my position, so to speak.

"They sounded fun on the phone," said Jenny. "I'm very curious."

"I'm sure you are. I'm sure *we* seem curious. Well, the long and the short of it is, Rosie was ... bullied, pushed around, *abused* ... and, um ..." I couldn't finish.

"*Hey*. You ok?" Jenny asked.

"Long story. Difficult story," I said.

She came over, close to me. "Tell it later, sometime. I really want to hear it. Let's meet your people, now. And *eat!* Ok, Red?" She looked at me a moment, and hugged me.

There was a shave and a haircut knock on the door, accompanied by some syncopated dog barking.

That got Jenny and me laughing, and we were *still* laughing— our robes, and my apron, still decorated with pancake mix, a splash of syrup, there was a piece of eggshell somehow in my hair—when we swung the door open.

Five faces, wide-open smiling, beaming at us, and three dogs likewise! Rosie stepped out from the group.

"Is this Jenny Sue Skiptewmaylewe?" she asked.

"That's me! Welcome! Come on in," and they all came in. I started the introductions.

"Jenny, this is Rosalita, her handsome husband Alberto (he did a small bow), Serge, *Officer* Serge Controllente, of the Pasadena Police Department (who did a short, official, but friendly salute), and over here is my elegant old friend Fyodor and his wife, the dancer, naturalist, gardener, and show tunes singer, Ruby (she did some kind of balletic spin) Taillights."

"SO good to meet you, Jenny Sue. Not sure I'm much of a singer, but I do it anyway! We saw you last night at the cafe, saw you and Red burning eyeballs back and forth. It was fun to watch! I thought you two would hit it off, and I think you did!" said Ruby, checking out our robes.

"We did. We do," said Jenny.

"We *will*," I said.

We all fell silent under the heavy weight of these three sentences, short as they were, but carrying a lot of info. The silence held, smiles all around, then we heard the sound of dogs licking—licking syrup off Jenny's robe.

"Let's eat!" yelled Jenny.

"Oh and," I continued the introductions, "that's Kansas, Missouri ..."

"And Oklahoma?"

"That's *Felix,* Jenny. That's Rosie's dog. We just like singing that song, for some reason, ever since we made Kansas."

Fyodor came over and put an arm around my shoulder. "Say, Red, they *really* like Jayhawks around here, don't they? The motel, I see them all over town, in windows and bumper stickers, and—I like your apron. Is it *alive?"*

We pushed Jenny's two tables together and all sat down to a loud, messy, beautiful bonanza of a breakfast, Jenny and I touching toes under the pink Formica table, Fyodor nudging me from one side, Rosie from the other, Serge winking at me, Alberto *thumbs-upping* me, Ruby gabbing away with Jenny, all of us at some kind of new family breakfast, for the first time; some kind of family that fell together, from California to Lawrence, Kansas.

What a relief, I thought. Something I'd been looking for for a long time, even before the night I walked out of the lonely basement in Eagle Rock, looking up at the moon—pretty, wearing earrings, but nobody up there, either. Maybe some of my new family felt this way, too, sometimes.

I was in love. With Jenny. With *all* of them.

Of course, then we all fell asleep.

I'm not sure how it happened, since I think I fell asleep first. Don't know who went down first, but the breakfast was so satisfying, so filling, so fun, so happy and *heavy*—in maple syrup and laughter and the bottle of champagne Jenny brought out at some point, the point at which Rosie and I decided to pass out—that in spite of the overload of coffee earlier, we all fell asleep.

All day.

I woke up to the music of Louis Armstrong, the light of the setting sun slanting into Jenny's house from her western window. I lay in her bed, a pillow up against the wall, the dogs asleep by the fireplace, and watched Jenny—laughing, talking to my friends, and *dancing* to the jazz.

We were spending another night in Lawrence!

We stayed up late that night. Fyodor and Ruby pushed a couple of couches together, bedded down in each other's arms, talking privately, face to face, right in the middle of the party; Alberto and Serge played cards in Jenny's kitchen area; Kansas, Missouri, and Felix explored the backyard; Jenny, Rosie, and I sat down by the fireplace. Rosie and I (mostly Rosie) told her the whole story, Mr. Hamptons, Charlie Parker's napkin, why we were on the way to Kansas City. Or as much as we knew that night, about why, and what we were going to do.

Jenny listened closely, quietly.

When we got to the part of the story where Mr. Hamptons raped Rosie, Jenny froze, silent, and stared into the fireplace, took a breath.

This was the second time I'd heard this story in a week, and Rosie told it clearly, and quickly; I suppose she'd found a way to carry it, she'd *been* carrying it for a few years. But it was hard to hear it again. And Jenny, who'd I known for *one day* at that point, showed me another side of her; it was hurt, haunted, compassionate, soft—and angry.

The card game broke up in the kitchen, Serge and Alberto started going through Jenny's record collection, they put on Los Lobos, which got Fyodor and Ruby out of bed and dancing, and Rosie, finished with her story, was up and dancing, too.

Jenny stared into the fire.

Someone turned up the music. The dogs tore through the backdoor dog door and jumped into the dance too, paws in the air. The party was in some sort of *third* wind, but Jenny pulled me over to her bed by the fireplace. We slid under the covers and watched the dancing from bed. We weren't going to be sleeping, because Fyodor, Serge, and Alberto were LOUDLY serenading Ruby and Rosalita.

The idea of *what time it was* didn't matter to anything or anybody, but I knew we were leaving for Kansas City in the morning. I told Jenny that, she looked sad.

Then, she laughed. "You're a detective? That seems so sort of out of character somehow, for you!"

"I know, and what do *you* do? We haven't even gotten around to that yet, have we? And no, I don't think I am a detective anymore. I'm I guess the artistic type—which means that *whatever* I am changes on a daily basis, if not faster. Is that an answer? But no, I'm not a detective. What about you, Jenny?"

"I'm the artistic type too, and in my case, it changes on a *second-to-second* basis, any snap of the synapse! The next snap might have me off to LA—though you may have thrown a monkey wrench into that—but here in Lawrence, at the University of Kansas, I teach two things: English Lit and Landscaping. Tomorrow's class, at 9 a.m.— *Yikes!*—here I am staying up late and falling in love—did I just say that? *Yes! Anyway* ..."

She *did* just say that, and the thrill of hearing it sent me into orbit! Or maybe *out* of orbit! I saw sparkles in the air around Jenny's face, felt sparks up and down my spine, and I heard some kind of fizzy carbonation sound in my ears—*all of this really happened*— meanwhile, I was listening to her voice ...

"... in the morning I'm teaching a class I invented myself—it was *months* getting approved by the administration—teaching the writings of Erica Jong, Patti Smith, Jill Soloway, and Diablo Cody. The class is called *Renaissance Women: Laying down their lines!* I even had to fight for that exclamation point on the course title. My department head calls it a cluster course. Whatever. I call it *fun*, and it's about fucking time, you know? I mean, when was the last time someone talked about a Renaissance *woman?* It's always *men of letters*, and *gee*, what a Renaissance *man* he is!"

"I love that, Jenny! And I love those women. Maybe I should cut Kansas City to attend your class."

"Yeah, why don't you? You can slip in the back row. I'm teaching another class that I invented, called *Twain, Dickens, and Dostoevsky: Three Troublemakers from The Wrong Side of the Tracks.* In the spring, I'm teaching all about the great singer, songwriter, and musician—Melody Gardot."

"Melody Gardot. I don't know that one, yet. Can you teach a musician in a literature course?"

"*I* can. I'll slip her in. You need to know about *her*, Red, if I have anything to say about it."

"You have everything to say about it, Jenny. Oh, and you teach landscaping?"

"Yeah. I know about trees and plants, plant grafting, and I try to relate it all to architecture, art, *anything*, expand it beyond just the green thumb zone. And I'm developing another class about Emily Dickinson I call *You Don't Have to Leave the Fucking House to Change the World*. I love Emily, the English Department will probably approve it, though they may want me to change the title a little. We'll see. Hey, Red ... wow ... I like calling you by name ... this is all so new."

"I'm falling in love with you too, Jenny."

Sparkles in the air.

In her eyes, too. "Um, do you know about the Flint Hills, here in Kansas? Did you drive through there at all?"

"No, but I've heard of them."

"It's a beautiful thing to see, I go there often, get calm. I was having a nice, peaceful breakfast one morning last year, after watching the sunrise in the Flint Hills, and looked down and saw that in my plate ... the hash browns, toast, bacon, even the bits of parsley looked like the waving grasses that morning. I told the waitress—this was in Blanche & Mabel's Cafe, of course—that they should call what I was having the *Flint Hills Plate*. She told her manager, and they *did!*"

"I'm in bed with the woman who invented the *Flint Hills Plate?* Hot damn!"

"And I am in bed with the man, the ex-detective ..."

"*Yeah*, ex—a few days on a *nobody-dunnit!*"

" ... the *man* leading a bunch—*a happy few*—to Kansas City! All funded by the Charlie Parker cocktail napkin! Hot damn is *right*. I may have to rip off your apron, Red, I think I'm horny again!"

She looked at me: I was, too. *We* were, so we did. Under the covers. Have sex, surreptitiously. Sideways, smiling all the while at the happy few. Otherwise occupied.

Then we slid into sleep.

Goodbye, for now

We woke up yawning, kissing, the sun coming in the windows from the other side of Jenny's house this time—the *east* window, of course. I got dressed quietly by the bed, Jenny tiptoed between the couches and the fireplace in her robe, the fireplace almost out but still smoky and crackling a little, everyone still asleep, sweet and peaceful. My happy few.

And a new one—Jenny.

"Coffee?" she asked.

"Yes, please. You know, Jenny, when I say goodbye here, in an hour or so? It's goodbye, *for now*. Ok?"

"Ok. Good. I'm glad. I can tell. I want that."

"This feels more like hello than goodbye. I guess I'm dragging this out, but I've known you for a night and a day and last night and this morning and I am going to *miss* you."

"I miss you already, Red. But I think I'll see you again soon. *Now,* I must get ready for class."

The others were waking up, making the same stretching, yawning, standing up noises as us, and watching us say goodbye over and over.

"Awww, *you guys,*" said Ruby.

Jenny waved and smiled *aw shucks,* kissed me, untied her robe, went into the bathroom, shut the door, and turned on the shower. There was a moment of silence—except for the sound of running water—and Alberto yawning out loud, like a coyote. Then I smiled in a *Hallelujah, I'm in love!* sort of way at Ruby and the others, went into the kitchen area, and started to make breakfast.

"Red?"

I turned around; Ruby was holding up the Jayhawk apron.

"Need *this*, don't you?"

I was still making breakfast, slinging plates and slicing strawberries, making toast and coffee (*"Flint Hills Golden Roasted— from Downtown Lawrence!"*), my new family watching from the tables by the now rejuvenated, blazing fireplace, when Jenny came out of the bathroom in a cloud of steam, bounced barefooted through a door into her garage, and rattled things around out there. We all waited, wondered, looked at each other, heard the sound of paper bags rattling, bottles *dinging* together, cans clattering. All those noises stopped short, and Jenny came bouncing and skipping out with armloads of bags, bottles, and cans.

"Recycling day!" she sang at us, dancing out the front door in her robe.

I served breakfast.

"Hi Morrison," I said to the van an hour or so later, after breakfast. We hadn't been split up for a night ever, except for the occasional visit and overnight stay (maybe a tune-up, or oil change) at Fire Jose's Gas Station in Pasadena. "Have a good night? Ready for the last leg to Kansas City?" I asked the van, patting the hood. The reflection of the sun, like an eye in the van's windshield, winked *yes* at me. I turned around and I was facing east, and Kansas City, also everyone happily spilling out of Jenny's house.

"Ready?" I asked.

"Yes we are!" said Rosalita. "And Red—I want to drive us in. This last stretch of road, into Kansas City." She was quite serious about this; I handed her the keys. "Rollin' rollin' rollin'…" she sang, then yelled, "RAWHIDE!"

"I'm surprised you know Westerns, let alone their theme songs, though I don't know *why*," said Jenny, coming out the front door, towel-drying her hair. "Since it's *you*, and I think you're probably real unpredictable."

"Yes, you never know with Rosalita, she *will* surprise you," said Alberto.

"I'll say," I said.

"Jenny, I know Westerns, Easterns, Southerns, and Northerns!" said Rosie.

"I believe it," said Jenny, giving Rosie a very big and *holding-tight* hug.

"See you later, somewhere, somehow," said Rosie.

"Yes, I think you will. Soon. Good luck in KC."

Rosie got in the driver's seat, started the van, the dogs peed in the front yard, then they and everyone else got in. Everyone but me. I walked Jenny back up the steps to her porch.

"Bye Jenny!" everyone yelled from the van.

"Jenny Sue Skiptewmaylewe!" sang Ruby.

"Ok, *my darling*," I laughed. "This is it."

She touched my cheek and we were close, face to face, both of us smiling, excited, sparkling tears in our eyes.

I hugged her and felt her laughing and crying, or was it me?

"This is GOOD!" I said.

"This IS good!" she said.

"You have my cell phone number."

"Yes. And you have mine."

"I'm so glad I met you."

"I'm so glad you came to Lawrence!"

"I really like you."

"Oh, I really like you, too."

"They're so cute," I heard from the van, the driver's seat.

"Look how happy Red is. Well, *both* of them," from the back seat.

"You two are under arrest," shouted Serge. "You have the right to remain *buoyant.*"

"I'll call you from Kansas City," I said.

"Good, do that. You're only about an hour away."

"This is just bye, *for now.*"

"I know it."

"Here we go again."

"Dragging it out, I know."

"Ok," I hugged her. "Teach well, light some matches!"

"Ok," she kissed me, "I will! They've such *flammable* imaginations!"

"Ok ..."

"OK!"

Ignoring the steps, and going for flamboyance, I launched myself off the porch down to the van and jumped in up front, next to Rosie; from there I could see Jenny wave once more and wipe her eyes, but she was also *jumping and skipping* (and laughing!) into her house.

But just before the waving and wiping, jumping and skipping (and laughing!), I saw her looking at something, really focusing, on the back end of the van, or the rear tire.

Something.

Rosie drove north on Massachusetts Street, right into the middle of some kind of agricultural parade—tractors growling and grinding along on both sides of the van; we were talking, reminiscing about our couple of days in Lawrence, laughing, also singing again (not *Oklahoma* now, instead, "... *all we are is dust in the wind ...*" by, yes, *that* band: *Kansas*), looking for the highway sign, finding it, getting up the ramp onto the highway again, Rosie accelerating ... 35, 40, 45, 50 ... then ... *bang bang bang bang bang!*

We pulled over. *Bang, bang, bang,* tinkle, tinkle ... tink, *dink.*

We all got out, walked around to the back of Morrison, and there —by the hand of Jenny Sue Skiptewmaylewe, no doubt—were a dozen beer cans tied to the back bumper under the Beatles bumper sticker, wedding day style!

"Ahhh, of course," said Fyodor, bending low to the asphalt. "There it is again, that bird. *Jayhawk Beer, locally brewed, in Lawrence, Kansas!* it says, on the can."

"Man, you can't escape that bird around here, can you?" I asked.

"Tell us about it," said Alberto, pointing at me. Pointing *low.*

I was still wearing the University of Kansas Jayhawk apron, from breakfast.

"Well," I said, "I'm sure as hell not taking it off *now.* Let's go, Rosie!"

We untied the cans, for now, all got back in, Rosie got the van up to 70 miles an hour, and we were on the way, almost there, almost to Kansas City.

I thought about the cans (which Fyodor had untied and saved for me, an eccentric and romantic keepsake) and laughed again.

"I love that woman," I said.

"*Tell* us about it!" said Rosie.

PART THREE   *Over the Moon*

Kansas City

Three or four *loud* rock and roll songs later, Rosie turned off the radio. It got quiet in the van, I got way deep into a meditative state.

Rosie pulled over into a rest stop. "I'm sorry, Red, I can't do it," she said, ignition off.

"What? You want to go back to California?" I asked, suddenly way *out* of my meditative state.

"Oh no, not that. But it only took me fifteen minutes to find out —I can't drive in Kansas. The speed limit is 70 miles an hour. I was down to *forty*-five a minute ago. I thought the *rock and roll* would break this wave of somnolence. Will you take over?"

"What's that word she just used?" asked Fyodor.

"Somnolence," said Alberto. "You know—*sleepy!*"

"Sure, Rosie, let's switch," I said.

We got out of the van to trade seats. In front of the van, crossing paths, she said, "Sorry, Red, this is like driving across a ceiling. Do you know what I mean?"

"I *do*," I said.

We got back in the van, me behind the wheel.

It got quiet again and I got meditative again, thinking about this new woman, Jenny. I was already falling in love with her, thinking ahead to Kansas City, and whatever was about to happen there, and as excited as I was about all of that, the *meditative* turned to *boredom* (driving in Kansas, still no Kansas City skyline rising anywhere ahead) as I squinted down the highway. I thought I saw Kansas City rising over the curvature of the earth (even in Kansas), but it was only a silo. There seemed to be many more cars on the highway, I saw the city limits sign, and I began to feel the gravitational pull of Kansas City (even from the zero-gravity, Kansas side). I was feeling another kind of gravitational pull—to fall asleep—but I kept my eyes open and my foot on the gas.

Around a twist of highway I saw tiny silver buildings on the horizon.

"*There it is!*" I yelled. "Kansas City!" And though it was *me* yelling, I startled myself into a swerve and light bump on the highway retaining wall.

"Retain yourself, Mr. Jumbo!" laughed Rosie.

I laughed too, but my eyes were rolling down the highway. "I think I see Union Station!"

The sun was shining yellow golden *bright* out of a high blue sky, Kansas City and the hills around it looked open, wide, expansive, and friendly, getting closer. Obviously, I was in a good mood, I even *sped up* a little.

Rosie was smiling, tears inside her sunglasses.

I drove us over the river bridge and the sun flashed off the tops of the skyscrapers. I saw Union Station waiting down the hill, south.

Not too close, but close enough

The bartender glides down the ladder and over to the Hamptons table. His shirt is as blindingly white and stiff as their table cloth and his thick yellow walrus mustache comes down to his elbows, seemingly. He has eyes like cue balls, a little blue chalk mark in the center of each, rolling right into Mrs. Hamptons eyes.

"Good afternoon, M'lady! What are we drinking, if you please?"

"I'd enjoy a Stolichnaya Vodka Martini, please," says Mrs. Hamptons, flattered by the bartender's elegant attention, charmed, and flirting back, a little. Mr. Hamptons stares at the floor-to-ceiling ladder in front of the glowing golden backbar wall of bottles in the Union Station Bar, not charming or seeing anyone to flirt with.

"And for the gentleman?" asks the bartender, his sly fox smile sliding more towards Mrs. Hamptons.

"How tall is that ladder? Twelve feet?" asks Mr. Hamptons.

"Yes, exactly. Twelve feet. Good eye, sir! And how 'bout them Chiefs, eh?"

Mr. Hamptons is amused by the bartender's attempt at male bonding and "masculine" topics of conversation—bringing up football. He'd been more subtle with his talk of ladders. He's also a little suspicious of the bartender's tone, but decides to up the ante with beer.

"You got any local beers I should know about?"

"I suggest Boulevard Beer. Would you care for a wheat beer, or a hoppy wheat beer, maybe the Oktoberfest beer or Nutcracker Ale, or ..."

"No no no, nothing like that, just a beer beer, alright?"

"Of course, sir, maybe a pilsner is what you'd like. A straight-forward pale beer, a guy-guy's beer, like the good old days of Schlitz, and Old Style out of Chicago, and ..."

"Schlitz was shit beer. Piss. So ... but yeah, ok, bring me the pilsner."

"Yes sir. By the way, my name is Paul, and I'll be right back."

The Hamptons watch Paul as he climbs up the ladder again, then brings down a bottle of Stolichnaya.

197

"This is where that man Roscoe works, right?" asks Mrs. Hamptons.

"Yeah. That's what I heard Rosalita say."

Mrs. Hamptons is enjoying Paul's bartending. "It's fun to be staying right across the street," she says, watching Paul as he jumps off the last rung of the ladder, snapping his fingers and a bar towel on his thigh. He makes her drink swiftly and precisely, draws a perfect head of beer, then he's on the way with the drinks.

Paul arrives with their drinks on a tray and flips two crisp white cocktail napkins spinning on the table in front of the Hamptons. When they stop spinning, he places the drinks.

"Stolichnaya Vodka Martini for you, young lady, and an ice-cold Boulevard Pale Ale for you, sir,"

"Paul?" Mrs. Hamptons is almost batting her lashes.

"Oui, madame?" he answers.

Mrs. Hamptons squirms a little, Mr. Hamptons glares a lot.

"There was an older African-American fellow, another bartender, we met here last time we were in town ... what was his name ... oh, yes—Roscoe? Does he still work here? He was so ... oh, I don't know ... pleasant.*"*

"Yes, he is! And he does. Work here. He works nights. He'll be in later this evening. About five. Will you be having lunch, would you care for a menu?"

"No," says Mr. Hamptons.

Paul bows, clicks his heels, starts back towards the bar.

Mr. Hamptons leans over, close and confidential to Mrs. Hamptons. "We'll come back here and have a late dinner, order dessert, some after-dinner drinks, try to get a table not too close to the bar, but close enough."

"Then follow this Roscoe guy home?" asks Mrs. Hamptons.

"Oh yeah." Mr. Hamptons relaxes back into his chair.

Mrs. Hamptons calls out to Paul, still on his way to the bar. The bartender stops, spins in place, stands up so straight, so regally, and does it so quickly, his mustache flies back over his shoulders, seemingly. He walks back to Mrs. Hamptons' side. "Yes, M'lady?"

"Paul?" tugs Mrs. Hamptons coyly, on his stiff, white, shirt sleeve. "Question. We'll be coming back for dinner this evening. Will we be needing a reservation?"

"Oh no, I shouldn't think so. What time will you be coming in?"

"When do you close?" Mr. Hamptons snaps, interjects, like a corkscrew.

"We close at ten, sir."

"Oh, we'll be in way before ten," says Mrs. Hamptons quickly, laughing.

"Do you work tonight too, or is it only Roscoe's shift?" Mr. Hamptons snaps again, like a bar towel.

A bit of the regal slumps out of Paul. His eyes go to Mr. Hamptons, but the rest of his body isn't interested.

"No, sir, I'll be off tonight. Roscoe will be closing up this evening." Paul looks at Mrs. Hamptons. "Would you like to make a reservation, ma'am?"

"Well, why not!" she bubbles up. "You only live once!"

"I'll be right back," says Paul, who puts on glasses, walks to the maître d' station and starts flipping pages in a leather ledger book. "What ... day ... is this? ... Oh yes. Here we are. Well, it's pretty open tonight, but busy later on, around eight-thirty."

"How about eight?" asks Mrs. Hamptons.

"Eight it is. Name?"

"Hamptons."

"Very good, Mrs. Hamptons," says Paul, writing it all down in the ledger. "Oh, and how are the drinks? Mr. Hamptons?"

Mr. Hamptons sighs and takes a drink of his beer.

"It's beer. What can you say about a beer? Can you bring over the dinner menu? I want to know what I'm going to have tonight, and also how much you people jack up the dinner prices."

"Oh LOOK!" Mrs. Hamptons squeals, then giggles, her eyes keenly peeled on something happening across the dining room.

Two men are finishing lunch; one of them folds his napkin and stands up to leave, the other rises with him, and they are kissing goodbye.

"KISSY KISSY!" squeals Mrs. Hamptons again.

The men hear her, but finish their much more interesting kiss.

Paul pulls a couple of dinner menus out from under the ledger book and starts back to the Hamptons table. "Reservations for Hamptons, table for two, at eight o'clock!" he announces in the late afternoon peacefulness, cool jazz muzak of the bar.

Mr. Hamptons snatches the menu without thanking or even looking up at Paul, who walks back to the kitchen, talking to himself.

"I have reservations, too," he says.

Red's Alert

I hit the brakes.

Loose change, empty coffee-colored Starbucks cups all the way from California, Colorado, and Kansas, everyone in the van, and all three dogs slid toward the front.

We stopped near the Union Station, in front of the Crown Center Hotel, at the curb of Washington Square Park, George Washington up on his bronze horse, looking down on us. Or down on me. Even his horse's head was bowed, knowing George Washington couldn't lie, but that maybe I *had* been, at least by omission, and that my lying had been bugging me since Lawrence, even Colorado, probably California. My dishonesty was not news to George and his horse, and they were giving me the "evil eye."

Which is what had made me hit the brakes.

"I've been lying to you," I said—*out loud.*

No one said a word; I thought this must be a shock, a disappointment to everyone in the van. Silence. A pedestrian skywalk connecting the hotel to the train station was just above the van. I saw families in holiday clothes walking through there, kids running, moms and dads smiling after them, going to their room, the pool, the movies, lunch, shopping, wherever—a wherever I'd never been any part of, as a kid, and never would, as a dad. But I thought I'd finally found *my* wherever, these people behind me in the van, I'd felt it finally, strongly, in Lawrence. I'd felt it up until this moment, and now I was worried that telling them the truth would shut me out alone again. Back in the basement.

"I'm sorry everybody, I'm not really a real detective."

Silence. But I saw a flicker of movement in the corner of my eye; Kansas and Missouri had crawled and squeezed (and slid, from my sudden braking) to the front, sitting on the floor in the space between Rosalita and me. My loyal dog friends, they'd stick with me.

But the dogs weren't looking at me. They were gazing in wonder behind me.

Cocking their heads, left, right. Left again. I turned around and saw what they were gazing at, something maybe inscrutable to them, but not to me.

Because what they saw were the wonderfully funny (though to the dogs, probably *strained*-looking) human faces of my friends trying not to laugh—*out loud.*

Which *is* a strain, until the laughing starts, and it did. Loud enough that the van seemed to be rocking left and right, like the dogs' heads, people on the sidewalks and in the park watching us.

I was laughing too, relieved, but then something *else* layered itself onto my many-layered brain. Rosalita saw that, tried to stop laughing ... breathe ... and speak.

At last, she got there.

"Now *listen*, Red ... " but then she started laughing again, composed herself, and continued, "... we're not laughing because we don't think you *could* be a detective if you wanted to be one. And I, for one, think you've had many detective-*esque* moments on this trip. We're laughing to think you'd worry that *we'd* take that so seriously."

"Exactly," said Fyodor. "Anyway, I think we already knew."

"And anyway, you're something better than just some detective, and I've known a few," said Officer Serge Controllente, from somewhere in the van.

"Aw Red, it's true, it's *true* we *knew*," Ruby was singing again, "either way, we *do* love *you!*"

"Hurray for pocho!" yelled Alberto, from right behind me, right in my *ear.*

"You're *Red Jumbo,*" said Rosie. "Anything else is just some job title."

This felt good, of course.

I looked up at George Washington, who said, in a relaxed yet statuesque way, *"See?* See what happens when you *tell the truth?"*

The horse nodded.

Astronauts, aliens, and animals

The dogs started barking like crazy. They seemed to be barking at something in the sky, but it was in the sky*walk*; a bunch of very small dogs running loose through the tube into the hotel.

I got out of the van. "I'm going to walk Kansas and Missouri. Felix? You wanna come, too?"

I walked the dogs into the park and let them off-leash to prowl and pee; they prowled all the way to the fence edge of the park where the railroad tracks cut through downtown Kansas City, started to pee, but when a heavy, red-rusty freight train came earthquaking down the tracks, the dogs ran for the van in a stampede! (In my head, I heard wild banjo music as a soundtrack to the stampede.) We all got back in the van, I looked up at the skywalk.

"Look at this thing. It's like science fiction, isn't it? Cities of glass tubes connecting ... and ..." I stopped. A couple had walked into the tube.

"There they are," Rosie said; she saw them too, walking into the tube from the Union Station side, on the way to the hotel. Both of them staggering a little.

"There they are," agreed Alberto.

"So, they're here," said Ruby.

"I wondered where they were," said Fyodor.

"And look where they're coming from," I said. "Is Roscoe working today?"

Rosie pulled out her phone, dialing.

We watched the Hamptons walk out of the tube and gone, into the hotel.

"Roscoe? Hi."

We all waited, listening to Roscoe's Volkswagen voice on the phone. I was looking at the end of the tube where the Hamptons had gone.

"Yes, we're here, in front of Crown Center, close to Union Station. Where are you? Are you at work ..."

A chain of children came into the skywalk from the hotel side, walking (some of them hopping!) in line, holding hands, all in Halloween costumes; astronauts, aliens, and animals, crossing overhead one by one into Union Station. It was one of the sweetest sights I'd seen in months.

"... because we just saw—oh ok, good, see you in a few minutes," said Rosie, ending the call. She looked at me. "Bryant's Barbeque, Mr. Jumbo, step on it."

I turned the key, turned us downtown, came to 18th Street and turned east.

It had been a long time since I'd been to Bryant's, but I knew the way, knew all the low, red brick buildings along the way.

"Rosie, you haven't seen Roscoe since Briar Patch, right?" I asked.

"Yes. The last time was on his release day. Out on the front steps, just before he walked down to the bus stop. He kept waving back at me, *'Bye Rosie! See you later, someday, maybe ...'* "

"And here we are," I said.

"And here we are," said Rosie.

A mile doesn't take long and *there it was.*

The red brick building on Brooklyn, the big red *Bryant's Barbeque* sign, the red and white awning under that, and under that, there *he* was. I knew it was him. Roscoe.

Big and friendly as the building, hands on his hips, he wore a bright white shirt and a black and white horizontally-pinstriped wool vest, so that he looked like the front page of a newspaper, hot off the press! Deep furrows across his forehead like the bold black lines of a musical staff, he had eyes (light brown, golden-*glowing* in the sun) that looked like they were coming from the top of a high mountain, seeing just about everything from that high and far away, and a smile that looked like Christmas morning, or something else festive and rascally. And like the building, he was also flashing some red, from big red cufflinks. He started waving with both hands up off his hips as he saw us drive up, Rosie waving back from out her window.

The man knew all of our names as we eased out of the van.

"Red Jumbo! You look good! Healthy. *Better* ... Fyodor, sir, welcome. I love Russian novels! We'll talk about that later ... And *you* must be Ruby, welcome to Kansas City ... Serge, OFFICER Controllente! You look like a rib man! Got 'em right inside ... Alberto, my man. So good to finally meet you. Heard a lot about you."

Roscoe shook hands with Alberto, then he saw Rosie. He hugged her for a long time, backed up a few steps, and took a good look at her, his eyes twinkling with tears.

"Hello, Rosalita, my friend. It's *so* good to see you again."

I didn't really remember Roscoe, but I liked him right away. I had liked him on the phone, in my imagination, and I liked him a lot, in person.

"I can't believe you're all here," he said, "I'm so *happy*, so glad you're all here. It's all gonna be alright, now."

The man was an emotional cup runneth over, and maybe a bottomless cup, at that.

He put an arm around Alberto. "Alberto, as an old friend of mine *Stacy* used to say: *'Everything gonna be alright!'* I met Stacy up on Hospital Hill here in Kansas City, when we worked together in a hospital—I worked in the morgue, Stacy was a janitor—and one night I was a *patient* in that hospital for a stab wound, just before I came out to California, about a month before I got clean. I came in that night bloody, and Stacy, my man from *Environmental Services*, came and mopped *me* up. He *cheered* me up!"

Roscoe laughed and hugged Rosie and Alberto together, lovingly, like he was marrying them! He hugged each of us intimately, individually, though it felt like he was hugging all of us at the same time, blessing us, however he pulled *that* off. I don't know if that's what he intended, probably not, but it *is* how it felt. I bet we all felt that way about Roscoe's welcome. He was one friendly and, I found out later, *poetic* guy.

We walked into Bryant's Barbeque.

Arthur Bryant's Barbeque

What a room! I'd forgotten. Dull, really; white walls and tables, red chairs, a TV turned on up by the ceiling, the kitchen at the other end; this was the famous Bryant's Barbeque.

But *something* was always happening in there.

Something was happening down in that kitchen. Black men and one woman, in red hats and shirts and green aprons smiling back at us like Christmas morning. (Here it was again, twice in a few minutes, my Christmas morning fixation, seeing Christmas in happy moments, imagining Christmas morning, don't know why, I didn't have many happy ones as a boy. Maybe that's why. I'm still looking for it, everywhere.)

We were in line, under the lit-up menu, the men and one woman looking at us, waiting, their hands on their hips or on lush red piles of beef and pork. A simple menu, in black and white and red letters, but we *studied* it.

Roscoe and I were the first in line, Ruby and Fyodor right behind us, Alberto and Rosie behind them, then Serge, and behind *him,* a pair of leathered-up Black men carrying motorcycle helmets. Everyone's lips moving, and salivating, as they read the menu. Bikers, too.

"By the way, Red, someone will be joining us," said Roscoe. "I've got a friend coming."

"Oh yeah? *Oh yes*—" I said, shifting my attention from Roscoe to a saucy plate going by, then to the order window, "—I'll have the pork sandwich and fries, *thanks!* So, who's the friend?"

Roscoe didn't answer, he was looking at the men in the kitchen, their hands on the meat, their eyes on something behind us.

I turned around and back there, in the front door, I saw *someone* —in a bright white pantsuit and a tall, wide, white sailboat of a hat. Under the white hat, she wore white-framed glasses with cool-blue-tinted lenses, a white jacket with wide lapels, and a tall collar that ridged up around her face, while down the jacket a line of buttons like small snowballs led to her silky white pants, flowing all around her feet, in white leather boots!

"There she is. *That*, Red, is Aunt Arctica," said Roscoe, in obvious awe.

Ruby and I looked at each other. *"Aunt Arctica,"* we whispered.

Everyone was dazzled, staring at Aunt Arctica, bikers, too. She was looking at me.

"Hello, hello, hello all—and are *you* Red Jumbo?" Aunt Arctica was in front of me in a *white flash*; long, bright white hair, a silver, twinkling touch of makeup, and a fresh, clean scent ... like an evening of snow on the way. She had a wide smile and deep dimples, long lines in her cheeks, full of tiny blue and green sparkles; I thought she was a bit older than me, maybe closer to seventy. I looked up into the clearest, bluest (even with her blue-tinted glasses now taken off), most *alive* eyes I'd ever seen. "Roscoe told me you're the man with the plan."

"Well—hi. Aunt Arctica."

"You can call me Auntie."

"Ok. And yes, I am Red. But I think I'm just the man with the *van.*"

We shook hands. A warm, strong hand coming from all the frosty, gleaming white.

She squinted at me. "I think you're more than that, Red. Roscoe told me a little about *you*. I understand you come from a long line of Jumbos."

I gulped. "Well, it *is* a long line."

"Uh-huh," said Aunt Arctica. "That's what they all say. So, Mr. Jumbo, you're the man with the van that brought Rosalita all the way here, brought her back to life again, from her fake death, and away from some—*motherfuckers?*—can we safely say that's what they are? And which one of you is Rosalita? I want to meet *her.*" Fyodor happened to be right next to her, so she looked at him. "Not you, I guess?" But they shook hands.

Rosie walked up to Aunt Arctica from the back of the line with her hand out. Auntie took it, and shook it.

"You're Rosalita?" she smiled.

"I am. And yes, they *are* motherfuckers."

There was the general sound of uh-HUH from Alberto, Fyodor, Ruby, and Serge, and the men and the woman behind the counter laughed conspiratorially. They couldn't know what they were conspiring in (or could they?), but they were definitely *with* Aunt Arctica, in anything. Obviously, Aunt Arctica had been to Bryant's before.

She put her glasses back on, making her eyes *double blue.*

I put *my* sunglasses on, to contribute to the style and drama of the moment.

"Hungry?" Auntie asked Rosie.

"Oh yes." We all said, one way or another.

"This is all on me," she said, walking past me, putting her face in the order window. "We'll have a couple of the meat trays, a couple of slabs, coleslaw, bake beans, potato salad, a pint of pickles, anybody want sandwiches?" she turned to us, *counted* us, "oh give us a smattering of beef and pork sandwiches, ten total, make it *twelve*, in case someone needs a midnight snack, *extra* sauce, and uh—those two guys in the back—?" The bikers pointed at themselves with leather fingers, *us?* "—whatever they're having. And, uh ... beer anyone? I mean not *some* of us, but anyone else? You guys wanna try the Boulevard Pale, believe me! So, *Bytha*—" she was down the line to the woman at the cash register, and they hugged as much of each other as they could, both squeezing through the window "—Bytha, we'll take a pitcher of beer and a pitcher of iced tea—lemon please —and how the hell *are* you, anyway?"

Bytha and Aunt Arctica talked a little, while the rest of us carried the pitchers of beer and iced tea out to a long Formica table under the big black and white framed photograph of Count Basie playing piano, and—at the end of the table, out the window—the Kansas City skyline. The Kansas City skyline ... *and* ... the dog-eared skyline of Kansas, Missouri, and Felix looking at us, from the van.

"Oh shit!" I jumped up, as our plates and slabs and racks and sauces began to arrive, via the *entire staff* of Bryant's.

"Not to worry," said Aunt Arctica, her hand on my shoulder, "sit down, *eat,* and let me have your car keys, Red. I saw those cuties on the way in, saw the California plates, and knew they had to be part of the gang. I've ordered some burnt ends and some fresh bowls of water for them. I'll help, and we'll take it out to 'em, yeah, guys?" she asked them respectfully, twisting arms, charmingly.

One of the guys, laying a long rack of ribs in the middle of the table, flanking it with a reddish-brown squirt bottle of sauce, looked out the window, and said, "yeah ... we could, *or ...*"

"Bring 'em in here?" winked Aunt Arctica, marinating the moment, playfully.

"Bring 'em in here," one of the other guys confirmed.

"Most definitely," said yet another guy. "After all, this is *Bryant's,* man."

"Car keys, Mr. Jumbo?" Aunt Arctica stood over me, hand out. I coughed up the keys. I looked at her, and at these *great guys,* these chefs of barbecue.

"Thanks, Auntie,*"* I said, "thanks, fellas. I mean, is this Kansas City or *France*, letting the dogs in? Thanks a lot, *everybody."*

The fellas laughed. "It's not France!" yelled Bytha, from the cash register.

"Not really Kansas City, either," said Aunt Arctica. "But it *is* Bryant's Barbeque."

A minute or two later we heard the crazed clicking of dogs running, skidding, and stopping at every spot on the floor with even a memory of spilled sauce. They skidded to our long table, and under it, to their plates and bowls.

We ate.

Come slither

Mr. Hamptons sits on the toilet feeling dull and mid-afternoon drunk, listening to Mrs. Hamptons snoring in bed in the other room, and tries to enliven his fantasy from the glass hotel elevator.

He tries to remember it—sometime a couple of hours earlier in the afternoon, coming back to the Crown Center Hotel from the Union Station Bar. He remembers that Mrs. Hamptons had gone ahead of him while he went to the lobby men's room, then he took an elevator up alone. But not alone. There was a young woman, and he thinks maybe he had talked to her.

He had.

He thinks she had a tiny baby girl in a stroller, and that he might have flirted with that little girl on the way up, innocently, of course.

He did.

He had moved to their side of the elevator, moved close, made baby talk down on his knees with the little baby girl, maybe two years old, then stood up, breathing alcohol into the face of the young woman in a corner of the elevator, baby looking up from her stroller.

"You have your mama's pretty lips," he'd said, looking down at the baby girl, who was beginning to cry.

The woman stopped him instantly, put her hand on his chest and shoved hard, which shot him across the elevator, the back of his head slamming into the glass wall on the other side.

Mr. Hamptons remembers sliding down the glass onto the floor, laughing, saying, "C'mon pretty girl, I came to Kansas City and I'm about to become a millionaire all over again, so play with me, ok? I just wanna play! See—?" And when he said "See—?" he tried to pull his penis out of his pants, but jamming his zipper with his shirttail.

He remembers right.

What Mr. Hamptons doesn't remember is that the woman was long gone by then.

In the bathroom, Mr. Hamptons reaches into his underpants, grabs his penis, and rubs and strokes himself, getting harder and hornier. Losing his train of thought, he grabs a wine bottle off the sink, drinks, pours wine on his penis, drops the bottle on the floor, smells his hand, and masturbates.

He laughs again, like in the elevator, and says, "Fuck, baby, I just wanna playyy."

He hears snoring, tries to stand up, pushing with his free hand on the toilet, then on the sink, he's up and staggers into the bathroom door, the chrome robe hook just missing his eyes. Still holding onto his penis. Laughing and masturbating.

He turns off the bathroom light and pulls the door open—almost falls backwards into the bathtub—and staggers out into the dim gray darkness of the hotel room, the curtains drawn tight shut. He focuses on Mrs. Hamptons on the bed, still in her clothes, face down in the sheets. He sways, stumbles to the bed, steps out of his underpants and pulls off his shirt.

Looking at the back of his wife's head but trying to see those lips in the elevator, he jerks himself hard, fast, slobbery breathing bubbling in his mouth hanging open, drooling down his belly and penis.

Mrs. Hamptons turns over, pulls a leg up in the sheets, and yawns.

Mr. Hamptons arches his back, looking up into the spinning ceiling, and comes—all over her. A lot of it in her hair. He's all done, looking for someplace to lie down. She's waking up.

Besides her hair, there's a big glob of his semen on her cheek.

"There's something on my face," says Mrs. Hamptons, blinking. "What is it?"

"Some of your lunch," he says, lying down, his back to her.

"Oh fuck you, my lunch. Wipe it off, whatever it is."

"You're a slob when it comes to eating, you know. You got drunk, sloppy drunk, I did too, but still—I've always thought that about you. For years. I can't even look at you when I eat."

"Just get it off. If it's some of my lunch, you can just eat it off me."

He ignores that, and lies down. They fall asleep.

Off leash

I leaned back and looked around; everyone's food—the ribs, the sandwiches, the saucy slabs, even the generous piles of brown and golden french fries that had looked like little Van Gogh haystacks all over the table—all of that was *leveled*.

We were so satisfied we couldn't speak. We were probably glowing!

"This is *my place*," said Roscoe.

"Mine too, believe it or not," said Aunt Arctica, taking a long swallow of iced tea.

"I know it," said Roscoe.

"Well, I thought maybe I don't look the type."

"Auntie, I knew it the first time we met, *right here in Bryant's*," said Roscoe, looking around at us. "She was a couple of people behind me in line, and we struck up a conversation. Been pals, since!"

"You don't look like *any* one particular type to me, Auntie," said Rosalita.

Aunt Arctica's sudden, sparkling smile looked like an alpine sunrise. "Where are all of you staying this evening?" she asked.

We all looked at each other, but we didn't know.

Aunt Arctica leaned back. She put on her blue-tinted glasses.

"Why don't you all come to my place?" she said. "I have a *large* house. Well, I'll admit it, it's probably a mansion. Ten spacious bedrooms, maybe more, bathrooms *en suite*, and that's just upstairs. Big well-stocked kitchen, we can do some communal dining, breakfast and dinners! Very close to Loose Park, you could walk these sweet doggies there, but it's not off-leash, but then not too much is off-leash in this part of the country. But my huge backyard *is* off-leash. Of course, inside my house is off-leash as well, if you know what I mean. *Inside.* No rules. No borders. In every imaginable way."

I looked over at Fyodor, Ruby, and Serge ... Rosie and Alberto were smiling at each other; this seemed to really touch them. We all knew what Aunt Arctica meant.

"This is so nice of you, Auntie," I said. "But we don't want to interrupt, or, *intrude*."

"No no, it's a *large* house. You can all spread out and have privacy. I'm on a massive lot, lots of trees, two gazebos, little pebble pathways, places to go off and be alone, reflect, and so forth."

"That sounds good, your mansion," said Rosie. "After being out on the road."

"And I have a big old *long* table, in my big old *wide* kitchen. Guillaume brought it over from the south of France, from his father's farm out in the countryside. Perfect for all of us to sit around and talk. We have a lot to talk about. But first, let's get you all back to my place."

I was loving this woman. We all were, all smiling and gazing at this woman. What a surprise at the end of the trail in Kansas City.

"Roscoe, you have your car here, or do you wanna ride with me?" asked Aunt Arctica, standing up.

"My car's around the back. They let me come in through the kitchen door. I'm like part of the family here."

"Shall we caravan, Auntie, with you two in the lead?" I asked.

"Yes. What do you think, Roscoe, Troost Avenue? To 55th Street, then I'll turn right, *west,* over to Loose Park, past Pennsylvania Avenue a few blocks. You know my place."

"Sure, but why Troost?" asked Roscoe.

"Feels symbolic. It's *still* the boundary in Kansas City, isn't it? The dividing line?"

"Yeah, Auntie, that it is. White people to the west, a lot of the rest of us over here east of Troost. *Still.*"

"And this—*project*—why you all came here together in Red's van, is about a sort of *un*dividing, am I right? In that spirit. Kind of, *hands across the water?"* Aunt Arctica paused and looked around the table at us all. "This is so nice. Shall we go?"

She led us out to the van (saw my bumper sticker, said: *You like the Beatles, too, eh?*) and Roscoe went through the kitchen towards his car, out back. The *Bryant's* men and Bytha waved us big smiling goodbyes.

"I think we're gonna have some fun," said Aunt Arctica, gracefully sliding down into her icy blue MG sports car, racing the engine.

"Where's Roscoe?" I said, wondering, scanning the alley and Bryant's parking lot. "I wonder what he's driving?"

"He's a big guy, I'm guessing it'll be a big *car* to stretch out in," said Ruby. "Let's wait for him."

Aunt Arctica was waiting, but revving. A little red and black Smart car came out of the alley and rolled up, tucking in behind the MG. It was Roscoe, waving and tooting the horn.

"Wow, that's a *small* car," said Rosie.

"Yeah," laughed Ruby. "It's like he's wearing it!"

We all jumped into the van because now Roscoe was revving. Aunt Arctica was quick in her zippy little car, but Roscoe stayed behind her and we stayed behind him.

Down Troost Avenue—low red brick buildings, storefronts of vacuum cleaner repair shops, barber shops, Taco Bell and Texaco, a bar and then another, and another, churches and liquor stores, more low brick buildings, and some taller ones, hopeless looking apartment complexes—then right on 55th Street, into the Country Club District. Large, tall houses and even taller trees fanning out a *deep blue-green shade;* it was calmer and cooler here. Aunt Arctica slowed down and waved for us to look and see: Loose Park; a long, rolling oasis of trees and ponds and people and kids and ducks and dogs, and our dogs leapt on the windows, barking wildly.

We turned right and left and left again and then we were at Aunt Arctica's house. It had a gate, but it was open; there was an intercom box, but the wires were hanging out of it.

The house was massive, looked like four stories high, but I wasn't sure about that because it kept climbing and winding and layering up in eccentric angles into tall pine trees that soared even higher. There were windows all over the house, different sizes, openings, like friendly *eyes*, it seemed to me, watching us drive up the driveway—saying: *come on in!*

That's what *I* saw anyway, it had been a long, long drive.

Aunt Arctica parked her MG, and a big, bright-white dog flew out the front door of the house, which had just opened by itself. Or so I thought. Behind the dog appeared a short, round man with black *black* hair, a white *white* mustache, and heavy white eyebrows, dressed in all white.

The dog was on the way to us, the man was on his way to Aunt Arctica and he kissed her. They talked for a moment, the friendly dog was all over the van, licking the windshield (so friendly I had to use the wipers) trying to get in Rosalita's window, and the man walked over and said, "I am Guillaume. Welcome. I must go. A new sauce this evening. I will see you tonight or in the morning. Goodbye."

"This is my special friend, everybody. He comes over every other night or so, pretty much lives with me now. He'll be moving in soon. Guillaume is a chef down on the Country Club Plaza, opens and closes the restaurant, it's his, he owns it, runs it ... also, he has a key to my house. And he knows which bedroom is *mine.*"

Guillaume smiled quickly, started away, but Roscoe wandered up from his car. The two looked at each other.

"Are you Roscoe?"

"Yes, hello. I *am* Roscoe."

214

"Enchanté. I am Guillaume. But I must go prepare now. Something new, a velouté sauce, with a twist, all my own! I am so nervous to get it precise. I'm sure you understand, being a bartender. I've heard about you, from chèrie. I *go*, but maybe I see you later tonight. Maybe we come in at the same time. A cup of cocoa in the kitchen, perhaps? As a nightcap." He turned and was off to an old Mercedes, parked farther down along the circle drive. He motored away.

We were all out of the van and together, we backed up a few steps into the yard to look at the house, to take it all in. I felt peaceful, happy, ready to move right into Aunt Arctica's mansion. Something about this place had me feeling right *at home*; I was wondering if it was something about a past life, the more regal one I must have lived sometime, *at least* once before.

I must have said something *out loud*.

"You can move right in, Red," said Aunt Arctica. "Welcome, all of you."

There was so much house to look at, and we kept looking at it.

"Great house, isn't it?" asked Auntie. "My grandfather was in on the start of the Kansas City Southern Railroad, *in on it* in a big way, I'd guess, from the size of this place. I don't know much about what my grandfather did or what my father continued when he took his place in the company—as a woman, like my mother and grandmother, we didn't get much information, we were supposed to, you know—*know our places*—but then, speaking of places, I got *this* place!"

We all laughed at this very extended bit of wordplay.

"I'll give you a little tour, and then get you into your rooms," said Auntie.

"Um, Auntie," began Ruby, carefully, "I take it the family name is not, um, *Arctica?*"

Aunt Arctica laughed out loud *so loud* she lost her hat! Somehow she'd kept it on even in that little ragtop MG (with the rag down), but now it was off, rolling down the driveway, and all her white-blonde hair came flying free (hat off, we saw her wild blonde flares).

"No—*Ruby Taillights*—it's not the family name, that's for sure! Now look, we can go in and scout around for rooms to all your individual tastes and quirks of personality—and I see a van-load of those here!—or maybe you want to look from here and point up to whichever window or even what *floor* intrigues you?"

"Yes, well, *I* like that little window up near the chimney, tucked in behind that huge Douglas fir," said Serge.

"All yours, officer," said Auntie.

"Auntie, this second-floor room, looking out over your garden, *that* one looks cozy to me," said Rosie. "What do you think, Alberto?"

"Rosie, *si,* very cozy, I agree."

"That's a nice room in the morning. Take it, you two. You'll get a lot of the old *el sol*, por la mañana!"

"Good for the *soul!*" beamed Alberto.

"Bueno para el alma, si," nodded Auntie.

"I like that window way up on top," said Roscoe.

"A nice long attic room, all knotty pine walls, yes, a good room, my grandfather's getaway, I'm told. With a view over the park and all the way to downtown. You'll be the closest to the moon up there tonight, Roscoe. What about you guys? Red? Fyodor? Ruby? Hey, where are your dogs?"

I looked and saw that they were running with Auntie's dog into a long, fenced-in meadow, around the side of the house. Running and leaping in happy arcs, like goats.

"My dog's name is *Bipolar*, by the way. Polar, for the continuing Icelandic motif, and *bi*, because I think he goes both ways!"

She picked up her hat and walked to the front door. We got our luggage out of Morrison.

We walked toward the front door, I was trying to select a room from all the windows flirting various mysterious settings and moods and scenes inside the house, and my phone went off. I knew who it was. Or, I hoped I did. I looked at the phone, and I was right!

"Jenny Sue Skiptewmaylewe! Hello! Well—let me *tell* you where I am, you'll never believe it!"

I heard Aunt Arctica's laughter echo in the huge foyer.

Mama is gone

The Hamptons, asleep downtown in the Crown Center Hotel, lying on their backs, mouths wide open, vending machine candy bar wrappers and open wine bottles on the bedside tables, air conditioning on full blast.

Their room is like the inside of a musty refrigerator with the light bulb out.

Mr. Hamptons pants and underpants are down around his shoes, still on his feet. Mrs. Hamptons has a thumb in her mouth—her other hand is on Mr. Hamptons hand, his other hand is holding his balls and penis—and she's talking in her sleep.

"Mmmmama ... mammma," she moans with the thumb in her mouth, loudly licking and smacking her lips around it. "Mmmam— maaa." She moans and moans, seems about to cry, jerks suddenly awake, squeezes Mr. Hamptons hand, and his other hand squeezes his penis, hard.

"OHWOWOWWW!" he yells, rolling out of bed, struggling, his feet handcuffed by his pants.

"What, Mama? Where are you?" cries Mrs. Hamptons, kicking the sheets off. She sits up in bed, sees Mr. Hamptons, and Mama is gone.

"Ok, ok ... well, we better wake up and get ready, anyway," she says, pulling a comb out of her purse on the floor. "Get back down to that bar."

"What time is it? When's our reservation?"

"Eight. It's not even six yet."

"So we'll be early. Come on, get up out of that bed."

"OK, ok," says Mrs. Hamptons, getting up, over to the bathroom mirror, applying red lipstick. She puckers at herself in the mirror, wipes off some excess red with a toilet tissue, and laughs.

Mr. Hamptons yawns and looks at Mrs. Hamptons in the bathroom mirror looking back at him; she drops her lipstick on the sink.

"Though I guess a little nap before wouldn't hurt," he says. "It is early. We'll get there when we get there."

She turns off the bathroom light, slumps smiling out of the bathroom, and falls back in bed. He undoes his shirt, drops it to the floor, and rolls back in with her.

She pours out the end of a bottle of wine into a pair of plastic hotel cups, hands one to him.

"Little nightcap?" she says.

"Or nap*cap," he laughs, coughs, wheezes, drinks, and swallows, all loudly.*

"I've always loved your sense of humor. I've always told people that you're witty!" says Mrs. Hamptons, tickling his belly, her fingers getting into something sticky.

The air conditioning downshifts to off; it's cold, silent, and dark in their hotel room, they fall asleep. For all her attention at the bathroom mirror, there's still a spot of his cum on her cheek.

The marijuana train

After a long tour of the basement, corridors and tunnels flying off in all directions, walking on uneven cobblestone and rough brick floors, Aunt Arctica led us up clanging black iron stairs to a long, *Lake Tahoe blue*-carpeted grand stair that flowed up to a smaller circular wooden stair that creaked higher and higher to the top floor.

Up there, I chose the highest room, at the end of a hall on the top floor; a massive white brick fireplace across the entire wall opposite the wall of windows looking out over Loose Park, a steeply vaulted ceiling, and a black bearskin rug on the floor, the head still on, and facing us—*growling* at us—as we all walked in.

We all jumped, all but Aunt Arctica.

"I know," she said, noticing Rosalita frowning at the bear rug, "I don't approve of it either, killing animals, *any* animals—to tell you the truth, I wish the bear had won—but Granddad shot him first. Still, it lends a certain rugged atmosphere to the room, I suppose. Will it be a problem for you, Red?"

"No, not at all," I said. "Though I wouldn't have shot him, either. Him or *her*. I like bears. I have a stuffed bear from childhood that I'm particularly fond of, from a London toy store. I still have him, brought him with me."

Aunt Arctica smiled and walked over to me. "Aren't you some sort of a detective? Isn't there shooting sometimes?"

"I was *almost* a detective, for a couple of days. I gave it a try. I began with Rosalita's murder case. But she turned out to be alive, and now we're friends. But there never *was* a gun."

I was looking out the windows at Loose Park, but I knew Aunt Arctica was looking at me. I could feel her smile.

"A London toy store?"

"Yeah. My dad got a big promotion and his company transferred him to London, right around Christmas. The teddy bear was my first Christmas present in England, but my father died two months later, so that was our last Christmas in London. My mother brought us back to the states, eventually here, to Kansas City. Near here, actually."

It got quiet, so I looked down at the black bear rug, but it was looking somewhere else.

"I'm sorry, Red," said Aunt Arctica, touching my arm. *"So ..."* she shifted gears, brightening, "...when was the turning point, Red? Was there a moment when you knew the detective life wasn't for you?"

"It happened today, downtown, outside Crown Center. I came face to face with George Washington, and his horse."

"Yes, I know the park. Sort of a moment of *truth* then, literally?"

"Exactly. But by trying to be a detective, I got to meet Rosalita, and all the rest of you—and, of course, *you*, Aunt Arctica," I said.

"Not to mention Jenny Sue Skiptewmaylewe," said Fyodor, with a chorus of *Yeahs!* and one *I'll say!*

"She's invited too, Red," said Aunt Arctica. "I heard the way you talked with her on the phone downstairs ..." (I may have blushed right there, when she said that) "... but let's go on with the tour." I threw my travel bags and jacket on the huge bed. The bags bounced.

"Yeah, Red, you'll *like* that bed," said Auntie. "You and Miss Skiptewmaylewe. If that isn't too forward of me."

"How many rooms are there in this house, anyway?" asked Alberto, wide-eyed.

"Who knows, Alberto, fifty maybe, including all the bathrooms. I was never here all that much as a girl, being sent off to camps and schools and various family-related houses to *summer,* as they used to say. I'm still discovering rooms and even whole *wings* in this place if you can believe that!"

We walked down the hall, twisting this way and that, and came to an open door emitting a rich red glow out into the hallway.

"What's this one?" asked Ruby.

"Allow me," said Auntie, flipping a switch near the door, which turned on the sound of a locomotive, starting up. We looked into the room, into the red light, and *up*—to a model train getting up steam on a track running along the walls near the ceiling. The train ran around in a square, going faster and faster through toy towns and trees along the tracks, a bright beam of light coming out of a light in the engine, and throwing up thick plumes of smoke. The plumes shot up, settled, then drifted down into the room.

We watched, then we *coughed.*

"What is that, is *that*—?" asked Ruby, and answered.

"Yes, it's *that*," said Auntie. "This is Guillaume's room, his QUOTE, *study.*"

I couldn't stop coughing, but I was trying; I wanted to hear her explanation for this, or *that,* coming out of a *model train.*

"The man loves his marijuana, and he's smoked it every which way you can— joints, pipes, bongs, hookahs. But he wanted to devise a way to smoke it without the work; the rolling and the lighting, and so forth. So we invented a hands-free way to smoke, combining pot with his model train hobby."

"Wow!" inhaled Ruby.

"Go on," coaxed Officer Serge, officially, but grinning.

"Well, inside the train's engine is a device we concocted using a flint and lighter fluid—just like a Zippo lighter inside—and the toy coal car behind the engine has a supply of marijuana which moves through a tube into the engine, lights, and puffs up through the smokestack. Guillaume comes in here, flips the switch, sits down, and goes for a ride."

Aunt Arctica, finished with her presentation, quickly stepped out into the hall and turned to us for a reaction, but we could barely see each other. Rosie and Roscoe and I followed Auntie into the hall, coughing, but out of range. We couldn't see Fyodor and Ruby, Serge and Alberto, but we could hear them coughing—and by the sound of the deep inhaling—really *savoring* the smoke.

"I'm off *that* train for good, know what I mean?" said Roscoe laughing, clearing his throat.

"Me too," agreed Rosalita. "That train has left the station!"

"I should turn it off," said Auntie. "It's getting a little thick in there."

"I'll turn it off!" Ruby piped up, appearing in the thick red fog, eager to assist, *lingering* at the switch.

"Thank you, Ruby. I do enjoy that fragrance. Let's finish the tour." Aunt Arctica looked up and down the hall, like she was trying to remember something. We waited for her lead, very lost in her massive maze of a mansion.

Then she walked down the hall to a small Chagall hanging on the wall.

There was a red button and a black button by the painting, both shiny and grimy. "Here goes," she said, and pushed the red button.

The wallpaper moved to the left, revealing a faintly-lit elevator car, flickering, with a weak fan humming above.

"Shall we?" invited Auntie. "Climb in!"

"All of us? All (I counted) eight of us?"

"Can it hold us all?" asked Rosie.

"Let's find out! *Ready?*"

We gradually got in, the elevator gradually dropped an inch or two, and we flickered and hummed downstairs.

The Elevator Epiphany

It was a slow, quiet ride, except for the flickering and humming. We were quiet in the beginning moments of the descent; I think we could all sense the slow side-to-side sway of the elevator car, bumping the sides of the elevator shaft.

"I like your house, Aunt Arctica!" said Alberto, with sudden, ice-breaking exuberance.

"Oh yeah, it's fantastic!" said Fyodor.

"Quite impressive," said Serge.

"You live in such eccentric luxury!"—Rosie.

"I could move in!"—Roscoe.

"*Can* we move in?"—Ruby.

I was feeling a strong wind of comforting romantic imagination blowing through me, being in Auntie's house.

"I feel like I've lived here before," I said.

Aunt Arctica turned, shuffled a step, craned her neck, and focused on me through all the heads in the elevator. "Truly?" she asked.

"Yes."

The elevator floated down a few more feet.

"Really?" asked Rosie.

"Yes," I said. Everyone was looking at me, and I wanted to explain it, but how? And could I? I took a moment, a breath, the elevator continued flickering and humming, and I cleared my head of stock phrases about reincarnation and cliches about past lives. I wanted to make it personal. I turned off all this thinking and started talking.

"Well, how should I say it? It's like I'm feeling a strong wind of comforting romantic imagination blowing through me." I liked the line in my head, so I took a chance with it in the elevator.

"Oh my, I *like* that," said Aunt Arctica.

"You said something like that out in Colorado one night," said Rosalita.

"Wow, let me write that down ..." said Ruby, "... Fyodor, do you have a scrap of paper?" as she started going through his jacket pockets.

"Can you elaborate on that, Red?" asked Aunt Arctica.

Roscoe periscoped his head over everyone and said, "Yeah man, go *on* with that!"

"Well, it's something very strong, kind of sweet—moving, for *me*—and it got me through my shitty childhood." This came out of me unprepared—unlike the line about the strong wind blowing in me —and I felt like I might cry. They were all looking at me, listening, waiting for me to go on. I was worried about stuttering, trying to get it all out, talking too fast if I spoke. But *fuck it*, I thought, and spoke.

"In a nutshell, I was alone, scared, attacked with constant criticism at home, violence at school. On a good day, I was ignored. So I'd hide. And while hiding, I had lavish, far-off, romantic fantasies about a life or lives before my shit childhood, and I *knew* that life ahead, later, somewhere else, sometime else, was going to be better than where I was."

The elevator swayed a few feet lower; it was quiet, soft smiles all around me.

"I lived by that," I said. "Still do. Even if it's a fantasy, a delusion, an illusion, a pretend life, it worked then, and still does. Why stop now?"

"Don't stop now, Red." Roscoe was with me.

"I think you mean imagination more than delusion." Ruby understood me.

"No way, pocho, don't stop, keep it *alive!*" Alberto was with me, too. "I have all sorts of laughing, bucking bronco, blue-sky movies in my head, but it keeps me happy and *peppy*, right, Rosie?"

"Yes, my love," smiled Rosie. "You keep *me* very happy and peppy."

Rosie, Auntie, and Ruby were passing Kleenex from Fyodor, who kept pulling more out of his jacket.

"Whether it's true or not," I said, "I've been here before. And I'm here now. Thank you, Auntie! Thanks, all of you."

The elevator landed—*hard*—the light went out, the fan stopped humming, and everyone but Aunt Arctica tumbled to the floor.

"Oh yeah," she said, in the dark. "I forgot to warn you about that."

Nooks and Crannies

The elevator door slid open to a view of a far kitchen wall of rough red uneven bricks and sagging shelves of spices, dark brown wooden beams leading up to more beams crossing a white wood plank ceiling, and through a low, wide door (also framed in rugged brown beams) we could see a long, wooden country table with loaves of bread, green-tinted carafes of bubbling water, newspapers, and in the center, a French flag and a vase of red roses.

"Mmm, that smells *good*," said Alberto. "The bread or the roses or both!"

"So, Aunt Arctica, are you French, too, on top of everything else?" I asked, from the elevator floor. None of us had stood up yet, taking in the view and the warm (bread!) aroma.

"Nope, that's Guillaume. I'm just a honky, like—well, like *you* Red! The rest of you are all the other spices, I'd say. What about you, Ruby?"

"I'm Jewish, Auntie!"

"Of course. Ruby Taillights. An old Yiddish name, I should've known!"

"Goes way back," laughed Ruby, still on her back.

"Well, I better get up and get myself together," said Roscoe. "I gotta get ready for work pretty soon."

"Cup of espresso, first?" asked Aunt Arctica. "For the road?"

"Sure! I'll just go check out my *suite*, ok? Be right back," said Roscoe, looking at various other doors in the kitchen, seemingly trying to figure out which way to go to get to his room. "Or, I'll just have a seat," he said, giving up, going through, and sitting down at the long table.

"Beautiful kitchen," said Serge, also still on the elevator floor. "And you're right, Alberto .... *nice smell!*"

"It *is*," said Fyodor. "How fresh *is* that bread?"

"Makes me hungry again," said Ruby, smiling, eyes closed. "I don't know how that's *possible*, after Bryant's ..."

"Oh, that bread, *mmm*," said Alberto.

"Shall we have some? Mi casa is *su* casa," said Auntie.

"It's a whole lotta casa!" laughed Rosalita, standing up.

"Thanks, Rosie. Make yourself at home, have a seat at the table."

We all emptied out of the elevator to join Roscoe at the table.

"Hey Roscoe, can *we* drive you to work?" I asked. "Me and Rosalita? I mean, if you *want* to go, Rosie."

Rosie nodded, "Mmm-*hmmm*. Oh yes, Red, I want to go."

"Well, *yeah*, Red. But somebody'd have to pick me up. I'll be closing tonight, won't get off until, maybe midnight, after I clean up the bar and ring out. I'm usually the last one out, so might be late."

"Guillaume could maybe come downtown and get you, if he gets finished first," yelled Aunt Arctica, over her excited, frothing espresso machine.

"Or *we* could come in a little later, have dinner, and wait for you," I said. "And then, if the Hamptons happen to come in for dinner, we could watch."

"Watch? You think they'll come in tonight?" asked Roscoe.

"We saw them going back to the hotel from Union Station, in that *tube* thing, the overhead walkway."

"The Link. Yeah. Ok. But there's a lot in Union Station. You think they were already snooping around for me?"

"They were *staggering* in the tube," said Rosie. "Are there any other bars in Union Station besides the Union Station Bar?"

"No. So if they'd been drinking, it could have only been in my bar. They know what I look like?" asked Roscoe.

Rosie shrugged. "They know you're the bartender, the Black bartender, unless there are other Black bartenders?"

"No, I'm it, for Black bartenders."

"They probably were snooping," said Rosie, "so they'll be likely to show up sometime, but *watch them*, Red? Do we wanna be seen yet?"

"I thought of that," I said. "But I think we need to get a bead on 'em—where they are in the hotel somehow, what they're doing—get a *read* on them."

"How do we do that?" Rosie asked.

I wish she hadn't asked *that*. I didn't know what to do. Or what the Hamptons were going to do. Or what was next. We all looked at each other, Aunt Arctica brought the espressos in.

"Maybe you and Rosalita could go in *disguise*," she suggested. "If I'm surmising right, that what you two want to do is observe these people—the Hamptons—*they*, in turn, will be coming to the Union Station Bar to identify and observe Roscoe. Roscoe, being the bait, will remain indelibly *himself*, easily observable, while you two, as I said, observe *them*. Preferably from a distance, and in disguise. And from whatever you can deduce this evening, we can go forward with that information. Food for thought for our pneumatic meeting. Yes?"

"Yes ... *yes*. So," I said, getting ideas, wondering what she meant about a pneumatic meeting, "if *Roscoe* is the bait—"

"And they're after my money, *Red*—"

"You tell them where it is, *Roscoe*, in so many words—"

"But to someone *else*, casually, at the bar—"

"Like you have no idea they're there, the Hamptons, overhearing all this—"

"Red? Roscoe?" asked Aunt Arctica.

"Yes?"

"Yes?"

Aunt Arctica sat down at the head of the long table. She took a sip of espresso, put the cup down with a dinky clink, and looked at Roscoe.

"I know you have to go, that there isn't time for all this right now, but maybe you could give them just a hint of your pneumatic idea."

"Yeah, what is all *that* about anyway?" asked Ruby.

"*Our* pneumatic idea, Auntie," said Roscoe, winking slyly, at Auntie. "Ok, listen everyone. The money—my so-called *Charlie Parker Cocktail Napkin Money*—is downstairs in Union Station. In the sub-basement. Right where I found the napkin. Right now. It's been there all along."

I couldn't believe it. Looking around, I saw that none of us could believe it. Even Aunt Arctica's mansion couldn't believe it. Probably all of its windows were as wide open as our eyes were, sitting at the table, and I heard a sharp *creak* from one of the upper floors.

"It seemed symbolic to hold the money in the spot where Bird had left his note. For protection, his angel watching over it. There was so much focus and noise from the press on me and how much I'd gotten—one million dollars—and what I'd do with it, and how it would change my life—all that talk, people talking and wondering where I'd put it, if I'd donate it, which bank, etc etc etc—and then it got out that I'd said I didn't really trust banks, which isn't entirely true, I was just being evasive, protective about the money, it was nobody's business, but there was so much pressure and attention ... so I had it cashed out, *discreetly,* at my bank, the bank I've been at since I got my first account, in high school, opened with busboy tips, and the same woman that opened my account, now the bank manager, was the *discreet one* that handled the transaction."

We listened, Roscoe continued.

"She gave it to me in shrink-wrapped stacks of bills in boxes, hugged me, wished me luck, didn't question a thing about it, and I drove it to Union Station. I worked my shift that night, cleaned up, cashed out, then I cashed out my *car!* All those boxes of cash in that little car out there, under blankets, under the parking lot security camera. I know Union Station *upstairs and down* from when I worked on the restoration crew after that Robert Altman movie got made back in '95—the movie, *Kansas City*—and I knew some areas were still untouched from when it closed in the eighties, rooms of old furniture, rotting desks, ancient train timetables, nooks and crannies all covered with decades of mold and dust. And I knew how to get down to those nooks and crannies. The nooks and crannies where I found Bird's note one night, exploring one night during a break from drinking at the bar upstairs. So there I was, months later, way after midnight, down a dark marble stairway, built before Charlie Parker was *Bird*, taking his money back down and hiding it, all those boxes, deep in the nooks and crannies. It's very deeply hidden."

I—well, *we*—were all alert and quiet, listening.

"So then, when you called, Rosie, about the Hamptons coming here to steal the money, we got to making a plan. Auntie, now we can get into the technical details of pneumatics—I just have what you called the *broad strokes* of it—this is your area, your expertise, I can tell by that marijuana train upstairs—but my idea, speaking of bait, is to lure the Hamptons downstairs at some point, letting them know, *indirectly,* of course—as they eavesdrop on me *confidentially* telling someone about it, a casual conversation at the bar—that the million dollars is downstairs, and that I entrusted Rosalita to remove the money for me, secretly. So the Hamptons will follow Rosalita down to get the money."

"And the pneumatic tubes? Where does that come into play, *one might ask,"* asked Aunt Arctica. Roscoe smiled. Auntie smiled. So did the rest of us. The mansion creaked again.

"I don't know if I should give it all away yet," said Roscoe.

It got even quieter in the mansion. I heard the elevator cables dangling in the shaft.

"I know," she said. "It's pretty good, this part of the plan. Maybe we should wait."

"Yeah. Let's hold off on that," said Roscoe.

We all stared. On the edges of our seats. I looked at Rosie. "Man, this is a real nail-biter," I said.

"A cliffhanger," she said.

"A page-turner," said Ruby.

Aunt Arctica smiled at each of us, one at a time, dragging it out. "No, go on, tell 'em."

"Ok, Auntie, I will!" Roscoe stood up and started slowly walking around the long table. "But hey, my friends, listen: I'm no Frank Lloyd Einstein here, ok? I just got this idea last time I was at my *ex*-bank, making a withdrawal at the drive-through window. It reminded me of the old days, back in the eighties, when the cash came shooting out in pneumatic tubes. *Whoosh, bam!* Remember? Per *your* design, Auntie, the tubes suck the cash out of their boxes and out of the sub-basement—to somewhere else, upstairs or outside of the Union Station—somehow simultaneously detonating, blasting, *cracking* the structure down there, collapsing the ceiling in that part of the sub-basement, nothing above it or anywhere else, *just that room*, crushing the Hamptons. They'll be empty-handed, and dead."

Rosalita's mouth was wide open. Mine was too. I wasn't willing to go that far. Aunt Arctica was still smiling; it looked like *she* was willing to go that far.

"Anyway, those are the broad strokes," said Roscoe.

"Pretty good broad strokes, Roscoe," said Auntie. "Kind of *Franz Kline* broad strokes, if you get my drift."

"I do, I *do*," said Roscoe. "There was an exhibition of his last summer, at the Nelson Art Gallery. Bold!"

"Bold," agreed Auntie. "Simple yet sophisticated. Vibrant."

"Violent," I added.

"Dead," said Rosie.

Everyone looked a little shocked. When I looked at Rosie, there was a flash of something in her eyes. And as startled, hesitant, *scared* as I was at the thought of killing the Hamptons (I felt incapable of doing that), I felt a flash of something, too.

It felt good. And bad. I needed to talk about it. "I guess that was the *Pneumatic* meeting, but I think we need another meeting. A *We're going to kill the Hamptons* meeting. I need to talk about that."

"I know, Red," said Auntie. "We will."

"I think I do, too," said Alberto.

Roscoe jumped up. "Got to go to work! If you guys are giving me a ride we gotta *go!"*

I nodded at Rosie and we downed our espressos.

Fyodor, Ruby, Alberto, and Serge fanned out into the mansion, to their rooms, Aunt Arctica hugged each of us, and said, "See you later on tonight, or in the morning. And welcome. I'm so glad you're here."

Rosie and Roscoe and I walked out on the driveway. Our dogs were with Auntie's dog in the backyard, sleeping in piles of autumn leaves raked up, red and yellow. We looked at the van, then at the Smart car.

"Which car shall we take?" asked Rosie, looking back and forth between the vehicles, with a straight face.

"Probably Morrison," I said. With a straight face.

"Morrison," said Roscoe. "Morrison. *Hmmm.* Oh, the van. I get it. Hey, why don't *I* drive, ok? You've come a long way."

We agreed to that, I handed him the keys, and we climbed in, me in the back seat for a change. As Roscoe and Rosie strapped into seatbelts, I looked all around at the grounds of Aunt Arctica's mansion, remembering this part of Kansas City, and especially Loose Park. I'd gone for a walk there one very excited fall morning many years before, the morning after the first date with my first ex-wife. A beautiful morning. A beautiful woman. I thought we were going to be married forever.

"Well, *this* has been a long day," I said, remembering more than just the day. I saw myself smiling in the rear-view mirror. I was excited, nervous, upset about this murder talk, wondering about that, ready for everything to begin. Roscoe started driving the van jiggling along the cobblestone drive, then he hit the brake.

"Hey wait. What about your disguises? I can have you seated sort of, off to the side, a little in the dark, but what about disguises?"

"HANG ON!" someone shouted, from the mansion. We turned and saw Aunt Arctica running down the driveway, fabrics flying from one arm, carrying an old striped hat box in the other. *"Wait!"*

Roscoe backed up slowly, met her halfway, she put the hat box down on the driveway, and we got out of the van. The dogs strolled over, curiously.

"How about these?" Auntie said, out of breath from excitement and running down the driveway. She held out a white Nehru jacket for me and a fur stole for Rosalita. "Try them on!"

Roscoe helped me on with the jacket, Auntie slid the stole across Rosie's shoulders.

"Um, Auntie, are they a married couple?" asked Roscoe, standing back and looking at us, squinting one eye.

Aunt Arctica walked over and stood next to him, squinting both of hers.

"Diplomats, I should think. What do you think, Roscoe?"

"Yes, I agree. Isn't there a grain exchange around here somewhere?"

"The Kansas City Board of Trade, not far from here, on the Country Club Plaza."

"Oh yeah. Perfect! And maybe they're staying with you, as honored dignitaries, if it comes to that."

"Well, it *shouldn't* come to that. These are disguises, not party invitations."

"Right, Auntie. I was getting ahead of things. Diplomats. What country are they from?"

"It won't come to that either, I hope. These *Hamptons* fuckers shouldn't even take notice of them, unless it's to *see* them, register: *diplomats*, then move on, and *forget* them. We sure as hell don't want the Hamptons to want to *meet* them," concluded Aunt Arctica, coming out of her squint.

The Nehru jacket fit elegantly, I had to admit I looked good, a little *international*, in my reflection in the back window of the van, but I still felt conspicuous. "Hats?" I asked. I'd just seen mine, sitting in the back of the van, beyond my reflection.

"Of course!" Aunt Arctica picked up the hat box from the driveway. "Rosie, a *midnight blue* pillbox for you—replete with feathers, and a deep indigo veil, for mystery!" She crowned Rosalita with the hat, fitting her perfectly, the veil dropping low across her eyes—then Auntie looked at me.

"I *have* one!" I got my top hat out of the van and put it on. "Do I look good?"

"Red Jumbo, you'd look good in jail!" said Rosalita.

"That's what they all say," I said.

"They *do?*" asked Auntie.

"We'd better get downtown," said Roscoe, jingling the van keys, climbing back into Morrison.

"I'll alert Guillaume that you might need a ride later," said Aunt Arctica. "In case *the diplomats* get called away."

"Thanks, Auntie. We'll work it out. Tell the others goodnight, we'll see them in the morning."

"I will. And have fun, do good—Mr. Towne," she said, shaking Roscoe's hand. "And *lay low,* you two!" she said to Rosalita and me, picking up the hat box and walking back to the house with those sweet, patient dogs; first wagging goodbye at us, then turning and escorting Aunt Arctica through the front door.

We got back in the van and started downtown. Roscoe knew the way.

We were *on the way.* I was nervous.

The Union Station Bar

Roscoe took the lead. He opened the polished glass brass doors to the Union Station Bar—inside it was calm, a hint of Miles Davis in the air, *Kind of Blue* (that song again) drifting down from high, ornately carved and creamy ceilings, the aroma of pepper and fish, the perfect white tables and silverware all lined up waiting for the evening to begin. The entire downtown cityscape of Kansas City filled the floor-to-ceiling north window, tangles of railroad tracks below.

"We're early, so let's see—I better go downstairs and change. What time is it, anyway?" asked Roscoe, a little distracted, a bit jittery I thought, overlooking his wristwatch, *underlooking* the big gold clock suspended from the ceiling.

6:30 it said, with bold black hands.

Rosie and I looked around, and up at a balcony of tables for two. "Nice up there," I said, "though a little conspicuous."

"It is a bit conspicuous, Red," said Roscoe. "Even if you *are* in deep disguise. How about back there?" He pointed to a wall of private booths—black leather seats, low chandeliers with tallow candles being lit by a busboy, various paintings of stockyards and some individual cows—each booth with a red velvet curtain, brass rings on a rod, ready to pull *closed.*

"Yes, that'll do," said Rosie.

"Done!" said Roscoe. "Here are some menus, care for a drink before I go downstairs? Red? A *Bloody Club*, perhaps?"

"How-How'd you know?" I stammered, sweetly surprised, then I looked at Rosie.

"Don't look at me," she answered, with a shrug for me, a wink for Roscoe.

"*Bloody Club:* Just the thing for visiting diplomats," announced Roscoe, behind the bar, beginning to mix, "visiting *dignitaries* actually—San Pellegrino Blood Orange and club soda, half and half. With a twist."

"Of what?" I wondered, out loud.

"My hips!"

"I look forward to the drink and especially the twist!" said Rosie.

231

"Make it two, please, Mr. Towne," I said.

"Two, it is. Have a seat, I'll bring the drinks out to you. Take the booth nearest the window, I can see you better there, from the bar. Clear eye lines, and I think we'll need to see each other this evening, if the Hamptons arrive. And since I don't know them yet, we'll need a signal, to let me know it's them, when you see them come in."

A man skipped down the stairs from the balcony in creamy-faded blue jeans, holes in the knees, tufts of blue floating around his kneecaps like feathers. As he came lower and closer, his eyes hit me like a ton of bricks. Wide-open and bright, like Easter eggs, *white* but painted with an intense splash of *blue* in the center. Remarkable eyes, maybe his best feature. But then he had that mustache, too.

"Hey Roscoe!" he sang out, through a heavy mustache that seemed to come down to his knees.

"Paul. You off?"

"Yeah. Gotta get downtown—K.D. Lang and Rufus Wainwright tonight! Off tomorrow, gonna make a night of it!"

The two hugged, and did some even *newer* combination of handshakes and slaps I didn't know about.

"Paul—these are my LA friends, Red and Rosie. Red and Rosie —Paul."

"Red and Rosie, from LA! I like the clothes. Are you actors? Or, are *you* an act? *Street theatre?"*

Roscoe laughed, we did too; Paul was about to, but he checked our faces first, to make sure it wouldn't be insensitive.

"They're diplomats, in disguise," said Roscoe. "I'll explain later, you look rarin' to go, buddy!"

"Yeah, I better bust a move. Do people still say that? Nice to meet you two, *oh!* Hold on—are you eating? I can see by your menus that you're thinking of it. The K.C. Strip is very fine tonight. Perfectly pink, sumptuous, with subtle, spare, crescent moon slices of red onion, and light scatterings of black pepper. Also, the catfish with a daringly delicious dribbling of saffron. For dessert, Philadelphia Cheesecake, crust as delicate and light as pale edible moonlight, but so assertively flavorful—you can hear the Philadelphia bell ring!"

"Bravo!" I cheered, and began to clap. *"That* was an act! Acts one, two, *and* three! *Encore,* Paul!"

Paul laughed, we all laughed. Even the busboy laughed as he lit the candles, which flickered.

"Go have fun tonight, and sleep in," said Roscoe, an arm around Paul's shoulders.

"Thanks, Roscoe. I'd better go. See you all later maybe, if you're around again this week—Red and Rosie: *Good evening."* He dove from Roscoe's arm into a deep bow.

Paul came up out of his bow, turned, and walked out through the gleaming glass and brass doors—they swung shut with a cottony soft click—then they swung open again, to Paul standing there again.

"Uh, Roscoe? You're an *older African American* aren't you?"

"Why yes, I am. Though a little toward the *January end* of older."

Paul came back into the bar, the doors clicked shut again.

"Two were in earlier today, asking, I think, for you. I told them you worked tonight."

"What were they like?" asked Roscoe.

"Drunk. Loud. Homophobic. The woman was flirting with me a little. The man had what I'd call an unfortunate mouth. *Ugly.* They made reservations for eight o'clock."

"Catch the name?"

"Let me check." Paul walked to the ledger book on the bar. "Hamptons."

"Bingo," said Rosie.

Roscoe looked at his watch, then at Rosalita and me.

"I'd better get dressed, why don't you two get settled over there. Paul, would you do me a favor and make two *Bloody Clubs* for our friends here? Special drink: San Pellegrino Blood Orange and club soda, half and half. With a twist. I realize you were just leaving, but could you?"

"Of course, you'd better get downstairs to *wardrobe.* Ha! I'm in a theatrical mood tonight! I'll make the Bloody Clubs. Good luck tonight. With—the Hamptons. Whatever *that* entails. And I have a feeling it entails all three of you."

"Thanks, Paul. Say hi to Rufus and K.D. and all the gang!"

"*Hallelujah*, yes, I will!"

Rosie and I walked over and slid into the leather booth, candlelight flickering in the silverware. Paul was already on the way with the drinks.

"Here you go," he said, setting down our drinks, clicking his heels, moving "*bye for now!*" swiftly through the doors again, the doors closing with their cottony click across the Union Station Bar. We sat in that silence for a few moments, looking at the painted stockyards.

"What time is it now, Red?"

We both had watches on, but needed to make conversation, I think. We looked up at the big clock.

6:45 Those hands were crawling.

Silence again, except for some soft and bouncy Duke Ellington music in the air, the tinkling of the busboy with forks and knives and spoons. We sat a little longer, read the menu. Waiters and waitresses were drifting through, customers beginning to drift in.

"You ok, Rosie?"

"Oh, I'm very ok. I'm ready to get into this. I've been having dreams, since seeing them—especially *him*—in Glenwood Springs. You hungry, Red?"

"I am, even after our soiree at the world-famous *Bryant's Barbeque.*"

"I would like a K.C. Strip. Isn't that the special?"

"It is, Rosie. But I have a hankering for seafood."

"I don't know, Red. Seafood in the middle of the country? In Missouri? Or are we in Kansas?"

"Missouri. But Kansas is close."

"I'm going to order the Strip Steak. Here you go, Red, look—seafood, next page."

"Pan-Roasted Baja Bass, Cashew and Quino Crusted Salmon, lobster, tiger shrimp, oysters on the half shell, diver scallops, hackleback caviar … *that* intrigues me … I wonder what the catch of the day is? Hey Rosie, look, there's Roscoe."

"Wow, *look* at him!"

We took him in, head to toe; black shoes shiny as wet sharks on the prowl, black pants with a red stripe up the side, bright clean white shirt, sparkling red cuff links. Small red bow tie. A heavy, white-gold wristwatch, which he checked for the time.

Roscoe stepped behind the cash register at the bar, a phone rang, he answered it, talked a little, then came over to our table.

"I'll send a waitress over," he said.

"Roscoe, you look elegant," said Rosalita.

"Thanks. I'm a little nervous."

"You'll do fine," I said. "But we should figure out what our signal is, to let you know when they walk in."

"I can have the maître d' alert me when they check in. Like have him announce, a little louder than usual, *'Hamptons, party of two!'* "

"Maybe something more subtle," said Rosalita.

"Yeah, you're right. A lighter touch. Let's see. How about this: when you see them come through the door, you two—very casually —turn and look at this painting. These two cows standing together in a field. Sort of point to it, discussing the art, or cow breeds, or whatever. You could just be miming, we're pretty far away from the front door here. I'll go hit the dimmer switch for these booths too, just a little *darker.*"

"That could work," said Rosie.

Roscoe pondered something. "We *may* need to talk, discuss strategy. If I need to talk to you, can you see that backbar ladder?"

"Yes," I said. "Wow, how tall is that? Ten feet?"

"Twelve. I'll move it, walk up six rungs, and turn a green Tanqueray bottle, label to the left."

"Got it." I began to gaze at the green bottle but snapped out of it.

"So Red, Rosie: if you see the *Ladder-Tanqueray Signal,* meet me in the kitchen—I'll tell the cook, the dishwasher, the wait staff and busboys, they'll know it's ok, and they should appear nonchalant if you go back there."

"But we shouldn't all go in at the same time. *Conspicuous,*" said Rosie. "Right?"

"Right," I said. "We'll be nonchalant, too. We may not need to meet at all. We just want you to get a look at the Hamptons, Roscoe. Then, depending on how close to the bar they are, you could—as you were describing it to Auntie and us earlier—casually, nonchalantly, even secretly, talk to a *special, trusted someone* about your secret stash—the maître d', a waiter, a customer you know, a regular that you trust, tell all about where you *really* have your infamous *Charlie Parker Cocktail Napkin Money.* It's a casual, *confidential* conversation, but within earshot of the Hamptons. What do you think?"

"I like it, Red," said Roscoe, "but what's to stop them from running down there this evening, and grabbing the money? And we don't have the pneumatics set up yet."

"Yeah, Red. It's risky, we're not ready yet," said Rosie.

"You could be not only nonchalant, Roscoe, but also completely vague about exactly where it is downstairs. You're just *piquing* them."

"But what if they wanna go have a *peek?*" asked Rosie.

Roscoe laughs, "It's a maze down there. They don't know how to get down, and anyone who would see them would question them wandering around, nosing around the exits, the *authorized staff only* doors, if there are any."

"So it's just giving them some information," I continued, "without them knowing you're giving it, and then—and I'm not sure if I even have it all figured out yet, I'm thinking as I go—Roscoe, *you* say that sometimes you make little withdrawals, just a little walking around money, or that your dear old friend, just arrived here from Los Angeles, named Rosalita, *she* needs a little walking around money. And you could say, to whomever you're telling this to, that on a certain night—she'll go downstairs."

"So they'd have to wait for Rosie to do that. We could do it day after tomorrow, Friday's payday, and they wouldn't able to find the money unless they followed her," said Roscoe.

"That's right," I said.

"I'd *lure* them down, right to the spot—" began Rosie.

"But we'd have a way *out* for you—" I continued.

A waitress came up behind Roscoe with a basket of hush puppies. A cute ingenue Audrey Hepburn kind of waitress.

"Well, you all look like you're in a spy comedy caper," she laughed. "May I tell you about the specials?"

"Bon apetit," Roscoe winked at us, strolling *nonchalantly* to the bar.

After the waitress told us about the specials, Rosie ordered her KC Strip, and I ordered Shark, which was one of the specials, *not* on the menu.

"One Kansas City Strip steak, medium rare, one Shark, two house salads, anything else right now?" asked our Audrey Hepburn waitress, with a tattoo of one of Marc Chagall's flying lovers on the inside of her forearm.

"No, that's all, thanks *Dee*," said Rosalita, reading her name tag.

Dee smiled, whirled around and sped off to the kitchen. The door fluttered shut, open, and she was on the way back to us.

"I detected a look of apprehension on your face, sir, about the Shark dish, but I *promise* you it's magnifique!" said Dee. "It's flown in on ice each day from the coast. East or west coast, not sure which. Ok?"

It *was* ok, then she was gone, sliding our order ticket through the window to the red, round, womanly chef (merry eyes in a pink smiling face, beaming through the window), then pushing through the swinging doors into the kitchen.

"Rosie, are you ok with being the bait?"

"I feel fine being the bait. But not like a worm. More like what you ordered."

"Shark?"

"You got it, Red."

7:30   Maybe it was me, but the closer it got to the Hamptons reservation, the bigger the numbers seemed to appear on the clock.

The darkening skyline of downtown Kansas City was beginning to sparkle blue, white, and red in the floor-to-ceiling windows. We were gazing at that, then Rosie looked from the window to me and smiled.

"Red, I am so glad we met."

"I was about to say something like that. No, Rosie: I was about to say *that*."

"About a week ago—is it that long? more or less?—I was trying to be dead, or *pretending* to be dead, to escape my life with the

236

Hamptons. Me and Alberto, trying to get out. And not back to Mexico. Now look where we are."

"I know just what you mean. A week or so ago I was trying to be dead, too. I was more than halfway there. But yes—look where we are. It all started for me, with Mrs. Hamptons, on the phone."

"Or, it all started with me, Red."

"Yes, you're right. I beg your pardon. And thank you for jumping off the Colorado Street Bridge. Strange to say that, but this has all been fun."

"And *freeing*, right?"

"Absolutely."

"And the fun's just begun. You know, back in Lawrence the other night, when you were with Ms. Skiptewmaylewe, Alberto and I were up late talking, about ... everything. We hadn't had a good talk for weeks, hadn't had a talk that didn't have something to do with fear, or the Hamptons, or *escape*, and we started talking for the first time in a long time about having a baby. When all of this is over. And ... Alberto is so fond of you, you know ... he wants to name our baby after you. Male *or* female. What do you think of that, Mr. Red Jumbo? We have some other ideas, though—*Rojo* is on the table. I like *Azulejo*. I hope that would be alright with you, so *whenever* we get pregnant, oh—*Awww,* Red ...'"

It was too late, I was already feeling this, what she was telling me, and tears were in my eyes. If I was already having fun, feeling free and more *in life* than the week before, this sent me even deeper into my *wide-opening* heart.

"I've been crying more than usual lately," I said. "You don't *really* have to name your child after me, but that's about the nicest thing someone's said to me in a long time. I couldn't have imagined it a few weeks ago. Thank you, Rosalita."

"You're welcome, Red. I hope you'll be around, later. To see our child born and grow. You'd be a very important person in her or his life."

"I'll be there, somehow. I promise."

Rosie lifted her almost-empty Bloody Club, and I grabbed mine. *"To getting pregnant!"* she said.

Dee brought out our salads, the plates of steak and shark, there was some light and friendly conversation with her about Marc Chagall ...

7:40 ... and the Hamptons walked in.

Both of them wearing sunglasses, collars pulled up (both of them), looking slyly towards the bar. Roscoe was not there as they made their entrance; I'd seen him glide around a corner and into the kitchen, bar towel waving like a flag from his back pocket, just before they came in. The maître d' escorted them to a booth near the bar, passing by an island of greenish-bronze statuary (a mermaid with seabirds on her shoulders), palm trees, and a few evenly spaced lampshades, *lit up.*

As the Hamptons settled in, they seemed to be adjusting in their booth, sliding low for inconspicuousness (like Rosie and me) but with a clear line of sight to the bar.

They hadn't seen us, they were seated in the booth facing away from us. Rosie passed me the basket of hush puppies. She looked nervous, but I think she was also having fun. I was about to try talking her out of using my crazy name for her *eventual* baby with Alberto when Roscoe came back into the room.

He flew around the corner, full of energy, smiling, bright white shirt, bar towel billowing, saw *us;* so Rosie and I casually, nonchalantly, glanced up at the painting of the two cows, like we had just discovered the artwork, I said: *"Oh,* look!" and we began to discuss the painting, putting down our forks and knives, doing lots of pointing and gesturing; Roscoe nodded: *signal received.*

We tipped our heads at the Hamptons, he looked that way, and he slowed down.

Roscoe turned to the backbar wall of bottles and began to neaten them up, spacing them perfectly. He picked up a pen and pad on the backbar to *check inventory,* looking quickly yet discreetly in the direction of the Hamptons table. They were *reading their menus* behind their sunglasses, as Rosie and I continued to *discuss the painting.*

"This is like good dinner theater," I said to Rosie.

"Or a movie. I'm glad we're in the back row."

"I thought we were on stage!"

Roscoe did more inventory, pulled out drawers, ran the water faucet, and rinsed some glasses. Two women at the bar waited for him to turn around. The Hamptons were deep in their menus, still in their sunglasses.

"I think we need to do some quick casting, Rosie."

"Do we? We need to do *something,* Roscoe looks a little startled. They got here early."

"That's what I mean. He needs that person to talk to, *privately,* about his secret stash."

"Privately, but *theatrically?"*

"Right, and don't forget nonchalantly."

"Privately, theatrically, verging on *loudly?"*

"But not *too* loudly."

"Naturally, casually—as if to a friend?"

"Hey wait a minute. Dee!"

"Red, she's perfect for this, I like her. Ok, when she comes over —*here she comes*—we'll tell her what's going on, what we're doing, she probably already knows about the *Charlie Parker Cocktail Napkin* and the million dollars. We'll tell her to let Roscoe know what's happening, she could pass him a note—I'll write it now— telling him that she's his, how did you put it?"

"His special trusted someone?"

"Yes, that's right. And she seems game. She said we looked like we were in a spy comedy caper. She knows we're up to something."

I whispered, "Cheers, Rosie!"

"¡Salud, Red!" she whispered back.

After being briefed and accepting her mission, Dee walked very casually, very smoothly, smiling, sauntering almost *sashaying* through the dining room of the Union Station Bar; she perked up, *jumped* up, twirling a little on the way back down, at the music coming from the dining room speakers, ecstatically whispering: *"Oh, Antonio Carlos Jobim!"* as she sailed on towards Roscoe, who was polishing glasses and watching her (she passed him *the note,* he read it, smiled and winked so clearly *at us* that we quickly went undercover, looking at and discussing the cow painting); then Dee, changing course, grabbed a water pitcher off the bar, and swung by the Hamptons table to fill their glasses.

Rosalita spoke low, out of the side of her mouth. "Is she overdoing it?"

"I mean, we said act natural, but that's the most *ostentatious* nonchalance I've ever seen."

"Maybe she's an artist, Red."

Dee finished pouring water, smiled over at Rosie and me, a smile asking *how am I doing?* and Mr. Hamptons took off his shades. "Thank you, young lady," he said in a full, slurry voice. Mrs. Hamptons took off her sunglasses. Dee walked over to the bar.

"Ok, it's working, so far," said Rosie.

"Yeah, now it's Roscoe's turn."

He was at the other end of the bar, still polishing glasses, whistling. His eyes flickered at Rosalita and me, at the Hamptons, then he put down a *very* polished wine glass, and started his own version of *casual sauntering* down to Dee, who was leaning on the end of the bar, looking around, up at the ceiling, even yawning.

"They're not very *subtle* actors, are they?" I said. "I wouldn't mind if this was a movie, because then it'd be just a movie, but this is *life.*"

"Tell me about it. Maybe life and death," said Rosie.

The Hamptons traded sunglasses for reading glasses, looked a little at their menus, a little *over* those menus to watch Dee and Roscoe at the bar.

"So, Roscoe. *Sup?*" asked Dee.

"Ah, you know," said Roscoe, mysteriously. "I mean, everything's cool."

"Yeah? Well, what's new?"

For casual conversation, they were really *projecting*. We could hear them from across the room, but the Hamptons seemed to be leaning in, towards them, still reading, or maybe pretending to read their menus. Dee looked back towards us for a moment.

"I wish they'd stop looking back here," I said.

"I know, they're going to blow our cover," whispered Rosie.

Trickery, in the key of Dee

"Are the Hamptons looking at us, Rosie?" I whispered back.

"I hope not! But what do we care? We're visiting dignitaries. I hope *they* see us that way."

"I'm not sure about these hats, though. These would be more fitting to dignitaries of the 19th century, Gilded Age types, you know?"

"No, Red, we *are* dignitaries, we wear what we want. So, like actors say—let's *inhabit* our roles. Anyway, no, I don't think they're looking at us, they seem to be focusing more on Roscoe and Dee."

Roscoe dumped (loudly) a bucket of ice into a bin behind the bar, smiled at Dee, and started their conversation.

"Well, Dee, I'll *tell* you what's new. Because something is. New, I mean."

"*Do* tell," said Dee.

"It's a little bit confidential," Roscoe said, in a stage whisper—*for the balcony*. He looked both ways, left and right, for privacy. Dee looked around too, gestured for lower voices, and leaned in close to Roscoe.

"I have a new hiding place," he said, in the same voice.

"For?"

"Well, let me put it this way. *The Bird has flown the bank.*"

"Are we talking about the *Charlie Parker Cocktail Napkin?*"

"We are, Dee. I always want to keep a low profile, now *even lower*, away from the world of banking, financial advising, advice, counsel, good intentions, etc. Away from the world."

"Back to the source."

"Exactly. Back to where I found it. Back to the exact spot, the room where Bird left his note."

"That's beautiful, Roscoe."

"Feels right."

The Hamptons were really into their menus; very quiet, very focused. Eyes down, ears up.

"Is it safe down there?"

"Yes, it's well concealed. And that place is a maze. No one could find it."

"Does anyone else know about it?"

"Yes, one. One very good friend."

"And you trust this friend?"

Over in our booth, Rosalita's ears were up.

Roscoe continued. "Completely. We've been through a lot together. I met her in rehab, out in California."

"Oh, so that's a special friendship."

"Indelible."

"Incredible. That *is* special. Is she in California, or—in town?"

Rosalita slid down a little in the booth.

"She's in town. She just arrived. With her husband, Alberto. A good guy."

The Hamptons menus jiggled a little, but they were focused behind them, reading.

"What's her name, if I can ask?"

"Rosalita. *Rosie,* I call her. But I go back and forth, we all did out there in California—Rosalita, Rosie—it's that kind of name, you know, she's that kind of *person,* I should say. Laid back, unpretentious."

"So, she knows where your *Bird's nest* is, so to speak?"

"Yes. I occasionally make deposits and withdrawals. I cash my paycheck and add it to the—what did you just say, *Bird's nest?—yeah,* so I *feather* my bartending money into the nest, and make withdrawals when I need to. Rosie and Alberto will need to get set up here in Kansas City with a place to live, and we'll draw from the nest for that, too. I owe her a lot from those rehab days. And I have a feeling that Charlie Parker would want me to spread his cocktail napkin money around with love and generosity, and for the benefit of *good times,* in the here and now."

"But not so much spread money around for, say, a new jazz museum, a Charlie Parker center, or some sort of, say ... institution."

"That's what I sense about Bird."

"He was for *the moment.*"

"Yeah, Dee. Don't you think? So I don't wanna hold it all—all that money—for only *my* moment. You hear me?"

"I absolutely hear you, Roscoe. So only you and Rosie—or Rosalita—know exactly where the money is? Not even the Union Station security guards know?"

"The guards know I found the note down there, like everyone else does by now, and they know I like to go down there and sort of *talk* to Charlie Parker, feel his presence, and thank him. They respect that."

"Where is the napkin *itself,* now?" asked Dee. "Do you even know?"

"It's somewhere in a temperature-controlled display case in a museum in New York ... or was it Paris? Or someone's mansion out in the French countryside? I can't remember."

There was a sharp *DING!* from the kitchen.

"Hang on, I have an order up. Oh, Roscoe—I need a Stinger and a Martini, *real* dirty."

Roscoe began to mix the drinks; Dee danced to the kitchen for the DING; Rosalita and I watched the Hamptons, whose dark glasses read the menu while their eyes darted all around. They hadn't seen us. We hoped.

"Now what?" asked Rosie, ventriloquistically. If that's a word.

"We wait," I whispered.

So we waited. It was quiet. Lester Young's soft sax, a train pulling through the station, cutlery gently touching plates, Rosie and I waiting, not talking. I thought I saw cows move in the paintings.

Dee came speeding out of the kitchen hands high with white napkins and white plates on a tray trailing white steam, swooped low with the food to a couple waiting near us, glided to the bar, floated the drinks over to the Hamptons, and took out a pen and order pad. The Hamptons mostly pointed to their menus, mumbled a word or two. Dee wrote down their orders, talked a little, very friendly, laughed, while the Hamptons silently stared at her through their dark glasses until she glided back to the kitchen again. They watched her go.

Dee came out of the kitchen, this time back in full nonchalant mode, and wandered over to Roscoe at the bar, who appeared relaxed enough to fall asleep.

"Well, sooo, Roscoe ..."

"Oh yeah—where were we?" he asked, pouring mini-pretzels into a bowl.

"I wanted to thank you for telling me this story, " Dee turned her body slightly, opening it up to the dining room a bit more, opening up in the direction of the Hamptons table, "... and I'll respect your privacy. You can trust *me*. I'm so lucky to call you my friend, Roscoe, and I'll be honored to meet Rosalita. I won't tell a soul what you said."

"Well, I appreciate that, Dee. And you *are* a good friend."

This was all completed with an affectionate fist bump across the bar. I was worried these two were playing the scene too broadly, but when I checked on how the Hamptons were reacting, I saw they were again leaning toward the bar, straining to get all the information. Rosalita noticed me noticing.

"Yeah, I think it's working, Red. But it *is* a little bit Vaudeville, the Dee and Roscoe Show."

I laughed, and choked on my Bloody Club—Rosie shushed me, but she was also laughing. The Hamptons, so intensely *focused*, were a million miles away.

Roscoe and Dee, just a few nonchalant feet away from the Hamptons, were talking again.

"So, I'll introduce you to Rosalita. On Friday—payday. She'll sit up here with me, so we can catch up, then at some point she'll discreetly slip downstairs, deposit my pay, pick up some *feathers* of her own from the nest, then return here for dinner and more conversation. We have a lot of talking to do."

"I look forward to it, Roscoe. I can see she's a special friend."

DING!

"Be right back."

Dee went into a sort of pirouette away from the bar, and as she spun past the Hamptons, she made a gun with her finger and thumb, pulled the trigger at them and said, "Hamptons order UP!" blew out her finger, then danced away into the kitchen.

At this, the Hamptons took their sunglasses off. They looked at Roscoe. He smiled and waved grandly at them, his large red-jeweled cuff links flashing red and gold in a swipe of motion through the dim dining room light.

"Good evening, folks!" Roscoe fully vocalized across the room, in his Roscoe Lee Browne voice, which I'd never heard him do before.

A little later, after closing time, we couldn't stop laughing in the van.

"So, *where* do you live, Dee?" asked Roscoe, at the wheel, out of control and over the center line now and then, because of his out of control laughing. We were taking her home after closing the bar.

"Rockhill Road, near the KC Art Institute. I live in a carriage house behind a mansion. You'll see, just take Broadway to 43rd and turn left," said Dee, giggling.

"Got it. I know the neighborhood. So, how'd we do, Red?" asked Roscoe, laughing and turning left, for some reason, on *39th.*

"You two were great!" I said. "You really pulled it off, pulled them *in*, though when you were done, I thought they'd never stop eating."

"Or drinking," said Rosie. "Or *leave!* I've never seen them out in *public* getting drunk like that. I knew they were taking secret nips all over the house back in Pasadena, and they'd end up plastered, but I've never seen them like *this!"*

"Where *are* we?" asked Dee, trying to catch her breath, trying to stop laughing.

"I think I turned too early," said Roscoe.

"It's cool, we'll get there, *this is fun*—way better than my usual lonely bus ride home. Anyway, you know where you're going. And Roscoe—when you went GOOD EVENING FOLKS! like you did, I almost lost it right then, so glad I was around the corner, in the kitchen!"

"If only *they* knew that I know *them!*" said Roscoe, followed by, "and know that *they* know me and that I know all of that, but they *don't!*"

"I think they took the bait," I said. "They're definitely going to be there Friday, and *ready*. Looking for you, Rosie."

"I was worried we were being too obvious," said Dee. "Were you, Red? I didn't dare look back at you and Rosalita to see how we were doing."

"No, it was perfect. I've never seen so many—what do they call them in the theater?—psychological gestures."

"Red's right, Dee," said Rosie. "And the Hamptons were *leaning in,* on the edge of their dining room seats."

"I was worried they were going to recognize you two back there," said Roscoe, in the rear-view mirror.

"Nope. Diplomats. We were in deep clandestine mode," I said. "And we know how. After all, I used to be a detective, and Rosalita here is what they call *illegal*. Right, Rosie?"

"Right. And damn proud of it!"

"Ok, Roscoe, bear right up here, after the stop sign," said Dee. "Go slowly through here—lots of dogs and cats and rabbits around here, also drunk art students—then follow the curving road up ahead. This is Rockhill Road. You'll see my place, you'll know it, believe me!"

The street grew dark after we turned, away from the downtown lights and neon along Broadway; this street was clustered with large old houses, tall, thick trees, and lit windows glowing through the branches. We had finally stopped laughing so wildly, but we were still smiling in the dark.

"There it is!" pointed Dee. "Home sweet home."

Roscoe slowly pulled the van over to the curb, crackling dry leaves and acorns popping on the street. There, just beyond the streetlight, was a large, *tall* Shirtwaist house—*seemed* like there were fireplaces burning in every window—and behind it, in a bunch of pine trees leaning all around it, was the carriage house.

Glowing blue, from the upper windows.

"What *is* that, Dee?" whispered Roscoe.

"My new work. My new piece, very multi-media."

"It's beautiful, even from the street," I said. "What do you call it?"

"I call it: *Kind of Blue*."

"Great title," I said, watching the undulating blue upstairs.

"I kind of stole it, from a great musician. A great artist."

"I think *you're* a great artist, Dee. I like *that* art, *up there*."

Dee turned around in her seat. "Red. Thank you *so much*." She turned back around, looking through the windshield, down Rockhill Road, and sat a moment. She wiped her face with the sleeve of her jacket, then she turned around again, smiling. "And thank you, all of you, for making me a small part of this project. Thanks *a lot*."

"Maybe it's a bit of performance art, eh Dee?" I said.

"Hey, Dee! *Look!*" said Roscoe, pointing up at the windows, crouching down at the steering wheel. "Shhh."

"What is it?" Dee asked, crouching down, too.

"Is there someone in your house? I see movement up there!"

Dee laughed; Roscoe came out of his crouch, a little.

"That's part of *Kind of Blue*—a department store mannequin traveling around the room on a small train track. Not a *toy* train track, mind you, but something I bought used from the zoo, a little train the zoo was getting rid of that kids used to ride through the ape house, or something. The zoo's replacing it with a *virtual* train ride or some shit."

"Wow, you Kansas City people really like your trains around here," said Rosalita.

"Well, it *is* a rail hub," said Roscoe.

We got quiet and watched the blue glow of *Kind of Blue* ebb and flow up in the upper carriage house windows, the mannequin passing in front of the window every so often, riding the train round and round.

"Well, *to bed!*" said Dee, breaking our spell. "See you Friday, ok?"

She was out of the van, into the pine trees, gone in the dark, up the walk and when a door opened downstairs, more blue light spilled out.

"She's the best," said Roscoe, starting the van. "Ahhh, youth!"

"Ahhh, art," Rosie said.

"Ahhh, *blue!*" I said as Dee closed her door, cutting off the blue at the door, intensifying it in her windows above.

Roscoe drove down the curving road, past the art gallery—full moonlight gleaming, glowing *silky* on the marble walls—past the art institute, past the conservatory of music and dance, and Roscoe said, "I think someone is following us."

I turned around and saw headlights.

"Should I look, too?" asked Rosie. "Or play it cool?"

"No, please do, *look*," I said.

"Yes, please confirm, tell me I'm not getting paranoid again," said Roscoe.

No other cars on the street, just these two yellow headlights, a little dim, like the eyes of an old fish, underwater.

"What do you think, Roscoe?" I asked. "We don't want to lead this car, whoever it is, back to Aunt Arctica's place, do we?"

"No. I don't think it's a police car, though. Every time the driver accelerates, the lights get really dim, almost go out."

"I saw that, too," said Rosalita, turning around, facing front. "And the motor sounds like a popcorn popper."

"You thought that, too?" I asked, also turning back around, facing front.

"*Plus*, I think I *smell* popcorn," said Roscoe. "Oh look: he's flashing his lights!"

He, or *she*, was flashing the headlights alright, and the effect of the high beams was like the eyes of *two* old fish underwater instead of just the one.

"Oh shit, he's speeding up! He's accelerating!" yelled Roscoe. So, back to one fish, diving deeper.

"Should we try to lose him? Or *her?*" I asked.

"It probably wouldn't be hard, but now I'm kind of curious," said Roscoe, braking a little. "Oh, hey man, now she's trying to pass us, overtake us!"

"Now she *or he* is going to lose the headlights altogether," said Rosie.

"I hope this isn't going to be a hate crime," I said.

The popcorn popper sound moved right alongside us.

"Who *is* that? Who's in that car?" Roscoe asked us.

I didn't know, but Rosie looked at me and shrugged. "Try to appear friendly, just in case," she said, waving at the car.

"In case of what?" I asked.

"*Bonsoir!* Rosie! Red! Roscoe! Hi! Remember me? It's me, Guillaume!" he yelled, switching on his dome light, totally draining his headlights.

"Hi!" we yelled back.

"Man, that's an *old* Mercedes, a classic," yelled Roscoe.

"*Oui*, it *is!*" Guillaume yelled again. "There have been many fine cars in automobile history, but none can hold a candle to this one!"

"*This one* can't hold a charge," Roscoe didn't yell, to us.

"Hey Roscoe! You were going to phone me for a ride home, no? Or was I to call you? I forget. But no matter, hot cocoa in the kitchen, my specialty—five minutes—follow *me!*" Guillaume waved, switching off the dome light and accelerating ahead of us.

"Welcome to Kansas City!" yelled Roscoe, laughing, but keeping close to Guillaume's dull red, Christmas bulb taillights.

Then ... all the way from the sunny, love-dazzled morning in Lawrence, Kansas, waking up with Jenny Sue Skiptewmaylewe (only the *second* morning of our lives together) to Guillaume's smooth and creamy cocoa just before bedtime (it really *was* one of his specialties), we said goodnight and drifted upstairs into Aunt Arctica's house (I was feeling smooth and creamy too), through the halls, a whole city of nightlights inside ... to our dark, velvety rooms.

Nightlight City

Up the hill from Union Station, down the other side, rolling south a few miles out of downtown Kansas City, under bright, cold moonlight, a hint of snow and fireplace smoke in the air, to Aunt Arctica's mansion, everyone (Aunt Arctica, too) is fast asleep in a kind of Nightlight City in the dark.

They are tired from the road, still sleepy-satisfied from Arthur Bryant's Barbeque (and the Union Station Bar, for a couple of them), feeling safe and sound (for the first time in a long time, for all of them) in the hospitality of Aunt Arctica, and spread out through the four floors (maybe more!) of the house. Fyodor and Ruby are snuggled up close in their room; in another room on a lower floor, Alberto is snoring on one side of a massive bed while Rosalita breathes softly on the other side, her breathing passing through her lips like the sound of a gently dripping faucet; Serge is upstairs, dreaming of skiing in the Sierra Nevada; Red's asleep up on the top floor, dreaming of Jenny; and the dogs—Kansas, Missouri, and Felix —are sleeping, slowly breathing ... in ... and out ... on a furry rug and a furry sofa near a softly diminishing but still crackling fireplace, on the first floor. Dreaming of something, by the looks of their paws pawing the firelight.

Throughout the mansion, Aunt Arctica's strategically placed night lights (light-sensitive!) blink on, one by one; some red, some blue, some white or flickering golden-yellow, some green ones in the shapes of pine trees, a blinking cityscape in the dark, within the house, within the hushed hills south of Kansas City.

A calm, quiet, beyond midnight landscape lit up inside the mansion; expansive but secret, and safe—the effect Aunt Arctica is trying for—and if one of these guests gets up tonight, starts walking around, looking for the bathroom, peace of mind, a glass of water, or trying to remember where they are, they'll probably see it like that.

Aunt Arctica, usually very insomniac, is very asleep, smiling in cotton-soft sleep, her house full of people, something big about to begin, tomorrow.

Time for the meeting

A bell rang. A little silvery tinkling, gentle, like the bell on a baby goat sweetly bouncing around on a grassy slope in the sun. Also, there was something spoken, *sung*, in full voice.

I was groggy—deep sleep satisfied and smiling, sunk inside the fluffiest, soft cloud of a bed—I couldn't make it out at first, that voice. I didn't hear any follow-up, no footsteps or creaking in any of the floors of Aunt Arctica's mansion, so I waited. The bell started ringing again.

"Réveillez-vous!" It was Guillaume's deep French voice, singing up the stairs.

"WAKE UP!" It was Aunt Arctica's also large voice, saying the same thing. Then, the bell ringing again. Then, both of them laughing.

Then, footsteps and creaking from all the floors, going down.

Downstairs, Rosalita and Alberto were already seated at the long, wide, fork and knife-battered country table in the kitchen. Sipping steamy coffee, they waved as I walked in. They looked fresh, sparkly, and cheerful. Alberto's thick black hair was combed back perfectly and so shiny (*Tres Flores Brilliantine*) I could see the candles—burning in the big, black, wrought-iron chandelier slung low over the table—burning in his hair! His hairdo was spectacularly glowing in the early morning sun and candlelight.

It was a warm, friendly room; Aunt Arctica and Guillaume cooking and banging around.

One by one, the rest of the traveling posse came in—Fyodor, Ruby, Serge, then the dogs, Kansas, Missouri, and Felix clicking along on the red tile floor. A minute or two later, Roscoe came yawning in.

"Good morning!" went flying around the table (it was noon) but with more snappy verve and sincerity than when we were out on the road, especially out in *flat Kansas.* And we were all smelling *something* simultaneously, making *those* sort of delighted faces—eyebrows up curiously, sniffing, eyeballs rolling delightedly—then those *somethings* were brought to us, carried in overloaded arms first

by Aunt Arctica, dressed all in white again, with white apron, and white puffs of flour across her cheeks, followed by Guillaume, humming, in a tall white chef's hat.

"FIRST, Quiche au Fromage," announced Guillaume (full voice again), as he placed plates around the table, nodding at Aunt Arctica's armload, following him, "*and* Le French Toast." He was intensely in the chef's role, so much so that he lit the tip of his tall chef's hat in the chandelier, a tiny flame beginning to burn.

Aunt Arctica, staying cool, blew it out, and kept coming with Le French Toast.

Guillaume delivered the plates, went back across the kitchen, and returned with two platters of beautifully chopped fruits, vegetables, and some rawhide strips; I was wondering about the rawhide strips until he slid them under the table for the dogs. We all sat down and ate.

And ate.

And eating like this didn't talk at all, dogs included. Pitchers of juice and the Bubbles of Vergèze went both ways around the table, and coffee. All of us smiling, dogs included.

Guillaume broke the contented silence, and offered champagne.

Aunt Arctica looked at him—*Not yet.*

Guillaume looked back—*But why?*

She looked at him, then at all of us. The look was clear. It was time. Time for the meeting.

Aunt Arctica sat at the head of the table, while Guillaume cleared dishes and poured coffee. His hat was still smoldering a little. She looked down the table at me.

"I'm—well, *namaste,* you might say—as the next man, or the next woman. I'm anti-war. I'm a pacifist. An *almost detective* without a gun, and I'm *almost* a Buddhist. And it makes me mad how the Hamptons treated you, Rosie."

"Me too," said Roscoe.

"But *kill* them?" I asked.

"I hate the Hamptons," said Alberto. "But no, I can't kill them."

"Do you really want to drop Union Station on them, Roscoe?" Fyodor asked softly, after a moment of silence.

"Of course not," he said, smiling and looking at the floor. "I couldn't kill them or anybody else. That was just, what's the word?"

"*Hyperbole,* no?" suggested Guillaume, sitting down at the table with his silver coffee pot.

"Right," said Aunt Arctica. "Roscoe's a gentle soul."

Everyone smiled around the table. One of the dogs was snoring. A sudden gust of wind blew a wall of crispy autumn leaves up against a window, shading the kitchen a little redder, flickering the chandelier candles. I was so relieved we weren't going to kill anyone. But I wanted to be sure.

"So—*not* killing the Hamptons?" I asked—*anyone.*

"No, no," said Roscoe.

"Wow, *thank god,*" exhaled Ruby. "I mean, I hate the prick, but no way!"

"Right," nodded Serge. "And besides, then I'd have to arrest you all. Who wants to go through all that?"

"I don't have killing in me," confessed Fyodor, "how about you, Alberto?"

Alberto looks surprised to be asked. "Oh, no! I am so peaceful. Do you remember that old Trini Lopez song, *Lemon Tree?*"

There was a pause at the table. Aunt Arctica broke it. "*I* do!" she yelled.

Alberto put his arms out as gnarly branches. "I am just like that tree, Auntie. You can put me in your sangria drink! Here to make life sweeter, if I can, *when* I can, come into my own fruition, day by day. Do no harm."

There was another pause at the table. Ruby came over and kissed Alberto on the cheek.

Rosalita hadn't said anything. We all noticed that, and waited.

"I don't need to *kill* them," she said. "But, fuck. Something. I need to do *something* to them. I don't *need* to, but yes, I do *want to* kill them. Him."

I looked down at the table. We were all looking down at the table, all quiet. Rosalita was looking out the window. I felt terrible— angry, sick, sad, helpless—when I thought about what Mr. Hamptons had done to her at the Rose Bowl. But I'd never feel all that she felt, the way she felt it. Every time it gets triggered in her.

Rosalita watched the red leaves blowing against the window; a big wind came and cleared it, and the room lit up again.

"But no. I don't kill people," she said.

What a relief. I think we all started breathing again. I know I did. Aunt Arctica looked at me.

"Red? Is something still wrong? You look a little out of sorts."

"I am. I don't know why. Well, *yes,* I do."

"What is it, Red? Tell us," said Rosalita, eating a fresh beignet from a basket Guillaume was now cheerfully trotting around the table.

I looked around the table. These people were my friends. I looked each one of them in the eye. How was I going to tell them?

Rosalita swallowed. Guillaume sat down.

"I'm not handy. Ok. There, I said it."

"What do you mean?" asked Auntie.

"I don't know how to help. I guess I can help carry the tube, if there is one, or *tubes*, a ladder or something, but that's the extent of my handyman skills" I said, looking around the table.

"Hell, me neither, I mean, I'm good with a hammer, sometimes," said Fyodor.

"Good with garden tools, but I'm not technical," said Alberto, very seriously. "It's just the way it is, you have to take me as I am, ok?" He said the last part to Rosalita, who laughed and choked a little on her beignet.

Serge looked down at Aunt Arctica and Roscoe. "As a policeman, I can stand guard maybe, make it look legal and official, whatever we're doing. I packed a uniform."

I looked at Fyodor, sitting next to me. He smiled and shrugged. On the other side of the table, Serge and Alberto looked at me, then at Fyodor. All the men, looking at each other, for validation. I know *I* was. Ruby smiled, and laughed.

"These *men*, gotta love 'em," she said to Auntie, "always thinking they have to be so handy, always feeling that male pressure, and competition, whether it's cars, home repair, or even pneumatic tubes under train stations!"

"Not me!" said Roscoe. "I admit it freely, like Red—I'm *not* handy."

"And by the way, Auntie," I said, "I wasn't meaning to imply, I mean—I wasn't going sexist on you or something—"

"None of us question your expertise, Auntie, I think Red's trying to say," said Fyodor.

"That goes without saying," continued Serge.

"Without saying," said Alberto. "Although we will say it. We *are* saying it."

During all of our confessions and explanations, Aunt Arctica, Ruby, and Rosalita were laughing, wiping away tears, trying to sip coffee, stopping short for fear of spraying it on each other.

But still, I needed to say more. So I did.

"I didn't mean to imply something, or presume something, or assume something. Or something. Saying I'm not handy, as if you needed me to be, to get this done. As if, without us men, can it happen? I didn't mean anything like that. I just want to be able to help, and—"

Fyodor waited to see if I was finished, then said, "—and, if Red's like me, he's worried he'll be in over his head. Or discovered to be incapable. Right, Red?"

"Or get embarrassed," said Alberto, looking down, at the table.

"Found out," agreed Serge.

"You guys worry too much," said Aunt Arctica.

"I'll say," said Rosalita.

"That's for sure," said Ruby. "We know you guys are ok, right, Auntie?"

"Right, Ruby. I can tell already. We all have to deal with all the same social mores, but I don't see you, Red, or any of you men, all hung up in them, in those roles. I don't feel disrespected."

"And I wouldn't have driven across the west with a bunch of male chauvinist pigs," said Rosie.

"Good!" laughed Aunt Arctica, *"Whew!* I'm glad we got *that* cleared up! Now that that's out of the way, what *I* need to do is to get a lay of the sub-basement land, so to speak, so if you can take me there—now, Roscoe? After the meeting? I can take some pictures, make some measurements, draw up some plans, then take it all to my inventor slash sculptor slash *madman*—I'll call him in a few minutes —and he can send it to his fabrication team for production and get it in place for tomorrow night. He's smart, efficient, talented—come to think of it, he *is* the fabrication team—and a good soul. Also a little shady, so he owes me for some trouble he got into on Beacon Hill one night back in 1985 when I was at M.I.T."

"You went to M.I.T.?" said Ruby, pausing to pour cream in her coffee and spoon it in circles.

"I did. I had a blast! I fooled around a little in *all* the departments. Graduated Magna Cum Laude. Or Summa Cum. Or whatever. Didn't go to the graduation ceremony. I had my own ceremony *off campus* with my pals at The Sevens pub down on Charles Street."

Guillaume flashed into the room in a new chef's hat (singing to himself, what sounded like "Like a Virgin," in French) and poured coffee.

Roscoe sat down next to Aunt Arctica. "Ready to go see that sub-basement?"

"Yeah, Roscoe," she said. "Let's get started."

Guillaume was up, picking up plates, clearing the long table. "Champagne *later!"* he said, and he was singing again.

"Can we go too?" asked Fyodor.

Aunt Arctica looks at the women. "I don't know, should we let these unhandy men tag along?"

There was a *long* pause. I almost got triggered by this, almost stopped breathing again, but then I saw Auntie's bright white smile under her blue, blue eyes.

"Absolutely!" laughed Rosie. "You guys drove a long way. You're damn well going to be a part of it all!"

Roscoe looked at his gold wristwatch. "Let's see—1:30. The guards, there aren't that many of them, they all know me, I'll just tell them I'm giving you all the nickel tour."

"Not the *million-dollar* tour?" joked Auntie.

"Yeah, *that* one," he said. "Come to think of it, why don't we go right in the front door? The grand entrance on the Crown Center side of Union Station," said Roscoe.

"You know what used to be there, where Crown Center is now?" asked Aunt Arctica. "There was a hill, a bluff, and it was called Signboard Hill. Ugly really, crammed full of billboards. So when you got off your train, came through Union Station and out the front door, you'd see all these signs. The first time I came into the station I was a little girl—I had my little white gloves on, my little blue hat—and I came out and the first thing I saw was a gigantic *rat!* It was a sign for a Kansas City exterminator, and so here was this big black rat that went across the entire hill down there, across the street from the station—with *big red flashing eyes!"*

"Oh god, how terrifying for a child," said Rosie.

"Yeah, it was. But it cracked me up too, at the time. I started laughing as soon as I saw it. And I remember the look on my parent's faces when I started laughing."

"What was the look?" asked Ruby.

"My father seemed to be afraid of me. First time I saw that. He looked at me a lot like that until I got older and then he detached altogether. My mom, on the other hand ... though we were in a train station, she looked like an internationally-famous American movie star on her first flight to Paris—I know this was a fantasy of hers—landing, deplaning, smiling, and coming out into the airport where everyone is waiting for *her*, fans and paparazzi, lots of cheering children ... and she's fluently chatting with everyone in French—she could too, Mom was fluent in three languages—so there, back in Kansas City, at Union Station, when I fearlessly laughed at the rat, she looked down at me *so proudly* with her cosmetics counter, movie star smile. Jesus, *that* was a mouthful."

Aunt Arctica stared out the window, eyes glazed for a second, leaves blowing and crackling around outside, red and yellow circles in the wind.

Her eyes unglazed and the wind picked up.

"Come on Roscoe, come on everybody," she said. "Let's go downtown."

Fuck Thomas Kinkade

In the Nelson-Atkins Art Gallery—uptown from Crown Center (once known as Signboard Hill) and the Union Station—the Hamptons are killing time, looking at the art. Walking from one painting to the next, Mr. Hamptons jingles his car keys, making Mrs. Hamptons nervous.

"That's not art," she says. She says it again at the next work of art.

Meanwhile, Mr. Hamptons grunts, jingles, checks his watch. ,

"Not Friday yet. Relax, idiot," she says. She says it again in a few minutes.

Upstairs, in the men's room off the Modern Art Collection, Christopher is taking his break in the spacious handicapped-only stall, two art books spread out on the black-and-white tile floor.

He doesn't see any handicapped coming, so he gets relaxed in the stall and continues his self-directed men's room art classes. He looks at Klee, Miro, Cassatt, Gauguin, Kahlo, Hockney, Chagall, and Artemisia Gentileschi; after a few minutes, he checks his watch. Time's up, fifteen minutes goes fast, break's over, he closes the books —bookmarking with strips of toilet paper the Chagall chapter in one, the Van Gogh chapter in the other—gets up and out of the stall, straightens his tie in the mirror, and walks out of the men's room. He feels great, alert and alive, even a little cool in his museum uniform, out in the gallery, smiling and scanning the centuries of art across the walls.

Though he still doesn't like the tie.

Back in guard position in the Abstract Expressionists Room, but loosely strolling, he turns to the side and—seeing his framed plexiglass reflection in a dark red corner of a De Kooning—thinks that his Grandma is right, that he does *look like that guy, that artist, Jean-Michel Basquiat.*

"This stuff isn't really art," says Mrs. Hamptons, as they enter the Abstract Expressionists Room.

"Yeah. Where's the Thomas Kinkade?" said Mr. Hamptons. "Let's ask that guard over there."

The guard is already looking over at them, friendly and receptive.

"He's *not gonna know,*" says Mrs. Hamptons. "Anyway, I gotta pee. That white wine wants out of me. Here he comes, ask him where the little girl's room is for me."

Christopher walks over.

"Oh shit, he probably heard me," she says.

"Hi folks, uh, yes—I did hear you, and the restrooms are right over there, by the beautiful De Kooning the gallery has just acquired. But no—sorry sir, ma'am—we have no Kinkades."

Mr. Hamptons makes a nasty little Elvis Presley curl with his lips.

"What did you say that painting was over there, De—who?"

"De Kooning," says Mrs. Hamptons. "We have one of his, remember? Anyway, I'm gonna pee, you talk art with Obama the security guard here, maybe you'll learn something," she says, swaying and giggling toward the bathroom door, passing too closely by a nude Henry Moore sculpture and flicking it with her finger—making a loud BONG sound in the room.

"Ma'am ..." Christopher begins, trying to guard.

"Never mind her, she won't hurt the art, hey—what's your name?" Mr. Hamptons is too close to him, looking around on the guard's jacket for a name tag, too close, getting closer, breathing wine in Christopher's face.

"Sir, I—"

Mr. Hamptons comes even closer. "You don't know art—come on —who are we kidding here, Obama? Right? Hahaha!"

"Sir, please lower your voice a little, other people here are trying to—"

"Hey!" Mr. Hamptons grabs the gallery guide out of his back pocket and rips it open, ripping it in two. He looks up and tries to find the guard's face again. When he finds it, he yells, "Van Gogh! Where was he born?"

There's a loud crash, silence, glass breaking—Mrs. Hamptons laughter echoes out of the women's room, some women run out. An alert, charismatically audacious woman in eccentric, electric clothes walks in; she is—on the way. You can hear it in her shoes, see it in her eyes; the way she walks through the door, focused, in her salmon, slingback pumps.

"Van Gogh. Come on. Where was he born?"

"Sir, I need to see what's happening in the restroom, please excuse me."

Christopher tries to leave, but Hamptons has his arm.

"You don't know art. You're a guard. That's all you're gonna be."

"Christopher?"

Christopher looks down, his hands are shaking; Mr. Hamptons is still holding him by the arm.

"Christopher?"

A bright, bold, bodacious woman in a dusty sage, double-breasted pinstripe jacket (name tag on her lapel: Karla Linda Hall) and pumpkin-orange silk pants (not the usual art gallery guard uniform) comes between them; she removes Mr. Hamptons hand.

"Christopher, why don't you take a break? I'll help this man and his friend OUT of the gallery."

"Out of the gallery? Oh no no no no no, I think not," Mr. Hamptons counters, confused.

"Oh baby—sir,—this entire situation is so past tense," Karla concludes, confident and in control. "Go on, C. You need a breather. From the fumes, if nothing else!"

She has her hand on Hamptons like a wrench. A very stylish, red-nailed wrench; a dash of Chanel No. 5 on the wrist. She has fierce, smiling eyes on him, too, but turns around and smiles at Christopher, softly.

"Go on, buddy," she says, also softly, "I'll put these two in the parking lot."

"You'll what?!" bellows Mr. Hamptons, the "what" echoing between the gallery walls followed by "OW!" which also echoes, getting the attention of the mingling art patrons and maybe a couple of the portraits.

Karla Linda Hall has Hampton's arm in a squeeze, tight as a tourniquet.

Christopher smiles at all of that, backs out of the situation, turns and walks over to collect his art books from under a bench in a corner of the room, and goes quickly toward the stairs, passing Mrs. Hamptons staggering and yelling her way out of the restroom, being taken out of the restroom, by the eccentric, electric woman in salmon pumps (she too has a name tag: Karin Cecille Hall; looks just like the other guard), who walks Mrs. Hamptons over to Karla Linda Hall.

"Wine glasses," Karin tells Karla, "probably left over from the retrospective black-tie party last night. Which was a ball, by the way, wasn't it? Those dance lessons are really working for me! Anyway, she threw the glasses against the mirrors. Broke both mirrors, too. Fourteen fucking years of bad luck."

Karla Linda Hall and Karin Cecille Hall, bookending the Hamptons (identical dazzling twins, in identically electric clothes, each daringly themselves, completely disorienting the woozy

258

Hamptons), walk them out of the gallery, Mrs. Hamptons yelling, Mr. Hamptons staring silently and furiously, back and forth.

At the twins.

Who couldn't care less. Who are singing a Sia song. The song is "Beautiful Calm Driving."

The hems of the silky pumpkin pants swing and snap heel to toe in time with their salmon slingback pumps as the twins stride the Hamptons to the exit, Karla saying, "We smell abuse on you, from you. Time to go, time to get in your car, time to do some ..." then both of them, singing "... beautiful calm driving ... beautiful calm driving ..."

Christopher is down a stairway to the gallery basement, through the tunnel into the underground parking lot, to his car.

He throws the books in the backseat. He throws them hard, the Van Gogh book splits apart in two pieces.

He starts the car, drives it fast, too fast, engine noise roaring around in the underground concrete. He takes the ramp up fast, bursts out into daylight, and is at the 7-Eleven in a minute.

Inside, he buys a 12-pack of beer.

Outside, in the car, he pops open a can, the foam running down his arm.

Hang on, *he says to himself.* Hang on a second. Stop.

Christopher puts the can between his legs, starts the car, backs up, waves at the 7-Eleven clerk watching him through the window, and drives back to a side street by the art gallery. He turns off the car and sits quietly, crispy red leaves blowing across the windshield. Something moving in his rear-view mirror.

He sees a spray-painted van pull up behind him and empty out one after another tattooed art student—purple hair, blue hair, green hair, red hair, no hair—carrying bags of food and wine into the Kansas City Art Institute across the street from the gallery. Christopher gets out of his car.

"Party?" he asks them.

"Oh yeah. Hey—you look like Basquiat," says one of them, a Chagall tattoo on her arm.

A Chagall tattoo. He likes her already. "I can donate some beer to the cause," he says.

"Well—cool! You wanna come? We've got a lot of food here!" says one of the other art students, the purple-haired one.

"Aw that's nice of you, thanks, but I gotta get back to work. You know, guarding the art."

"Ok, we understand. And we appreciate that, you guarding the art," says the blue-haired one.

259

"You guys make the art, I'll guard it." Christopher reaches into his car and pulls out the 12-pack of beer.

"Or you could do both," says the Chagall one, the one who thinks Christopher looks like Jean-Michel Basquiat, the one looking very interested in this art guard. She steps up, takes the 12-pack, and sees his art books in the backseat.

"Maybe I could," says Christopher.

"Why not?" they all say, in various encouraging ways.

"Have a great party," he says, getting back in the car. He smiles at the Chagall one. "See you later, maybe."

"Hope so," says the Chagall woman, who turns and points at the new student residence hall across the KCAI campus. "See that window over there, all crazy-lit up? That's where the party is. It'll probably go into the wee hours, come find us, if you like. I'm Dee, by the way," she says. "See you."

"Christopher. See you."

He drives back down the ramp into the underground lot and backs into his space, pours the can of beer out the window.

"Fuck Thomas Kinkade," he says.

Christopher is looking forward to the party.

260

Hello, Dalai!

I went into what they call "take charge" mode. I got some of us into the van, took the wheel, Roscoe next to me up front, Rosalita, Guillaume, and Aunt Arctica following in the Mercedes, everyone in sunglasses, and after driving out of Auntie's long loop of a driveway, down several side streets, then side streets off the side streets, down to actual *alleys* (we were sneaking downtown, a little worried, wondering where the Hamptons might be, didn't want to accidentally run into them, though Ruby Taillights laughed at us, saying she pictured them sacked-out and hungover in the Crown Center Hotel— *did we really imagine them taking in the local culture?*), our caravan rolled up to the front door of Union Station.

Aunt Arctica coasted to a stop alongside us, her and Rosalita looking mysterious in their shades, Guillaume in the backseat in sunglasses and his chef's hat. The *shorter* one, for driving.

My cell phone went off and everyone jumped.

"I hope it's not *them*," said Fyodor.

I looked at the phone and my heart jumped; I think maybe my ears stood up!

"Jenny *Sue!* Hi!"

"Hi there, Red!"

"Who?" I heard Roscoe ask the backseats.

"How are ya? *Where* are ya?" asked Jenny.

"About to enter the belly of the beast," I said.

"You're in Union Station?"

"Out in front of it. About to go in, downstairs."

"Anything happening yet? Have you seen those people—the Hamptons?"

"We saw them, we're getting ready for them, we're in the research stage now."

"Alright, good. I don't know what *that* means, so I guess I better let you go."

"I'll call you back. How are *you?* I miss you."

"Well, I'm great hearing you say *that*. I miss you, too. I still smell of you."

If my ears weren't standing up, something else was about to.

"I still smell of you, too. I won't say I haven't washed my hands since we met, but I haven't taken a bath yet!"

Roscoe turned around to the backseats. *"Who* is this?"

I turned to him. "It's Jenny Sue."

"Tell him the rest of her name, Red!" Serge piped up from the back.

"What's going *on* there?" laughed Jenny.

"It's Jenny Sue Skiptewmaylewe!" said, or rather, *sang,* Ruby.

"Is Ruby using my name in vain?" Jenny continued, laughing.

"She'd better not!" I said.

"I'll let you get on with it, and I've got to my next class, don't get in too much trouble. *Some,* but not too much."

"No, Jenny, we won't. We're keeping a low profile."

"Yeah, I bet. Red Jumbo and Ruby Taillights, et al—a real *low* profile!"

"Oh no, we're being slinky and surreptitious."

"Uh-huh. "

"I do miss you, Jenny."

"Um, *Red?"* I heard Alberto ask, from the back.

"I miss you. I like you, Red Jumbo."

"Detective Jumbo?" Now it was Serge. "We have business to attend to in the sub-basement ..."

"I like *you,* Jenny Sue."

"Bye, Detective."

Quiet in the van, quiet in the Mercedes next to us, a lot of sunglasses looking my way.

"Where'd you meet her, Red?" asked Roscoe.

"Lawrence, Kansas."

"Aha. Good. Lawrence is a good place to fall in love."

"Is it?"

"Sure is. Worked *this* time, didn't it?"

"I think so. Can it happen this fast?"

Roscoe removed his shades. "You're asking us? Hell, we're not the ones with our ears standing on end! Oh, here comes the guard. *Everybody down!"*

We dropped below the van's windows, I signaled *down!* to Auntie's Mercedes, and they dropped out of sight, except for the top of Guillaume's chef's hat. I squeezed up in my seat, looked where Roscoe was looking, and saw a very large Black man in uniform, striding our way. He was *big,* middle-linebacker big, and he looked as if he was coming to (maybe) tackle us. He walked up close to the van and peeked in.

"*Heyyy,* Roscoe buddy!" he boomed down at us, his voice deep and friendly, echoing in the canyon between Union Station and

Crown Center across the street. His big, beatific smile shining at us, gleaming right through our sunglasses.

Now what? I was wondering.

"Hello, Dolly!" said Roscoe, laughing, rising in his seat. "I was just teasing you, playing hide and seek! How are you, man?" Dolly, looking over his shoulder at the Mercedes, waved playfully at Guillaume, Aunt Arctica, and Rosie, rising in the windows.

"Dolly, is it?" I asked Roscoe.

"We used to just call him Patrick, but he's gone seriously Buddhist all of a sudden, so now he likes it if we call him Dalai."

"Oh. I thought you meant, I thought you said *Dolly.*"

"I can see how'd you think that, hear it that way."

"Especially when you say *Hello, Dolly!*" Ruby chipped in. "Now I feel like singing show tunes again."

"You say he *suddenly* went Buddhist?" asked Serge.

"Yeah. And he's deep into it now. Something happened, or he saw something. He doesn't go into it, changes the subject. Dalai even got rid of his guns."

"That's quite a change, getting rid of his guns and turning Buddhist," I said. "I mean, I like it, I *admire* it."

Dalai was over at Guillaume's Mercedes, talking with Aunt Arctica.

"Wow, I think maybe I've seen you before, Miss—?" he said, removing his sunglasses, smiling at Aunt Arctica in *all white* and her blue shades.

"Arctica. But call me Auntie," she said.

"I love this woman," giggled Ruby.

"Me too," said Fyodor. "I think I'm going to change my fashion sense, maybe my name."

We all got out of the van.

"Welcome to Union Station," Dalai said, making eye contact with Roscoe, who gave him the *OK* sign. "Friends of Roscoe's are my friends, too!"

Roscoe introduced us all to Dalai, who asked what we were up to.

"I want to show them around down in the sub-basement, and where I found Charlie Parker's note," said Roscoe.

"I hear ya. But be careful where you walk, it's kind of a mess down there. You know your way around. But maybe I oughta go with you? It's dangerous, kind of *raggedy* down there. The power should be on, you know where all the light switches are, right, Roscoe? You need flashlights or anything? Hey! I'll go get some hardhats. Let's see, how many are there of ya? You, Roscoe, then Miss Arctica ... three, four, five ... uh, ok, I'll bring a bunch! But first, everyone: *welcome.* Follow me."

Dalai escorted us into Union Station, through the crowded main lobby, and down to a door at the end of a corridor.

"Is this unlocked?" He twisted the doorknob and opened the door. "Ah, *yes!* Mr. Charlie Parker says come on in!"

One at a time, we all stepped through the door, down the stairs, into the dark *cool* beneath Union Station.

"And Mr. *Dalai* says, come on in and *namaste* awhile!" we heard, from the top of the stairs. "Hang tight, everyone, I'll be right back with the hats! The light switch is down there at the bottom of the stairs, Roscoe. You know where, buddy."

He shut the door and walked away. We all stood there in the dark as his footsteps faded away.

"*Where* is the light switch?" asked Roscoe.

We were all feeling around for the switch; I heard us shuffling around, the sound of tin cans being kicked, falling over, then I found something with my hand, but it felt warm, not cold concrete, not splintery wood, and it was moving.

"Hi Red, that's me you're groping," said Rosalita.

"Oh shit, *sorry!*"

Someone took their phone out and waved its light around. The switch was found.

The lights flickered lit, went out, then tinkled back on— fluorescent blue.

"Ah-ha!" said Roscoe.

The first person I saw was Rosie, blinking in the flickering light, looking around.

"Sorry about that, didn't mean to grope you. I thought you were the switch for a moment there."

"That's what they all say. Wow—*look!*"

White. Ghostly. Curtains of spider webs waving in the chilly air, surrounding us. Roscoe put a hand through the webs, and they floated down on our heads, gritty, full of tiny spiders, crawling down our arms.

"Ahhhhhhh!" we screamed, unanimously.

We brushed the spiders away, brushed each other off, and stared into the dark. Dark gray walls like prison walls. Dungeon walls. Dark in the corners, along the ceiling, darkness everywhere but around the fluorescent bulbs, and the glowing spider webs, collapsing around us. We didn't know where the floor was, or where it might end. Squares in the walls, jagged glass around the edges— windows. Into black.

"Wild, huh?" said Roscoe. "Upstairs it's all finished, but down here, it's another world."

"It's creeping me out," said Alberto.

"It smells like the forties," said Rosie. "Do you know what I mean?"

"I do," said Ruby. "Like how a forties movie would smell, if you could smell it. Or Robert Mitchum's T-shirt."

"This isn't the spot," said Roscoe. "We have to go farther, deeper in, and down. Through, uh—*there*. That tunnel, over there."

Roscoe led us out of this first room, the tunnel sloping slightly downwards, getting colder, darker, echoing everything close. Like our breathing.

"You're gonna laugh at me," he said, "but if we all join hands— here, excuse me, let me get through here, oops, sorry Red, is that you?—like in kindergarten, I'll get us through the dark. Down this tunnel, down two flights of stairs, then we're in *the room*."

We walked in a line in the dark, underground, hand in hand, in silence.

"Hey, are we all still together here?" I asked, worried because we'd been in the tunnel for what felt like a few minutes, and I hadn't heard all of us speak. I didn't want us to get separated now, after everything we'd been through.

"Yeah, let's have a roll call," suggested Roscoe. "Aunt Arctica?"

"*Here!*"

"Guillaume?" Roscoe continued.

"Oui!"

"Rosalita?"

"Or Rosie, either way."

"Alberto?"

"Si!"

"Fyodor?"

"Hi!"

"Ruby?"

"What?"

"Officer Serge?"

"Back here!"

"And … Red Jumbo."

The line stopped, our chain of hands broke, and we burst into applause. It was loud in the tunnel, and I was glad it was dark because I was getting *very* choked up. We'd all come a long way together. And not just in the tunnel.

The applause stopped.

"Red Jumbo?"

"Oh, Here! Sorry, I got caught up in the moment."

We all laughed, and re-clasped hands.

"A little farther, the stairs down are just ahead," said Roscoe. "There *should* be a light, below."

Deep down in the sub-basement, colder, something dripping, darker, and mostly black but with the shade and smell of rust in the air, we walked into a room, out of breath, and ... *cold.*

Roscoe flicked a switch. Dim, dusty light yellowed-up the air; there were cubby holes in the walls, ancient papers drifting out of them onto a long, red, cracked-leather countertop, a desk, chairs—broken, sideways on the floor, upside down—and all white. Like it had snowed, and frozen in time. *The Kansas City Star*, front page, 1956, dusty on the floor.

We looked at each other, then back at the room.

"So, this is where you found the note?" asked Rosalita.

"Right there, that desk," said Roscoe. He walked across the room and clicked another switch in the dark; the dim yellow light slowly turning white-yellow bright.

"Bird's note was in that desk. Dalai told me not to come down here, that the walls were structurally weak and getting worse. And though there had been new construction upstairs and outside, and that there were plans to remodel all of this too, that nothing was happening down here, yet. *Dangerous* down here, he warned me. They can get bills passed for the cosmetic and flashy and sexy stuff *upstairs,* but for the out-of-sight, out-of-mind, and underground—*down here*—Kansas City taxpayers don't care."

"That's probably a metaphor," said Aunt Arctica.

"Definitely," said Serge.

"But the city council," continued Roscoe, "says that it wants to expand the Union Station development, below street level. More shops, an underground mall, and movie theaters. Even *windowless condos*, which are being pitched to the young, to the hipsters, Millennials, and Generation Z, as sexy and daring. They're calling it *Postmodern Living, Subterranean Savoir Faire*, something like that."

"I doubt they'll get to it," said Aunt Arctica, "But my madman friend can easily and safely do your plan up, *pneumatic.*"

"And can he somehow make it not only pneumatic, but a little *something else?"* Rosie asked.

"One triggering the other? We can figure something out. But something, although not lethal, maybe *symbolically uncomfortable* for the Hamptons?" she suggested.

"Both happening simultaneously?"

"Oh, I think so, Rosie, *yes.*"

"I wonder what Charlie Parker was doing down here, so far underground?" I asked, looking around.

"Don't know. Maybe practicing. But late one night, I was drinking at the bar, and I heard a saxophone. Got a chill down my spine. It's a funny thing about jazz music, it's always comforting to me. Later, when I first got sober, anytime I heard jazz, I wanted to drink. Not anymore, but jazz still feels like music for the lonely and the left out, sometimes the drug-addicted, middle-of-the-night music, and when I heard a sax down here, I felt that comfort, like someone reaching out to me. So I followed that saxophone downstairs, opened that door, walked into this room … it was a mass of spider webs, wall to wall, a curtain, like upstairs, full of spiders. And of course, no saxophone player. I cleared through, found the desk, pulled out that drawer, and found his note left here from back in the thirties."

"*Charlie Parker Cocktail Napkin!*" said Ruby.

"So, Bird himself led you down here with his saxophone playing?" I asked.

"Yeah, I think so. A dead man." Roscoe laughed, holding up his hands. "I guess he wanted me to find the note, to help me. Maybe because I *asked*. I was so low that night, so drunk, and lonely, that I actually asked *out loud* for a sign, some kind of inspiration. That's when I heard the music."

"That's marvelous, Roscoe," I said. "Where *is* the Bird's Nest?"

"*That* drawer." pointed Roscoe.

"The same one where you found the napkin?"

"Seemed right, Red. Poetic. Safe. Like Bird's watching out for me, and … us."

Roscoe reached up into the ceiling, took down a hidden silver key hanging on a hook, opened the drawer and pulled it out, a long, deep drawer with compartments, full of old papers, rusted staplers, and pencils; he pulled it all the way out to the end, and at the end—a stash of black plastic garbage bags.

"One million dollars. More or less. Right there. So, Rosie—*"*

I was staring at the black bags and Rosie nudged me; she was pointing at the bags and staring at me. I looked at her, gesturing—*I know! The Charlie Parker Cocktail Napkin Money!*

"Yes, Roscoe?" she said.

"Friday, tomorrow night, you'll come down here, secretly, but not so secretly that the Hamptons can't see you and follow, you come down here, *see* the money—and then ..."

"The plot thickens—*pneumatically!*" laughed Aunt Arctica.

"... we have the money placed on this table so they can see it, the opening of the tube is somewhere nearby—*these are just rough ideas so far*—then Rosie, you step back here, giving them a chance to grab the money, and you get in here, through this door ..."

Roscoe pushed a button in the wall, and a dark green metal door slid back, opening into a small elevator. A weak, maybe 10-watt bulb burning inside.

"You get in here, and as they approach the money, maybe you give us some kind of signal, or they trigger something, and that activates the suction, sucking the … *Charlie Parker Cocktail Napkin*

Money ... out of their hands, out of this room, to us, which also activates something else which brings some ... what did you call it, Auntie?"

"Something symbolically uncomfortable."

"Yeah, that. Brings *that* down on the Hamptons."

"So, Roscoe, I'll be in this elevator?" asked Rosalita, peeking inside it.

"Yes, and you'll get upstairs quickly."

"Is this thing quick enough?" I asked, also peeking inside.

"Looks old," said Alberto, coming back into the light.

"It's old but it *moves!*" said Roscoe. "But you'll have to be quick on the controls, Rosie."

"Where does it go?" she asked.

"Right up into the kitchen, in the back—the dish room. It gets so foggy and steamy in there during the dinner rush, no one will even see us. Or care. Anyway, the kitchen staff will all be *briefed,* as they say. You think it'll work, Auntie?"

"Oh yeah, Roscoe. I *do* need to take some notes and make some quick sketches, figure out the placement of the pneumatic tube, etc."

"Does your madman friend need to come down here?"

"For the installation, yes. But my schematics should be enough for the fabrication stage."

Aunt Arctica was looking around the room, making mental notes. Rosie was snug inside the elevator car, peeking through the dirty circle window, getting a feel for the small space; the place she'd be when she'd escape the Hamptons for the last time, *going up.*

It was quiet in the room, with all the thinking going on; Roscoe started laughing. "It's kind of an over-elaborate plan, isn't it? A little overkill, not *literally* but, a bit outlandish?"

"Yes, that's *true,* Roscoe," said Aunt Arctica. "It's a little unlikely." She looked around at all of us, finally at me, and winked. "But it *will* work," she said. I winked back.

"But I have a question," said Rosie, in the elevator, looking like a courageous astronaut. "*What* are we doing? To the Hamptons, I mean."

Aunt Arctica and Roscoe looked at each other. They shrugged, but they looked confident, on top of things.

"It'll be a surprise. From all of us," said Roscoe, "for *you,* Rosie."

There was the sound of wheels in the sub-basement. Rolling our way. Louder and louder, clattering closer. And whistling. A grocery store cart rolled into the room, full of safety helmets, Dalai smiling his white smile at us through the dark like a lighthouse.

"*Safety first!*" he yelled into the room, enthusiastically.

Red wine and the Bubbles of Vergèze under a flickering chandelier

We put the hardhats on, made measurements and notes, Rosie did a few test runs up and down in the elevator, and Dalai stayed with us "for security and safety reasons." (And *good company*, he added, speaking for himself, not for his bosses upstairs.) Ruby walked across the street to Starbucks, brought back a latte for Dalai, asked him about his name and that got him talking.

"I used to have a lot of bad nights and bad days," Dalai said, "hollering and hitting people, women, children, men, dogs and cats, forgot to feed my fish, didn't feel a thing about it. I didn't feel a thing. *Ever.* Collecting guns and collecting grudges. Then I saw that, *first off*, everyone was crying around me, uneasy around me. Then I saw that they were hiding from me, avoiding me, *then* ... everyone was gone. Gone away. Lonely for company, I went to a family reunion outside of Kansas City, out in the countryside, out in Missouri, got a good look at some of the family tree, *took a good look.* Blew my mind. Got back in the car, didn't say goodbye to anybody, and drove back to town. Crying my eyes out all the way home on I-70, but I got back. A few weeks later, I met some people at one of those First Friday art festivals, became sort of a *once in awhile* Buddhist, if you can believe it. Changed my name and just about everything else."

Dalai finished there, exhaled, and smiled contentedly. We were finished too, so we dropped the helmets in Dalai's cart, single-filed back through the tunnel, up the stairs and out the front door, made our caravan back uptown to Aunt Arctica's mansion, *then*—Auntie at her drafting table in her art room off the kitchen (a glow, that *Lake Tahoe blue* again, pouring out of the room), but within earshot—we all relaxed around the long table again, the dogs asleep under it, Guillaume in his *tall* chef's hat (a night off from work) lighting the chandelier candles and spreading small plates around for us, announcing: *"Balsamic Bruschetta* ... and now, the *Blanquette de Veau.*" He uncorked a bottle of red wine, looked around at us.

"Well, *I* will drink! I understand some of you can*not*, but—"

"I can!" Ruby perked up.

"Aha, Ruby, ok then," said Guillaume, pouring. *"Bon!"*

Serge pushed his wine glass forward.

"Officer," Guillaume poured for him and looked at Alberto.

"Please, Señor. I mean, Monsieur," he said.

"I will answer to either, my friend," Guillaume smiled proudly; he was deep in sommelier mode. "Red? Your usual Perrier?"

"Yes, of course, the Pink Grapefruit one, if you have it."

Guillaume looked upset. "Of *course* I have it!" he said, for two seconds pissed, but it passed. "Rosalita?"

"I'll have what Red's having. The *pink.*"

"Perrier for me too, Guillaume," said Roscoe, "that is, the Bubbles of Vergèze!"

Something fell on the floor in the art room. We heard Aunt Arctica laughing.

"Alright, I'll have that, too …" she called out, "… the *Bubbles of Vergèze!"*

Guillaume looked in her direction, asked her if she needed help with whatever dropped, then he looked at us, as she *continued* to laugh; finally, he walked over to the kitchen sink, where *he* dropped something, this time with glass breaking.

"Merde!" he boomed, lightly vibrating the silverware.

"Well," said Rosalita, "I guess it's that time of the evening when gravity kicks in."

Aunt Arctica dropped something else, and her laughter got refreshed. Guillaume tinkled broken glass by the sink, sweeping; there was also the sound of pouring, and low chuckling. He returned (also *refreshed*) with a perfectly balanced tray of fresh glasses and the Bubbles of Vergèze. He looked like he was in a much better mood, licking his lips, burping a little, and smiling.

"Voilà!" he said. "I was not *really* angry with you, Red," he said, on the side.

I looked over at Ruby, as Guillaume poured the bubbles perfectly, even cheerfully. "Hey, Ruby?"

"Yes, Red?" she answered briskly, maneuvering around in her chair to fully face me. *"Ha ha*—it just dawned on me—you and I are close on the old color wheel, eh?"

"Me, too!" said Rosie.

"Yes, we are. But my question has to do with your *last* name—Taillights," I continued.

"Oh. Yeah." Ruby maneuvered away, a little.

"I liked it when we met at the Beverly Hills Hotel. I thought it was flamboyant, playful. Fun."

"Yes. *They* did, too, Red. My so-called audience." Ruby's smile faded as she did a slow ring-around-the-rosie with a finger on her wine glass.

I was sorry now that I'd brought it up.

"But, for you, is it also sexist?" asked Rosie.

"It is. And it became—after the playfulness and flamboyance wore off, and it wore off pretty fast—it became insulting."

Aunt Arctica walked back into the kitchen and sat down. "I bet it did," she said.

"The world is full of misogyny parlors," said Rosalita.

Alberto leaned forward, smiled sweetly at Ruby. "When I first came to Los Angeles, first started working for the Hamptons, they didn't use my name at all for a long time. They didn't call me anything. Later, Mrs. Hamptons began to call me Alberto. Mr. Hamptons just called me *Taco*. It's not the same thing, but it hurt me."

Ruby smiled at Alberto, also sweetly. "It's pretty close, Alberto. I'm sorry. And thanks for sharing that."

"What's your real last name?" asked Rosie.

"Rosenfeld. Ruby Rosenfeld. "

"I like it!" said Aunt Arctica.

"I like it, too. It has a lot of *rrr!*" said Rosie.

Ruby grinned. "I'm going to change it *back* to that, soon! I was thinking of doing that anyway, but this conversation, *thank you very much,* has decided it!"

"Nice to meet you, Ruby Rosenfeld," I said, standing up. "A toast."

At the far end of the table, Guillaume set down his tray and raised a glass. Then, Roscoe raised his.

Then, Alberto.

Serge.

Fyodor, also standing up.

Aunt Arctica got a glass from Guillaume's tray and raised it.

Rosalita stood up with her glass and nodded *ready*.

"To Ruby Rosenfeld!" I toasted.

"RUBY ROSENFELD!"

Our glasses raised high to just under the chandelier, the candles flickering with all the ceremonial movement, we drank to Ruby. Fyodor set down his glass and hugged her.

Guillaume dropped his glass (more broken glass; I wondered if it was a ceremonial French tradition, in honor of Ruby), cried out, "Beignets!" and shot to the oven.

We all sat down, Fyodor refilled Ruby's glass, Serge poured for Alberto, and Roscoe watched everybody, smiling.

"How about *you*, Red Jumbo?" he asked me. "You have a certain distinct look, but I wouldn't say it reads *red*."

Ruby put her feet up on the table, following Aunt Arctica's lead. "I *like* his look," she said, squinting across the table at me. "That nose could part the waves for a school of schooners, and the hair styling is definitely what I'd call wind-tossed, tousled, and seaworthy. I mean all of this as the highest praise, Mr. Jumbo, of course!"

"Of *course!*" I said.

"But those clear blue eyes, oh my. They're very Caribbean-clear. Actually, they're even bluer, blue like when I first saw you from the elevator at the Beverly Hills Hotel."

"She's flirting right in front of you, Fyodor," Auntie said to Fyodor.

"So I see," he said. "It's ok, we've all been through the Rockies together. Then Kansas, so ..."

"Red, I think I will call your eyes *Maliblue,*" Ruby concluded, and yawned, dropping her head on Fyodor's shoulder, falling fast asleep.

After a while, after more red wine, beignets, and Bubbles of Vergèze, Aunt Arctica went back to her drafting table; we could hear her on the speaker phone with her design partner, or as Auntie referred to him, the *improvisational carpenter*. I couldn't quite make out what he was saying, but he was using words like yes, and to be sure, and *oh absolutely, Auntie!* I heard him say he was going to set up an emergency meeting with his "*production team*," meaning himself, that he'd call her back, etc., and he said goodbye. It was quiet in the drafting room.

"How you doing in there, Auntie?" I asked.

"Super!" she said. "Making great progress. My blueprints look like a Dr. Seuss book, but it'll all work. I trust my guy."

"Can he do it all by tomorrow?" asked Roscoe. "I guess it doesn't have to be *this* Friday."

"Yes, *this* Friday, tomorrow," said Rosalita.

"Yeah, we should go tomorrow. We've set the bait," I said.

"True," said Roscoe.

"*Very* true," yelled Aunt Arctica, squeaking up out of her swivel chair, her footsteps coming our way again.

"He says he'll be up all night tonight," she said, leaning in the doorway, smiling at us. "Roscoe, can he meet you at Union Station sometime tonight, maybe *late,* for installation, to place the tubing and ... our surprise? I'll give you his phone number."

"Sure. Do you need to be there, Auntie?"

"No. I'm emailing him everything he needs to know, so if you'll just guide him through the back door, down the tunnel, down the stairs, and so on—will there be guards around?"

"I've already told Dalai to expect him, but I'll go down to introduce them. If he sees me, it'll be cool."

"Even if he sees someone carrying some sort of tube into the sub-basement?"

"He trusts me, Auntie. Trusts all of you. And after all the things that have happened to him, well—he's a guard, but he guards what he wants to at this point."

"It won't take my guy long to set it all up, he's been into these kinds of things before, *disruptions,* and such. He's my age, and left-wing."

"You mean, college campuses, administration buildings, and so on, right?"

"Precisely, Roscoe."

My attention was drifting until they said that. "But we're still *not* blowing up the Hamptons, right?"

"Oh *no!*" Roscoe and Aunt Arctica said together, laughing.

"Do we know what the *surprise* is yet?" I prodded.

"Almost," Aunt Arctica winked at Roscoe.

"Ideas comin' in all the time," he winked back.

"We'll bring you guys in too, don't worry."

"Ok, Auntie. Well, so—*Friday,*" I said, toasting again.

Rosalita stood up."Friday!" Her glass was empty.

Guillaume was on his feet, and after a few minutes of his circling and pouring, we all lifted our glasses again.

"FRIDAY!"

Aunt Arctica lingered in the doorway, we all drank and mused in silence for a moment. Thinking about what was coming. Tomorrow night.

Fyodor looked up at Aunt Arctica. "He'll be up all night, huh? Your guy?"

"Yes, Fyodor. He's like that. Passionate," said Auntie. "He lives in that laboratory of his, sleeps there, back and forth between there and his little adjoining factory—thinking, tinkering, *thinkering,* oiling, and fixing."

"Kind of an eccentric man," said Ruby.

"Just what we need," said Serge.

"Just like us," I said.

"When does he sleep?" asked Alberto. "*Does* he?"

"I don't know, Alberto," said Auntie, sitting down next to him. "Good question. I drove by his place one night, it was late, *really* late, I was on the way home from a rock concert. It must have been three in the morning. I was in his neighborhood, so I drove by, stopped, and parked. All the windows of his laboratory, and his sort of *lean-to* brick and aluminum factory building, were lit up, glowing golden, kind of flashing and flickering with accompanying clanging and banging sounds. I could see him walking around inside, back and forth through the windows, hair a mess, shirtless—he might've been naked! A wild place. I could hear it kind of *humming* a block away, as I drove home."

"Does he have a name?" asked Rosie.

"Chainsaw." Auntie took a beat and looked at us. "Yeah, *Chainsaw.* I mean, the man *is* intense and muscular, has crazy, spinning eyes, in my experience with him he can't sit still, but he quotes Chögyam Rinpoche Trungpa and listens to Eva Cassidy records. He says that one of his customers, actually it was some department of Hallmark Cards just a few blocks away from his place, someone there nick-named him Chainsaw, because he tends to complete jobs *overnight,* and to perfection, no matter how large."

"I have a feeling he *will* be ready by tomorrow night," said Rosie.

"*Oh* yeah," said Aunt Arctica. "And if we can't sleep tonight, or even if we can, he might wake us up, because we're likely to *hear* him, across town, as he fires up his factory and begins the fabrication of our instrument, um, *tube.*"

"Where are we," I asked, "while all this pneumatic stuff is going on?"

"Dinner at the Union Station Bar," said Roscoe.

"We'd go to dinner while Rosalita is um, *being followed by* the Hamptons downstairs?"

"Exactly, Red. Well, that's where we'll all be. At a table. Waiting for Rosie, who's just *stepped away* for a few minutes, to return."

This didn't feel right. "I don't like it," I said. "I don't like Rosie being alone, followed by the Hamptons."

Serge nodded. "Detective Jumbo should accompany her."

I agreed, only, "I don't know that I can find that Nest again. Can you, Rosie?"

She shook her head.

"I'll break away from the bar and lead you both. Hopefully, the Hamptons' greed will still be enough that they'll follow us."

"Where am I?" asked Rosalita. "*After* the surprise. Still in the tiny elevator?"

"Yes, you, I mean us three, will take it upstairs to the kitchen, everyone else will be there to greet us."

"Can I say something?" asked Auntie Arctica. Something about the way she asked, the mansion went silent. Except for logs crackling in the fireplace down the hall.

"Of course," I whispered.

"Friday night is my birthday. I turn seventy. I'd love to celebrate it with all of you. Is that alright with you?"

We all went off!

"*Oh,* of course, Auntie!" cried Ruby, beginning to cry with joy. "I love a party!"

"Hell yes!" Roscoe said, coming around the table with a bear hug. "We'll make a fuss, cause a commotion in the bar, come tomorrow night! Happy birthday, my friend!"

"Not yet," said Auntie.

"And I'm right behind you, a few years. I actually *like* this getting older jazz, you know? This thing everyone seems to be so afraid of. I think I'm just *starting* to loosen up!"

"Me too. I'm ready for more, Roscoe, *a lot* more, a whole new decade, at least!"

I noticed, down the table, Fyodor and Alberto grinning at each other.

"I'm not telling my age," said Fyodor.

"Neither am I," agreed Alberto. "I'm going to remain a man of mystery."

Something else went off—a phone somewhere—sounded like it was vibrating on Aunt Arctica's drafting table.

"Oh, that'll be Chainsaw," said Auntie, swinging her legs off the table. "My *crazy naked partner.*"

"He'll be up all night," said Rosalita.

"I think we will too," I said, getting excited, picturing some wild, dramatic, absurdist—*dangerous?*—hopefully cathartic event that would be Rosie's victory in the sub-basement, then Auntie's party in the Union Station Bar.

"I know *I* will!" said Ruby. "I want to listen for the crazy man in his factory tonight! Fyodor? You good?"

"Hell, yes! I'm tired but I'm wired. Officer Controllente?"

"Oh yes, I'll be right *here*, right on the edge and *eve* of history! How about you, Alberto?"

"Si. I wouldn't miss this night. I may stay awake all the way to Saturday morning! I'm a long way from Pasadena, from the Hamptons Mansion, and I'm on a mission!"

Aunt Arctica was watching us, listening to us, standing in the blue glow of her art room door, letting her tears roll right along, because why wipe those kinds of tears away, anyway?

Aunt Arctica's Mansion (Two hours later)

"Zzzzzzzzzzzzzzzzzzzzzzzzzzzzzzzzzzzzzzzzzzzzzzzzzzzzzzzzzzzzzzzzzzzzzzzzz zzzzzzzz."

"Wow," says Aunt Arctica, alone in the dark kitchen, chandelier candles flickering, almost out.

"Zzzzzzzzzzzzzzzzzzzzzzzzzzzzzzzzzzz."

"They all conked out! I can't believe it. They were so excited, so awake. *Now this! Gone. Upstairs asleep. Can you believe it? Guillaume?"*

"Zzzzzzzzzzzzzzzzz," snores Guillaume.

"Guillaume?"

"TARRAGON! Zzzzzzz."

Aunt Arctica pours a fresh glass of the Bubbles of Vergèze, bubbles sparkling silver in the yellow candlelight. She kisses Guillaume on the forehead, then licks him there, sensing rosemary, sits down next to him, strokes the bellies of Kansas, Missouri, and Felix, all three also conked out; paws flicking and twitching, dreaming. She sits there in the dimming candlelight, stretched out, wiggling her toes; smiling and anticipating, dreaming.

Guillaume's eyes open.

"NO! Much more garlic! Two Thyme Sprigs! Quarter cup, cognac!"

His eyes close, a candle smokes and goes out.

"Zzzz."

Aunt Arctica steps back into her room and picks up her phone.

The Factory

*Hmmmmmmmmmmmmmmmmmmmmmmmmmmmmmmmmmmmmmmmm
m m m m m m m m m m m m m m m m m m m m m m m m m m m m m m m m m m m —
r r r r r r r r r r r r r r r r r r r—s s s s s s s s s s s s s s s s s s s s s s s s s s s s—
grrrrrrrrriiiiiiiiiiinnnnnnndddddddd — bang bang hammer hammer,*
BANG!

Jingle!

*Chainsaw picks up his black, paint-splattered rotary phone on
the first ring.*

*"Hello? Yes, Auntie, I'm nearly done! It is almost finished!
OW!"*

*The man leaps, hops up and down on the cold concrete floor,
stops, and exhales gradually into laughing at himself. His puppy
hides behind a case of beer, under the machinery.*

*"Oh, it's fine, I just backed up into the lathe, and it's been
running all night.* HOT! *Beg your pardon? Yeah, I'm afraid I am in
the buff again. I work better this way, unencumbered. Of course, I
suppose I should be careful. Lots of sharp machinery around here—I
could end up, unCUcumbered, if you catch my drift."*

*The little steel wool fluff of a puppy comes from behind the case
of beer and jumps up at the naked man, who begins skipping the long
phone cord on the floor, skip-rope style. The puppy hops and barks.*

*"Hello?" says Auntie through the phone. Chainsaw snugs it back
up onto his naked tattooed shoulder, against his tattooed jaw, and
keeps on skipping the cord.*

*"But yeah, it works! I tested the tube for pneumatics, and it
really sucks! And uh ... I figured out the other thing. The Hamptons
Surprise. You're gonna love it. Ok, see you tomorrow. Sleep tight. If
you can! Good night, Auntie!"*

The Crown Center Hotel

Bedside lamps and the TV still on, the Hamptons lie apart in their underwear, mouths open and snoring, sputtering.

Mr. Hamptons drools down his neck a little stream of fluid, draining down across his belly into bits of sandwich and french fries and an empty peppermint schnapps bottle in the sheets.

A Make America Great Again *bumper sticker dangling out of the pocket of his coat, draped on a chair by the TV.*

Shining, brilliant, and golden

Rosalita and I sat at the actual *bar* of the Union Station Bar, just the two of us, in the soft, fading evening light. Staring into the backbar mirror.

I was feeling a little surreal. No, *surreal* is too fancy. I was *scared.* I was worried about being followed by the Hamptons, especially Mr. Hamptons, who was big, and angry when he was drunk. We were about to do some kind of a *surprise* to the Hamptons. Not knowing what that was scared me as well ... since it was about to happen.

I was dressed in a new double-breasted pinstripe jacket (sage green, piñon pine pinstripes, felt like good *natural* karma), new Levis blue jeans (brand new, for luck; I was breaking out in superstition), and my red (symbolic, wearing my name) pearl-button cowboy shirt from a feed store high in the Sierra Nevadas (a nice California memory); Rosie was dressed in *her* brand-new clothes: a *Yellow Like Van Gogh* pantsuit (the official name of the color, I remembered it in capital letters because it was also the name of the shop), red leather sneakers (Roscoe had pointed out some red pumps but she had said simply, *Ouch!, I'm supposed to walk around down in the Union Station sub-basement in pumps?)*, and a string of pearls.

Roscoe had taken us shopping on the Country Club Plaza that morning, after he woke us up. We took the van; Roscoe said he was anticipating a *"trunk show* load of clothing," and he paid for everything, said money was no object for Rosalita's "Luring Look."

"Not that long ago, you were in deep diplomat disguise, just so we could get a *bead* on the Hamptons," he said as he drove us back up the hill from the Plaza, past Loose Park, back up to the mansion. "Now you're dressing so they can see you coming!"

Back at Auntie's mansion, another feast from Guillaume was on the long table for lunch; this time *Steak Diane* and *Basque-Style Fish with Green Peppers and Manila Clams,* followed by *Pear Tarte Tatin.* Roscoe had paused for a moment, sniffed, smiled, almost sat down with us, but said, *"no, gotta go, lots to do,"* then took off in his Smart car with Aunt Arctica in the passenger seat, making notes in a notebook.

After lunch—where we'd all tried to make casual conversation and pretend it was just another day but it was clear we were all thinking about tonight—Alberto, Serge, Ruby, and Fyodor drifted away satisfied, like the slow, savory steam drifting off Guillaume's cooking; they were going back upstairs to their rooms, they said, to rest up for the big night, just a few hours away. But on the way up, I'd heard them getting hijacked by the jingling of frantic dog tags on the stairs, needing a walk.

Then, Rosalita and I went down to the Union Station Bar in Auntie's MG.

"I could really use a drink right now, Rosie," I said, eyes rolling up and down the golden floor-to-ceiling backbar of bottles.

"*Tell* me about it," she agreed. "Here comes Roscoe. One bartender who *won't* give us one."

"I guess Auntie's still downstairs with Chainsaw, checking one last time. And how *about* that man? She says he was down there early this morning, working away, him and Dalai. Apparently, they totally, *karmically,* hit it off. When Auntie arrived, Chainsaw still hadn't gone home, and he was with Dalai—who was on his lunch break—meditating together out by the fountain in front of Union Station."

"Hey, you two!" Roscoe flashed up fast in front of us on his side of the bar, happy and wired, in his bright white shirt and gleaming red cuff links.

"*He* doesn't look nervous," I said.

"Yeah. No. He doesn't. Hey Roscoe, we were just talking about a drink."

"*Hell* no!" Roscoe frowned at us, but his smiling overruled his scolding. "We sobered up for days like this! Where is everyone, Red?"

"Well, Alberto and Serge, Fyodor and Ruby took the dogs out for a long walk in the park across from Auntie's mansion. Let 'em run around free, chase some chipmunks, etc. They'll be down here in a bit, the dinner reservation is for eight o'clock. Also, they needed to gas up Morrison along the way."

"And the Hamptons?" asked Rosalita, looking around the dining room, smiling her *dare of a smile* that she had smiled the first time I met her in the Polo Lounge. "They here yet?"

"Soon. Seven. Very soon. Actually, now. There they are."

Roscoe saying that was like an ice cube down my back.

"Good evening, folks!" he sang out, walking briskly toward them. "Good to see you again, you have a reservation, I believe?"

Behind us, I could hear the shuffling feet of the Hamptons, Roscoe's mixed in, walking towards what had become *their* table.

Then the sound of seat cushions wheezing. Rosie and I were still, silent, gazing up at the wall of bottles, sneaking peeks in the mirror.

I was having that *this is it* feeling.

"Did they see us?" asked Rosie.

"Hard to say. They probably will, any second. Or they'll act like they haven't until we go downstairs. And then it'll all begin. But you know, Rosie—they're gonna *see* us, in these clothes. Especially you, Ms. Yellow Like Van Gogh!"

"And you, Mr. Red like Jumbo!"

"Nice rhyming scheme there, Rosalita."

"Red, it already *has* begun. So ..."

"Let's really *wear* these clothes?"

"Yeah. And let's really wear *ourselves*."

In a few minutes, Roscoe came back to the bar with a face full of fun, of hiding our big secret.

"Drinks?" he asked, loudly. "Mr. Jumbo? *Rosalita?* Your usual?"

"Yes, Mr. Towne," Rosalita answered loudly. "The ... *Bubbles of Vergèze.*"

"Excellent choice!"

Time was crawling, the Union Station Bar was filling up, getting louder. I wanted to get into the action; I had been drinking coffee and *the Bubbles* since morning, and now my nerves were talking amongst themselves.

Roscoe and Rosalita were making small talk for the Hamptons to observe. The Hamptons were drinking, looking angry and restless at their table (they'd *definitely* observed us), waiting for their dinner orders to arrive. But I hadn't seen the *stage* yet, the Charlie Parker Room. I wanted to get a look at *The Tube*. Now.

"Bloody Club, sir?" asked Roscoe, *bartending* me, smiling widely for the Hamptons.

"Yes. I'll have another. Slice of lime, this time."

"But of course, my fair gent, if that's your bent!"

Rosie looked at me, then at Roscoe. Then again at me. "Wow, you two. Such rhyme and meter."

"I'll be right back," I nudged Rosie. "Gotta pee," I said, but I was really going downstairs to see the stage. "It may take a detective like me fifteen minutes, but I'll be right back." I didn't want Rosie to feel abandoned in this tense, last-minute moment.

I started to get up from the bar. I could've sworn I heard the Hamptons teeth grinding at their table. But when I looked slightly in their direction, I saw it was only the ice cubes clinking in their cocktails. I got up and got to the back hallway of the restaurant and made for the kitchen door; the staff knew me by now.

Dee came out of that swinging door with a tray of food up high, trailing delicious white clouds.

"*Mmm,* what's up there?" I asked.

"KC Strip, Coq au Vin, Jumbo Shrimp," she said, gliding by. "Good luck, tonight, by the way!" She stopped short, but the tray continued to float, somehow not spilling. Dee started to laugh and turned around. The tray rotated on her axis, swirling the mixed aromas.

"It just occurred to me—that's an oxymoron. *Jumbo Shrimp.* Hahaha, no offense, Mr. *Red* Jumbo!" She turned and glided down the hall, laughing, toward the dining room, the tray still completely balanced and steaming.

"It's a night for corny jokes," I said out loud to myself, and the kitchen door swung open again. This time—Guillaume, in the full white chef's outfit, and hat.

"Oh, I have one for you, a corny joke!" he said, stopping in his tracks, with an arm full of brown and blue eggs in their cartons.

"What are *you* doing here?" I asked.

"Oh, borrowing these eggs, my restaurant ran out, can you believe it? Must get back there now, many reservations in the book tonight! Oh! Red! I am curious: is it all about to begin? The *sabotage?* Ooo, I am excited for you!"

"It *is* about to begin, I was just coming back here to do a last-minute check on the tube."

"Ah, oui, it's just over there, you see? So, anyway, before I go, this corny joke: do you know the one about the three-legged dog?"

"Can we do that later, after the sabotage?"

Guillaume looked both ways and patted me on the shoulder. He moved in close enough to kiss me, then he *did,* on both cheeks.

"Certainement! I leave you to your devices, and—to your *device!*"

He held the door open for me and pointed, with a flourish, toward the distant shining, brilliant, golden object. "Voilà! Yes, it is finished. Mon chérie's friend, *Chainsaw,* he is crazy, but he works fast!"

Then Guillaume was gone, out the door into Union Station, back uptown to the Plaza.

I walked into the kitchen. It was busy—noisy, sounds of water running, plates ringing, silverware clattering, food frying, cooks and waiters talking back and forth—it was so busy I felt complete privacy in the midst of it all.

The object that was shining so brilliantly in the corner near the dishwashing machine ... I realized what it was.

I walked over closer. What a great idea.

It was perfect. It was funny. It was beautiful to see, and very moving.

Coming up from the floor in the back corner of the kitchen was the tube—gleaming golden brass, flowering up and fanning out into the shape of the bell ... of a saxophone.

This was the end of the tube that the *Charlie Parker Cocktail Napkin Money* was going to fly out of.

Now I had to go downstairs and see the rest of the tube. But I'd have to be quick.

It was almost time to begin.

I hurried into the small elevator. "Good evening, *Otis,*" I said. I pushed a red (DOWN) button, the door closed, the car jerked with a mechanical-metallic *clank,* and floated down to the Charlie Parker room.

There was a low, steady hum in the room. I felt around, flicked the switch for the light, and the bulb eased up brighter, little by little. The room had changed a lot since our last meeting.

Immediately before me, suspended in the air right at *mouth* level, was a shiny black saxophone mouthpiece. There was a sign hanging over it that said: "Blow." But even without the sign, you sort of had to blow on it, the way it was situated in the room. I almost did, too—blow on it, I wanted to—but I noticed some wires coming out of it, leading into the ceiling, and the beginning of the tube: the shiny golden neck and body of this oversized saxophone, curving gently down then gracefully up and into the ceiling, and then *more* wires, spreading everywhere. I edged carefully around the mouthpiece, not even exhaling around it, figuring it was part of the *surprise.*

From the mouthpiece, the body of the saxophone flattened out into a long, gleaming, transparent box, suspended at *hands* level, where there was a small plexiglass door with a shiny silver latch. Inside, softly but clearly lit by tiny pin lights, were many tall, neat stacks—of crisp, green, five hundred dollar bills.

Above the transparent box was a black mechanism hidden high up in the ceiling, small red and green lights blinking off and on. I figured it must be part of whatever made a pneumatic tube pneumatic. Or—something else. Seeing that gave me a cold sub-basement chill.

I looked at the money again. Was that really one million dollars, the *Charlie Parker Cocktail Napkin Money?*

Now that I had seen the stage, it was time to get back upstairs with the rest of the actors. I turned off the light, stepped into the elevator, pushed the button, and traveled slowly upwards a few floors, swinging slightly left and right in the shaft, and came to another rude metallic stop at the top.

The door opened, steam floated in and I started back to the bar. But froze. Something was moving around in my brain. The detective part of me that I never turned completely off. Something was not in place. *Something*—I raced back through the clouds of steam and pulled open the elevator door, reached in, pushed the black (DOWN) button for the lowest floor and closed the door, I heard it jerk and descend. Whew! It would be waiting for us when we got there.

The steam floated in and carried me through the kitchen and out to the bar, just as the play was beginning.

Rosalita looked relieved that I was back. It was insensitive to leave her alone at such a time, and I was about to apologize when the curtain went up and Roscoe was *on stage*.

"Rosalita, would you like to stroll down and pick up a stack or two of our *Charlie Parker Cocktail Napkin Money?*"

The Hamptons, at their table near the bar, were watching. Glaring at us in the backbar mirror.

The Hamptons Surprise

Dee glided into the mirror and paused for a moment with her pen and order pad, looking like the most mischievous trickster of the Kansas City Art Institute.

"Dessert?" she asked the Hamptons. "We have fresh strawberries and cream, also a delicious white chocolate mousse!"

The Hamptons (watching us) said nothing. Their silence meant no. It was time to go.

Downstairs.

Roscoe (watching everything) saw that and made the first move. "*Well*, Rosie, shall we go visit the *Bank of Bird?* It's Friday, I'll deposit my paycheck, and we'll make a little withdrawal, for you."

"Oh, I've been so anxious to see this! So, this is the very spot where you found Charlie Parker's note?"

"Any after-dinner drinks?" Dee asked. More silence. I could sense that the Hamptons were about to snap. Their table was crowded with before, during, and after-dinner drinks.

"Yes! The very spot!" Roscoe answered and looked at me. "Red? Would you like to come with us? You're a jazz fan, aren't you?"

"Well, sure, is that alright with you, Rosie?"

"You're ready for the check, then?" asked Dee.

"PLEASE!" Mrs. Hamptons blurted. "YES, BRING THE CHECK!"

This was loud. The dining room was full, including the barstools to the right and left of us, which swiveled now, towards the Hamptons. But not Rosalita, not me, we didn't swivel. And not Roscoe, talking, laughing, and pouring drinks, as if he hadn't heard this outburst.

I saw the Hamptons in the mirror; Mrs. Hamptons was red in the face, clenching her jaw, staring out the north windows of the restaurant. She got up, jarring the table, tinkling the glasses, spilling a couple, and said she was going to the restroom. And nearly ran out of the dining room.

"I'll get the check, sir," said Dee, in the friendliest voice I'd heard from her yet. But I heard a trace of treachery in it. She looked *ready.* For it all to begin.

"Just a second," said Mr. Hamptons, grabbing Dee's arm. She asked him to let go and he did, smiling drunk, in her direction, but missing her eyes. He was sitting sloppy, half on his chair, half off, teetering, writing on a cocktail napkin, pressing down hard and tearing it, grabbing the napkin under Mrs. Hamptons drink, starting over. He finished, held up his credit card and the note. As she reached for them, he took her hand, and kissed it.

With a little bit of lick, a little bit of tongue.

"Yeah, Red. Let's go downstairs," said Rosie in a low, charged voice. Clearly, she'd seen the lick, too.

"*Very well.* So—" Roscoe had seen the tongue too; we had the backbar mirror, but he had his bartender's eyes, watching everything, "—shall we?"

We began to stand up, slowly, stretching, yawning, waiting for Dee to come back with the check for the Hamptons, waiting for Mrs. Hamptons to come back from the restroom, not wanting to get too far ahead of them; going slowly …

Dee came back, smiling, pretend laughing, flipped her note from Mr. Hamptons to us (behind her back!), sailing it perfectly landing on the bar between Rosie and Roscoe and me, and delivered the check to the Hamptons table, just as Mrs. Hamptons was returning; puffy-eyed, weaving, *heavily rouged.*

Roscoe picked up the note, read it, crumpled it, and glared down at the bar top. He pushed the crumpled note over to us, flattened it out, we read:

I'd like fresh strawberries and
MY cream on YOUR "mousse" —
It IS white chocolate, isn't it? LOL! I know it's delicious baby!
(Crown Center, Room 701. Knock once, wait for me to cum. Ha!)

Rosie's mouth was tight and her eyes angry. She whispered, "Let's go."

Roscoe came around from behind the bar and we *eased* into our exit, casually talking about whatever, something, anything—acting completely "unaware" of the Hamptons as they "spied" on us from their table.

Rosie was looking at me with the slyest look in her eyes, she led us dangerously close to the Hamptons table, and when we got there she bumped it with her hip, jiggling and tinkling the glasses again.

Not that the Hamptons noticed. Mrs. Hamptons was fumbling with her purse and Mr. Hamptons was inspecting the check, figuring the tip, checking the total: their attempts at appearing not to see or hear us.

We kept moving, pushing through the brass doors and into the wide expanse of the Union Station.

Roscoe pointed across the lobby to an exit and we walked towards it.

"Are they taking the bait?" asked Roscoe. "Are they coming?" he asked again, *excited.*

When we got through the door, on the other side of it, we let it slowly, slowly begin to shut, though *this* door was not closing cottony-soft; the three of us crouched at different heights, peeking through the door which was taking forever to close on those groaning, ancient, rusty hinges, and just before it shut, we saw the Hamptons; *they were coming our way!*

We stood up out of our crouches, the Hamptons footsteps echoing off the red-rose marble lobby floor, getting closer. Roscoe cracked his knuckles, I flinched, and Rosalita looked at me.

"Ready, Rosie?" I asked.

"I'm remembering the Rose Bowl and every other thing including that note to Dee a moment ago. I'm very ready."

"Let's go," whispered Roscoe, the Hamptons echoing even closer.

We walked, zig-zagging down three flights, into a long hallway of light bulbs zipping past us overhead, into the dark tunnel. Rosie, with her red leather sneakers, didn't make any noise, so Roscoe had to scuff and stomp to make sure we were heard. Every once in a while we would pause to listen to the footsteps behind us, Roscoe stayed out in front, leading us out of the tunnel, then we turned left, into *the room.*

"Careful, don't touch anything!" Roscoe whispered, standing in front of the floating, oversized saxophone with the "Blow" sign, then —*"Rosie, Red; you two get in the elevator."*

So, *we two* (who else?) ran over and got in the elevator, waiting, wondering *what next?*

Roscoe smiled and said, *loudly* and cheerfully—

"SO *ROSIE,* if that's enough, if that's all you really need, you sure you don't want another stack of hundreds? No? How about you, Red? No? Well, then let's go back upstairs and have another drink to celebrate." Roscoe jumped in behind us as the elevator door *purred slowly* closed, revealing a round, dirty window. We all clustered close around it to peek through the old, yellowed glass.

Shhh. One of us said. Like one of us needed to; we were still, silent, waiting.

Footsteps, slower, hesitant; step ... step ... step. Then we saw the Hamptons at the door of the Charlie Parker Room.

They were wide-eyed and staring at the big golden saxophone.

They stared at the mouthpiece, at the sign suggesting they *Blow* on it, then (*There it is!* Mrs. Hamptons pealed, startling us) at the money inside the transparent box.

Mr. Hamptons looked at the fresh green stacks of bills without expression—he didn't seem overjoyed, for some reason—then he was reading the sign and studying the mouthpiece. He wasn't enthusiastic about that either. Standing there in the elevator, I realized that since the first day I'd met him at the Lanyard Hotel, I'd never seen him overjoyed about much of anything.

Mrs. Hamptons looked around the room; looked at our elevator, saw the window, cloudy and yellowed.

"Where'd they go?" she asked.

"Back upstairs, I guess."

"How?"

Mr. Hamptons looked around the room; he saw the elevator, too.

"Guess they went up that way. Whatever. But now we know where the money is, and how to get down here. We'll come down here later, tomorrow, before the bar opens, when none of them are around, and get it all bagged up. Bring the travel bags down here, fill' em up, roll it all upstairs and out to the car."

Mrs. Hamptons frowned and started pacing, came right up to the elevator window, turned, and stopped, with her back to us.

"Now that I think of it," she said, "is that gonna look weird, if someone sees us, rolling our suitcases up from down here? Right out into the lobby?"

"We'll act like we're lost, like we just got in from the airport ..."

"And we'll say, isn't this the Crown Center Hotel? Where's the front desk? We have a reservation, *goddamnit!* Ha ha, brilliant!"

"Yeah, just a couple of confused, stupid, Midwestern tourists."

In the elevator, behind the clouded yellow window, we were only inches away from Mrs. Hamptons!

"Right. Sounds good. Anyway, I guess it's not going anywhere, the money," said Mrs. Hamptons, walking over to the transparent box. "So we can take it slow, come back tomorrow and get it. That's a lot of money, just sitting here in this saxophone thing. And what *is* this thing? It's like a shrine or something. A shrine to this guy Bird. I remember him, some drug addict, singer, or whatever he was. Harry Parker."

"Charlie."

"Huh?"

"Charlie Parker."

"Ok. Charlie Parker. Some dead, drug-addicted musician. What a cliche. Who cares? I need a cocktail."

"Let's get back upstairs," said Mr. Hamptons, walking toward the door.

In the darkness of the elevator, Roscoe put a finger to his lips, mouthed *wait*. Rosalita and I watched through the cloudy window, holding our breath.

Mrs. Hamptons was smiling, not moving, delicately touching the plexiglass door to the *Charlie Parker Cocktail Napkin* stash.

"Can we take a little, now?" she asked in a baby doll voice.

"Yeah. Or a lot," said Mr. Hamptons, eyeing the saxophone mouthpiece.

"Go on," said Mrs. Hamptons.

Mr. Hamptons smiled a tiny smile. Big for him, as far as I'd seen, so far.

"Should I?" he said, licking his lips.

"Go *on.*"

Get ready, whispered Roscoe.

"What if they hear it?" asked Mr. Hamptons.

"Awww, they're all the way upstairs in that noisy bar. We're way down here. Go *on.*"

"Ok, I will. I don't give a shit about Charlie Parker, but I do like music. Always thought I had some in me." Mr. Hamptons moved close to the mouthpiece. He took a deep breath, I was still holding mine.

"I have a request, honey," said Mrs. Hamptons.

"Honey? You haven't called me honey in decades." His tiny smile got a tiny bit warmer.

"Play *Lover Man.* Play it for me, since you *are* one."

Rosie flinched, and gasped. The Hamptons heard it, looked around the room, at the elevator window, but not through it. Rosie inhaled deeply, through her nose.

Mr. Hamptons licked his lips, inhaled—and blew hard into the tube. The note that Mr. Hamptons sounded was like a wet fart through a plastic bag.

"Guess I'm too drunk," he said, looking embarrassed, another new look for him. His eyes startled and sharpened, he was hearing something. We were all hearing it, a sound something like a long rush of air; a sound like something *pneumatic.*

With a loud WOOOSH—the *Charlie Parker Cocktail Napkin Money*, each neat stack of crisp bills—one million dollars—*flashed* up the tube, in a flurry of light yellow-green, into the ceiling, *out of the room.*

"Hang on," said Roscoe.

The saxophone empty, the fogged-up plexiglass door popped open, puffing steam. Above the mouthpiece, red and yellow lights flashed in the ceiling, a whirring sound was growing, and the wires were crackling, sizzling, starting to smoke. Even in the elevator, we could tell, the room was *hot.*

The Hamptons looked at each other in fear. They moved toward the door. A blast of flames and smoke filled the entrance. They jerked back, cowering. A booming roar filled the room.

"Is this the surprise?" I whispered to Roscoe.

"Part of it," he whispered back.

There was a big thud and the room jolted, and shook hard. Sounds of grinding stone or concrete. Another, even louder boom —

"STOP!" yelled Rosie.

She opened the elevator door, walked through the quivering Hamptons to a flashing red button up amid the wires, lights, and machinery in the ceiling, and pushed it. The red and yellow lights faded out, the whirring whirled down, and the flames and smoke and booming dissipated, spread out, thinned out.

Rosalita turned, looked straight at the Hamptons, and walked through the sputtering flames in the doorway, out of the room, and into the dark hallway.

Roscoe and I looked at each other, didn't say a word. The Hamptons had their backs to us, standing in place, swaying drunk, swaying along with the turning Earth. The four of us, frozen in time and silence, then—footsteps—sounded like many feet, coming back down the hall, getting closer. Rosie showed up in the dim light carrying two old wooden chairs, and she kicked them into the room, nodding *thanks* at someone in the darkness beyond the door. She looked at the Hamptons.

"Sit *down*," she said.

Mr. Hamptons raised his right arm like he was going to protest, but then he swayed sideways into Mrs. Hamptons, and they fell backwards into the chairs, knocking and bouncing the chairs around so that when they got seated and settled, they were looking in our direction, Roscoe and me, in the elevator. But they weren't looking at *us*.

Their large, unfocused eyes; drunk but awake. Watching Rosalita.

She walked in a circle around the room; a tighter circle around the Hamptons; she walked in front of them and stopped.

"You raped me, so *fuck you,*" she said.

Mr. Hamptons raised his arm again and again Rosie said, "Fuck you. Shut up."

Mrs. Hamptons, quivering chin, quivering everything, looked at Mr. Hamptons with horrified eyes. He had been looking at Rosie, but now he wasn't looking at anyone, or anything.

"Fuck you. I'm not going to tell you how that made me feel, how I *have* felt, alone with it for a while but not *anymore*, and how walled-in the world got for me. And I sure as hell won't tell you how I've been getting it and *not* getting over it, but while I'll never forget that you raped me in my car on a beautiful day, I will forget *you*. Both of you. Even if you *are* beginning to cry, Mrs. *Whatever the fuck your first name is.*"

And yes, Mrs. Hamptons was crying. One of her shoes had come off, she was shaking, moaning, rocking in her chair. Mr. Hamptons was red, his head like a balloon, blowing up.

Rosie was not crying.

"I'm not afraid of you anymore. "I faked my death to get away from you. A dress dummy went off the bridge, not me, but I'm away from you and you can't do shit to me anymore."

"Please, let me …" said Mr. Hamptons, falling out of his chair. Mr. Hamptons was on the floor, clutching himself. Mrs. Hamptons crawling around and *on* him.

"Fuck you," said Rosie. "There is only one thing I want from you and that is for you both to GO AWAY!"

"You heard her," said a voice in the dark.

A voice a little boozy, but a lot strong. Something or *someone* large floated into the room, a big man in a wine-stained white shirt, and he got behind Rosie.

Out in the hall, there was a low growling in the dark—a sort of *MMMMMMM* electric razor sound—and another, thinner man came in, in a black suit, also got behind Rosie, next to the first man, and said, "Hi, Hank."

"Hi, Bill."

A flock of butterflies flew through my stomach and my jaw dropped open. I grabbed Roscoe's arm, and he grabbed the arm I was grabbing him with back, *tight.* We held onto each other and looked at each other, pop-eyed.

"Are you seeing this, too?" I whispered, still holding onto his arm. Roscoe nodded yes, crazily grinning at me, then turned back to the spectacle of everything that was happening.

"Damn," he said, shaking his head. "I thought something would happen. I mean, I *asked,* but … *damn!* Something in the air. Power and light, man."

We relaxed a little, took a deep breath, and let go of each other, smiling. We looked over to where Rosie was standing, right in the middle of everything.

She looked relaxed but fierce, and taking it all in.

The two men looked at the Hamptons and checked their watches.

"Say, Bill, What time does the mail come around here?" asked Hank.

"Can't say," said Bill.

"What do *you* say, Roscoe?" asked Hank, looking at the Hamptons on the floor.

"Anytime now, Mr. Bukowski." Roscoe turned to me, shaking.

There was a soft sucking sound, getting louder, coming closer, the sucking sound rising, something clanging, banging, ricocheting, coming our way, then there was a streak of white and a pneumatic canister slammed into the transparent plastic box.

Hank walked over to the box, opened the door, pulled out the canister and removed an envelope. He took reading glasses from his shirt pocket, wiped them on his shirt, put them on, opened the envelope, and took out a piece of paper. He cleared his throat.

"It's for you, Mr. and Mrs. Hamptons. From the law firm of Burroughs, Bukowski, and Bird, in Los Angeles. The bottom line is that your house burned down and you've lost all your money. Says here that your front gate was left open, your house was unlocked for some reason, so some guys got in, ransacked the place and burned it to the ground. There's a lot of legalese and bullshit, but there's something here about securities fraud and tax evasion, and the I.R.S. has been alerted. This correspondence has been cc'd to a *Mr. Chainsaw,* inter-office. Says for you to call him at your very earliest convenience."

The Hamptons were small on the floor, getting smaller. They couldn't speak, couldn't make their mouths work. Their eyes were wet, unfocused, darting back and forth between Rosalita and the two men standing over them.

"They're going to the slammer, eh, Burroughs?"

The thin man laughs. "Damn straight."

Hank tore the letter and envelope in half and laughed. "Just kidding."

The thin man pulled back his jacket an inch or two, and there, on his hip, the shine of a long, silver-barreled handgun.

"Hey, Mister. Remember me?"

Mr. Hamptons clutched his inner thigh.

"Remembe*r this?"* Another voice. A warm, full voice, from somewhere. From a man not in the room, but filling it, and Union Station, and Kansas City, and on and on all the way to Paris and back.

Something caught my eye, and I nudged Roscoe. Something glistening on the mouthpiece of the saxophone; glistening and moistening.

The softness of the sound of breathing, silence, a brief inhale, then the opening notes of *Lover Man* lit up the sub-basement. The unmistakable sound of Charlie Parker.

Roscoe closed his eyes and smiled. "Oh man, there's that sound again. Mmm ..."

A few minutes later, when the song was finished, the big, warm voice said, "As you see, I take requests. Now I'd like you two *Hamptons* on the floor to take Rosie's request, and go away."

Roscoe opened his eyes and we looked at each other again.

The Hamptons were looking at each other, too.

Rosalita stood her ground.

The warm voice said, "Dalai?"

Summoned by the invisible but very present voice of—it *was* Charlie Parker himself—the Dalai of Union Station walked in the door, filling it, and extended a hand to the Hamptons.

"Come on, folks," he said, smiling softly, "let's get you up and out of here. You're having kind of a bad night, aren't you?"

The drunk Hamptons struggled up, staggered and scissored sideways, but Dalai had each of them firmly in hand; left hand in Mr. Hamptons' hand, right hand lifting Mrs. Hamptons to her feet.

I looked over at Rosie; she was standing straight and strong, watching. The two men that had been behind her, Hank and Bill, were gone. Just Rosie, standing there. Waiting for the Hamptons to be gone.

"Back to the hotel," said Dalai, leading them by the hand, around the pneumatic tube, past the suspended saxophone mouthpiece, to the door of the Charlie Parker Room, "and back to California. But not back to normal. You two must die, but *we're* not gonna kill you. You die, then you must start over. Get some help. "

Dalai took them by the hand, out of the room, into the dark hallway, gone.

Roscoe slid the elevator door open and we listened to Dalai walk them away. Dalai was still talking. "You need professional help to get yourselves broken down and killed off. Worked for me. You'll see."

Then, footsteps echoing, fading through the tunnel, and up the stairs. All quiet.

Then, footsteps coming back. Down through the tunnel, slowly.

And then there was Mr. Hamptons, bracing himself in the frame of the door, trying to speak, looking at the floor. "I want to apologize, Rosalita. For what happened."

He backed into the hall, saw me in the elevator and did a double-take, gave me what might have been a dirty look (though with tears in his eyes, and I think maybe mine, I don't know if I was seeing him clearly), then he looked away, and walked away.

I was frozen in the elevator door, didn't know what to do next. I wanted to go down the hall after Hamptons. I was moved, but confused, and it wasn't good enough, I thought. What he'd said. I wanted to go down the hall for Rosie, to fight for her, defend her, but she was handling everything perfectly, so I kept still.

Rosie was staring at the dark, empty door. The hall was quiet. So quiet we could hear music, people talking upstairs in the bar. But then I heard something in the hall. I looked at Rosie, and we looked at each other like we'd been waiting for, but never really expecting this sound. It was only just beginning.

Roscoe was nodding and smiling, *yes*.

The sound of *sliding*; long, slow sliding down a wall somewhere in the hall, or the tunnel, sliding and collapsing on the floor; the sound of something coming up from inside Mr. Hamptons; retching, gagging, coughing, spitting sounds, young boy moaning, followed by a long, deep breath, a high, loud howl, and then hard sobbing …

… he cried for a long time. And we waited for him.

After a while (he seemed to cry forever), he blew his nose on something, we heard him struggling to stand up, and he was coming our way.

Mr. Hamptons, in the door again.

He *looked* like Mr. Hamptons, but like some other, softer man. He looked softly at Rosie, and red as his eyes were, they were larger now, and very clear.

"Rosalita. I'm sorry. I'm sorry for raping you. Because *that* is *what happened*, as I *didn't* say, a few minutes ago. I raped you." He was starting to cry again, but tried to stop, for the moment. "There's something wrong. *Something* wrong in me. I wake up the same way every morning. I hope Dalai's right. I hope I can do something …" Mr. Hamptons let go, crying again."… no, I *will* do something," he said, clearing his throat, and maybe his mind. "I'm sorry, Rosalita. I'll go. Unless you want to say something."

Rosie shook her head no, she didn't. Mr. Hamptons nodded *ok,* tried for a soft smile, which it was, looking first at Roscoe, then at me. Not with a soft smile exactly, but in the neighborhood of friendly, for the first time.

"Goodbye, Mr. Jumbo. I think you're probably good at your job after all, *whatever* it is."

I saw Rosie and Roscoe checking me out, probably also wondering what that job was, and when I looked back, Mr. Hamptons was gone.

"Maybe my job is to be your elevator operator tonight."

Rosie and Roscoe smiled at me, and each other, looked around the Charlie Parker Room again … at the dark, empty door … and entered the elevator.

"Going *up?*"

"The elevator *jumped*, and began to climb; I turned to Roscoe. "Roscoe, were those men, those writer guys—the *late* Charles Bukowski and William S. Burroughs, along with the voice and music of Charlie Parker—were they part of the surprise?"

Roscoe, relaxed and rascally reclined in a back corner of the elevator, jumped his eyebrows twice and chuckled.

"I planned the letter in the envelope and used their names as the lawyers in our plan to terrify the Hamptons, but those guys actually showing up *themselves*—that was a surprise to me," said Roscoe.

"But I've always been one to ask for help and usually I get it— no matter the source. I'm glad they came."

The elevator window getting brighter, yellow light drifting down from above, also laughter, music, and ... a sort of *cheering.*

The elevator came to a sudden stop and—*ding!*

The door slid open to the bright, busy kitchen—all porcelain, silvery, steamy, black and white tile—with the chef, her assistant chef, the dish man, three busboys, Aunt Arctica, Guillaume, Alberto, Serge, Ruby, and Fyodor turning to us, frozen in the moment; their faces curiously looking at us, hands still in the air, mouths open in the middle of cheering, and a flurry of millions of dollars (*give or take*) flying out of the golden bell of the pneumatic saxophone tube.

"What happened?" asked Aunt Arctica.

"He apologized," said Rosalita.

"*No,*" said Auntie.

"Yeah," said Rosie.

"Is that good enough for you, Rosalita?"

"Yes."

Everyone standing there, dazed by this news, kept *on* standing there, being dazed. Alberto and Serge, dazed by this but now laughing at the sight of all the flying money, began grasping in the air at the floating bills, trying to collect more from the floor, while Dee and a young Black man in a Nelson Gallery museum uniform (and a name tag: *Christopher*) eased back and relaxed along the side of a big bludgeoned (juicy) butcher block table. Dee began to laugh, and drink wine. Christopher was dazed, too, looking a little *out of the loop,* but enjoying Dee's laughter.

As for me, I felt fantastic. And on the verge of tears. I felt free. I *felt.*

I wasn't *really* a detective, never had been, but I was something else now, something better than a detective, or an elevator operator, or any other job description, something finally, forever free.

I could live upstairs, or anywhere, now.

As the millions (more or less) floated through the kitchen— landing in salads, bits of butter, slices of bread, coq au vins, the dishwashing machine—I flashed on that *other* sub-basement, that basement in Eagle Rock in my house in California. I thought of the night I came up out of it, right up to the moon. Me and the dogs. And the night blooming jasmine. Then, as I flashed on *where are those dogs?,* Kansas, Missouri, and Felix came stampeding into the kitchen from somewhere and jumped up at a baguette sticking off the edge of the butcher block table. They didn't need to; the chef and her assistant drew three fresh *puppy-sized* baguettes out of the oven, and dropped them on the floor.

But back to me.

Just a little while ago I was there. I'd go for days and nights and weeks in that basement out west. Facebook. Porn. Angry, hopeless news. Liquor store. It was a lifetime ago.

Not where I was now, in the kitchen of the Union Station Bar. Surrounded.

Someone turned up the music; Rosalita danced with Alberto, Ruby danced with Fyodor, Aunt Arctica danced with Guillaume, then with Serge, Dee danced with Christopher (who pulled off his tie), then also with Serge.

The red round womanly chef came to me through the kitchen steam and floating money, hands extended, *wanna dance?*

Oh, *did* I! Puffs of flour burst as we clasped hands.

It was *peaceful*, this music, I felt like I was floating in outer space, in a way where I wouldn't necessarily want to return to earth, not *yet*, anyway. I asked the chef what the music was. She whirled me toward Aunt Arctica, who said, "It's Mozart's piano concerto, number twenty," and whirled away.

"Köchel listing 466, right?" asked the chef, whirling me dizzy.

"Yeah—uh, that's what I thought," I said.

"Yes, exactly, in D minor," said Dee, floating in from the other side, dancing now with Guillaume, "the second movement—ROMANCE!"

Then *she* floated away. I loved this music, loved seeing Dee dancing and looking romantic herself, especially after that note from Hamptons. She was giving special looks to the museum guard Christopher and he was giving them back. Roscoe was leaning against the wall, watching everyone, looking happy and peaceful. I looked around again for Rosalita, to see how she was doing, and saw her in the far corner of the kitchen, dancing with Alberto. Her husband. Her lover. They were dancing close, smiling at each other, like a tremendous load was finally off, a big weight.

The Mozart concerto softly tinkled down in piano notes like snowflakes (that's what I thought, then *said,* to my dancing partner, the chef; she looked a little dazzled by the poetry of the line, but maybe she was dazzled by everything else going on in the room) and ended. We all applauded, bowed, curtsied, etc.; the dance was over.

We'd all had a weight lifted.

There was a sweet silence in the kitchen, except for a dripping faucet. The wall phone rang in the kitchen. Roscoe answered it. He perked up and covered the receiver with his hand, whispering. Laughing and excited. He hung up, did a little twirl on the tiles, and danced out the door. We watched him through the order pick-up window as he danced to the bar and turned off the jazz music softly playing in the dining room.

The customers looked up a moment, Roscoe waved and announced complimentary champagne (*or* Bubble of Vergèze) for everyone; the customers smiled, nodded, and went back to eating, back to talking.

At the bar, Roscoe opened a drawer, took out a CD, slid it into the CD player, looked back at us through the order window in the kitchen and announced: "*Places*, dancers. And ..."

With a flourish, he spun what I'd correctly guessed was the volume knob, because the speakers popped and the customers jumped in their chairs.

"... burn, baby, *burn*."

The song ("Disco Inferno" by The Trammps) came on LOUD, filled the dining room, spilled into the kitchen, Ruby screamed, Rosie laughed, Roscoe jumped from the bar to the big brass door, flung it open, *and*

right there, in the door

Jenny Sue Skiptewmaylewe (in a sparkling red sequin pantsuit) ran in then *slid* past all the barstools along the linoleum, her eyes on me all the way, the slide ending just a few feet short of the order window, where she stopped, looked through, and said, "Hi there, Red."

"Well, *that's* some kind of a woman!" said Aunt Arctica.

The kitchen burst into dancing. I ran to the kitchen door, Jenny met me there, and we collided in a big hug which lasted until we bumped our heads on some pots hanging from the ceiling.

Roscoe, amazed, smiling and delighted, ran and jumped into a slide of his own, but in his excitement he veered off course, off the linoleum where it ended at the carpet, where he stumbled into the dining room tables, and customers, and he rolled, tumbling and laughing into a professorial old man in a wheelchair, and they both tipped over onto the floor.

Dee inhaled suddenly, alarmed.

"Oh shit," she said, laughing out loud, "that's Dr. Hoffmann, Chair and Professor Emeritus of Renaissance Art History at the Kansas City Art Institute."

The song ended. There was what I would call, if I had to describe it, a scholarly silence. One of the dogs trotted across the tiles with a one hundred-dollar bill in his mouth.

Dr. Hoffmann looked down at Roscoe splayed beneath him (like he was looking down from inside a gilt-dusted art gallery frame, yet appreciative of Roscoe's exuberance) and asked, "Excuse me, *Mr. Towne,* but would that complimentary champagne be Veuve Clicquot, by any chance?"

Roscoe was up off the floor, after brushing himself off, uprighting the professor's wheelchair, selecting new music, finding the case of, yes, Dr. Hoffmann, *Veuve Clicquot,* and pouring free champagne at every table in the Union Station Bar.

The music was "Parker's Mood," and Jenny and I were dancing.

"I'm *so* glad to see you. You just drove up?"

"Just got off the train. Lawrence to KC, bullet train. Sort of. Sort of a slow bullet. But, Mr. Jumbo, here I am!"

I was in love already, *really* in love with her. With everybody. And *everybody* was dancing.

"What happened?" asked Jenny. "Down in the sub-basement?"

"We lured the Hamptons with the money, then pneumatically sucked it away. Kind of silly, needlessly elaborate, but kind of *fun*, I thought, and *funny,* in its improbability. Just a few minutes, or an hour ago. There we were, and I saw all this machinery, this pneumatic *thing* light up, suck the money out of the room, trigger this wild amount of fear-inducing special effects, flames and smoke … it's funny, Jenny … at that moment, the tube thing started sparking, wires crackling, smoking, and the room got *hot*, so I didn't know if the machinery was malfunctioning, or if it was actually working the way it was supposed to, if someone was about to get hurt, but anyway—at the last second—Rosie *stopped* it. Pressed a button, turned it off, sat the Hamptons down, got in front of them and told them: *fuck you.*"

"Good for her!"

"From one second to the next, I couldn't believe what I was seeing. Or hearing. But I—*we*—heard Charlie Parker speak, then play our partially pneumatic saxophone. I still can't believe it. Two other guys were there—*writers,* of all things—I recognized one of them, I'd spoken to his wife, Linda Lee Bukowski, in a bookstore out in Pasadena, and the other guy had a pistol, it was your man Burroughs, around the corner from your house, then they both disappeared … I don't know how any of this could've been—Charlie Parker, Burroughs, Bukowski are all dead—but they were there and Mr. Hamptons apologized."

"Gosh."

"Yeah. He did. Not at first. But then he broke down. They both did. Completely. They were very drunk, but their sobbing was deep, felt real."

"Jesus."

"Mr. Hamptons said he was sorry. Twice. The second time more a lot more honest, and … *vulnerable.*

"*Fuck.* What did Rosie say?"

"She told the Hamptons to go away. And they did. As I said, they were fucked up. They were drunk and looked *tired.* So then—with *perfect timing*—Dalai walked in from out of the darkness down there, and helped them up and out of the room, quite compassionately, back to Crown Center."

"Dalai? as in Hello, or His Holiness?"

"Neither. You'll probably meet *this* one later."

"Alright. Good."

"I hated the Hamptons, Jenny. I hated them a couple of hours ago. I've probably always been a little optimistically naive about how much people can change, and I thought these two were simply ugly, vile, gross. Beyond anything. But when they began to cry ... I don't know these people, what went wrong, what's wrong with them ... but I've never seen people cry like that. It wasn't manipulative crying, I've *seen* that. Probably *done* that. They must have been saving it up, holding onto it since ... a long time."

"Parker's Mood" ended, melancholy and inconclusive.

"How do you feel, Red?"

"Like celebrating! I didn't know you were gonna be here tonight! I love dancing with you."

"Me too, with you."

"Also, I feel ... I'm glad it's over. And I'm glad Rosie turned that thing off, that thing with the flames and all."

"I'm glad she stood up them."

Percussion, guitars, and a spreading, soothing, sexy synthesizer.

"Yes. *Yes.* I am proud of her. I love this song. Who is it?"

Jenny put her arms around me. "There's probably quite a lot more crying to come for the Hamptons. I don't know this song, but it's sexy to dance to."

"*Bryan Ferry,*" said Roscoe. " 'Don't Stop the Dance.' "

"We won't," said Jenny.

The song faded away but Jenny and I continued dancing, swaying, holding hands, fingers interlaced.

"Rosalita must feel relieved," Jenny said.

"I guess I feel relieved, too. I want to go home, go to bed."

Jenny looked alarmed.

"Well, home for *now*. Sleep in. Talk about all this later, or maybe in the morning. I'm exhausted. I think we all are."

I looked around the dining room; Roscoe cleaning up behind the bar, preparing to close, customers drifting away, Dr. Hoffmann wheeling himself out, tipping his tweed Irish walking hat to Roscoe (they knew each other, they were already pals, it turned out, from Roscoe's recent artistic adventures in a workshop at the art institute), Rosie sitting in a booth with Alberto, gazing out the north windows at the twinkling Kansas City skyline, Dee and Christopher kissing in a booth. Only Jenny and I were still dancing.

"But I'm happy, Jenny. Want to go home with us?"

"California?"

"Aunt Arctica."

Jenny was *re*-alarmed.

"Not *that* Antarctica. The one you met tonight. Who loved your entrance. *Aunt* Arctica is much closer, much warmer. Has a big house about fifteen minutes south of here."

"Of course. I thought *that* name rang a bell."

Roscoe's face was lit up by his phone. "Dalai just texted me. He got them to their hotel room. Even tucked them in."

Rosie and Alberto got up out of their booth, Ruby and Fyodor came over from the bar with Serge, and Dee and Christopher watched from their booth until I motioned for them to join us; all came close, we got in a quiet circle. The dogs broke through to the center of the circle and lay down.

In a dim corner, Aunt Arctica rose from a booth, stretched, and yawned. "Let's go back to my house," she said.

Jenny squeezed my hand.

The kitchen door swung open and out came Guillaume, trailing steam; also very *loud* music.

"By the way," he said, swinging a pair of large, black, scuffed-up saxophone cases, one in each hand. "I give you—the *Charlie Parker Cocktail Napkin Money!*" he said. "*Most* of it. There may be a few hundred here and there, in the salads and sauces, pots and pans, but we'll get it all, Roscoe."

"Thank you, Guillaume. Help yourself to a *salad*, if you like. We couldn't have done it without you."

"Let's get up the hill to the mansion," said Aunt Arctica. "Light some candles. There are fresh sheets on all the beds. But we'll be up late, I think."

I squeezed Jenny's hand.

Roscoe began dancing with the music coming from the kitchen, he danced his way to the kitchen door, stuck his head in, said goodnight, and danced back to us. Jenny nudged me, I nudged her back; we recognized what the kitchen staff was blasting—the soundtrack from *The Rocky Horror Picture Show.*

"You're not strictly jazz, are you, Mr. Towne?" asked Auntie.

"I'm not *strictly* anything," he said.

Jenny and I squeezed *each other's* hands.

We all quietly left the bar, the front brass doors of the Union Station Bar clicking cotton-soft shut behind us, the dogs clicking curiously ahead across the marble lobby floor. Through the glass, at the top of the arched windows of Union Station, I saw the full, Halloween-orange moon.

She had her earrings on.

South, to Aunt Arctica's

We got out to the parking lot and I looked for our old friend Morrison, easy to spot; I called it—*Still Life: White Van in Orange Moonlight*. Still there, waiting for us.

If I was ever going to get sentimental, romantic, or attached to something in *wheels*, it was going to be this van. From Eagle Rock to the Hamptons mansion, from the Beverly Hills Hotel across the Rockies, then across Kansas (zzz) to here; I walked up and patted the van on the windshield.

The wipers seemed to move and speak, "We've come a long way, eh, pal?"

I came out of conversation with Morrison and looked around the Union Station parking lot. Guillaume putting the sax cases into the back of Roscoe's car, the two of them briefly hugging, then Guillaume and Aunt Arctica getting into her MG (ragtop *up*, snow forecast—Guillaume changing into his shorter chef's hat, the one for driving); Roscoe squeezing into his small car, revving his small engine, *Smart*ly; Christopher escorting Dee (and opening her door) to what *for me* is the perfect car—a classic Volkswagen Bug—and when he started it, the sound of that engine triggered a deep breath in me and I inhaled all the way back to college. (I'd had six Beetles, all fun, all totaled. And I'd been in Jenny's, where she'd totaled *me!* Delightfully.) The rest of us got into Morrison.

I looked at the gang in the rear-view mirror; the faces of Alberto and Rosie, Serge, Fyodor, and Ruby snuggling in the back—Jenny Sue riding shotgun—all of them quiet, smiling, peaceful.

"That's all behind us now," I said. "Well, *mostly*."

"I wonder what's ahead?" asked Alberto, in a soft voice. Soft, but more wondering (maybe even dreaming) than worrying.

"Anything," I said.

"Fun!" said Ruby.

"Freedom," said Officer Serge.

"Peace of mind?" asked Fyodor.

I heard the dogs snoring somewhere in the van; they were already there.

"Oh yeah, peace of mind. Love, too," said Jenny.

"A place to live?" asked Alberto.

"Anything's possible," I said, pushing my theme. "A larger life. A big, alive, *Jumbo* life!"

"With a rosy outlook!" said Rosie.

There was a significant pause in the conversation. Jenny entered it. "Gee whiz, you two are not only fun, you're *symbolically named!*"

"And fun is always possible," said Ruby, pushing *her* theme.

"So is freedom, and there are always ways," winked Serge, *off-duty.* "To get free."

Jenny was laughing. "I haven't said gee whiz since I was seven!"

"It's that kind of an evening," I said, grinning up at the orange moon, which seemed to be grinning back; a couple of jack-o'-lantern grins.

"Anything is possible, like Red says. Everything. *Anywhere.*" said Rosie.

I started the van, put it in gear, but didn't drive.

"Freeing, then being yourself, at last—no one can touch that," said Jenny, philosophically, in the dark.

That was the coda I was looking for, so I drove slowly out of the Union Station parking lot.

I led the way and took us up the hill from Union Station, through midtown Kansas City on Broadway, past the Uptown Theater, through rowdy, boozy, musical Westport, over to Main Street, and down the hill towards a glittering music box of neon and Christmas lights blinking on and off, and on.

"This is the famous Country Club Plaza," said Jenny. "They must be testing those holiday lights. They light them up on Thanksgiving night—wow, that's *soon!*—and these Kansas City people go nuts for it."

I was feeling wide open wild and fresh—seeing everything *new.* Kansas City felt fun and lively, even friendly maybe, though I could picture my little house waiting out in California, the moon above the glittering music box ahead also filling my windows out west; windows watching for me and the dogs to come home.

We pulled up to a major intersection, 47th and Main Street, and stopped for the red light, the famous Plaza to the right. Then, I saw a sign.

A literal sign, a *sign* sign, and a symbolic sign; a sign in every sense of the word.

The light was still red, but the sign made me want to accelerate.

It said, simply, energetically, encouragingly: RIGHT ON, RED.

I smiled, got a tear in my eye. Maybe I *could* live in Kansas City again. Or wherever I wanted to. A car honked behind us. It was

Auntie, in her MG. Guillaume stuck his head out the window and yelled something in French, laughing, with hand signals, waving his chef's hat. Behind them, Roscoe honked. I heard the distinctive sound of the Volkswagen horn *honk*, and there was a line of cars developing behind Dee and Christopher, right up the hill on Main.

"Um, Red," Jenny said. "You *can* go."

I looked at the sign, this time with no comma.

Still, it felt good, comma or not; I wiped the tear away, and turned right.

I drove us through the Country Club Plaza, through the music box—each jeweled window full of holiday-hungry people eating, drinking, already getting merry, doing early Christmas shopping—then we went up the hill toward Loose Park; darker up there, quieter, the treetops tall and hedging high against the blue night sky and the moon, rolling high and bright white. I drove around the edges of the park, found the narrow lane to Aunt Arctica's, cut the ignition at the top of her driveway and rolled down to the mansion, electric candles glowing waxy yellow in all the windows.

"It's so peaceful up here, so quiet. I want to be quiet, too," I said.

"Yes," said Ruby, in the dark.

"Me, too," said Rosalita, "I can feel it."

"I can too," said Serge. "First time in a long time."

Headlights flashed into the van from behind, then Aunt Arctica was next to us. Guillaume was smiling, about to say something, but when Auntie saw our dreamy faces, she stopped him. And cut off her ignition. Roscoe arrived on the other side, smiled in at Jenny, turned off his car, and lights. I heard a Volkswagen a street or two away, then it rolled in silently behind us.

I looked up at the tall white house, all those rooms inside, velvety dark blue windows in the moonlight. It was Fall, and cold, leaves sparkling like water in the wind, blowing down the driveway.

We sat in our cars and listened to the sparkling leaves in the moonglow reflecting off the mansion, then the moonlight quiet breezed in again. No one spoke. I felt for Jenny's hand and found it. I didn't look, but I knew she was smiling. Her hand was warm; she squeezed.

Someone in the van inhaled deeply. Someone *else* inhaled (probably I did, too), then everyone exhaled at once, and started laughing. It got quiet again, only the wind.

Kansas, Missouri, and Felix began to snore on the floor.

Then, from the MG, Aunt Arctica clapped her hands and jumped out of the car. She left the driver's side door open and ran towards the house.

"The ROBES!" she yelled, laughing, running, unlocking—then *flying*—through the front door, the entire first floor lighting up!

The Robes!

I looked at Jenny. Then at Rosalita, in the rear view. Over at Roscoe in his car.

Guillaume lit a cigarette in the MG (a Gitanes, I could see the blue box; the moonlight was strong); there was the yellow flash of him striking a match, the billowing clouds of white smoke (a *Gitanes!*), then Guillaume disappeared in the fog, laughing.

It was *that* kind of laugh, like he knew something we didn't, and (if you can imagine this, *hear* this) his laugh sounded like a motorboat. An outboard motor on that boat, cackling along on the water and down around the bend in the river. Disappearing out of sight, but still laughing.

Something flickered in the corner of my eye; I turned to the mansion and the entire second floor was lighting up.

Then, the third.

Then a room higher, up at the top of the house.

Then that room went dark.

Then the third floor, then the second.

Naturally, my eyes (still some detective instinct there) went to the first floor.

I heard a car door open and close, and a cough. The motorboat laughing again. Footsteps coming, a fog bank moving in. *I* coughed.

"Shall we?" said Guillaume, looking eager and mischievous, pointing at the mansion with the lit red end of his smoky cigarette. *"Après vous."*

Something flickered in the corner of my *ear*, Aunt Arctica—out of breath, laughing, waving us in—had opened both of the front doors, Bipolar beside her and the dogs made a run for it, skittering through the moonlit leaves on the driveway, running right through her legs, sliding and skidding inside to food and water, with lots of dog tag *ringing and dinging* on the bowls.

"We shall," said Rosalita, walking toward the front door of the house, the rest of us following her lead, staying just ahead of a red-lit Gitanes.

Roses. We walked inside to roses. Roses everywhere.

On every flat surface, in all sorts of vases, the aroma of roses was *red-velvet heavy* in the air. We went into the dark library, just beyond the foyer, around the corner and down the hall from the kitchen, books from floor to ceiling but there may have been more roses than books.

And speaking of red velvet ...

Rosalita and the others were frozen, gazing around the library, but I saw Aunt Arctica at a desk in the corner with an armload of what looked like ... robes.

She caught my eye, winked, and walked towards us.

"Auntie?" said Rosie (looking I guess what I'd call: sweetly in shock. *I* was).

Aunt Arctica walked very slowly, very softly to Rosalita, and presented her with a robe.

It was red velvet, covered all over with woven roses, and with a small square of pale pink on the breast, monogrammed: *Rosie.*

"Welcome home, Rosie," said Aunt Arctica. "Wherever— *anywhere*—you want that to be."

You could've heard a pin drop in the library.

In fact, as Aunt Arctica draped the robe around Rosie's shoulders, she found a price tag still attached to it, said *"oops,"* removed it, and then—Auntie *dropped the pin.*

"See? You *can* hear a pin drop!" she said (looking at me; big tingle right down my spine). "Come on everybody, get in line— *Robes for Rosie!"*—and began to hand them out, all monogrammed; Alberto, Serge, Ruby, Fyodor, Roscoe, Guillaume, three small sweaters for the dogs (yes, monogrammed), me—she'd even had one made for Jenny. Dee and Christopher hung back in the corner of the room until Aunt Arctica waved them over. She handed them both robes.

"Of course I got extras, knowing this group and how they attract friends. And, Dee and Christopher, I'll get these monogrammed for you tomorrow, down on the Plaza. You know, I had these robes made in Paris, Guillaume knows a man there; they were marked as high priority, then over-nighted—delivered just this morning," she said, sliding on her own *Aunt Arctica* robe. Her eye on Guillaume, she said, "and speaking of my man here, the romantic, who loves surprises—hates to see them spoiled—he hid all these in his special *train room*—I think you may remember it—so that no one would see them too early. So they'd be presented at the right moment. It worked, my love, perfect timing. Warning: You all *may* get a little contact high."

Guillaume arched his eyebrows and lit a new Gitanes. "So, Rosie? You like? How do you feel, Rosie?"

Rosie was on a small sofa, crying.

In all this time, with all of this—everything that had happened, and what had happened before, before I'd met her, what she'd done to get away from the Hamptons, and all the things I didn't know about—I'd never seen Rosalita cry. Almost, a couple of times; behind the couch in the Hotel Colorado, on the highway at night sometimes, in the darkness of the van. But now, it was all coming down, and out. Real hard deep crying.

She was full.

Alberto sat down next to her, to comfort her, and began to cry.

The rest of us sat around them on the floor, in a half-moon, facing them. Rosie looked up after a minute or two and smiled a little, wiping her tears on the lapel of her robe.

"Sorry," she laughed. "Don't wanna mess up my new robe."

We all laughed, *"no no, go on!"* partially removing our robes, gesturing an offer of them to her and Alberto; our sort of *community Kleenex*. That started them crying again.

We sat there with them, as Rosalita and Alberto cried. Our half-moon got tighter, closer. I was holding Jenny's hand, had an arm around Fyodor, on my other side. Nobody said anything for a while. The dogs came in, looked at us, and lay down in front of the cold fireplace.

I lost track of time. The only thing I heard was the brisk cold wind outside the mansion, creaking the walls, whistling down the fireplace. A train through Union Station, rumbling up from downtown. The crying softened to sniffling. Guillaume's big belly gurgled.

Now we were all laughing as hard as two of us had been crying.

Aunt Arctica stood up, Jenny stood up, I stood up, Ruby gave Rosie a hand up and hugged her. Roscoe's laughter was out of control as he patted Guillaume's rumbling belly. Fyodor moved onto the sofa with Alberto, still softly weeping, wiping tears. Dee and Christopher leaned against each other, head to head. Serge was building then he *lit* a big fire in the fireplace, and we all turned golden; glowing in the wild shadows of the library.

"Let's all take a break, ok?" said Aunt Arctica. "Everyone want to go upstairs, freshen up, chill out, maybe crash? Then, come back down in an hour or two for a nightcap? Red, you can give Jenny a tour, if you like. Ok? Dee and … Christopher, is it? *Handsome man!* I have a special room upstairs for you two. Follow me!"

We fanned out into the big old mansion; up the stairs, down the halls, some of us up the old elevator, and roses were *everywhere.*

We took a break, and freshened up. I'd been exhausted an hour ago, but now I was *revived.* I took Jenny on a quick tour and zip (a *slow* zip, probably as zippy as her bullet train from Lawrence) up and down the elevator (and slow enough for some private, slow kissing), and in probably less than an hour we came back down. I think we all wanted to be together, to—

Celebrate.

Congratulate.

Talk; talk about anything.

Or not; Just be in one room together.

And what a sight we were! Jenny and I barefooted it into the kitchen, following trails of rose pedals on the battered wood plank floor, and everyone (except Dee and Christopher, and the dogs) was already there, sitting around the table, all in the *Rosie Robes,* like a happy, woozy rose garden. With roses, of course, dangling, falling out of the chandeliers; the chandeliers smoking candles like Guillaume was smoking his Gitanes. Aunt Arctica, her bare feet on the table, waved us in.

"Looks like Valhalla," said Jenny.

"Where?" asked Alberto, smiling and leaning back in his chair.

"Isn't that down in the Ozarks?" asked Roscoe.

"Or some sort of hall of fallen heroes, from some sort of old Norse folklore or something, maybe?" asked Aunt Arctica, knowing more than she was showing. "Though no one here is *at all* fallen. Come Red, Jenny—have a seat."

We were honoring Rosalita, so we put her at the head of the table, making a ring around our Rosie. She looked beautiful, and relaxed, her skin glowing (*rosy*) off her robe, eyes shining in the candles. s

So, here we were. All together, smiling at each other, sweetly, almost shyly, no one speaking. I wondered how the others felt about what had happened on this trip from California, what we'd just done downtown, at Union Station.

If they felt like me, they felt *good.*

Before now, we were always just *on the way* to this day, driving forward, figuring out, and now it was the evening—or maybe the morning after—the day.

I was so calm I felt like I was floating on rose petals. There *was* in the air—besides the heavy red rose aroma and the crispy yellow woodsmoke—a quiet, settled satisfaction.

Guillaume came out with drinks, spun his sommelier circle around us, and sat down. We raised our various glasses.

"To Union Station!" said Ruby. So, we drank to that.

"To Chainsaw and his tubes!" I said. "Shouldn't he be here?"

"Chainsaw isn't one for socializing," said Auntie. "Rather reclusive. Kind of a gregarious loner. He loves people, he's a good listener and he can talk all night, but then sometimes, he just disappears. But yes, *here's to Chainsaw.*"

Now I stood up. "I also want to make a toast to our sort of *astral* visitors, who arrived right on time ... here's to Mr. Charles Bukowski! ..."

Rosie lifted a glass, " ...to William S. Burroughs ..."

Roscoe stood up, " ...and to Bird. Mr. Charlie Parker!"

Everyone stood up, and we all drank, looking at one another, thinking of the visitors, acknowledging what we were experiencing, and sharing.

We sat down, settled quietly for a moment.

There was a sound, like breathing ... or wind ... soft ... then the distant pop of a cork, an MMMMMMMMMM sound vibrating protectively around us, and a swarm of warm, scattered saxophone notes, just a little closer.

We sat with that for a few moments, then Fyodor jumped to his feet. "And to Aunt Arctica, Guillaume, and to *this house!*" he said, looking around the room at the candlelit shadows winking and trembling on the dark wooden beams in the ceiling. We drank to that. "I don't want to leave!" he decided, after he swallowed.

"Well, you *know* ..." Aunt Arctica said, smiling, eyes closed, wiggling the toes of her bare feet up on the table, crossed at the ankles. She didn't say anything else.

I looked at Fyodor, he looked at me, then at Ruby, who shrugged, then she looked over at Serge, who ... anyway, we all looked at each other. *We* didn't know. Question marks floated in the air about what she meant by "Well, you *know* ..."

Then, after another minute or two of silence, Auntie opened her eyes and lifted her glass. "To Red Jumbo! For cracking his first case!"

Guillaume, right behind me, pounded me on the back *hard* and I almost geysered Bubbles of Vergèze across the table.

"SPEECH!" they all hollered.

I stood up. Cleared my throat. "Yes, friends. My first case. And my *last* case ..."

"NO! Please, *no!*" yelled Rosalita and Fyodor, everyone else laughing. Especially me.

"But I am so glad to have cracked this case, and I am *especially* happy to have discovered Rosalita—ALIVE!"

This brought everyone to their feet, cheering. The dogs started barking from one of the upper floors of the mansion. They came running down, sounding like they were getting lost, running down wrong hallways, at last arriving in long skids across the floor.

"I love you, Rosie," I said, and we toasted, "To ROSALITA!" We toasted, drank, and sat back down.

"I love you, too, Rosie," said Serge. But now ..." He paused, then walked over to the fireplace and looked into the flames, very serious, very *Officer* Controllente. I hadn't seen this side of him, and it worried me. Was he having a conflict about Rosie's immigrant status?

Serge turned abruptly, walked over to a window and paused there, watching trees waving their limbs in the wind, getting *stronger* now. A storm coming.

He delicately touched the window pane, paused, and came back to the table.

"... I need to make a special toast. To that clever trickster of a coyote in the arroyo beneath the Colorado Street Bridge, and," Serge, good at pausing, paused again, "to the brave, selfless department store mannequin from the evening wear department of Macy's in Pasadena."

I could see that since Rosalita knew Serge well, and well before her murder, she knew that he was joking when he dramatically paced and paused around the dining room, but the rest of us didn't see it coming. Aunt Arctica and I caught each other's eyes with a sort of *whew!* look.

Serge raised his glass. "To the mannequin, I say, *Vaya con vestidos!*"

Roscoe leaned in close to me, *"What?"* he whispered.

"Go with dresses, *I think,*" leaned in Jenny.

"Vaya con vestidos!" shouted Rosie, laughing.

"That's a corny joke, isn't it?" Serge asked.

Guillaume leapt to his feet. "Oh—my joke! *oui, oui, oui*—in the *old west*, the three-legged dog travels from town to town on his horse, looking for the bad guys, he has his revenge to take, and he comes to the *old west town*, goes into a salon—*saloon,* I mean—all gets very quiet and scary, and three-legged dog tells bartender and everyone else: *'I'm looking for the man who shot my paw.'"*

Now we were all laughing.

"*I* want to toast Rosalita," said Alberto. "I, um ... I didn't know what to do. Back then, before. When we were working for Hamptons, I was scared of them, but glad to have the work, and to have a place to live, to be making money, but I never was sleeping, and every day I start so much worrying about everything. I made my motto, 'Do good, lay low.' But I was so unhappy, you know? I didn't know what to do." Alberto thought of something and smiled, "I felt just like a turtle, but upside down!" We all laughed softly. "You know what I mean?" he asked us.

Rosalita took Alberto's hand, which startled him a little; he teared up, but continued.

"Thank you, my love, for taking care of us, for taking care of *you*, for pretending to get killed to get us away from there. From them. And for bringing Señor Jumbo into our lives, and ... for all of you. When I worked for Hamptons, I used to talk to myself all the time, to you, too, Rosie, but so much just to me. But now," he looked all around the table with a *big* smile (I'd forgotten how white his teeth were), "I talk to all of you!"

Guillaume was clearly moved by this, sniffling and snorting. Also still smoking.

Alberto stood up straight, lifted his wine almost to the ceiling beams. "Con todo mi corazón, Rosie, and *everyone*," he toasted.

It got quiet again. Something was blinking in the corner of my eye. I saw a small red light flashing on the phone by the espresso machine. Aunt Arctica, sitting across the table, parted her feet, looked through them at me, then over at the red light.

"A message," she said, "I never even check that thing anymore. I wonder who it could be?"

Auntie walked over, brushed some rose petals off the answering machine, and pushed the flashing red light.

"HI, IT'S VERA!" Ms. Similitude began, and stopped. We waited, heard footsteps, heard something metallic drop and clang, then roll, maybe into a wall and stop, there was a distant page: *"Dr. Claude, page for Dr. Claude, Dr. Claude, second floor please,"* then, nothing. Then, "NOW'S THE TIME, to call and hail you all, give CONFIRMATION to your success at the train station, I bet it was a HOT HOUSE down there in Kansas City tonight, it gives me STAR EYES to think of it, and how all you dear friends of mine—JUST FRIENDS—just the *best* I could ever have, though I have not met all of you, but I love all the rest of each you—each EMBRACEABLE YOU—and, um ..." and she stopped talking again. We could hear her fumbling with the phone, but not hanging up.

"Fascinating woman," said Aunt Arctica.

Roscoe was chuckling. "I love it. She's name-checking Charlie Parker songs."

"VERA HERE AGAIN! So, just wanted to let you know I'm happy for you and really for you, Rosalita. It puts a SEPIAN BOUNCE in my step, to know you are away from those people, that there will be no more SCRAPPLE IN *THEIR* APPLE and that you and your LOVER MAN Alberto can now be at peace. It doesn't take any ANTHROPOLOGY to know you'll be better without those people on your back, but—ha ha ha ha—" she stopped again, muffled the phone, this time with a fit of giggles, maybe out of control, "—but, ha ha ha, it might take some ORNITHOLOGY to know who to thank! Am I right, Roscoe? Am I right, Mr. Bukowski, Mr. Burroughs, Mr. Parker? Ha ha ha ha! Never throw away your cocktail napkins, even *I* know that!"

We all sat there wide-eyed in the candlelight.

"Well, that's all for now. Don't have to return the call. I have to wend and bend my way back down the hall and downstairs to my room here, where I am RELAXIN' AT CAMARILLO, and yes I know I'm not really in Camarillo but in Pasadena, but I wanted to say hi. And, I am glad they're *gone,* those people. Or that you're gone away from them, dear Rosalita. Ok, bye for now. Before I go to bed I'm going to go to the cafeteria and get some SALT PEANUTS!"

The message beeped an end and we sat quietly, smiling in the candlelight. Dogs snoring again, under the table.

Jenny, still wearing her red sequin pantsuit under her rosy robe, stood up.

"All I've got to say is I'm glad you all came through Lawrence. This is the wildest bunch of people I've ever met! I mean, I love my little literary life down in Lawrence—not so *little* really, come to think of it, that stuff, those books; there are books that saved my life, and go on doing that. The first time was when I read *One Flew Over the Cuckoo's Nest* ... I was still in my *parents'* nest, feeling cuckoo, and by the last page I knew I could fly. But *Rosalita.* Congratulations. And Alberto—Veni, vidi, vici. Fyodor, Ruby, Officer Controllente ... goddamn, what lovely people. Then, I get to meet the funky, sartorial, pneumatically poetic Mr. Roscoe G.T. Towne—lyrical bartender and *inventor!* A scrumptious French chef —that's you, Guillaume! Can I bum a Gitanes? And thank you, Aunt Arctica, for welcoming me into this marvelous, massive, mysterious maze of a home. I love it here. This place *looks* like you. And Rosalita, like dear Alberto said, thank you for bringing Señor Jumbo into *my* life. I ... kinda *like* Señor Jumbo, as you may have detected. Are you *all* detectives? Careful, Elvis Costello is watching!"

We all laughed, coughed, shuffled and scooted around in our chairs, took sips of our various drinks, moving for the first time since Jenny Sue Skiptewmaylewe began talking. But she had something more to say, and we settled back down for it.

"I mean, I don't know what I'm doing next either. I'm supposedly on a tenure track down at KU, loving it, starting up a whole new class—remember, Red?—the department approved it!— but tenure track or not, I tend to get sorta *off-track* sometimes, too, on purpose! And all this is fun too—*you guys*, I mean. Anyway, it's nearly Thanksgiving break. Maybe I can kinda come and go, Lawrence and here, finish out the semester, then ... for Christmas, Auntie? *Here* for Christmas? Time to rest, and think."

Aunt Arctica smiled a very clear *yes*, and Guillaume passed a Gitanes around the table (bucket-brigade style) to Jenny. Fyodor lit her cigarette and she curtsied and sat down. We all looked at each other, anticipating the next speech. Fyodor said, "Well, now what?"

"Yeah, that's what I was wondering," said Alberto. "Though I don't feel like moving at all. Even from this table."

"I *like* it here," whispered Ruby, from inside her velvety robe, her face tucked cozily down into it.

"Me too," said Fyodor. "How about you, Serge? I guess you have to get back to Pasadena."

"Oh, I'm off-duty. Maybe for keeps."

Everyone looked at him in surprise and glee. Alberto slapped Serge on the back and we all cheered.

Aunt Arctica and Rosalita were sitting next to each other, bare feet on the table. Auntie stood up, walked slowly around the table, came to me, and squeezed my shoulder. "May I have a splash of your *Bubbles of ...*"

"Vergèze? Certainly. I'll pour." I did.

She went about orbiting the table again. "I know you all have— aside from Ms. Skiptewmaylewe—your houses and your lives out in California. But you two, Rosie and Alberto, I guess you're floating free now. I imagine that feels good, yes?"

"Yes," said Rosie.

"*Oh* yes," said Alberto, eyes twinkling. I hadn't seen him twinkle before.

Aunt Arctica was passing just behind Alberto and she leaned down and kissed the top of his head.

"Good," she said. "I'd say there's no reason to hurry anything. You all need a rest. So rest, heal, sleep in tomorrow. Savor this moment. This new life."

She circled and sipped. We watched and waited; she was leading up to *saying* something to us, but was interrupted by Dee and Christopher, who silently seeped into the room like sauna steam. Silently, and grinning like Christmas Eve!

"Um," said Dee, "we were playing with your train, Guillaume. We shouldn't have, sorry!"

"*Tut tut*," retorted Guillaume, releasing an accumulated cumulus of Gitane smoke into the ceiling. "That's what it's there for, chérie!"

Christopher looked about to burst into laughter, but maintained. "Merci beaucoup, Guillaume," he said with a brief bow, but bursting: "ALL ABOARD! Ha ha ha ...!"

Dee and Christopher sat down next to me, I inhaled discreetly, and poured them each a glass of wine. Aunt Arctica was on the move again, hands on hips, seemingly thinking, seemingly trying to organize her thoughts into words, then seemingly ready. She was.

"Between this inherited mansion of mine," she began, "and— what is that Bible quote? Something about my 'Father's house has many mansions and I have prepared a place for you.' Well, anyway, I'm paraphrasing, but you get the drift. Between this place and

Roscoe's *Charlie Parker Cocktail Napkin Money*, making him nouveau—not to mention *pneumatically*—riche, you all have a lot of space and time to think it all over."

So *this* was the rest of the "Well, you *know* ..." moment earlier. I liked the sound of it.

"And by *it*, thinking *it* over I mean, of course, the question: what now?"

She drank the last of her bubbles and set the glass down on the table with a crack, like the period of a very *big* sentence. She walked over to Guillaume, fanned his cloud of cigarette smoke away, leaned down, kissed him, and headed for the door.

"I'm going to bed." She turned around. "Stay up, talk it over, sleep in. Rosalita, you and Alberto can go anywhere you want. That goes for all of you. But you don't have to go, yet. I'm just beginning to love you guys. I'd miss you. And you don't even have to *go*, at all. But, listen, if you can *go* up here," she tapped her head, "you can *be anywhere*."

"Cool," whispered Ruby.

Jenny squeezed my hand. I squeezed back. I was feeling tingly, happy, in love. Happy; and not even second-guessing it.

"Anyway, I'm going to bed. I'm too tired to be deep. *Good night*." Aunt Arctica left us, her feet patting trails of rose petals in the dark until we couldn't hear her anymore. The elevator clanked and hummed above us and away up into the mansion.

After a moment of silence, nothing ceremonial about it—it just got quiet for a moment—the elevator came clanking and humming back down to us, the door opened, footsteps down the hall, and there was Auntie again. Laughing already. She looked at Rosie.

"And Rosie? Anytime anybody from somewhere gives you any shit about all that legal *illegal* stuff, you tell them they're out of their jurisdiction, way out of line. Why? Because you're in *Aunt*arctica now!"

Then she was gone again, the elevator too; up, up and away.

I looked around at everyone, everyone looking sleepy. "Well," I said, "I guess this is it."

"Not necessarily," said Roscoe, eyes closed and smiling, blowing thick French smoke rings to the ceiling. "You just got here."

"That's *true*," I said, leaning back in my chair.

We were all leaning back in our chairs now, feet on the table. Guillaume had brought out a basket of fruit, he was working on a banana—the basket being close to him, I asked him for an orange. He tilted forward on his chair, snatched an orange, squeezed it, and rolled it my way. I stopped it with my foot, leaned forward, grabbed it, and we both leaned back again, feet on the table.

"Seems to me we can be anywhere, now," said Rosie. She turned to Alberto. "What do you say, guapo?"

"I say si, and I like it here, for now," he said.

"For now, for a while," said Roscoe, almost asleep.

"Ok by me," said Fyodor. "I say we sleep on it, though not quite yet. I want to savor this night."

Dee and Christopher were holding hands, still grinning, their eyes on a box of Swiss chocolate bars near the espresso machine.

"How are you two doing?" I asked. "Have to work tomorrow?"

"No, *thank goodness*," said Dee. "I traded shifts so I could work last night, so I'm off tomorrow. You're off too, yeah, Roscoe?"

Roscoe was asleep, smiling, starting to snore.

"I have the *weekend* off," said Christopher, focusing on the Swiss chocolate, poised like a bobcat. "And I really like our room, the special one upstairs that Ms. Arctica just showed us. Do you think I might stay over a night or *two*, with Dee? Don't want to be presumptuous, I'm kinda new on the scene, don't want to intrude on what seems to be a special moment for all of you."

"Kinda new, my ass!" laughed Dee, kissing Christopher on the cheek, licking off *some* of the lipstick.

"You absolutely belong here," I said. "Stay and savor our special moment, *your* special moment, your special room with Dee, not to mention Guillaume's special train!"

"I want to savor this night, too," said Ruby, getting up and casually going over to the chocolate, then casually slipping it to Christopher and Dee. "I want to explore this big old place, if it's ok with *you*, Guillaume."

He waved *of course* with his cigarette.

"I like this place," Ruby continued. "All the windows. All the ways of seeing out. All directions, any direction, some new ones, some higher than before. Which I guess is my metaphor for *me* in this moment, if it's not too strained."

I thought it over, I think we all did.

"I know just what you mean, Ruby Rosenfeld," said Fyodor.

"All the windows, no shutters, no blinds—*all clear*," said Serge.

"Wow. Poetic," I said.

"Not bad for a cop, would you agree, Mr. Jumbo?" asked Serge.

"Arresting, officer."

"Perfect imagery for what I'm thinking, feeling," said Rosalita. "My eyes are different, I see the same things, but my eyes, I don't know, something new."

"Si! Me too, what I see," said Alberto. "*Fresco!*"

"It *is* poetry, and I'm from the English Department!" said Jenny. "I like what you said, Officer Controllente!"

"Serge, Jenny. And thank you," said Serge.

"*Fuck*, these people are great!" Dee elbowed Christopher, who was grinning with a mouthful of Swiss.

We all fell asleep in the kitchen, but I can't remember when.

Sun

When I woke up we were still there, asleep, some of our heads down on the table, some of us still leaning back in chairs, feet splayed out on the table, some on the floor, some spilling over onto each other.

It had snowed in the night. The snow was beginning to reflect light into the room, a brilliant blueish-white glare through the windows, and across the dark wooden beams.

"Buenos dias," whispered Alberto, groggy, flashing those bright white teeth again. He was smiling all the time now, probably while asleep too.

"Hi," waved Fyodor, head down on the table.

Roscoe and Guillaume lay on the floor near the sputtering, orange fireplace, looking very uncomfortable, I thought. Side by side, together, very stiff and straight.

"They look like Olympic luge racers, don't they?" asked Jenny, yawning. "Morning, Red. Gosh, I'm sleepy. Do you hear a car?"

Kansas and Missouri roused up from under the table and pawed me. Little brown coffee bean eyes blinking, wide awake. Felix wandered over under Rosie's chair and went back to sleep. Bipolar was lying next to Guillaume.

"I'll take these guys outside," I said, kissing Jenny *good morning.* "They've never seen snow before." Then I heard the car.

Coming down the driveway, sounding through the fresh snow like milk pouring on Cheerios. Which made me hungry and look around the kitchen.

Roscoe stretched by the fire, rolled sideways and stood up. "Hear something?" he asked us, squinting then shuffling to the kitchen window. When he got there he looked out, chuckled, and waved. "It's Paul. What's *he* doing here? He's got a box, a present or something." There was a knock on the front door, and Roscoe went to answer it.

"What's going on?" asked Rosie, ruffling her hair and rubbing her eyes. "Good morning, all."

Guillaume and Bipolar were still asleep by the fireplace, as was Ruby, cuddled up in her robe in a chair at the end of the table. Dee's sleepy head was on Christopher's chest, his sleepy arms around her. Serge was the next chair down the table from them, asleep, arms folded across his chest, bare feet crossed on the table, a single rose stem between his toes. I didn't remember *that*.

Roscoe came into the kitchen with Paul and his big mustache, a smile very large for so early, and a gift box from Hallmark Cards.

"This is Paul, everybody!" announced Roscoe, in his full, rowdy, bartender voice. "I think you've already met Red and Rosie."

"Good morning, everyone," said Paul more softly, mindful of Guillaume on the floor.

"Hey, how was K.D. Lang?" I asked, in my corduroy morning voice.

Paul's bright blue eyes could've woken Guillaume just by looking at him. "Oh, she's the best!" he beamed. "Yes, sorry to disturb, so early, but Roscoe told me about—*last night*—and he asked me to let him know if anything came up. Any further developments. Any reactions from Mr. and Mrs. Hamptons."

Guillaume stirred a little by the fire, still asleep. *"Where's my ratatouille?!"* he shouted.

"He's having chef dreams again," I informed Jenny. "He's alright, it'll pass."

"Anyway, *this* came up," said Paul, gently setting the box in front of Rosie. "I'll get on out of here, let you all get back to your morning, anyway I have to prep the bar, open for lunch. *Busy* downtown, Roscoe, the holiday crowd!" He shook hands with Roscoe, nodded at all of us, and turned back to Rosie.

"They came to the bar an hour or so ago, knocked on the door, I unlocked and asked them in—they looked pretty rough, a bit bleary —but they said no, that they were just leaving *this* for Rosalita, if she comes back in. Or if I could get it to her, to *you*, somehow. I said yes, of course. She, Mrs. Hamptons, smiled at me, and touched my arm. Mr. Hamptons put his hand out to shake, and yeah, I shook it. His hand was cold, shaking, but he gave me a good firm shake. Gave me a nice smile, looked over my shoulder and told me he loved the 'backbar wall of bottles, and that *ladder!*' Asked me again if it was 12-step, and that he needed one of those in his house back in Pasadena. Then they were gone. I watched them, followed them from a distance across the lobby, saw them walk back across the street to the hotel, arms around each other. I better go. Have a good day, everyone. Bye Rosie, *Red*. Later, Roscoe."

The front door closed, we heard Paul start his car, and drive away. Guillaume was awake, sitting up by the fire, and Aunt Arctica had quietly returned, was sitting next to him. Dee and Christopher were awake and looking at the Hallmark gift box.

A red box with a green lid. Rosie lifted the lid.

She pulled out some festive holiday tissue paper, then something mangled, and wadded up. A ripped bumper sticker. She flattened it out on the table: MAKE AMERICA GREAT AGAIN. Rosie wadded it back up, and pushed it aside.

She lifted an envelope from the box. Elegant, flowing handwriting; the letters nicely, openly spaced across the envelope: *From One Wounded Deer to Another.* Rosie opened it, pulled out a card. A very artful card, in the natural colors of deep woods; yellow, golden-brown, and green, some blue, maybe water beyond the woods, and a portrait of a beautiful woman in the woods. With antlers on her head.

Rosie opened the card, and began to read. As she read, her eyes got wide. She finished, took a breath, a moment, kept her eyes on the card, then went back to the top and read it out loud to us.

"She says: '*Dear Rosalita, I never told you my first name, and I want to. It's Frida. You never knew, but my mother was from Mexico City, and named me after her favorite artist, Frida Kahlo. My father, an American businessman, did NOT approve, but mother insisted. Maybe one of the few times she insisted on anything with him, and so I was named.*

'*I am sorry. For how we treated you. For how I treated you. I don't even understand now, how we could treat you like we did, but we got quite a shock yesterday—thank you, Rosalita, you did something I've never done, so far. Mr. Hamptons isn't as bad as he seems—though he reminds me of my father sometimes—but we're talking, and we apologize, to you. For everything. Thank you, Rosalita. I'm moved, I'm changed, by your courage. Your courage to tell us off. Or more precisely, to fuck off! Ha ha ha.*

'*Best always to you, Rosalita. Truly. Yours, Frida.*'"

None of us said a word, silence in the kitchen, a log rolled in the fireplace spraying crackling sparks and Guillaume jumped, but Aunt Arctica didn't.

"That's a very good letter," she said.

"I like it," said Rosie. "Especially the part about 'something I've never done, *so far.*'"

"May I see your card?" asked Christopher. "That painting showed at the Nelson. We have those in the Museum Store."

"She's come a long way," I said. I was flashing back to the first day I drove up to the Hamptons mansion and met Frida Hamptons. "But maybe she was already there, and hurting. I can't really know. What a wonderful letter she wrote."

Dee passed the card to Christopher; Fyodor, Ruby, and Guillaume read over his shoulder. All in happy tears.

"*Wow,*" said Ruby. "I *like* that."

"Me too," said Alberto.

"Me three," said Serge.

"Me *eleven!*" laughed Roscoe, wiping up *his* tears. "I mean, don't we *all?* Hey Guillaume, throw me a Gitane, I wanna celebrate."

"I do too!" I stood up and said, "I want to get up, get outside, start the day! But first, shall we have a toast?"

There was another one of those dramatic silences (except for the snapping fireplace) we were getting so good at, and we all looked at the table—all glasses and bottles empty—nothing to drink.

"Alright, we'll do that later," I said.

There was much standing up, yawning, stretching, hugging, talking, laughter, chairs being pulled out and pushed back into the table, Guillaume organizing (commandeering) a cooking class for the guys, announcing that women know how to cook intuitively (the women in the room rolling their eyes; "Not *me*," laughed Dee), a fresh cloud of French tobacco smoke overseeing it all, and Jenny and I and my dogs snuck off.

After wandering around, kissing, and otherwise *perusing* each other in the dark library, accidentally discovering a luxurious screening room—seats and curtains in blue velvet, *A Room with a View* playing with the sound off (we noticed the sax cases tucked into a dark back row of theater seating, safe and sound)—we went up in the old elevator. When the door slid open to our floor, I started out to walk Jenny down to our room, but she pushed me back in the elevator.

"I know where it is, my darling Red. You *LA* guys get out there in all that snow!" Kansas and Missouri were already up on their back legs in the elevator, trying to paw the DOWN button.

Jenny and I kissed until the elevator door cut in on us, then I heard her laughter receding above as the dogs and I floated downstairs in the elevator.

As we floated, I heard Aunt Arctica and Rosie talking somewhere, the elevator stopped, the door opened, Felix and Bipolar hopped on board, Auntie and Rosie waved without a break in conversation, and we passed below *that* floor.

We arrived at the bottom floor with a bump, the elevator door slid open slowly, and the dogs took off across red tiles of an empty cold basement room. They knew where to go! They ran, slid, and waited at the heavy wooden back door for me, and when I finally got there, when I opened it, threw back the heavy black iron latch, they went flying out into Aunt Arctica's wide, wild, rolling backyard—across all that fresh new *white!*

The sun was shining bright in blue sky as the dogs ran and ran, all over, everywhere, making Japanese writing in the new snow.

Everything was brilliant white against the sky going up and up and on and on, forever blue.

The sun looked like a full moon to me.

I whistled to the dogs, they came running to me, *at* me, leaving comet trails of snow behind them as they ran.

"Look at that sun," I said, pointing up into the blue. "It's not even noon yet, but already it has its gleaming gold sax strapped on!"

The sun was too high and too bright, too many light years away, so they concentrated on me, panting frosty air, snow in their whiskers, making miniature blizzards when they shook their heads, snow flying off their ears.

"Come *on!*" I said, my arms open to them. *Excited!*—they ran away from me, maybe twenty-five yards out into the snow, turned around, then Missouri came running back and at maybe ten yards, *launched* herself—right into my arms. I kissed her, she licked me, we made sweet eye contact—*pant, pant, pant*—I put her down. I heard another collar tinkling ...

Kansas came charging now.

He launched himself a little later than Missouri, a little lower, maybe at five yards, and shot hard—straight into my balls!

I was on the ground, saw the sun, some *stars*, and clenched my legs together as Kansas and Missouri mauled me in the snow. Felix and Bipolar were looking straight up into the sky, sniffing, tongue out, catching ... *snowflakes?*

I heard a glassy, clicking sound. The dogs froze and looked around.

Clicks again, three of them. Coming from up in the mansion. One of those windows? The dogs periscoped their heads around and up, saw where it was coming from.

I looked where they were looking and saw Jenny in the window of our room on the top floor, waving at me in her red rosy robe, behind the frosty glass.

She licked a finger and wrote in the glass: !ᗡƎЯ IH

Me and the dogs looked at each other.

They sat down in the snow, waiting for more information. Jenny looked at her message and laughed, signaling for us to: Wait, *hold on!*

Then she licked her finger and wrote again, above the first message.

HI RED!

I needed something quick—and looked around for materials. The dogs watched me, not sure how to help. The backyard was a field of twinkling white snow—pretty, but no materials, nothing to write with.

I looked back at Aunt Arctica's mansion and saw six big garage doors at one end, and a small backdoor, *open.* I got up and started running toward that ajar backdoor.

My shadow was running ahead of me, then it faded. I looked up and saw a low line of puffy round clouds riding overhead, like a team of flying snowmen: *it was getting colder.*

And it was snowing again!

A sign

I got through the backdoor, my eyes adjusted in the dim garage, I looked around.

Cans of paint, a green riding lawn mower, a red-rusted black motorcycle with flat tires, a wall of tools, most of them missing, a tight-packed yellow wall of National Geographic magazines, ladders, snow skis, water skis, a silvery-teal canoe lodged up in the rafters, a ripped parachute hanging down from them, and an old blue Porsche with— *a black and white Beatles bumper sticker!* (Snow and wet pine needles on the windshield; a bit of *after midnight* driving, Auntie?)

Tall sheets of wood leaning on a wall. A line of spray paint cans.

I took a full sheet of plywood and a can of black spray paint, shook the can, uncapped it, dropped the sheet on the floor and sprayed. It took a minute, it was done; I wasn't second-guessing it. It was *perfect art.* And it was a sign. I lifted it from the floor and ran back out into the blizzard, dogs running ahead through the snow like police escorts.

I was running with the huge sheet of wood over my head, catching snowy wind and taking flight for a second or two, landing, then running on, away from the house, up the hill to the back fence.

I slowed down, stopped, stayed on my feet, and planted my freshly-painted sheet of wood, my sign—my *note*—in the snow, leaning on the back fence, wedged into some low-hanging pine branches.

I looked down at Kansas and Missouri. Felix and Bipolar, too. They looked up at me, tails wagging explicitly, barking joyously.

Together, we all walked down the hill a few steps and looked up at Aunt Arctica's mansion. A tall, wide, *warm* house inside, windows lighting up in the sudden snowstorm.

Jenny still up there, in our window. She saw my sign:

!

A wind swept quick, full of *more* snow, cutting through the pines, knocked the sign down, and it slid down the hill, scooping up the dogs—and *me*—sledding us back down towards the house. The dogs spread their legs on the sign and braced.

I was laughing, hanging on, letting go.

Jenny cranked her window open. "I'll be right down!" she said.

"I'll be right *out,*" said Dee from the backdoor.

The dogs and I (and the **! SLED**) came sliding down to a rest in the snow.

"Me too," said Rosie, from another window.

"Me too, *wait for me!*" said Ruby, from another.

I saw Guillaume's tall white chef's hat crowded into a lower window, surrounded by the guys; cooking class interrupted.

A tiny window opened at the tallest triangular peak of the mansion.

"Anyone *else?*" yelled Aunt Arctica, in a frosty exhalation of exhilaration.

And all the windows opened, blizzard or not.

Chris Coulson is the rowdy writer of *Nothing Normal in Cork, The Midwest Hotel, Go With the Floe,* and *A Bottomless Cup of Midnight Oil.* He's been writing his way out of trouble since kindergarten.

Made in the USA
Middletown, DE
13 May 2023

30076378R00205